KAREN

TEABAGS & TEARS

EMPIRE
PUBLICATIONS

First published in 2012

This book is copyright under the Berne Convention. All rights are reserved. Apart from any fair dealing for the purpose of private study, research, criticism or review, as permitted under the Copyright Act, 1956, no part of this publication may be reproduced, stored in a retrieval system, or transmitted, in any form or by any means, electronic, electrical, chemical, mechanical, optical, photocopying, recording or otherwise, without the prior permission of the copyright owner. Enquiries should be sent to the publishers at the undermentioned address:

EMPIRE PUBLICATIONS
1 Newton Street, Manchester M1 1HW
© Karen Woods 2012

ISBN 1901746 917 - 9781901746914

Printed in Great Britain.

*"Come and share a pot of tea,
my home is warm and my friendship's free"*

ACKNOWLEDGEMENTS

Wow, where did all this come from? Since writing Broken Youth I just seem to be going from strengh to strengh. The public are loving my work and I have a lot of fans and followers. Without my readers I would have probably given up a long time ago, so thanks to all my avid readers.

A big thanks to Rose who reads my tarot cards, she's always bang on and prepares me for the days ahead. Thanks as always to my PR Judith Broadbent who is always behind me, to John and Ashley at Empire for believing in me.

To my family, thanks for being amazing - big hugs and kisses to them all; Ashley, Blake, Declan and Darcy. I love you all with all my heart. To James for all his support and my parents Alan and Margaret for all theirs. Not forgetting my grandchildren Dolton, Cruz and Marci - I love you to the moon and back.

I always try to write from the heart and tell it how it is. I'm still writing raw, gritty books and love how people are getting behind me. A big thanks to Glen Mortimer and all the actors at Stirling management. Thanks to all my facebook friends, and twitter. My website is somewhere where you can all get in touch with me too. karenwoods. co, or you can follow me on twitter @karenwoods69.

Teabags and Tears is dedicated to all us women who have been hurt in the past by men. You are not alone and always remember, friends are for life. My last thanks as always is to my son in heaven Dale. You're always in my heart.

1

"Fucking hell, hurry up will ya, we're gonna be late." Sandra always wanted to be on time but no matter how much she tried the minutes just ticked away. Rushing, rushing, rushing.

"I'm nearly done. Just a bit of aftershave and I'm all yours," a man's voice shouted from upstairs.

Kevin was one cocky fucker Sandra thought as she huffed at the bottom of the stairs waiting for him to come down. Her hand rested on her hip as she trudged towards the mirror that hung from the wall in the hallway.

She stood yanking her Lycra dress away from her gut. She felt fat. Tugging at her knickers through her dress, she shoved her overweight belly back inside her passion killers. As her eyes focused on the mirror, she sucked her stomach in and turned to the side. "You fat twat Sandra" she whispered under her breath as she shook her head. Kevin, her husband, was coming down the stairs now. He was whistling some tune he'd heard on the radio. Pushing her away from the full-length mirror he stood admiring his outfit. Kevin was all about looking good. His dark jeans fitted him like a glove and Sandra commented that his bollocks looked strangled inside them. He smiled and grabbed at his crotch with his hand. "You're just jealous coz you know the chicks will be looking at them that's all." Sandra gritted her teeth and shot him a look. She knew he was right, all the women fancied him. They gathered like flies round shit whenever he was near.

"Come on then lard arse. I'm ready when you are."

Reaching for her handbag Sandra took one last look in the mirror and sighed. Kevin dragged her away by her arm. "Posing bitch! And you have the cheek to call me vain!" he chuckled. Heading to the car Kevin chewed rapidly on his gum. It had just started spitting and Sandra held her handbag over her head as she ran towards the car. One drop of rain on her hair would cause it to frizz beyond belief.

Squeezing herself into the passenger seat she could see her stomach bulging out in front of her. Kevin saw her fidgeting. "What's fucking up with you now? You look fine, stop worrying." Shaking her head she scowled at him.

"I don't fucking feel fine. I look like a beached whale."

Turning the engine on, her husband sniggered. "Well what do you expect? You're always in the fucking fridge."

She became defensive. "You cheeky bastard. I've lost two pounds this week."

Kevin pulled out from the driveway and continued. "Two pounds! That's a fucking fart. You need to get to the gym and burn some of that blubber from yer arse."

Her heart sank. He was so cruel with his words and he never thought about how he was making her feel. Trying to get comfy in her seat she punched at his arm with force. Her face was red with anger. "Av Mr fucking 'All About Me'. Where's the support? I wasn't always like this, remember." Kevin turned the music up and jerked his head as he sang along. She was now in a strop and pulled the mirror down to check her make-up.

Sandra was forty-two. She considered herself average looking and always tried to keep herself smart. Her hair was auburn with several blonde streaks scattered through the front of it. It always looked dry and heat damaged. Last night she'd tanned herself from head to toe and as she held her hands out in front of her she could see where she'd applied too much of it. "Fucking hell" she whispered. Dipping her finger in her mouth she rubbed vigorously at her knuckles trying to remove the dark brown tan from her skin.

"What times this fucking party starting then?" Kevin asked. Sandra glanced at her watch and tutted.

"About half an hour ago," she huffed.

Kevin crawled out from the junction into the traffic and replied in an angry tone. "Don't fucking blame me! You were the one in the bath for over an hour, whatever you were playing at." He raised his eyes towards her. Sandra looked pissed off. She knew to keep her mouth shut. She was in the bath for ages but she didn't want to tell him that she'd shaved her fanny. She wanted it to be a surprise for him later on that night. She gazed from the car window and ignored him.

Pulling up at "Billy Greens" pub you could see a few people stood outside. Kevin quickly checked his face in the mirror and opened the car door. He could see one of mates and headed towards him. As he heard Sandra close the door behind her he placed his arm over his shoulder and pressed the central locking. His walk now changed and Sandra frowned as she followed behind him like a lost sheep.

"Yo! What's happening lads?" His mate Martin shook Kevin's hand and spoke in a bad arse manner.

"I've just got here mate. It's hammered inside though. I just got a pint and come out here for a bit of space." Sandra was still pulling at her dress and hid her handbag in front of her stomach. Kevin patted his mate's shoulder and told him he would see him later.

Inside the music was pumping and the DJ Reggae Ronnie was playing all the latest tunes. Tonight they were celebrating Sandra's sister's birthday. Sandra heard screaming from across the pub. As she looked through the crowd she could see her sister Tracy waving her arms frantically in the air. They both moved towards her through the crowd of people. The birthday girl now squeezed them both in her arms. Sandra opened her black leather bag and pulled a pink birthday card from it. She pecked her sister on the cheek as she wished her happy birthday.

Tracy was gorgeous and Sandra envied her sometimes. She was everything she'd wanted to be. Sandra had always been unhappy with her body and moaned in the past at her mother asking why her two daughters were so different. Sandra's legs were short and plump where Tracy's were long and slender. It had been a family joke for years and Sandra had learnt a long time ago that she would always take a back seat to her confident sister.

Kevin was his usual flirty self with Tracy. He was all over her like a rash. There had always been some kind of connection between them but Sandra just thought it was a brotherly love. Kevin left them both to go to the bar. Sandra watched her sister's eyes as they followed her husband's perky arse towards the bar. Tracy dragged her sister by the arm over to their parents. Sandra's mother checked her watch as she saw her. Her eyes looked at Sandra with a disapproving look.

"And what time do you call this?" Sandra ignored her and sat down. Anita, her mother, was back on her case. "I thought with it being your only sister's birthday

party you would have made the effort to be here early?"
Anita was tutting and shaking her head. Sandra looked
inside her handbag trying not to give her eye contact as
she replied.

"It wasn't me it was Kevin. You know what he's like.
He's a tart when it comes to getting ready." Kevin could
now be seen holding three drinks heading back towards
them. Placing the glasses on the table he picked one up
and passed it to Tracy with a big smirk on his face.

"Oi, birthday Girl, get that down ya neck." Tracy
smiled and kissed her brother-in law on the cheek.

"Orr thanks Kevin. You shouldn't have. I've already got
two drinks from Uncle Pat and Auntie Jean." She pointed
to the drinks and smiled. "I'm gonna be so pissed tonight
yanno." The birthday girl swigged the glass of Vodka in
one gulp and slammed it on the table. "Bring it on" she
ranted. A song called "What's my name" by Rhianna now
played and Tracy grabbed Kevin's hand for a dance.

"Come on Kevin. Let's see what dance moves you've
got." He tried to get out of it at first but she didn't give
up that easily. She was tugging at his hand leading him
towards the dance floor. Before long the two of them
were bumping and grinding to the music. Sandra sat
looking around at all the people in the pub. She felt
lonely. The last few months had been hard for her and
she just couldn't pull herself together. Her marriage had
gone stale and she knew it wouldn't be long before Kevin
traded her in for a new model. He abused her physically
and mentally and he'd drained any self-confidence from
her. Sandra had just given up caring.

Sandra worked as a nail technician in a local sunbed
shop and loved meeting people. She'd worked there for
over five years. The money was good and it kept her out of

debt. Sandra had been married to Kevin for over twenty years .Her two sons were more than a handful. They kept her on her toes every day they breathed. She knew deep down inside that one day that one of them would end up behind bars.

Kevin was a bit of a wheeler and dealer in the area and had his hands in more than one pot. He'd spent several years in prison in the past but it never deterred him from earning a quick few quid. The family lived on a Manchester council estate in Monsall. Sandra's family all lived nearby and she never thought about moving away.

"Fucking hell wallflower, move over!" Sandra's best friend Tina now came to sit by her side. Once she squeezed her arse into the small gap next to her she placed her drink on the table. Sandra smiled as Tina spoke. "Where's Kevin then?" Sandra's eyes peered over to the dance floor. Tina gazed over and saw Kevin and her best friend's sister having the time of their lives.

"Doesn't that bother you?" she whispered.

Sandra reached for her drink. Slowly sipping her Tia Maria and coke, "Oh you know what he's like," she answered, "he's always been the same with the women. I gave up caring a long time ago."

Tina screwed her face up. "Well he's a cheeky cunt. No way would I have my man acting like that" She was angry. Tina leant in closer so Sandra's mother couldn't hear her. Covering her mouth with her hand she whispered. "Tracey is just as bad as him. Look at her the little slapper!" Both of them now watched as Tracy was sliding up and down Kevin's body with her hands all over him. Sandra was hurt but tried to keep her calm. Her mother now joined the conversation.

"Just look at our Tracy dancing. She can't half move

her arse." Tina smirked and pinched Sandra's leg. They both knew Anita would never have a bad word said about Tracy. Even as a kid she was always the apple of her mother's eye. Anita turned to talk to another woman who'd just joined them leaving them free to speak. Tina was shaking her head in disgust.

"Fucking nothing ever changes does it Sandra? I mean your mam must see Tracy's nothing but a dirty little slut." Sandra giggled and loved how straight talking Tina was. They'd been friends since high school and she'd warned her off marrying Kevin right from the start. Even back then she hated him with a passion. She'd told Sandra in the past her husband was a womaniser. Sandra knew deep down that Tina was right, even though she didn't like to admit it. She'd always been the underdog in the relationship and felt insecure. Kevin and Tracy were back at the table.

"Top little mover you aren't ya Tracy," Kevin chuckled. He now sat down opposite Sandra. He was still laughing with her sister and she could see him weighing her sister up and down. Tracy was wearing a white dress that just covered her arse cheeks, and you could see the outline of her thong underneath it. Tina noticed Tracy's underwear through her dress. She coughed and cleared her throat.

"Fucking hell Tracy. I can see your draws through that dress." Tracy stuck her arse out behind her and tried to look. Tina continued. "It's not underwear that. It's more like a fucking cheese grater. You need some like these babies." Tina stood up and lifted her dress up revealing her big knickers. Everyone was laughing. She now paraded the floor with her skirt held up flashing her big black Bridget Jones style knickers. "Just wait till you're our age Tracy It will all change." Tina dropped her skirt and grabbed her drink from the table. Looking at her Sandra she smiled.

"Come on miserable arse. We'll show em how to shake arse." Sandra shook her head and looked anxious. Still yanking at her dress, she told Tina she couldn't be arsed. Tina huffed. "Fucking hell Sandra, get up here now. You know you're my dancing partner."

"For fucks sake," Sandra moaned as she admitted defeat. She squeezed between the two tables to join her friend. Kevin smacked her arse on the way past him. "Will you fuck off nob head" she scowled.

"Temper, temper. I'm only giving you a loving touch that's all" he snapped. She knew she'd overreacted and reached her hand to his hair. With a quick movement she messed it up. Kevin panicked and pushed her from his side as he tried to get his hair back in style. Both women headed to the dance floor.

"Tell you what Tina. If my life doesn't change pretty soon, I'm gonna die of boredom." The music was loud and Tina was yelling as she danced. "You need a toyboy Sandra. No relationship, just pure sex with no comebacks."

"I'm too old for a toyboy, love. I just need some excitement that's all." Tina chuckled.

"You're never too old for a bit of young stuff. Trust me Sandra you would never look back." Sandra sighed and carried on dancing but her mind was all over the place as she looked over towards her husband. "It's him that makes me feel like this. Him and his fucking ego." Tina huffed at her friend.

"I don't know how you do it Sandra. He's hard work. You deserve a fucking medal." Sandra now focused on Kevin. Her hands were waving in front of her. "I mean look at him." Sandra glanced over her shoulder as Tina shook her body next to hers doing some dance move she'd seen Tracy doing earlier. There it was right in front of their eyes. The bastard was all over her sister like a rash. Laughing at her and touching her legs. Sandra marched from the dance floor. Tina tried grabbing her back. "Hold on, where you off to? The song hasn't finished yet." Sandra was like a steam train heading towards Kevin with a look that could kill, held in her eyes. Stood in front of them she placed one hand on her hip as she bent her head in towards them both.

"Ay! Fucking octopus arms!" she ranted. Kevin lifted his head up and stared at his wife. His face was still filled with laughter as Tracy still kept prodding him with her finger.

"What's up with your boat race now?" he moaned.

"You're all over my sister again. That's what's fucking up with my face." Kevin's face changed and he looked like a wrongly accused criminal. Holding his hands in the air he spoke out loud. "I've done nowt wrong honest." He looked surprised.

"Orr don't start this shit again. Every time you have a few drinks you're always the fucking same" Sandra kicked at his calf as she moved past him. Tracy had a cunning grin spread across her face as she spoke.

"Sandra we're only having a laugh, don't be getting paranoid."

"Shut the fuck up you tart," she shouted in her face. Tracy now involved her mother and it wasn't long till the family was at war at the table. Anita tried to make peace. It was obvious from the start she was on Tracy's side.

"Sandra, I wish you would just leave her alone. It's her birthday for crying out loud. They were only having a laugh that's all. It wouldn't do you any harm to crack a smile every now and then too you know." Sandra looked alone and chewed on her lip as she tried to defend herself. Years of coming second best to the family slag was finally coming to the surface. She didn't care if it was her birthday or not she was getting the truth out once and for all.

"Oh I might have known she would have told her mummy," Sandra said sarcastically. Anita looked at her and hissed. Sandra now had Tina by her side and felt she could take the lot of them on. Taking a drink from her glass Sandra stood up and bent down towards Tracy's face. Her sister backed off and held her head back to the seat. "He's my fucking husband, not a doll for you to play with. You might have played with all my toys when we were kids, but not this time, trollop." Tracy was waving her hands in front of her trying to defend herself.

"What the fuck you going on about now? Do you want him sat here all night miserable as fuck, because that's what he is when he's sat with you!"

Sandra made a grab for her but Tina held her back whispering in her ear. "Leave her Sandra. You're better than that." Tina dragged her friend away from the commotion. "Come on let's fuck off from here." Sandra ragged her handbag from the chair and spit into Kevin's face. You could hear her mother shouting.

"That's disgusting. He's your husband not an animal." Sandra gave her an evil look and left the pub with Tina.

"Mam she's a fucking nutter. I mean we were only having a laugh wasn't we Kev?" Kevin was wiping the spit from his eye now and sat with his hands between his legs. He knew he'd been pushing Sandra for weeks and in a way, he had expected her to explode sooner than she did. He just couldn't help himself. Tracy was a darling and given the chance he would have ripped her knickers off in an instant. Shaking his head at Anita he got the sympathy vote he was looking for. He spoke in a low voice.

"She's a crank. That's what I have to put up with."
Tracy was by his side. Holding his hand she looked at him.
"Kevin seriously, what's her fucking problem with me?"
he rubbed her hand as she sat by his side.

"Ahhh she's a knob-head. Just ignore her." Tracy left
Kevin and went parading round the pub. She could now
be seen talking to The DJ Reggae Ronnie. He was as
black as the ace of spades but Tracy had a crush on him.
Many a night he'd taken her in the men's toilets and
shagged the arse off her and tonight didn't look like it
was going to be any different

Sandra and Tina headed to another local pub in the
area called the Queens on Monsall. She could be herself
there and never felt out of place. So what that it was her
sister's birthday party, she didn't care anymore the slut was
doing her head in.

The walk to the pub took about twenty minutes and
Sandra now felt comfy in her dress. The bulge she'd tried
to hide all night long just hung freely from her body
and she walked with confidence not having a care in the
world. Tina started talking.

"It's always the fucking same with your Tracy isn't
it? She's got to be the main attraction all the time. Your
mother doesn't help either." Tina was flicking her hair
from her face.

"Yeah well I've just about had enough of the little
slapper," Sandra sighed, "she'll get what's coming to her
don't you worry."

Tina looked shocked. This was out of character for
her friend and she carried on walking looking chuffed
that her mate was finally stepping up to the mark. For
years she'd seen her take abuse from Tracy and her mother

and it was about time she told them how she felt. They both entered the pub to enjoy the rest of the night.

Anita was always the same with Tracy. In her eyes she could do no wrong. She was her baby and she wanted to try and keep her that way for as long as she could. Her husband Graham could see the way she treated Sandra was different, but he always kept his mouth shut to try and keep the peace.

Anita was fifty-eight and looked well for her age. Her life with Graham had had its ups and downs but they had just about learnt to cope with one another. Anita hadn't worked for years due to arthritis in her hands. She'd worked as a machinist in the past and still made the odd pair of curtains to pass the time. The rivalry between her daughters had been going on for years. She knew deep down Tracy was a flirt and she'd seen her overstep the mark on more than one occasion. Anita just presumed Tracy had a good relationship with Kevin and thought Sandra should just stop being insecure. She wasn't aware that Tracy had shagged his brains out several years before and had his child aborted.

Sandra and Tina were the life and soul of the party inside the Queen's pub. You could hear Sandra's mobile ringing continuously in her handbag but she just kept ignoring it. The drinks came fast and furious and they were both pissed out of their heads. Both women now sat huddled together in the corner of the pub.

"Do you think I'm overreacting," Sandra slurred, as she leant on her friends shoulder at the side of her, "because if I'm being silly, just tell me."

"Nah, do I 'eck. She always does it. For years she's always been the same. If Kevin was my husband I would have twisted the bony cunt right up." Tina was rocking.

Sandra's mouth looked collapsed at one side as she spoke.

"I think they've had a shag in the past you know. Don't ask me how I know but I can feel it inside. Call it a gut feeling." Sandra pressed the palm of her hand onto her stomach. "I can feel it right here." Tina had thought the same for years and she'd heard rumours in the past that Kevin had shagged her sister but she kept her mouth zipped just in case she was wrong. Tina held her head to the side.

"Why don't you just come straight out with it and ask her? You'll be able to tell by her face if she's lying or not. She could never hide the truth, that one. Remember how her eyebrow always twitched when she was lying." Sandra agreed but sat staring into space. She could never ask Tracy outright and plus, even if she denied it she still wouldn't believe her. She was a lying slut who couldn't be trusted.

2

Kevin lay next to his wife in bed. He'd been awake for a while and wanted to get to the bottom of his wife's behaviour the night before. He wasn't arsed that she left the pub as he had a great night with Tracy but he wanted to seem concerned about their marriage. Rolling in behind her he tickled her side. "Wakey wakey!" Sandra could be seen moving about but she remained facing the opposite way from him. Kevin was leaning over her now.

"Sandra don't say we've fallen out again. Turn round and speak to me will you?" Sandra opened her eyes but remained still. Her head was banging and the night before was taking its toll.

"Just leave me alone will you."

Kevin hovered over her now. He could just about see her eyes. "I've done fuck all love. I only danced with her."

"Only did this, only did that," Sandra snapped, "it's always the fucking same." Her voice was sarcastic. Kevin huffed and banged his hand on the blankets.

"Oh so it's another day of fucking misery then?" He fell back on to the bed and dragged the bed covers back over him. He kicked his legs roughly and made it known he was angry. She felt scared. She knew he wouldn't think twice about punching her lights out. Sandra hated when they fell out and felt like she needed Kevin in her life to breathe. Slowly she rolled over onto her back.

The bedroom was painted in a neutral beige colour. Everywhere looked clean and fresh. The white cotton quilt cover was now pulled up under her chin. Her shoulders could be seen shaking slightly as she started to speak.

"Listen Kevin, it's all the time. You fancy Tracy and you can't hide it." Kevin sat up and pulled her closer.

"Babes, don't be a muppet. You're the only woman for me." His words made her smile. She knew he was full of shit but somehow she wanted to believe him. His kiss made her melt into the bed and she needed the love he was providing. As he made his move to make love to her, she tried to keep the covers over her body. She hated the way her fat fell at the side of her and she didn't feel one bit sexy. Kevin looked like a Greek God with his tanned, toned body. As he mounted her she felt as if it was a mercy fuck from him. As she watched him close his eyes she wondered if he was thinking about her sister. Shaking her head she tried to rid the vision from her mind.

Kevin had always been highly sexed. At first she didn't

mind because she was rampant herself back then but as the years passed she always complained about his sex drive. He was like a rabbit. Sandra met Kevin in school years before. As soon as she cast her eyes over him she wanted him for keeps. Sandra secretly got herself pregnant just to get her claws into him. Kevin came from Moston in Manchester and he had quite a name for himself amongst the local girls. Everything about him was top of the range and even though the years had passed he still looked tasty.

Lying beside her husband Sandra tried to shake off her mood. Kevin lay sweating at the side of her. Sandra didn't get much enjoyment from sex with him and she often pretended he was the best thing since sliced bread beneath the sheets. His sex was rough and fast and she often wondered why he never made love to her. She's seen it on TV so many times in the past and wanted the romance she craved deep down inside her. On occasion she did sometimes become a porn queen in the bedroom but that was mostly when she was pissed out of her head and didn't give a shit. Banging noises outside the bedroom door made her aware that one of her sons was awake. She yanked the covers over her and tried straightening her hair.

"Mam where's my black jeans? That nob head better not have em on." John was the older of her two sons. He was full of attitude and spoke as if he was black. Sandra was sick to death with the fights between her two sons and took a deep breath before she answered him. "How the fuck do I know. I put all your clean washing in your bedroom. I don't monitor whose wearing what." John huffed as he banged the door shut behind him. He could be heard moaning from outside the door. Sandra looked at Kevin for help.

"It's my day off work. I'm not listening to them pricks arguing all day long again." She sat up and searched for her knickers on the floor. Still keeping the covers round her waist she quickly slid her draws on as she moaned. "Why can't they just get on like normal fucking kids?"

Kevin was flexing his muscles at the side of her and looked at his arm as he spoke. "They will sort it out in time. Me and our kid were always scrapping. It's just part of growing up." Sandra stood up and grabbed her housecoat from the side. Perhaps she should have wasted her sister when she was younger, she thought. Then the little slag would have known not to touch her husband. Sandra was now making herself angry again. Anytime she was angry she reached for food, for comfort. Heading downstairs she shouted to Kevin she was making breakfast.

The smell of bacon soon filled the air. Sandra looked hot as she splashed the hot oil all over the eggs in the pan. Her son John now came to join her. Sitting at the dining table he spoke. "I'll have a butty mam. I just want bacon on it, no egg though." The radio was on quite loud and Sandra was singing along to it trying to get the vision of her husband with her sister out of her mind. Turning round to her son she bent down and sang into his face. John moved her away with a quick push. "Will you move, you're doing my head in" She smiled and knew he wouldn't stay around much longer. He was a miserable fucker and she often wondered if he was a full shilling. Her other son Paul was completely the opposite and he always smiled unlike John. Perhaps it was the weed John was smoking; it must have something to do with it, she thought as she gazed at him tying his shoelaces.

Kevin now came into the kitchen in just his black boxer shorts. One of his hands was shoved down the front of them as he spoke to his son. "I don't suppose you're gonna be looking for a job today, or is that too much to ask."

John screwed his face up and gave his dad a look of disgust. "Will you get off my back! It's weekend, the job centre isn't open until Monday ya muppet." John had been unemployed for months.

Kevin pulled his chair out from the table and grabbed the newspaper as he still spoke to his son. "Makes no difference what day of the fucking week it is. You're still a fucking lazy twat, end of." John grabbed a piece of toast that had just been placed on the table. He looked deflated.

"Right I'm out of this depressing place. You wanna look at your own life dad instead of getting on at me all the time" Kevin was ready to pounce on him but Sandra stepped in.

"Ay ya gobby fucker. Have a bit of respect." Her son was bouncing about the kitchen now and he held no fear from his father.

"Well it's true he's going on at me all the time and I can't see him working a nine till five job. He's just as bad as me. He sells weed. So like father like son, innit." He left the room and Sandra was holding Kevin by the arm as he was shouting after him.

"Cheeky little cunt. Tell ya what don't bother coming back here. Find your own fucking place to live." You could hear John shouting back but his words were muffled.

Sandra sat at the table and listened to her husband waffling on. "For fucks sake I'm sick of all this shit," she mumbled. Kevin heard her and went on one. Throwing his bacon butty across the table he left the room. He'd been extremely violent to her in the past and she knew to keep her mouth shut. Sandra stared round the kitchen as she nibbled her breakfast. The sound of a message alert could be heard and she scanned the area for the mobile phone. Reaching to the kitchen side she pulled Kevin's phone from the work surface. Quickly checking he wasn't around she pressed the buttons to reveal the message.

The name of her sister was at the side of the message. Quickly scrolling down, the words strangled her.

Thanks for last night Kevin. We must do it again sometime.

She felt sick and stood pacing the kitchen floor. She'd been in bed pissed the night before and never knew what time her husband came home. She didn't think for one minute he was still out with her slut of a sister. Gripping her arms she stood staring. Half of her wanted to kick off but she knew he would deny the message and say she was reading too much into it. No she had to be calm and cunning and catch the bastard in action. Throwing the phone back on the side she could hear him coming into the kitchen. He looked angry as he frantically searched for his phone. The bastard must have known he'd left it in the kitchen and looked eagerly to find it. Sandra knew she shouldn't have but she quickly spoke as she yawned trying not to look at him.

"What time did you end up getting in last night then? I was wasted I didn't hear a thing." Still rummaging around Kevin replied. "About two-ish I think. I was bladdered and just got my head down"

"Lying, lying cunt," she whispered. "Did our Tracy stay until the end or did she get off home. She looked pissed as a fart when I was there so God knows what she was like later on." Her eyes were on his face now as she watched him try and hide his sins. Guilt was written all over it. She knew he was guilty before he even tried to speak. "I dunno, I wasn't sat with her. I was with my mates as soon as you left." He was now stretching his arms above his head and pretending to yawn. She watched him locate his phone and he quickly left the room.

Sandra grabbed her mobile and pressed the buttons at speed. A ringing tone could be heard. "Tina it's me. Where are you, I need your help" Tina sounded as if she was still in bed and her words were slow.

"I'm still in bed. Why what's up?" Sandra was on the verge of crying.

"It's that dirty slut again. She's been with Kevin last night. Tracy just sent a text thanking him for the night they had together. Orr Tina I want to kill her. The little slut. What am I gonna do now?" Tina paused and you could hear her coughing. Once she had regained her breath she gave her advice.

"Right girl it's time to catch the scum-bag in action. No point in causing World War Three for fuck all is there? Give me an hour and I'll come to yours. Is Kevin still home or what?" Sandra was livid and her words were shaky.

"He should be going out any time now. Probably going to meet Tracy for all I know."

"Right like I said give me an hour," Tina replied, "I've just got to get ready and get rid of this guy who I brought home last night. Fuck knows who he is." They both giggled and the call ended. The text message was being repeated in Sandra's mind. With every word she felt sick and knew that this time she would have to face her demons.

Tina threw her mobile phone on the bed, stretching her legs across the unknown man at the side of her she looked at his face. He wasn't that bad looking she thought and she'd shagged a lot worse in the past.

The man was about forty years of age and looked quite rough in the face. She cringed as the night before came flooding back to her. Tina had been a dirty porn star with him and covered her face with her hands as she softly kicked his legs. "Come on you. I need to go out." The man moaned and pulled her closer. He didn't know her name and called her love as he spoke. "I'm still fucking pissed love. Don't you fancy another mind blowing shag before I go home?" Tina smiled. Usually she would have kept him there all day, but her friend was in need and she told him straight. "I can't sweet heart. My friend needs me. Maybe we can meet up again sometime?" The man was covered in tattoos. Tina held his hand and examined them in more details. She commented how nice they were. The man now told her his name.

Steven was a tattoo artist and had his own shop in Manchester city centre. He told her he would do her a nice design for her back if she wanted. Tina always liked tattoos and told him she would definitely be up for it at a later date. Quickly glancing at the clock on the wall she told him again she had to go.

Watching him climb from the bed she admired his firm toned body. She licked her lips and gave a second thought to shouting him back to bed. His arse was perky and she could see he worked out. Pulling his faded jeans over his arse she watched him tuck his large penis inside them. Searching the floor he found his black t-shirt and came and sat on the bed next to her. Tugging his top over his head he fell back onto the bed.

"So do you want to do this again? We had a good time didn't we?"

Tina chuckled. She couldn't remember the night before but the burning sensation in her vagina told her she'd had a good time. Steven had piercing blue eyes and she was staring into them as she spoke. "Yeah okay why not?" A quick kiss on her cheek and he stood up. Pulling his mobile phone from his pocket he asked for her number. She hesitated at first but he looked an alright kind of guy and she finally gave in to his request. The door could be heard slamming and she kicked the blankets from her body. Running into the bathroom she could be heard farting loudly. Tina laughed out loud at the noises she was making. All morning she could feel the wind trapped inside her and now Steven was gone she couldn't wait to get the gas from her arse. She let rip.

Looking in the mirror Tina ran her fingers through her bleach blonde hair. All her make-up was still on her face from the night before. Licking her index finger she rubbed underneath her eyes and tried to remove all the mascara that was now sat there. Running the water into the sink she quickly swilled her face. Reaching for a towel she was struggling to see. With a quick rub of it she was dried and all she needed to do now was brush her teeth. Sticking her tongue out into the mirror she squirmed at the yellow coating on it. She tried to brush it off with her pink toothbrush. Grabbing her jeans she slid them on and searched for a top to wear. Tina was the same age as Sandra and her body was well in need of a session at the gym to tone her wobbly bits up. Tina had had her fair share of heartbreak in the past and the last time she'd been in a relationship it nearly killed her. Her ex-partner had cheated on her loads of times and was never scared of beating her to within an inch of her life. She'd promised herself from that day that she would never let a man treat her like that again. Tina was ready and headed to her best friend's house.

"Where have you been slug? My head's been all over the place, you need to help me Tina." Sandra closed the door behind her friend and led her to the kitchen. She placed her finger over her mouth as they sat down and gesticulated that Kevin was still in the house. Tina asked for a cup of a coffee. The sound of running water could be heard and you could see Sandra putting the contents into the cups. Leaning on the side Sandra turned to face her. She looked worried.

"He's definitely been shagging her Tina. I don't care what anyone says." Tina just watched her friend's face and knew exactly what she was going through. The sound of someone coming down the stairs could be heard. Kevin appeared at the kitchen door.

"Where are my car keys? Have you seen them Sandra?" Shaking her head she wanted to run at him and head butt his cocky face. Was he going to meet her sister she thought, as her face went red with temper? Her blood was boiling. Twisting her wedding ring round her finger she told him she hadn't seen them. He was angry now and she could see he was in a rush for something as he kept checking his watch. Speaking in a low tone she looked at him.

"Perhaps you should re-trace your steps back from last night. Think about what you done when you come in."

Kevin shot her a look. "I can't remember last night you nob head. I was pissed." Gritting her teeth she tried her best not to speak her mind. Tina was watching her and shook her head as a signal for her to be quiet. Kevin left the kitchen. The sound of shaking keys could be heard, he was back.

"In my coat they were. Right I'm getting off see ya later." He quickly leant to kiss Sandra on the cheek. He was gone within seconds. Tina listened to the front door slamming. When she was sure Kevin had left she started to speak.

"I knew it ya know. You can tell a mile off something is going on between them both." Her words were like hot stones being dropped into Sandra's heart as she collapsed onto the kitchen table. The sound of sobbing could be heard and Tina realised she could have been a little more subtle with her words. "Orr Sandra. Come on love. I didn't mean it to sound like that. He's just probably made a mistake." Sandra lifted her head up and yanked at her oversized t-shirt.

"Mistake" she screamed. "I'm the worst mistake he's ever made. Look at me compared to our Tracy. I don't stand a chance."

Tina screamed as she held her closer. "She's a dirty trollop. She's your fucking sister. Where is her respect?" Tina stood up. She reached for the kettle. She quickly poured it into the cup and walked to the fridge for the milk. Sandra was now sat at the table lighting a cig with shaking hands.

"We need a plan Tina." Holding her cup of coffee Tina joined her. Once she'd lit her cig she agreed as she took a deep drag from it.

"Don't get angry love, get even. That's what my dad always used to say to me." Sandra nodded her head slowly.

"I want to ruin him Tina. I want to hurt them both badly."

Silence filled the room for a moment and Tina tapped

her fingers on the dining table. "I agree we need to think this out and make sure we pay them both back. If you approach her, she will just deny it point blank. You know her of old, the lying dirty slapper. Arghh! She makes my blood boil." A look of malice was etched on their faces as they sat like witches round a cauldron plotting their next move.

3

Tracy lay in her bed and smiled as she thought about the night before. She'd betrayed her sister in the worst way possible but held no remorse for her actions. She wanted Kevin and nobody would stand in her way of getting him, not even her own flesh and blood. The sound of her mother's voice outside the room made her hide her head under the quilt cover. She was still pissed and couldn't be arsed listening to her mother moan about her sister's behaviour the night before. Searching for her phone, she checked it to see If Kevin had replied to her last text. Her face looked frustrated as her hands came from underneath the covers to place her phone back on the side.

Tracy was a man-eater, without a doubt. She'd been shagging Kevin on and off since she was sixteen. At one point she was pregnant to him and was really up for keeping the baby until he made her see sense. He must have loved her, because after all he went with her to get an abortion, he stayed with her until it was over.

Tracy had told her mother she we was going to stay at her friends on the day she had the abortion planned and her mother didn't bat an eyelid as it was quite normal for Tracy to stay over at a friend's house. Kevin didn't stay with her all night. When she came out of hospital he just put her up in his mate's house and fucked off until the following day. After all this was his wife's sister and he knew if Sandra got wind of it, all hell would have broken loose. Tracy didn't see Kevin a lot these days as she was sleeping with any guy with a pulse to fulfil her sexual needs.

Kevin had taught Tracy a lot in the bedroom and she was quite hot between the sheets. She had no inhibitions and would try anything to make her man happy, unlike Sandra. Kevin sometimes felt guilty at what he was doing with her sister but he could never say no to Tracy. She was like a drug and he was addicted.

Tracy grabbed her phone from the bedside cabinet and sighed. "Where the fuck is he? He's taking the piss." Checking the bedroom door she pressed the tiny green buttons on her phone. She could hear it ringing and waited for him to answer.

"Hello it's me" she whispered.

"Tracy what have I told you about phoning me. I could have been at home."

"Oh shut up Kevin. You weren't saying that last night was you?"

Kevin backed down. "Well, I'm just saying that's all." His voice sounded stressed and you could tell by his voice he wasn't in the mood to talk to her. "Are you at the grow house today?" she sniggered. Kevin hesitated but finally told her he would be there later on in the day.

The grow house was where Kevin grew his crop of marijuana plants. Every day he would go there to make sure everything was okay. The house belonged to his friend but he was away on holiday so she knew it would be a good place for them to meet up and have sex. Tracy sounded excited. "Right what time are you there? I'll get ready and meet you." He wanted to say no but the ache in his groin was ruling his mind and he finally agreed to meet her a few hours later. Tracy ended the call with a smile on her face. Stretching her body fully she began to sing. Her mother now entered the bedroom.

"It's nice to hear you singing love. What's made you sing and be so happy?"

"Kevin's going to shag me all over the place and our Sandra hasn't got a fucking clue about it," she wanted to shout out but she just smiled back at her mother with her secret stuck firmly to her tongue. "I'm just happy that's all mam. I've opened all my birthday cards and I've got nearly one hundred and fifty quid in them. I'm buzzing. I might even book myself a holiday."

Anita looked excited. "Oh that would be nice. At least you'll see something for it. Who's going to go with you?" Tracy's face looked like she was thinking. She didn't have many friends due to the fact she'd shagged all their boyfriends and the ones she did have were always skint all the time. Tapping her teeth with her fingernail she looked like she had someone in mind. Bolting up from the bed she rubbed her hands together.

"I might ask Beverley from down the road. She's a good laugh and I've been away with her before." She stared at the wall as if she was thinking again. "Yeah I'll ask Bev." Anita left the bedroom after she'd scraped Tracy's washing up from the floor. You could now hear someone coming into the house. Her face looked stressed. "For fucks sake that's all I need" Tracy huffed. Sticking her head from the bed she could hear her sister's voice in the house. She could also hear the loud laughter of Tina, Sandra's best mate. She held her head to the door listening to the conversation downstairs. Sandra could be heard speaking in a loud tone.

"Mam you have to understand why I get pissed off. Imagine if your sister was all over my dad. You just wouldn't have it. Would you?"

Anita was defensive and walked away from her. "They were only having a laugh Sandra. It was her birthday for Christ's sake."

Sandra was fuming. "Well what about the other week when we were all sat in here?" She was pointing her finger about the front-room. "Tracy was sat on his knee. Remember? She's a fucking flirt?"

Her mother sighed and raised her eyebrows. "There was nowhere else for her to sit that's why." Sandra twisted her fingers together as Tina was getting ready to put her two pennies worth in. Sandra was still fuming as she continued.

"So why didn't she sit on my knee?" Her head swung back as she ranted with temper. "I'll tell you why mother because she knows what she's doing and that it winds me up big-time." Sandra blew a laboured breath and tried to calm down. "Mam seriously I'm gonna do her in if she carries on."

Anita huffed. "Oh Sandra, she's you're sister. Why would you think that about her? You should have some trust in her." Tina cleared her throat and placed her full palm on the table as she spoke.

"Anita, Tracy does it on purpose. I've seen it too. She fancies the arse off Kevin. You can't deny it?" Sandra's mother sat down at the table and all of them lit a cigarette. The kitchen was filled with smoke within seconds and Tracy waved her hands across her face as she walked in to join them.

"Fucking hell. Open a door or summit. I can't breathe

in here." Tracy started choking. She was going right over the top. Sandra could now see her face and she stared at her ready for action. Tina was now kicking her under the table to behave herself. Tracy was full of herself as usual and continued in her quest to break her sister's temper. "You calmed down now psycho?" Tracy chuckled. Her eyes focused on Sandra. Tracy was now stood with one hand on her hip. She was wearing a short t-shirt that barely covered her stomach and nearly all her legs were visible. Tina gawped at Tracy's long slender legs and slowly stroked her own thighs wishing they were a bit thinner.

"Who are you calling a fucking psycho?" Sandra spat, making sure she could get to her sister if she carried on with her cheek. Tracy checked she had her mother's full attention and continued with her cocky attitude.

"You Sandra that's who. What was last night all about? Kevin is my brother-in-law. I would never do that that to you." Anita looked at Tracy and gave her a small smile. She was putting on a good show the little slag and Anita was buying every word. Tina licked her lips to speak but Sandra was in there first.

"I can't wait until you get a fella. Just let's see what you're like ay, when I'm all over him like a rash?"

Tracy laughed out loud. "Don't make me laugh. I would never get stressed over a man, especially over them talking to you!"

Sandra gritted her teeth. She was fuming. What did she mean? Was she saying that I'm a fat cow and that no one would ever look at me? Clenching her fists under the table, Sandra's knuckles turned white. Everyone had heard the insult, so she was well within her rights to kick her fucking head in surely. Sandra leant forward to stand but Tina pushed her back and took over.

"Tracy you are bang out of order. You're always flirting with Kevin. I've seen it loads of times." Tracy now opened the back door to let some air inside. She knew Tina was a fighter and that she wouldn't have thought twice about opening a can of whoop ass on her. Tracy tried to back pedal.

"If it's a problem, I won't speak to him again. But imagine when everyone knows why we don't speak. You'll look a right paranoid twat then won't you Sandra?"

That was it, Sandra had heard enough. She jumped up from her chair and leapt onto her sister. Anita was screaming for her to stop but it was too late, Sandra was ragging her about the kitchen, screaming as she pummelled her fists into her face.

"Paranoid twat, I'll show you who's paranoid!" she shouted, as she twisted Tracy's long blonde hair into her grip and dragged her about the kitchen. Anita was trying to pull her off but Sandra was like a fighting machine and was letting her have it big time. Tina was stood with them both and was in no hurry to end the fight. After all, the tart deserved it.

Sandra was soon wasting Tracy. She finally threw her to the floor and sat on top of her as Anita tried pulling her body off from behind..

"Sandra get off her you're gonna kill her," Anita screamed and spun her head back to Tina for some support. "Tina please help me." Sandra was now in Tracy's face, her teeth were gritted together and bits of spit sprung from her mouth as she shouted.

"Not so gobby now are you? Tell ya what. If you ever, ever go near my husband again I'll do jail for you. You fucking scrubber." Sandra was harsh but she meant every word of it. Tracy was screaming underneath her and she was wriggling about furiously trying to escape. Tina now stepped in and pulled Sandra from her sister. Anita was yelling at the top of her lungs. As soon as Tracy was free she gripped her and pulled her closer protecting her like a lioness would protect her cub. Anita now shook her head as she snarled at Sandra.

"No fucking need for that Sandra. Since when have you become this violent woman? You have serious issues you do. You need to seek medical help." Tracy, now feeling brave knowing that Sandra couldn't get at her, hid behind her mother as she shouted abuse.

"Fucking fat porky arsed bitch. No wonder Kevin doesn't come home to you, you're a fat fucking mess." Tracy was now jumping about behind Anita, her hands waving in the air. Sandra looked at her mother's face and knew it was time to go. Grabbing her coat from the chair she gave Tina the eyes to follow her. Tina looked at Tracy and shook her head. They left the kitchen as Tina spoke the final words to Tracy.

"Little girls shouldn't mess about with big women, otherwise they'll get hurt. Do you get me?" Tina nodded her head slowly at Tracy as she left with a look of hate held in her eyes. Tracy looked scared now because Tina had just threatened her. She'd heard stories about what she was capable of and fell onto the floor crying as her mother nursed her wounds.

Anita grabbed a cloth from the side and slowly placed it on her lip. Her hands were trembling and she was shaking from head to toe.

"I can't believe that your own sister would do this to you. Is she on drugs or something, because it's not like her one little bit." Quickly wiping the blood from her mouth Tracy jumped up from the floor. She couldn't wait to tell

Kevin what had happened and hoped he would back her up once he'd seen the state of her face. Anita was chasing her round the kitchen still trying to wipe the red blood from her t-shirt.

"Mam, will you fuck off now. I'm alright." Anita started to sob. "You're not alright, look at the state of your face. You need some ice on it to take away the swelling. Wait there while I get some from the freezer." Anita ran back to the fridge as Tracy bounced up the stairs locking herself inside the bathroom. Standing behind the door she struggled to breathe. Her heart was racing. She could now hear her mother shouting from outside.

"Tracy open the door. Let me get this ice on your mouth."

"Mam I'm fine. Just leave me alone will you?" Tracy moved towards the mirror. She looked a mess. Sucking her bottom lip to stop the bleeding, she started to get washed. Once she'd removed all the signs of blood from her face she quickly applied some black mascara to her long lashes. Her hand was shaking as she held the long brush to her eyes. Quickly throwing her hair up into a ponytail she left the bathroom. Her mother must have been waiting in her bedroom because she was by her side straight away. Anita spoke in a frantic voice.

"I've told Kevin. I just spoke to him on the phone. He's going home now to sort her out." Tracy's face sunk. Her mother had just fucked up any chances of her getting a leg-over this afternoon. She was supposed to have been meeting him anytime now. What a fool her mother was. Tracy stamped into her bedroom and searched for her phone. She typed a message to Kevin asking him if he would still be at the house. Once she pressed the send button she sat on the bed with her mobile phone in her hands waiting eagerly for his reply.

★

Tina and Sandra headed back home. Tina was laughing her head off as they both walked with speed. Sandra had never been a fighter and Tina couldn't believe what she'd just witnessed.

"Fucking hell, since when did you become a warrior?"

Sandra raised a smile but as they walked up the road she began to cry. It was all too much for her. "I'm sick to death of it all Tina. Why do they think I'd just sit there and take the shit they throw at me? Do they not think I have feelings?" Tina could see the pain in her eyes and linked her arm. She offered her some words of wisdom.

"I've told you love. Don't get angry, get even. We can sort them both out so they never fuck with you again. You have to be two steps in front and one behind them love." Sandra looked deep into her eyes as if they were magic and hoped she would find the answer to end her nightmare. Approaching the house Tina could see Kevin stood at his car with the door open wide. He was resting one arm on the door and one arm on the roof as he watched them drawing nearer.

"There's Kevin." Tina whispered through the side of her mouth. Sandra looked uneasy.

"What's he doing back? I thought he was out for the day."

Tina stood tall and looked directly at him as they got nearer. "I bet your mam has phoned him to tell him what's gone on." Sandra shook off her tear and had a stern look on her face.

"Does this face looks like it gives a shit Tina?" Sandra

stood tall as she walked to the car. She could see him shaking his head and he didn't look happy. Tina knew they were going to have words and kissed her on the cheek.

"Right see you later. Phone me if you need me."

"Yeah alright, speak soon." As soon as Tina's back was turned Kevin grabbed Sandra by her coat and marched her in the house. She was struggling with him and wasn't going to let him get the better of her.

"Get ya hands off me, you prick. Who do you think you are?" His voice was angry and his temper boiled.

"You're mam has just been on the phone. What the fuck do you think you're playing at ay?" She snapped back at him.

"I'm playing at fuck all. I'm deadly serious. Don't think for one minute I'm gonna take anymore of your shit." Her head fell to the side as his clenched fist pummelled into the side of her face. Closing the front door behind them his reign of terror began.

"I'm sick of you showing me up. Look at the state of you. You're nothing but a big, fat bastard." His face growled down at her on the floor as his eyes peered menacingly at her face. Cowering away from him she held her hands in front of her face to try and defend herself but it was no good. Kevin dragged her hair all over the place and finally pulled her into the front room.

"Please make him stop. Please" she whispered, but no one heard her as she felt his foot kick into the depths of her stomach.

The beating was now over and she lay sobbing on the floor. She knew she was hurt but didn't know where the pain was coming from, as every bone in her body was on fire. Sandra could hear Kevin's rapid breathing nearby and heard the flickering of a lighter. The smell of tobacco now filled the air. Could she make a run for it? No, her body was too weak. Peeping through her looped arms she could see him sat smoking on the arm chair. The sound of her legs moving caused him to drop his head over the arm of the chair and look at her. Her eyes were swelled now and she was finding it hard to focus. Sandra sat up and pulled her back up against the wall. Drawing her knees up to her chest she was aware he was watching her movement, his chilling voice made her tremble inside.

"See what ya have made me do now. It's all you're fucking fault. What have I told you about getting me angry?" Her face remained looking at him as her thoughts went unheard. Oh I'm gonna hurt you so bad, you bullying bastard. I'm going to ruin you and that dirty little tramp of a sister. Her face looked anxious. Kevin now spoke to her as if she was a little child.

"So what do you have to say for yourself"? Sandra remained quiet. He picked up a nearby ash tray and launched it at the wall near her. "Don't fucking ignore me you sad cunt," he screamed. Her body was shaking and she knew he would hurt her further if she didn't reply. Her mouth was dry as she swallowed. You could see her blowing breath from her mouth as she tried to speak.

"She's the cause of it not me. Why are you treating me like this?" His body jerked up from the chair. Pacing the floor he came to the side of her and kicked at her shins. She yelled out in pain. He knelt down now and he looked directly into her face.

"If your Tracy would have me, I would be there in minutes you daft fat slag. But she doesn't, so I'm stuck with your sorry arse instead aren't I?" he ranted.

Bastard, bastard she thought. Sandra covered her ears

with her hands but he dragged them away so she could hear every word he had to say to her.

"If you ever touch her again I'll hurt you. Do you hear me?"

Sandra nodded. His fingers gripped her chin as he spit into her face. "You need to remember Sandra that the women out there want me all the time. Good looking ones as well, but I choose to come home to you. Fuck knows why." His face looked cocky as he stood shoving her head towards the wall. He walked away straightening his top. The clock on the wall was ticking loudly and it seemed forever before he sat back down. He told her to get up from the floor. She ignored him at first but as he shouted again she jumped up as if boiled water had been poured onto her.

Sandra sat on a nearby chair and kept her hand held over the side of her face. She saw Kevin checking his watch and once he'd sent a text message on his mobile phone he stood up. Bending down to her he asked for a kiss. She hated him with every bone in her body. She cringed as he leant in to her to connect with his lips. The sound of lips smacking could be heard. The dirty twat stuck his tongue into her mouth and seemed to be turned on by the whole episode. Grabbing his keys to his pride and joy he left. He was her lord and master.

Rocking in the chair, Sandra wanted to end her life. Her mobile phone started to ring and she could see Tina's name flashing on the screen. Holding the phone in her hand tears fell from her eyes. Pressing the answer button she heard the voice of her friend.

"Well what did he say about it all?"

Sandra began to cry. Her words were muffled and hard to understand.

"He's just kicked fuck out of me Tina. I'm a mess." The phone went dead and Sandra was shouting into it hoping her friend was still there. After a few minutes she gave up and fell onto the sofa. A wet patch was now visible where her tears had fallen. Sandra now lay sobbing her heart out.

Sandra jumped up as she heard the front door open and close again. She could now hear her son Paul shouting if anyone was at home. Quickly she placed the cushions round her face and pretended she was asleep. She could hear him at the side of her and felt him gently pushing at her arm. He didn't stay around much longer now he thought she was asleep.

Around an hour passed and Sandra had fallen asleep. There was a knock on the front door and someone was knocking on the letter-box as if their life depended on it. Sandra rolled her bruised body from the sofa and peeped into the hall way. She could see Tina with her face squashed up against the glass. Sandra trudged to the door and opened it.

"What the fuck" Tina screamed as she saw her friend's face for the first time. Sandra tried covering her eyes but Tina dragged them away to get a better look. "The dirty no good bastard. You should phone the police on the wanker." Tina was livid. Leading Sandra to the kitchen she switched the kettle on. That was the answer to a lot of problems they had and the only way Tina knew how to cope with a drama. A brew and a cig. Yeah that was the medicine her friend needed to calm her down.

It was war now and as they sipped their cup of tea a plan unfolded between them. Tracy and Kevin would be destroyed. They both knew they would have to be cunning to go undetected. It was just a matter of time before the two of them got what was coming to them. The girls smiled as they took deep drags from their cigs as Sandra nursed her face with a cold flannel held up to her eyes.

4

A few weeks passed and Sandra started to plot her husband's downfall. As she sat in work waiting for her next client she tapped her finger on her front tooth. The salon where she worked was boiling hot and the sound of the sunbed fans could be heard.

Sandra's table was set in the front window of the shop and she could see everyone who passed. Her black tunic felt tight round her chest and she promised herself that she was going on a strict diet as of today. Well that was after she'd eaten her sandwich and the chocolate éclair she'd just bought from the bakery next door. Kevin had been even more distant over the last few weeks and tonight was the night she had planned to follow him and see what he was really up to. A client now joined Sandra. She looked stressed.

"Oh Sandra, sorry I'm late I missed the bus from town." Pulling the cake from her mouth Sandra smiled and told Maxine to take a seat. Wiping the cream from the side of her mouth, Sandra searched the drawer at the side of her for a nail file. Maxine had been her client for over a year now and had become a good friend. She made Sandra piss laughing with some of the stories she told her. In fact the tales she'd heard from behind her nail station would make anyone's toes curl. The women saw her as some kind of therapist and never held back with their own personal problems. Maxine always had problems. She was around thirty eight years of age and was sunbed mad. Her skin looked like a rhino's. Maxine had hammered the sunbeds over the years and she looked orange. Since she'd been taking the new tanning pill on the market she looked like an umpa- lumpa. Maxine threw her finger nails into her face.

"My nails are minging love. I took the false ones off the other day. My fingers look as if I have picked a thousand spuds from a field." Sandra sprayed some antiseptic over her hands and began to prepare her nails for the false tips. Maxine's voice was quiet now. She looked around the shop with caution to make sure no one was listening. "I've got some dresses in my bag from Selfridges if you wanna have a look." Sandra nodded. Maxine was a shoplifter and had been for years. Everybody knew her and what she did. These days though she had to go out of Manchester to earn her living as all the security guards knew her in most of the stores. Maxine had been to prison a few times in the past and spoke openly about her sentences. Sandra knew she'd had a hard time with her boyfriend in the past and the scars on her arm told her just how bad it had been. Sandra told her she would have a proper look at her swag later. Maxine dropped the bag at the side of her and casually spoke.

"So what's new with you love, any gossip for me?" Sandra was filing her nails with her head dipped. She paused and looked up in deep thought. She wanted to tell her that her husband was shagging her sister but held back as another customer walked into the shop to use the sunbeds. She watched the middle-aged woman go to the reception desk and carried on with her conversation. Sandra kept her problems to herself for now. Maxine now filled her in on the latest traumas in her life.

"Well that wanker of a boyfriend I've got has been at it again. I caught the cunt bang to rights the other night" Sandra stopped filing her nails and listened with interest. Maxine didn't care who heard her and looked angry as Sandra felt her hands tense as she continued to file her nails. Maxine spoke in a loud voice. "He told me he was going to look at a new car with his mate. I was on to him straight away. I mean I wasn't born fucking yesterday was I?" Maxine chewed on her lip and moved closer across the table. With a giggle in her voice she whispered. "Revenge is sweet Sandra and I've already started to wipe the smile off his face. I've cut all the twats clothes up to start with. I mean I nicked most of them for him anyway and there's no way I'm dressing the tosser up for someone else to look at." Sandra's eyes lit up, she wanted to know more. She didn't realise it but she was squeezing Maxine's hand tighter and her client had to wriggle free to get the blood flowing again. Maxine continued.

"My mate Marcy from down our street put me on to it a few weeks ago. She said she'd seen him in the Claridon pub at the top of Monsall. You know where it is, don't you?"

Sandra nodded eagerly and replied. "Yeah I've been in there a few times with Kevin. It's rough in there isn't it!"

Maxine giggled. "Oh it was rough when I went in love let me tell you." Maxine now sat back in her chair. Her face was serious. "I stood at the door at first and didn't want to go in. You know what it's like don't you love? Half of me wanted to know but the other didn't. Anyway I thought fuck it. I needed to see it with my own two eyes."

Sandra started speaking now and she looked about the shop to make sure no one could hear her, after all she was at work and had to be professional. "Yeah that's the worst thing ever. Not knowing if he's cheating. It would drive me mad."

Maxine's face looked grey as she carried on. "I couldn't see him at first when I opened the door. But as I looked closer at a few of his mates they knew the game was over for Barry. They all sunk their heads down in shame because they all knew about his affair with her. I just followed their eyes to the corner of the pub and that's when I saw him. Fucking Romeo and Juliet had nothing on him. Holding her hand he was, staring deep into her eyes. He didn't even see me walk in." Maxine's face looked sad as she continued. "The pub was silent and I crept to his side without him batting an eyelid." Sandra was gripped by the story, as if she watching it on TV. She would have gladly eaten a packet of crisps and sipped a Coca Cola if she had any as she hung on to Maxine's every word.

Maxine blew a deep breath and run her fingers through her long red hair. "He was chatting shit to her and the girl was now looking at me. He turned to see what she was looking at and nearly had a heart attack when he saw me stood there. Everyone in the pub was waiting for my next move and I didn't disappoint them. You know what I'm like don't you?" she said with a smirk across her face. "I jumped on him there and then. His little slapper of a girlfriend looked shocked and tried to stop me. Well that was until I jawed her."

Maxine was giggling and held the bottom part of her stomach as she told her the rest of the story. "I ragged Barry's hair and there wasn't a thing he could do about it because he was sat down. His tart was shouting at the side of him now and that's when I told her who I was. She was a cocky little twat, I can tell you, because she didn't believe me at first. Six months she said she'd been seeing him. Barry was now on his feet by this time and denying it all to me right in front of her face. She fucked off once she'd heard that. He was stood like a prize prick in the pub now and you could see his mates with snide smiles all across their faces. I was calm you know, when I told him I would be sorting his clothes out and I wanted him out of my life as from today. I just left the pub then. I mean there was nothing left to be said was there?"

Sandra shook her head slowly. Maxine now looked sad. She pushed her hand back over to Sandra and you could tell she was close to tears. Sandra rubbed Maxine's hand slowly and called her ex a no good bastard. Maxine tried to break a smile. "Oh don't worry about me. I'll have the last laugh, don't you worry and he'll pay for every tear I've cried. Anyway once bitten twice shy innit." Sandra was intrigued and wanted to know more about this payback she planned for her ex-boyfriend. She'd already secretly searched on the internet and had a few revenge ideas for Kevin but Maxine looked as if she knew what she was talking about and she wanted to pick her brains. Filing her nails, she probed deeper.

"So what have you got planned for him now then. I bet he went mad that you cut all his clothes up didn't he?"

Maxine looked proud. "He's lucky I didn't cut off his cock off the prick. Because the way I felt Sandra, I could of you know." Sandra looked into Maxine's eyes and she could see that she meant every word. Sticking the nail tips on her fingernails she wanted to know more. Maxine was definitely a wise head.

The radio seemed to be playing lots of love songs.

Did the radio presenter know how they both felt, because every song that played was heartbreaking. As "Where D Broken Hearts Go" By Whitney Houston played Maxine giggled. "For fuck's sake turn this bag of shit off. I'm depressed enough without this kind of music." Sandra needed this woman's help and spoke in a low voice.

"Ay Maxine I think my fella is fucking about too. What do you think I should do?"

Maxine smiled cunningly. "Do you know what, you're about the third person who has said that to me this week. What's wrong with these men around here? Aren't we enough for them?" Sandra felt embarrassed now and started to apply the clear top-coat polish to her nails. As they were placed under the dryer Maxine nodded her head as she stared at her nails. "We could set up a business you know. We could call it 'Payback Slimey Cheating Bastards'!"

They both were laughing out loud now but Sandra was on it and the thought of helping other women like herself appealed to her. Sandra checked her nails and looked at Maxine with a serious face. "Tell you what. If you help me catch this fucker of a husband I'll set up a website for women with straying partners. We'll show the dirty fuckers. We can catch them red- handed or even just do things to them without them knowing what's going on."

Maxine's eyes lit up. She was excited too. She searched in her bag for a pen and scribbled her mobile number down for Sandra. She told her she was busy tonight but she would gladly meet up at a later date to discuss their next move. Sandra told her they had planned to follow her husband that same night and covered her face with her hands as the thought of catching him ran through her mind. Maxine stopped her dead in her tracks.

"Don't do anything yet. Let's catch him red-handed. Once you know he's cheating, then we can start paying him back. What's the point of letting the cat out of the bag straight away? We can ruin him and his tart big time." Sandra agreed. She would just go tonight and see for herself what the bastard was fooling around with, and once she knew for sure the games would begin to ruin him.

Maxine waved goodbye as she left the shop and winked at her telling her she would be in touch. Sandra now sat tapping her fingers at the table. Her husband was going to get what was coming to him and she couldn't wait to wipe the smile from his face and her sister's.

Much of Sandra's day went more or less the same. She looked as if she had something on her mind and she struggled to concentrate. Once she'd finished the last set of nails for a client, she went on the sunbed for nine minutes to try and relax. Stood inside the cubicle she started to undress. The full-length mirror stood from the wall and she couldn't help but look at herself. Turning to the side she breathed in and pulled at her fat trying to look as thin as possible. It was no good because no matter which way she stood, she was still the fat bastard she hated. "You need to stop eating you beached whale Sandra," she muttered. Rolling her bra down from her shoulders she threw it onto the chair and stepped inside the sunbed.

Closing the door behind her she looked at the tubes and slowly felt one to see if it was hot. Her fingers gently pressed on one and burnt her finger. Silly bastard she thought. She stood holding the two ropes from the ceiling as she squeezed her arse muscles together. This was exercise after all. The heat inside the cubicle was now taking effect and small droplets of sweat rolled from her brow. She was now fidgeting and stepped out of the sunbed to check the timer on the wall to see how long she had left. With four minutes remaining she stepped back inside and danced about as if she was stepping on hot coals. Phew it was hot! Once her time was up she jumped outside and wafted her hand in front of her face. Dragging her knickers down slightly Sandra checked her white bits. Sandra now sat down on the small wooden chair inside the cubicle for a minute. She felt sick and hung her head between her legs.

Once all her nail station was clean, she said goodbye to John the manager. He was quite fit and if he hadn't have been married, Sandra would have seriously thought about shagging the arse off him. So what, she thought, she was married too, but that didn't matter anymore because her husband was an out and out bastard. Perhaps one day, she thought as she gazed at him from afar. Her mobile phone started ringing. Searching her bag she headed out of the shop.

"Hello I'm just coming out of work now. Where are you?" It was Tina.

Sandra had arranged to meet her back at her house. She was scared and the thought of following her husband tonight was starting to have an effect. "Right, see you soon. I'm just getting in the car now." Sandra said goodbye and opened the door to her Black Corsa. Throwing her handbag on the passenger side she fastened her seat belt. Her hands looked shaky as she pulled off. She was that pre-occupied she didn't even check her mirrors and nearly hit a passing car. "Oh for fuck's sake pull ya self together girl" she moaned.

Opening the front door to her house she could hear Tina shouting behind her. She turned her head and saw her friend jogging up slowly. Once they were both together they entered the house. Sandra shouted to see if anyone was home. No one answered.

"Put the kettle on love. My mouth is like sandpaper" Tina laughed.

Sandra filled the kettle up and stood with her back to it. "I'm shitting myself you know. What am I going to do if it's true and he is with Tracy?"

Tina shoved a cig in her mouth and slowly inhaled. "You don't do anything. We'll just sit quiet until we're ready to make our next move." Sandra now filled her in about what Maxine had said earlier. Tina knew Maxine and smiled. "Well she's right love. What will you get if you go in all guns blazing? He will deny it all and make up some excuse. You know what Kevin's like."

Sandra finished making the brews and started to talk about setting up a business of paying men back who had wronged their partners. Tina was excited. "Yeah I'm defo up for that!" she chuckled, "and if Maxine's onboard I know it will be successful." Tina leant back in her chair and twisted her hair round her fingers. "She's a crank though, but I'm sure she has some great ideas. After all she's been through loads with men in the past and I've heard some of the sick shit she's done to them if they've fucked about with her."

Sandra looked as if she'd had a brainwave. As she passed Tina her drink she seated next to her and looked excited. "I'm shit hot on the internet as well. I could make a website, I've done one before so that's not a problem. Ay, we could be like detectives." She rubbed her palms together. Tina was laughing and spoke about some of the things they could do to pay cheating partners back. You could hear the front door opening and Sandra nudged Tina to be quiet.

Kevin walked in like a cowboy strutting into a saloon. He stood at the kitchen door and scanned the area. Scratching his bollocks down the front of his tracksuit bottoms he smiled. "Don't be making me any tea tonight, I've got to go and check the grow later so I'll grab summat while I'm out." Sandra couldn't look him in the eye. She'd never been one for lying and spoke to the table as he pottered about the kitchen.

"Fucking hell, when's this grow gonna be ready. You're always there. Surely it's done soon?"

Kevin walked to her side. She looked uneasy. "It's ready when it's ready. You won't be saying that when the cash is here will you? We should get about ten grand when it's done." She huffed. Sandra never got fuck all from the weed he sold and was nearly telling him that, but remained quiet, she didn't want to wind him up.

The house where the weed was growing was his friend's house. The bedrooms had plants in every room. She'd been there with him in the past and couldn't believe all the equipment that you needed to grow Marijuana. "Right I'm getting a bath" he said casually. Sandra screwed her face up at Tina as he left her side. Once he was out of sight and his footsteps could be heard going up the stairs she snarled at Tina.

"Washing his cock isn't he, for our Tracy. I want to go up now and kick off!"

Tina could see she was on the verge of breaking and grabbed her back. "Will you turn it in, stop tormenting yourself until you know for sure. As soon as he leaves tonight we're onto him. So don't spoil it."

Sandra gritted her teeth. She walked to the fridge and grabbed a Kit-Kat. "Do you want one Tina?" she held the biscuit up and showed it her. She declined. Sandra munched her biscuit at speed. "See what I mean, as soon as I'm upset I reach for food as comfort. I'll be fucking eighty stone before this is all over!" They both chuckled. Whispering now filled the kitchen as they both plotted to capture Kevin and his mistress.

Kevin said his goodbyes as Tina and Sandra watched the soaps on TV. Coronation Street was on and they both looked interested in it. They said goodbye to Kevin but kept their eyes on the screen. As soon as he was gone it was as if boiling water had been poured on the pair of them – they both jumped up and searched for the car keys. They knew where the grow house was and wanted to get there as soon as possible so they could see who went inside.

They were soon in hot pursuit. At one point they were nearly behind Kevin in the traffic and feared he might have seen them. "Fucking pull over" Tina shouted. Sandra quickly pressed her brakes and turned off from the main road. Her face was red and she looked anxious. "Right get back on him, just head to the house and park over the road where he can't see us." Sandra was driving like a maniac and her mind was all over the place. Once she reached her destination she pulled the keys out from the ignition and dipped her body down into the driving seat. Tina now also hid as they watched Kevin going inside the house.

Night-time was now falling and their vision was poor. Tina was sure she saw a car pulling up outside the house and forced Sandra to drive nearer so she could see properly. Once Sandra was closer to the house they both recognised the woman they saw stepping from the car. Sandra was livid and Tina had to drag her back as she tried to leave the car.

"Sandra, leave her will you. She'll get what's coming to her don't you worry."

Sandra wriggled from her grip. "Fuck off will you and get off me. She's gonna get leathered now the fucking tart." The two of them were now wrestling in the car.

Tina looked over to the house and shouted. "Look he's opening the door." Holding Sandra in a grip, Tina felt her friend deflate as she saw Kevin kissing Tracy before she went inside the house. Sandra screamed and Tina held her in her arms feeling every inch of her pain. She was heartbroken.

"She's a dirty little bitch. He's going to be sorry. The pair of them are!" Sandra was sobbing now and wanted to get away from the house because she knew if she stayed there a minute longer she would have gone over to the house and kicked the front door off its hinges. Placing the key back into the ignition her eyes were flooded with tears. Tina sighed. "Let's go to Maxine's, she'll tell us what our next move is. Are you in the mood for it?"

Sandra nodded. Her tears now turned into anger and her face looked like it was going to explode. "I fucking knew it. I don't know why I never ran over to the house. I need to pay him back big time. Do you hear me big time? I want them both to feel pain. The pair of cheeky cunts."

Sandra phoned Maxine's mobile and she told them she was in a nearby pub. The Queen's was round the corner from where they were so they headed there to meet her. The pub was quiet and only a few punters were in. Maxine was sat with a local piss-head and told him she needed some privacy when she saw the girls walk in through the door. Maxine could tell something had happened by Sandra's face. Tina went to the bar and Maxine pulled up a chair for Sandra to sit next to her.

"What's up love?" Maxine whispered.

Sandra shook her head and took a while before she could speak. "I've just caught Kevin with his knock off." Maxine sat nearer and wanted to know more.

Once she'd told her the other woman was her sister, she gasped. "What a sneaky fucker she is. Orr... I bet you want to kill her don't you?" Sandra held the tears back that had formed in her eyes. She was sick of crying and felt a relief that she wasn't going crazy anymore. For years people had told her she was imagining things but now she'd seen it all with her own two eyes.

The truth was out there now. Sandra was now on at Maxine. She needed help to hurt him and started to tell her about how and where she'd seen him with her sister. Sandra's words made Maxine smile. She told her all about the weed he was growing and how it was nearly ready. Maxine rubbed her hands together and spoke. She even knew the man he was growing the weed for. He was a main head and someone not to be messed with. Maxine chuckled.

"Oh, he is so going to be so gutted. Can you get the keys for the house where the weed is?" Sandra thought for a minute and told her she could get a key cut if needed but asked why. "Why?", Maxine ranted. She pulled her arm closer and became giddy. "Because we're going to have it away, that's fucking why. I can organise it no worries. I just need a key. Plus you can earn yourself some decent cash." Maxine burst out laughing. "He's gonna be so gutted. Let's hit him where it hurts." Maxine patted the pocket on the back of her jeans. "In his fucking pocket."

Sandra hugged her and started to thank her. Maxine spoke in a soft voice. "Don't you worry love, I told you I would help you. So let the games begin." Tina smiled at Sandra. Her face now seemed calmed and the sadness was lifting. Malice filled her face and she grinned at her friends. Sandra sat with her arms folded. She was rocking as she spoke.

"I want him and Tracy to pay. She isn't getting away with it." Tina now jumped into the conversation and she too had some evil plans for the pair of them. The three of them now sat chatting and before the night was over, Kevin's downfall was planned.

Sandra left her car at the pub. It wasn't that far home anyway and they could walk. The midnight air hit her face and she felt sick. Swaying about in the car park, Tina held her friend up. Her words were slurred as she tried to stand.

"I'm gutted Tina. I can't believe the cunt is shagging my sister. I mean, I did know, but I suppose I didn't want to face it, if you know what I mean."

Tina kissed her cheek. "He doesn't deserve you. You have me now and I'll never let you down. Best mates forever." Sandra cried and snot was dribbling down her nose as she tried to wipe it on her sleeve. Tina's mobile phone was ringing. Searching in her jacket she located it. She nudged Sandra in the waist and showed her the screen displaying Steven's name. Tina had told Sandra that she'd been seeing Steven for a few weeks now and lately he couldn't get enough of her.

"Hello" Tina replied. She was now laughing loudly and she could be heard telling him she would meet him shortly. She told him to meet her on Rochdale Road near the junction. He knew where she meant and the phone call ended. Tina was giddy and she was laughing telling Sandra she was going to get a night of passion. Sandra was in no mood for anyone else's happiness as she stood spewing her ring up near some garden wall while Tina was getting ready to leave.

"Right, goodnight. Don't you be worrying love. Keep your cool and we'll sort this shit out tomorrow." She pecked her on the cheek and Tina left her side.

★

Sandra pushed her key into the front door. She entered the house and could hear someone in the front room. With anger across her face she entered and saw her son John sat playing on the Play Station, shouting at the screen. "You German bastards get out of my way!" She couldn't be arsed with him and made her way to bed.

The bed felt as cold as her heart as she lay in it. She looked at the place where her husband usually slept. Clenching her fist she punched into his pillow. The photograph of them together now stared back at her from the bedside cabinet. It was as if he was laughing at her from the photograph. Gripping it from the side she launched the wooden frame at the wall. Splinters of wood now flew across the bedroom. Lying in bed she hugged herself tightly and tried to rid herself of the pain she felt inside. Even the thought of food now made her feel sick.

Nothing could give her the comfort she needed. She was a broken woman.

5

There he lay at the side of her, the dirty cunt. He was fast asleep and stank of stale beer. Her eyes now focused to the bedside cabinet at the side of him. She could see his car keys with the key to the grow house on them. Like a snake she slid from the bed and crept round to his bedside. Her hands were shaking as she picked up the bunch of keys. "Shut up fucking rattling" she thought as she held them tightly in her grip. Heading to the bathroom she hid the keys in her housecoat.

The keys made her feel sick as she stared at them. They were connected to Kevin's infidelity. Her face screwed up.

"Bastard!"

She knew she didn't have long and shoved on the clothes she'd worn the night before. The place where she was going to have the key cut wasn't far and she knew she could be there and back within ten minutes if she got a move on.

Driving to the shop she gripped the keys tightly in her pocket. She looked at his car keys and a plan formed in her mind. She would get his car key cut as well, after all it was his pride and joy and she knew without it he would be devastated. She would keep the car key for a future revenge attack.

The man in the cobblers wore long brown overalls. He looked like a pervert with thick lens glasses hanging from his nose. Sandra nearly started laughing when he spoke to her with a stutter. He was like Ronnie Barker from the TV show "Open all Hours." She passed him the two keys and paced the shop waiting for him to cut them. Once he was done she quickly paid him and headed back to the car. She needed to get the keys back to Kevin's side as soon as possible because if he thought for one minute she had them he would knock the living daylights out of her.

Creeping back up the stairs, she held her breath. She was panting like a dog and her nerves had taken over. Slowly she opened the bedroom door and sneaked inside. She held the bunch of keys tightly and tried to place them down without making any noise. The fuckers were noisy and kept rattling. Placing them down on the side Kevin opened his eyes and looked straight at her. She looked worried. She had to think fast.

"Where's your lighter?" she asked him. His eyes closed again and he mumbled where it was. She quickly headed back to her side of the bed. The job was done and she felt happier now knowing the twat was getting what he deserved. She could feel his hand on her body. She cringed. He now spoke to her with a cocky tone.

"Fancy a bit of slap and tickle?"

His eyes were looking at her. He could tell she was ready to make an excuse and dived on her before she had chance to speak.

"Get ya gums round my plums. Get ya smackers round my knackers" he giggled as he swung his hairy ball bag in her face. Sandra tried to raise a smile but she was struggling not to break.

"I'm not in the mood" she moaned as she pushed him away from her. Looking into her eyes he punched Sandra in the waist. He was angry.

"What again? You're never in the fucking mood anymore. I don't know why I even bother." She ranted back at him. "Well don't ask again then nob head. It's not as if you're some kind of 'Love God' or summit"

His face changed and she looked scared. Kicking at her legs he let her have a piece of his mind. "It's like shagging a wet lettuce anyway. I would rather have a wank. Go on fuck off out of here you fat cow."

Sandra struggled to get up from the bed. She feared he was going to beat the living daylights out of her. He'd done it before in the past when she'd refused him sex. As she stood up she was dying to let him have it, she didn't care anymore and nearly let the cat of the bag. "Keep it quiet Sandra, don't spoil it" she whispered under her breath. She walked slowly from the bedroom and you could tell she was still debating telling him what she knew.

Mastering her anger, she got in the bathroom. Leaning against the cold wall in the bathroom she jerked her head forward and backward just enough so it touched the wall. Her eyes were filled with tears and she wanted to run back in and let him have it. Her son had a baseball bat in his bedroom and she knew it wouldn't take long to go in and get it. Gripping her hands tightly she blew deeply and slowly to calm herself. Her mobile phone could be heard ringing. "Oh fucking hell it's in the bedroom" she huffed. Taking a deep breath she opened the door. She could see the bedclothes raised in the middle with Kevin's knees holding it up. The bastard was wanking. Quickly she walked to the side of the bed and grabbed the straps of her handbag dragging it towards her. She paused. She couldn't resist it.

"Hope you're cock goes soft. You wanker" His head now appeared from under the sheets he looked hot. He snapped at her.

"I wouldn't have to toss myself off if you did your job would I? Go on fuck off out of here!"

Sandra smiled and knew she'd broken his concentration. Her phone had stopped ringing now. It was a missed call from Maxine. She hurried out of the room leaving Kevin frustrated that he had to start all over again.

Checking her sons were still in bed, she hurried downstairs. "Hello Maxine, it's Sandra. Yeah, yeah I've got them. I'll meet you this afternoon about two o'clock at your house. Yeah, me too. Okay, see you later." The phone call left her struggling for her breath. Heading to the front room she turned on the telly. Her mind wasn't on it but the people speaking on it made her feel as if she was sat in company. Her eyes looked around the room. Shoes were all over the floor and plates with leftover food stared back at her. The signs of someone smoking weed was all over her glass table. She kicked the Rizla papers from the table with the side of her foot in disgust. The ash tray at the side of her was full with cig dimps. Searching her bag she grabbed her fags and lit one. She would have usually emptied the ashtray because she couldn't stand it when it was full, but today she couldn't be arsed.

She could hear his footsteps through the ceiling. Raising her eyes she knew exactly which room Kevin was in. He was now on his way downstairs. She could hear his thuds as he stamped down the stairs. Drawing her legs up to her chest she puffed hard on her cig. She could now feel him at the side of her. His hand reached to the arm of the chair and she could see him taking one of her cigs. She hated this man with a passion.

Sandra needed to make a move. Not a word was spoken between them as they both sat watching the TV. The thought of moving out of the room scared her. She wanted to be invisible and just disappear without him saying a word to her. "Invisible, yeah that would be good" she thought. She smiled as the thought of sticking her finger up her arse and wiping it under his nose. To be Invisible, now that would be an adventure. Coughing slightly she stood from the sofa. He looked over to her

"Make a brew ay and some bacon butties."

Sandra froze. Usually she would have obeyed his every need but today she felt different. She felt stronger.

"Nope I'm going out. Do it yourself." He looked shocked and turned his head from the chair to see her face.

"Orr come on Sandra. I'm knackered." The words were there again. Her mind was bubbling. Shagging my sister, shagging my sister. You dirty twat. With one hand on the doorframe she scowled.

"You had enough strength for a wank didn't you? So get off ya lazy arse and make your own fucking food. I'm nobody's slave anymore. I'm gonna look after me from now on, because no one else will." Her eyes rolled as she turned to leave. Kevin launched the remote control at her head and it just skimmed past her, smashing to bits on the wall. He was fuming. He was shouting at the top of his voice.

"Don't get fucking smart Sandra because I'll do you in. You fucking slut. Do you hear me?" She left the room. He was still screaming at her. "I don't know who you think you are lately. That Tina is rubbing off on you. Keep her away from this fucking house." Sandra smiled. For the first time in years she had refused to make him something to eat. She was getting stronger each day and she liked the way she was feeling. Raising her two fingers towards Kevin in the living room she rammed them up in the air.

"Fuck you arse-hole" she muttered.

After a quick wash Sandra stood in front of the mirror. She looked thinner. Bringing her face up closer she stretched her skin around her eyes. "I need some Botox" she whispered. Gripping the skin tighter she pulled it towards her ears. One last quick look and she was gone.

Walking out of the house she could hear Kevin shouting behind her. As she turned her head before getting into the car she could see him waving his hands up in the air shouting "Where the fuck are you going? I need my clothes ironing. Get back here." Opening the car door she gave him a smile and sat inside. She could see him approaching with speed. Locking her door frantically he was at the window banging on it with full force. Hands trembling she inserted the key in the ignition. "Keep calm, keep calm" she mouthed. Kevin's angry face squashed up at the window. Spit hung from the corner of his mouth as he stood there wearing nothing but his boxer shorts. His chest was bare and you could see his toned body turning red.

"Don't be smart Sandra. Get back in here and do my clothes." The banging was getting louder and she knew if she didn't drive away soon her car window would have gone through. He was banging harder. The car started to move and she kept her eyes on the road. She couldn't look at him. He was livid and at one point he was lying on the bonnet of the car smashing his fist against the windscreen. Heart pumping she turned the steering wheel and headed out of the cul-de-sac. One of the neighbours was out watching everything and she grinned as Sandra passed her. Kevin was left behind. As she looked through her rear view mirror she could see him still stood there with his hands on his hips shaking his head. She knew she would have to face him later on but for now she was free and that's all that mattered.

Her mood was low and as she turned the radio up, she smiled as her favourite song came on. Candy Statton "Young Hearts Run Free" now played at full blast. As she sang along she meant every single word. People next to her in the traffic smiled at her as they watched her singing her head off. To them she looked like the happiest person alive. How wrong they were! Maxine didn't live far away in Harpurhey. Ten minutes drive and she was there.

Harpurhey was a rough place to live. Monsall wasn't that much better. Sandra felt as if she was walking into the Bronx as she pulled into the small car park facing Maxine's house. Gangs of lads were sat about and they were kicking a football about. Turning the engine off, she debated waiting for a while until they'd moved on. Fuck it she thought, what's the worst that can happen? She stepped from the car. She could feel their eyes burning into her back as she stood slightly bent over, locking the door. Walking towards them she gripped her handbag tightly in her arms. She was already planning in her mind her fight back if they tried to rob her. She was next to them now and raised a smile at one of the lads. Spitting on the floor he carried on playing football. She was okay, they were leaving her alone.

Maxine lived on the edge of the Two Hundred estate. Each house looked the same. The net curtains hung from the windows with misery written all across them. None of the gardens were cut neatly and weeds grew through the gaps in most of the fences. A few dogs were running about on the field facing her and even they looked like they had mental issues.

"What's up with us all" she mumbled. Maxine's house looked straight at her. The windows looked like they hadn't been cleaned in years. The small garden at the front was full of empty beer cans and bottles. Tapping the silver letter box she stood back from the door. Maxine answered, she looked busy.

"Oh come in love. I won't be a minute, I'm just sorting these women out." Maxine went back into the front room and Sandra followed her. The front room was packed with knocked off clothing. Dresses were hung from doorframes and jeans and shoes were scattered all over the sofa. The two women were Maxine's buyers. They bought in bulk and got some really good bargains from her. Looking at Sandra they became apprehensive until Maxine gave them the okay.

Maxine had been busted lots of times in the past and the buyers always shit themselves when they were inside her house. One large lady with blonde bleached hair piled her clothes up and came to Maxine for a price. Maxine picked each garment up and you could see her adding them up in her head. Throwing the last dress on the sofa she looked at the woman. "Give us eighty quid. It's comes to roughly about two hundred but I know you and you're a good buyer so call it eighty." The woman dug into her black handbag and pulled out the cash. Counting it out in front of her she checked the amount was right.

"Have you got any black bags love?" the woman asked. Maxine now reached to the dining table situated at the back of the room and pulled two from the roll she had there. She always had bin- liners in the house and was never short of them. There were no Selfridge's or Harvey Nicols bags on this estate. It was a black bag or fuck all. The first lady left and as Maxine walked her to the door the other woman was holding dresses up to the light and examining every detail on them. Maxine returned and raised her eyes at Sandra. Maxine knew this woman of old and knew she wanted rock bottom prices. She was waiting for her to start her usual moaning. She didn't have to wait long. The other woman called Pat looked quite stunning. She was stood with her arms folded. You could smell her perfume all over the room. She was a dolly bird. False eyelashes, false nails and Sandra was sure her tits were false as well, as she examined them sticking from her tight black vest top. Sandra felt her own breasts and pushed them up with the side of her arm. Her own tits looked like spaniel's ears and she knew if she ever won the lottery new ones would be the first thing on her list.

Pat now started to pull dresses up from the chair at the side of her. "I like these but they are a bit dated." Her face screwed up as she stroked the material. Maxine looked stressed and Sandra could tell by her expression that she was losing patience with her.

"Listen Pat, don't fuck me about. You either want them or you don't. Every fucking time you come here you're always the same. I'm busy so hurry up ay."

Pat looked embarrassed. "Right, work out how much it is for this lot."

Maxine was at her side as she took the dresses from her hands. "Sixty quid."

Pat was going to argue the toss but as she looked at Maxine she could see she would be fighting a losing battle, giving in she paid her the money with a grin on her face. She knew she could double it when she sold them on and started to brown nose her. "Thanks love you're a star. If you get anything else ring me first. You know I always buy from you."

Maxine nodded. Pat was pissing her off and to tell you the truth she didn't like her anyway. She was too much up her own arse. Pat owned the local pub called the Top Derby and she was never short of a few quid. Everyone who knew her, knew she was a tart and she wouldn't think twice about shagging your fella. Maxine wanted her gone from the house and once her black bag was loaded up with her knock-off she carted her from the house.

"Thank fuck she's gone. She does my head in. Did you hear her trying to get the stuff for next to nothing? The cheeky fucking bint."

Maxine shoved some clothes from a chair and reached for her cigs from the table. Once she lit it she took a deep breath. Sandra was sat at the side of her staring round the front room. Trainers were situated at her feet and she knew they were the culprit for the cheesy smell she could feel strangling her nostrils.

Maxine was still dressed in her pyjamas. This was normal for her and she wouldn't think twice about walking to the shops in them or walking the streets. Pyjamas' was the code of dress these days for people who lived on a council estate. It wasn't that they had no clothes, it was the point of why waste your good clothes when you're just dossing all day. Bringing her knees up to her chest Maxine rubbed her hands together.

"So did you get them?"

Sandra shoved her hand into her pocket and jingled the two keys in front of her. "Result love. Oh he's so gonna regret ever messing with you. Right, let me make a quick phone call, we need this done as soon as possible." Maxine searched under all the clothes for her mobile phone. She dragged newspapers from the table and sighed as her eyes looked round the room. "For fuck's sake. Where the fuck did I put it?" She looked at Sandra. "Do me a favour love, phone my mobile." Sandra located her own phone and found the contact number she required. Holding the phone out in front of her she waited for Maxine's phone to ring. You could now hear the muffled sound of her ring tone. At first Sandra couldn't make out which tune it was but as it got louder she smiled as the Usher ring tone could be heard. Maxine was now on all fours searching for her phone. The sound was coming from underneath the chair. Sliding her hand under it, her face was side down on the floor. Her arm was now out of sight.

"Here it is. What the fuck is it doing underneath there? I don't know, I'm losing the plot me love." Sandra giggled. She was also always losing her phone and was glad to see someone else have the same problem.

"Mine is my keys," Sandra chirped in, "I must lose them about five times a day. I'm hopeless." Maxine was now wiping the dirt from her screen. Folding her leg underneath her she sat back down. Her eyes were struggling to focus as she tried to find the correct contact. Sandra was hanging on her every word. Maxine found the phone number she wanted and sat back on the chair. The phone was answered.

"Alright Barry. It's Maxine. Can you get round to my house as soon as possible. I've got some graft for you. Right okay. See you soon." Sitting looking at her phone Maxine grinned. "Right that's sorted. These lads are shit hot and don't fuck about. Kevin's going to crumble." Twiddling her hair Sandra sat on the edge of her seat. "I want them to put a video camera in there first. I want to get some footage of them twats together."

Maxine scowled. "What the fuck do ya mean? I thought you wanted them to get the grow tonight. They won't fuck about with all that shit."

Sandra looked angry. Twisting her fingers she looked at Maxine and spoke in a firm voice. "Listen love. They can get that later on. Kevin goes to the house tonight, so they can film him first then wait for him to fuck off before they get the weed."

"You're fucking hard work you are" Maxine sighed, "Have you even got a video camera?" Sandra sat in deep thought. "Yeah yeah, I have. Kevin's got one in the house. It's a bit old but it will do the trick."

There was a knock at the front door. Maxine shit herself at first and started throwing all the knocked-off clothing into the corner. She now shouted at Sandra. "Peep through the kitchen window and see who it is."

Sandra looked scared. Standing slowly she chewed on her fingernails. Approaching the window she held her body. Her head was now at the side of discoloured net curtain. She jerked her head backward as she saw one of the lads clock her. She stood back in the corner of the kitchen like a scared animal. A face could be seen at the window and she froze. The banging on the pane of glass made Maxine come into the kitchen. She now saw a familiar face and laughed.

"Fucking hell it's Barry."

Sandra looked as if she was having heart attack. Her face was red and she looked hot. Maxine left her to go and open the door. Standing in the kitchen Sandra looked around. It was a disgrace. Plates were all over the sides and the sink was full of dirty dishes. Dirty washing was piled next to the washer and the smell in the air was putrid. She walked back to the front room with a look of disgust fixed firmly on her face. Maxine was a scruffy cunt. Three lads were now stood pacing the front room. They only looked young and they were all dressed the same in tracksuits and trainers. The ring leader smiled at Sandra and introduced himself as Barry. What the fuck was she doing she thought. These lads weren't much older than her own sons and yet she was conspiring with them to commit a crime.

Barry rubbed his hands together as the other two lads made a joint. Sandra sat down and waited for Maxine to begin. Once she heard her telling them she wanted them to rob a grow of weed she knew she had to step in. Her mouth felt dry and she sucked on her lips to give them some moisture. With a slight cough she spoke.

"It's not just the weed. I want you to film him first."

Barry sat down next to her and laughed. "What the fuck are you going on about? We're here to have the weed away, we're not fucking film producers."

The others laughed. Her face turned sour. She knew what she wanted and continued.

"No filming, no weed. Simple."

Sitting back on the chair Barry looked at the others. There was silence for a moment and Barry could see by her face she wasn't going to change her mind. Gripping the joint from his mate he inhaled deeply and released smoke rings from his mouth. Sandra was tapping her foot nervously hoping they would agree. Barry spoke.

"Right so let me get this right. You want us to film someone, doing what exactly?"

Sandra sat up as if someone had shoved a pin into her arse cheeks. Her words were fast and furious and Barry had to tell her to slow down at one point.

"Basically, my husband is shagging my sister and I want them filmed so I have proof when the time comes to use it." Barry laughed out loud but when he saw her serious face he realised it wasn't funny. Sandra continued. "The video recorder has a timer on it. Just place it out of sight in the bedroom and fuck off until later. Once they leave the gaff just get the camera back, and then take the full grow. I mean the lights and everything, because they are worth something as well aren't they?"

Barry was excited and wanted to know more about the weed. Sandra now told them that each room in the house had marijuana plants growing in it. Now the simple task of doing a bit of filming didn't seem too bad and Barry grinned at Sandra. "Right yeah we can do that, but we need to talk cash now don't we and we need to know who wants what."

Maxine stepped in, after all she wanted an earner too. She stood to her feet and rubbed her hands together. "We'll have to see what's there first innit. We can split it five ways. We have to be careful about all of this because it's Zac Hanson's grow." Barry looked worried until Maxine told him she had a buyer. Sandra wasn't really arsed about the money and just wanted to ruin her husband but the thought of some extra cash made her face light up. She spoke to the group.

"There'll be enough for us all don't worry. Just get that filming done first and when the fucker leaves later on tonight you can go in and fleece the fucking lot."

Barry shook Sandra's hand. He told her he needed to know where the house was and needed to get the video camera set up before Kevin got there later on that night. Sandra looked apprehensive. She didn't know these lads and they could have had her over. She glanced at Maxine for her to take over.

"Right, me and Sandra will meet you here in an hour. We can let you in the house and make sure you set the camera up. Once that's done you can come back here for a bit and chill. Sandra will ring you when her husband gets home and then you can do your stuff. Have you got a van an all that?" Barry nodded and told them they had to find some storage for the plants. They sprang to their feet and told Sandra they would be back within the hour.

They left with a spring in their steps.

Maxine looked at Sandra. "Right you better get your arse in gear and go and get that video camera. They'll be back soon and we need to get it all set up before Kevin gets there tonight," Sandra huffed. She knew once she was back in the house Kevin would make her pay for the way she had disobeyed him earlier. He'd never hit her in front of anyone before and she had a cunning plan to take Maxine back home with her. Once she told Maxine her plan for her to come with her, she planned a story to tell Kevin because after all he was a nosey fucker and would want to know why Maxine was at his house and why she wanted the video recorder.

"Right we can say to Kevin that you're going to a christening and you want to video it. He won't say owt about that will he?" Maxine smiled. "Listen chick, I'm not arsed what you tell him. Are you scared of him or summit?" Sandra looked shocked. Was it that obvious to people that he ruled her life? She dipped her head and felt embarrassed.

"He's a control freak Maxine. I just do anything for an easy life." Maxine knew there was more to it than met the eye but kept her mouth shut. She had suffered domestic violence in the past and Sandra was showing all the signs of a victim. They both set off to Sandra's. She looked nervous and was forever checking her watch. She hoped Kevin was still out. As they pulled into her drive she knew when she spotted Kevin's car that her ordeal with him was about to start.

Rooting in her hand bag for the door keys, Maxine could see Sandra was agitated. She gritted her teeth and hoped the bullying bastard started while she was there. She wasn't afraid of no man and she would put him right in his place if he started with her friend.

They walked into the hallway. Music could be heard playing from upstairs and she knew by the song it was one of her sons. Walking cautiously into the kitchen they passed the living room. She could see Kevin sprawled out on the sofa playing with his phone. She showed Maxine into the kitchen and went into the front room. Kevin sat up as if he'd shit his pants. He was on his feet. He looked angry and walked straight up to Sandra. His large hands gripped her face. She wriggled to try and get away but his hands were firm. "Oh not so smart now are you slut." Her lips were squeezed together as she tried to speak. His head connected with hers and she fell straight to the ground. His voice was loud now and Maxine was now stood at the doorway. Her eyes quickly looked at Sandra and she looked as if she was ready to pounce on Kevin. His eyes now turned to Maxine and he looked like a kid who had been caught in the act. Sandra stood to her feet and didn't want any more violence. Her face raised a smile and she led Maxine back to the kitchen as if nothing had happened.

Sandra's hands were shaking and she was holding her head as she switched the kettle on. She felt faint and placed her hand on the side to steady herself. Maxine could hear Kevin rummaging around, she was fuming. A single tear fell from Sandra's face and Maxine was at her side within seconds.

"Love, don't get upset. He's a wanker and he'll get what's coming to him. Trust me, I've been like you and I know it's hard to walk away but if you stay here, what kind of a life will you have?" Sandra nodded, she was just about to pour her heart out when her son came into the kitchen. He could see a strange woman holding his mother and it didn't take long for him to work out what had happened. He'd witnessed the violence between his parents many times before and clenched his fist as he knew his father had been at it again, the anger was written across his face.

"What's up mam?" he was at her side and Maxine moved away sitting back down. Sandra controlled her tears and tried to cover up her husband's abuse.

"It's nothing son. It's just ya dad being a prick again. Don't get involved it's sorted now." His fist clenched as he banged it on the kitchen side. He was stood there in his shorts and his bare chest was visible. His body looked toned and you could tell he was no longer a child who'd let his father abuse his mother. He wanted revenge.

"Mam I'll twist him up I swear. I'm fucking sick of it ya know. Who does he think he is?"

Sandra placed her hand round his shoulder. She didn't want any more violence and told him so. "I've told you it's sorted now. Don't you go making things worse than they are. He's going out now anyway."

John flung her arms from his body. "Why do you always protect him ay? Let me sort it out. Trust me, he won't ever raise his hands to you again" Sandra raised her voice again as Maxine sat in disbelief.

"John just fuck off will you? You need to sort your own life out never mind mine." He was stood with his hands yanking at his hair. He looked frustrated.

"You deserve everything you get you know. Why do I even fucking bother!" He left the kitchen in a strop.

Maxine looked cold as she rubbed her arms. She had goose bumps visible all over her arms. Sandra was now in her "Everything in my life is fine" mode. She had become a great actress over the years and this performance deserved an Oscar. Sandra sat at the kitchen table once she'd brewed two drinks. Sipping her tea she spoke in an animated voice. "Oh fucking hell. What a day ay." Maxine shook her head and reached over to her arm. She squeezed it gently and that seemed to be enough to let Sandra know that she cared.

Kevin could be heard coughing as he came down the stairs. Sandra sat up straight and watched the kitchen door open as he stood there. She rubbed her fingers on the table and looked nervous. Kevin was dressed in a pair of faded jeans and a grey t-shirt. His trainers looked new and she could smell his Diesel aftershave from where she sat. He froze at first then slowly walked towards the kitchen side to grab a glass of water. He looked like he wanted to say something but Maxine jumped in first. She knew Kevin of old and knew he was a womaniser. A few of her mates had slept with him in the past but she kept that to herself, for now. Kevin looked at Maxine and nodded. He knew she had a reputation and was wary that she could shove a knife in his back at any moment. He gulped his glass of water and reached over to kiss Sandra's cheek. The kiss made her cringe. She didn't pull away because she knew it would only add fuel to the fire. He was acting like a different person.

"Right I'm off out. I'll be back about six for my tea. Make something nice ay," he said cheerfully, smirking at Maxine as he left.

Sandra was quickly out of her seat and up the stairs. Maxine lit a cig and huffed, "What a fucking day."

The mirror called to Sandra as she passed it. As she walked towards it she could already see a red lump beginning to appear. She touched it softly and you could see the pain in her face. Her eyes rose to the ceiling and she walked away thinking how much of a fool she really was.

Dipping her head into Kevin's wardrobe she searched for the video camera. It wasn't normal for her to go into his personal things and he had beaten her up in the past for doing it but today she didn't care anymore. Standing quickly she ran back to her bedroom door and banged it shut. No one must see her or know of her mission. Her arse was sticking from the wardrobe and she was virtually sat inside it. She was like a kid in a sweet shop searching through his stuff. Sandra sat holding clothes out fully and looked surprised. She hadn't seen any of these new clothes and realised how much of a separate life they led. A little black bag now looked at her and it looked like his shaving bag. Unzipping it slowly she revealed its contents. "Fucking vain prick" she mumbled. Lots of skin care products could now be seen. As she dug her hand deeper inside the bag she could feel small packets. As her hand brought the package from the bag her heart sunk. She'd found condoms. Not just plain condoms, fucking ribbed ones.

"Dirty cunt!"

She sighed. Sandra held the condom out in front of her and pulled a face. She walked up to her own set of drawers at the side of her bed. She was frantically looking for something. As her hand came from the drawer you could see a small shiny object in her hands. Sandra sat back down near the wardrobe holding a safety pin. She held an evil look in her eyes. Her hand held the condom up in front of her. Slowly she pierced it. She repeated this on all the condoms she found. Sandra now laughed like a witch casting a spell. Once she'd finished she threw them back inside the bag.

Eventually she found the video camera. It was in a small case at the very back of the wardrobe. She quickly grabbed it and threw all Kevin's clothes back inside without a care in the world. She'd ironed a lot of them previously and didn't give a shit that she might have to iron them all again. She was livid as she headed back down the stairs to Maxine. Hands held up in the air she screamed.

"The cheeky bastard has got condoms in his wardrobe, I've just found them!" Her face was white now and she couldn't get a cigarette into her mouth fast enough. "I don't believe it ya know. Have I been walking round with my eyes fucking shut?" Her hands were held out in front of her and Maxine didn't know what to say. She could have told her the truth and said that her husband had been shagging about for years but looking at her face she knew she didn't need anyone else kicking her while she was down.

Maxine interrupted her. "Did you get the video recorder, because we need to be back at my house soon before the lads arrive? I don't want to keep them waiting." Sandra produced the camera and grabbed her car keys from the fridge. Her mind was working overtime and she looked stressed.

"Can we go into the house with them? I want to make sure they put it in the right room and all that. I know there is a double bed in one of the rooms because Kevin has told me in the past and that will be the room he uses."

Maxine told her she would go with her. After all she wanted to see the grow and work out how much money they would all get from it when the stuff was sold. Driving like a mad woman she was back at Maxine's within minutes. They could see the lads waiting on a nearby wall. Sandra knew Kevin would be in the local pub for a few more hours yet and relaxed. That was his daily routine. Kevin also sold weed and most of his punters were in the pub. The punters knew weed was always on tap as long as he was still in the pub. Sandra could feel the hate running through her veins. She picked up her phone and relayed her findings to Tina. Tina wasn't shocked but tried to act the same as Sandra. She arranged to meet her later. Tina was with Steven and by the sounds of it he was shagging her brains out yet again. They were getting quite close these days and Sandra wondered if her best friend was falling in love.

Pulling up across the road, Sandra felt sick. She rubbed her neck vigorously. The house looked seedy with drooping, poorly fitted curtains hanging from the window. Sandra put her hand on her chest and commented to Maxine how fast her heart was beating. Maxine was calm and casually got out of the car. The area looked quiet except for a dog running about in the nearby park. Maxine gave the lads, who were sat in a white transit van, the nod. Only Barry came to join them. He didn't want to bring it on top and told the others to remain in the van. Pulling his hood up over his head he jogged towards them as all three of them quickly marched towards the house.

The key was new and it took a few times of twisting and turning it before they finally opened the door. They all quickly scurried through the front door. The house was warm and the smell of the marijuana plants hit the back of their throats. Sandra pulled her coat up over her nose.

Maxine went in every room and knew there was some decent cash to be earned. Barry was behind Sandra as she ran up the stairs. She struggled for breath as she mounted the stairs. Three bedroom doors stood facing her. As she opened each door weed plants were scattered everywhere. Bright lights were hanging over them and Barry examined the plants in more detail.

"They're ready these fuckers are. It's a good job they're going tonight. If you would have waited any longer we would have missed them." Sandra left him without speaking a word and opened the last remaining door. There it was, the double bed where her husband shagged her sister. The quilt cover looked dirty and everything about the room looked seedy. Empty condom packets were scattered all over the carpet. She felt physically sick and heaved a few times. Barry was at her side and placed a comforting hand around her shoulder.

"Don't worry love, this won't take a minute and we'll be gone. She passed him the video camera. His hands fidgeted with the small silver buttons and he could be seen checking his watch. "What time do you want the timer set for?" Her head tilted to the side and she asked him the time now.

"Half four"

"Set it for half eight then. Surely he'll be here by then." Barry messed about with the timer and once it was set he looked around the room for somewhere to place it where it would be out of sight. Sandra looked in a world of her own and didn't take much notice of him. The scent from the bed made her stomach churn. She sat considering whether to hide under the bed and surprise the cheating bastards but Maxine now came into the room and helped Barry set the trap.

The camera was hidden behind the long brown curtains. It had a full view of the bed and any action that would happen on it would surely be captured. Barry squeezed at his cock. He couldn't wait to see the footage. He was a man after all and any picture of a woman's fanny was enough to make his cock stand on end.

The smell of the drugs was now too much for Sandra. Even when Kevin smoked weed at home she made him stand outside in the garden with it as it made her feel sick. They all left the bedroom and headed for the front door. Sandra wanted to set the house on fire. She wanted them both to burn in hell.

Slamming the front door behind them they headed back to the car. Sandra now passed the key to the door over to Maxine. "Make sure they pick that video camera up later will you? And make sure they don't rip us off."

Maxine grabbed her closer. "Don't worry sweetheart. You're working with me now and these lads know I'm no dickhead." Barry told them not to worry and as soon as the job was done he would let Maxine know. He jumped into the van and waved as he drove off.

Sandra dropped Maxine off and headed back home. She remembered Kevin had told her he would be home for six o'clock and she wanted to make sure his tea was on the table to avoid any upset. Sitting down at the kitchen table she ran her fingers across the patterns of the grain. The table had seen so much sadness over the years and each grain had heard her pour her heart out on many occasions. She sat wriggling her legs about under the table. She was dying for a piss.

Heading upstairs she let out a sigh of relief as her arse hit the toilet seat. She seemed to be pissing forever. Glancing around the bathroom she saw Kevin's mouthwash. She stopped for a second and stood up with her knickers still dangling round her ankles. A smile filled her face as she reached over for his spearmint mouthwash. It looked like a green liquid. She screwed the lid off to smell it. It smelt fresh. Placing the plastic bottle in the toilet bowl she started to piss again. She was laughing her head off now and if anyone would have heard her they would have thought she was mental. She wiped the sides of it with toilet roll and placed the lid back on top of it. Shaking it gently she placed it back where she'd found it. Revenge was sweet and suddenly she started to feel a lot better. She was going to break her husband in two and although this was a very small thing, it all went towards making her smile more every day that passed.

Sandra went to lie on the bed. It was time again to confess all her secrets to her diary. She'd kept one for years now and she often found comfort in getting all her thoughts down on paper. She couldn't wait to tell her paper friend her latest traumas. Rolling the pen in her fingers she began to confess her sins.

6

Kevin came home at the time he said he would. He looked grumpy and she knew she would have to tread on eggshells around him. His tea was nearly finished and everything but his egg was cooked. She could hear him coughing in the front room and knew she would have to shout him into the kitchen. Flicking the hot oil over the egg she watched it changed colour. It was ready.

Sandra now walked to the kitchen door and shouted him in a loud voice. "Kevin your tea is ready." Waiting a few seconds she scurried back to the kitchen sink. The noise of pots and pans clanging together could be heard. She could feel his presence in the room before she actually saw him. A hand now smacked her arse and she cringed as she turned to place his food on the table. He looked bladdered.

"Pass me the salt will ya. I wish you would just leave it on the fucking table." Sandra opened the cupboard and searched for the salt. She could hear him moaning in the background. "Where's my chocolate milkshake. You know I always have one with my tea. What's fucking up with you woman, are you losing the plot or summat"? She felt useless.

"No I'm fucking not. I'll get it now. For fuck's sake give me chance, I've only just put your tea on the table." His eyes followed her with a hateful look. Sandra knew she was getting cocky with him and tried to back-pedal. Her hand shook as the chocolate milkshake hit the glass. It was cold, just the way he liked it. If Kevin hadn't have been in the same room she would have spit into it for sure.

"Here you go. Freezing cold just the way you like it." She watched him take a small sip and he smiled at her, letting her know she was now off the hook.

"Where's your tea?" His eyes were on her again as he sat up looking on the kitchen side for her plate.

"I'm not hungry yet. I'll grab something later."

He dug his fork into his chips. He ate like a tramp that hadn't been fed for weeks and she could see food all around his mouth. Sandra was now deep in thought as she inhaled deeply on her cigarette. Bet our Tracy doesn't see this side of you does she? Shit-stained boxers and farts coming from your arse every other minute. No. She just sees all the good things. Well, let's see how much she loves you when you have fuck all.

Kevin was talking to her now with his voice raised.

"Fucking hell are you listening to me or what?" Her eyes shook as she realised he was speaking to her. She had to ask him again what he'd said. He was now shoving his plate across the table with an evil look on his face. Bits of food were left on it. Patting his lower stomach he asked for a slice of cake that he'd seen in the fridge earlier that day. His son now walked into the kitchen.

"Is there owt to eat mam. I'm starving." Kevin looked at John and shrugged.

"Where's the please in all that. She's not your fucking skivvy you know." John knew he was after an argument. He was always like this after a few beers and on many occasion he'd wanted to kick fuck out of him. Sandra could see their eyes locked together as she pulled open the oven door. Grabbing a small tea towel from the side she gripped the hotplate and slid it onto the table. Kevin's eyes were all over John's food. He was a right jealous fucker and checked his son didn't have a bigger tea than him.

Sandra was now sat at the table making conversation with John. Kevin was jealous of both his sons and had said so in the past in one way or another. Sandra was his property and he made it well known he wouldn't share her, even with his own flesh and blood.

Kevin left the kitchen. John rammed two fingers into the air towards him and Sandra laughed. John had his faults but where his dad was concerned they both agreed he was a total dickhead.

"Where's Paul?" Sandra asked as she watched him scoff his food down.

Talking with a full mouth he chuckled "He's with his chick again. You know what he's like, as soon as he gets a bird, he shags them to death." Sandra laughed. He was right enough. Paul was so different from his brother. He was so caring and didn't really get into much trouble with the police unlike John. He'd had his moments, don't get me wrong, but he seemed to have quietened down a lot. Sandra smiled as she twisted her hair round her fingers.

"Orr bless him. He's in love, leave him alone." John laughed out loud.

"Mam, come on admit it. He's a fucking fairy." His mother raised her eyes and looked deep in thought. Her words were low and John struggled to hear her. "Oh to be young and in love, what I would give to turn the clock back." Kevin's voice could be heard behind her. She hadn't noticed he was there.

"Yeah me too. Perhaps then I wouldn't have ended up with a trollop like you. The women loved me back in the day. So we both have regrets don't we?" His eyes pierced into his wife's. Sandra dipped her head, she thought he was going to slap her and looked edgy. John jumped into the conversation, he'd heard enough.

"Yeah you might have been alright back then, but look at you now dad," John laughed raising his head.

Kevin hated anyone talking about his body and John was looking his dad up and down. Sucking his stomach in he ranted at John. "You would be surprised what your old dad can still get. The women still want it." He was now grabbing at his crotch behind Sandra's back. He walked away mumbling under his breath as Sandra felt sick inside.

It was usual for Kevin to go and have a sleep at this time and as she heard him going up the stairs she knew her plan would soon come to fruition. She looked sad and her son placed his hand on her shoulder.

"Mam, he's a cock. I don't know how you put up

with him. He thinks he's a young player like me."

Gripping the hand Sandra stroked it slowly. "Son, I'm used to his shit. He doesn't bother me anymore." Tears welled up in her eyes and John had to leave the kitchen. He couldn't cope with tears, to see his mother crying cut him up inside. He hated his father with a passion.

"Prick" he muttered under his breath.

Once the pots were washed, Sandra sat watching the clock. One hour to go, she thought. Reaching for her mobile phone she texted Tina.

Are you coming to my house? I need someone to talk to.

Placing her small black phone on the table she sat with her legs crossed wishing the rest of the day away.

Tina grabbed her phone from the side of the bed. Steven was shagging her brains out and she struggled to read the message as her head jerked about on the bed. His cock was like a baby's arm holding an apple and she cringed as he penetrated deeper inside her. Her eyes quickly read the text message and she flung it to the floor as the sex intensified. Steven was now upping his game and his arse was moving like a sewing machine. Tina was yelling with delight as her legs were now hung from his masculine shoulders.

Over the last few weeks Steven and Tina had become like a hinge and a bracket. Every spare minute they spent together. He was teaching her the art of tattooing and recently designed a pattern for the side of her foot. Each time she watched him at work she wanted to fuck his brains out. His face was always serious and the tip of his tongue always hung from the corner of his mouth when he was concentrating.

"Who was the text off" he asked as he lit two cigarettes up.

"Oh it was Sandra. Her head's up her arse at the moment. You know with Kevin and all that." She lay flat as the smoke seeped from her mouth. Steven was now by her side and the cotton sheets were placed loosely over their hot bodies.

"Why does she put up with him? From what you have told me he's a womaniser so why doesn't she get rid?" Tina smiled as she placed her leg over his. He now cradled her in his grip. She grinned.

"Oh don't worry love. He won't be smiling for long. Sandra has big plans for him." Tina felt like she could tell him anything. They were getting on well and she hoped he would be moving in with her pretty soon. They'd spoken about it a few times in the past and they were both eager to take their relationship to the next level. Tina squeezed him before she got up from the bed and stubbed her cig out. Her best mate needed her and she knew she would have to make a move. Steven tried dragging her back into bed but she declined telling him her fanny had had enough cock for one day.

Walking naked to the bathroom she could feel his eyes burning into her. She quickly turned back around and saw him hanging over the bed watching her every movement. She was in danger of falling head over heels in love with this man and it scared her sometimes that she'd let him get into her heart.

Relationships had been bad for Tina in the past and she'd suffered horrific domestic violence from her previous partners. Closing the bathroom door she hugged her body. She felt so in love and it showed all over her smiling face. Running water into the sink she smiled at herself in the mirror. The cold water splashed onto her face and she was blinded for a second. Head dipped into the sink as her hand searched for a towel. Once she located it she patted her face with the white fluffy towel. She could see again. Steven was now in the bathroom with her and you could see he was still rampant. Quick as she could she located her knickers and yanked them up over her arse. He was still smiling at her as he knew more sex was still on the cards.

With a quick brush of her teeth she headed back to the bedroom to find something to wear. She could hear Steven shouting her as she yanked her jeans up. She held her ear towards his voice.

"So should I bring my stuff over later or what? I may as well… I mean I'm always here aren't I?" Rubbing her hands together with excitement Tina tried to sound nonchalant. Her voice was high pitched as she tried to hide her excitement.

"Yeah, if you want. I won't be home until late tonight though. I have to help Sandra out." She punched her clenched fist into the air to celebrate. "Sex on tap from now on, get in there."

Sandra could hear Kevin coming down the stairs. She sat watching the TV in the front room. Turning her head slightly she could see him stood in his boxers at the side of her. His hair was messed up and he looked rough. Bending down near her he nicked a cig from her packet. He scratched his ball bag as he sat on the chair facing Sandra. She could feel his stare. Fidgeting she moved her body away from him. His coughing was loud and he struggled to cough up some phlegm that was lodged at the back of his throat. Kevin stood quickly and spat into the nearby bin.

"Dirty twat" she mumbled as her face screwed up. Looking back at her as he wiped his mouth with his hand he moaned at her.

"What's up with your face? I was fucking choking. What do you want me to do, die?" Her face gave him the answer to his question. Kevin snarled at her and made his way back to his seat. His phone could be heard ringing. Once he'd located it he looked at the screen and quickly walked out of the room before he answered it. Sandra stood to attention and looked like a sniper as she hid behind the door. His voice was low and she could hear him telling someone he would be there soon. Running like a frightened rabbit she sat back down trying to look disinterested. Her heart was pounding in her chest and she was trying to control her breathing. He was back.

Plonking back down he threw his phone onto the sofa. She was dying to ask who was on the phone but her heart told her who it was without her having to ask. The television was on and even though her favourite soap was just about to start her mind was all over the place. She couldn't concentrate. Her eyes watched the clock on top of the telly and she prayed Tina would be there soon as her nerves were all over the place. Kevin gave a yawn and stood up. His hands played with his nob in his boxer shorts as he spoke.

"Right I'm gonna get a bath. Any chance of a butty or owt before I go out?" Her eyes opened wide. She started to get up from the chair but his hand pushed her back down. "I don't want it yet silly. I mean when I get out of the bath. Fucking hell it will be as dry as your fanny otherwise." He chuckled and pushed her arm for Sandra to welcome his joke but she struggled to raise a smile. Laughing he walked away leaving her alone in the front room. His phone was staring at her and it felt like it was teasing her to check the messages. Tapping her fingers on the side of the sofa she rocked to and fro. She was debating whether or not to take her chance.

She could hear the bath water running. The sound of her husband walking across the landing could be heard. Creeping, she made her way to his phone. Hands shaking she pressed the message button. The name Peter was across each message. Her face scrunched up. She looked confused. Pressing the full messages all was revealed. The bastard had put her sister under a false name. Her eyes squinted as she focused on the words.

I think I'm falling in love with you. You need to sort this out Kevin, it's gone on for long enough.

She went bright red. The sound of knocking at the front door shit her up and she launched the phone back on the sofa. Taking a minute she tried to pull herself together. Sandra was panting. She walked slowly to the front door humming some song trying to be calm. Tugging at her t-shirt she pulled the front door open.

Tina looked at her. "Fucking hell you look rough." Sandra struggled out a smile and invited her inside. Tina was loud and her voice let everyone know she was in the building. Sandra told her to lower it and sat in the kitchen trying to flatten her hair. Catching a glimpse of herself in the mirror she knew Tina was right. She did look as rough as a bear's arse. She switched the kettle on.

In contrast, Tina looked as if she had some kind of glow about her. When the cups were placed on the side Sandra turned to face her. She knew instantly she had something to tell her by the way she was vigorously rubbing her hands together in front of her face.

"What's up with you?"

"Quick, finish making that fucking brew and park your arse down here," Tina said patting the chair at the side of her. Sandra chuckled.

"One minute love I have to make that cunt a butty" said Sandra raising her eyes to the ceiling letting her know Kevin was upstairs. Quickly she got the stuff for his sandwich and threw it onto the two white pieces of bread in front of her. She froze for a minute and turned to Tina with a slice of bread still held in her hands. Spit from her mouth now dangled onto the bread. When she had spat on it about three times she held her belly as she turned back to the kitchen side. Tina now stood with her and grabbed the bread from her hands.

"Give it here." She now snorted up through her nose and then spit whatever came out of her mouth onto the slice of bread. Sandra was pissing herself laughing. She quickly squirted some mayonnaise over it and placed the other slice on top. The two of them were hysterical. Once the sandwich was made Sandra cut it in half and placed it onto a small saucer covering it with a piece of tin foil. Sandra sat down. Tina grabbed her arms almost straight away and squeezed at them.

"He's moving in tonight."

"Who?" Sandra moaned.

"Fucking Steven. He said he was bringing all his stuff over later. Fuck me how will I cope? I haven't lived with anyone for years," Tina rocked her chair back on two legs and sighed. Sandra looked shocked.

"You haven't known him that long, are you sure?"

Tina was defensive and placed her hands on the table staring right at her. "I've known him months now. Why are you putting the mockers on it? For fuck's sake Sandra don't you think I deserve a bit of happiness?"

Sandra grabbed her cigs. She wasn't in the mood for an argument. She was happy for Tina but she wanted her to make sure she was doing the right thing. Tina had made so many mistakes in the past and Sandra didn't want to be the one who was picking up the pieces when it all went pear shaped. She gave her a look of concern.

"I do want you to be happy love. I'm just saying are you sure about it all?" Tina was lighting her cig and pulled it from her mouth in anger. Her face looked red as she opened fire on Sandra.

"Course I'm fucking sure. He's lovely, he makes me laugh and sex is brilliant. What more could I ask for?" Sandra smiled and leant over to hug her. Her mind was all over the place and she agreed with Tina that she did deserve some happiness in her life.

"Well if you're sure, I'm happy for you."

The two of them were still hugging each other when Kevin walked into the kitchen. You could taste his Armani aftershave at the back of your throat. The girls pulled away from each other. Tina sniffed loudly and shot Kevin a look. She hated him with a vengeance and made no secret that he made her cringe inside.

"Fucking hell you smell like a prostitute's handbag. Have you got enough of that shit on or what?" Tina spoke in a sarcastic voice. Kevin scowled. He walked further inside the kitchen and messed about on the side as he defended himself.

"It's Armani. You wouldn't know class if it hit you in the face. All your scruffy men wear fucking Old Spice or summit like that." He smiled as he found his sandwich. Tina was back on him, she was on form and wouldn't let him get the better of her.

"Ay, my men would give you a ten break. You're all

washed up now. Maybe back in the day you were alright, but now you're dated." Tina was laughing out loud and looking at Sandra who chewed on her bottom lip to stop laughing. Tina carried on throwing insults at him. "I've told Sandra she needs to trade you in and get a stud muffin like I have." Sandra couldn't hold it anymore and burst into fits of laughter. Kevin didn't look happy. He walked around the kitchen table so he could give Sandra the look. The look she knew that meant shut the fuck up or else. Creasing his face he sat down with his food and answered Tina.

"If Sandra wants to find someone new then off she can trot, but she knows where her bread is buttered and I can't see her moving anywhere can you?" Tina hated the way he put her best friend down and she could tell by Sandra's face she wasn't going to answer him back. She chirped in.

"Well don't be too sure on that. Sandra has loads of men drooling over her. I just hope she sees the light one day and kicks you to the kerb." Kevin grabbed Sandra's cheeks and squeezed them together. He was being playful.

"She won't ever leave her Kevin will you babes?" Sandra pulled his sweaty hands from her face. She couldn't be arsed with him. They both now watched him as he started to take a bite from his sandwich. With a mouthful of food he asked Sandra for a drink of his milkshake. He told her to put some ice cubes in it.

Tina smiled cunningly as the bastard bit into his sandwich. Sandra hid her face inside the fridge and had to put her hand over her mouth to stop the laughter escaping. Walking to the kitchen side she grabbed a glass. You could see her shoulders shaking with laughter as she poured his drink. Once she controlled herself she was back in view carrying his drink. Her face was red as she turned and passed him the glass. He looked like a pig in a fit as he scranned his food. Sandra sat down and Tina nodded her head with a smile on her face.

Kevin was all ready now and came back to kiss his wife on her cheek before he left. His kiss made her feel sick inside and she didn't know if she could keep it in for much longer. Grabbing his black leather jacket from the side he left the house with a spring in his step. Once the door could be heard closing Sandra broke.

"I can't do it Tina. I know that cunt is going to see our Tracy" she pointed her fingers towards the door. "And I'm just sat here like a prize prick. I should be up and behind him telling the twat I know his fucking seedy secret."

Tina rolled her eyes as she spoke. "What, and do you honestly think he's going to admit it to you? Get a grip girl. Just wait and break him down piece by piece." Tina was now at her side as Sandra stood with her back against the wall. The sadness was all over Sandra's face. She stood staring for a moment and finally burst into tears. Tina wasn't good at this kind of thing and patted her on the shoulder telling her she would be fine. A look now appeared on Sandra's face. You could see her nostrils flaring as her breathing started to calm down. Walking to the table she grabbed her cigs. Passing Tina one the women sat staring at the kitchen walls. The night was going to be long and Tina checked her watch. Secretly she wanted to get home to her new love but she knew her friend was a mess and needed support.

Tina smiled as she slowly placed her fingertip around the glass Kevin had previously drunk from. As she stoked it carefully she asked what drink was in it earlier. Sandra puffed on her cig as she told her. "Oh it's his fucking precious chocolate milkshake. He drinks it with every meal. He's like a big kid. I mean come on, fucking milkshake it's a kid's drink innit." Tina's eyes rolled about with excitement as she tilted her head to the side and tapped her knees. She wasn't listening to a word Sandra was saying. Slowly she placed her elbows onto the table and dropped her head into her hands. She had a cunning look across her face.

"Let's make him a right fat bastard." Sandra looked at her and didn't have a clue what she was on about.

"What the fuck are you talking about now? Make who a fat bastard?" Tina walked to the fridge and searched for the bottle containing the drink. Once she'd found it she casually walked back to the table and slammed it in front of Sandra's eyes.

"Make Kevin a fat bastard that's fucking who." She now read the label on the drink and laughed out loud. "Right first thing tomorrow me and you are going into town. There is a health shop there where we can get what we need."

"I don't understand what you're going about. Explain it again?"

"Right. Kevin always drinks chocolate milkshake doesn't he? And you know he loves his body the posing cunt?" she cackled as she continued, "so, let's make him put weight on." Sandra looked vacant. She still didn't get what she was on about but as she continued she smiled from ear to ear as the plan unfolded. After all, Kevin had called her a fat cunt for years and to see him looking like a Christmas pudding put a smile right across her face. Tina explained further. "There is this weight gain stuff that all the bodybuilders use. They use it to build muscle and I know a few lads who have had it. It puts pure weight on ya Sandra. We can have him fat as fuck in months." Sandra rubbed her hands together and her own anxieties disappeared. Standing to her feet she danced about the kitchen with Tina. They both looked mental.

Sandra spoke with hatred in her voice now as she stared at the kitchen wall. "I'm gonna break him in two, Tina. Everything he has ever loved is going to be taken away. Oh my God there is so much I can do to him!" She turned her head to Tina, "but let's just get tonight out of the way before I begin the rest of it ay?"

7

Tracy stood in the mirror turning from side to side. Pressing her face up towards it she checked her make-up. Her skinny jeans clung to her legs for dear life and her camel toe was more than visible. Her vest top revealed her perky breasts and her pink bra strap could be seen hanging from her shoulder. Flicking her hair back she danced about the room listening to Beyonce on her iPod.

Tracy had always been trouble. Even her own friends disliked her but they just put with her because they were scared of what she would do to them if she found out she wasn't liked. Her only true friend was Lesley. Lesley would do anything to please her and Tracy liked it that way as she was on call for her every need. The sound of someone knocking on her bedroom door could be heard. "Come in," Tracy shouted.

Her mother was now stood there holding a plate with her tea on it. "I wish you would eat downstairs with us love. It's not right you eating up here on your own. Remember a family who eats together stays together."

"Mam, will you fuck off moaning," Tracy scowled, "I'll eat when I'm ready. I'm not into all that stuff you make. I like pasta and healthy things." Anita looked deflated as the fish, chips and peas stared at her from the plate. She'd always cooked a hearty meal for her family in the past and she felt like she'd failed as a mother.

"Pasta won't fill you though. Look at you, you're a bag of bones" she grabbed at her arm pulling at her skin.

"Mother, if it was left up to you I would be massive. That's what happened with our Sandra, you fed her too much."

Anita tried not to smile but as she spoke the laughter came out in her voice. "Ay don't be saying that about your sister. She only put on weight after having kids."

"Yeah," Tracy sighed, "and the ten packets of crisps she was eating each day had something to do with it. Come on mam, she never stops eating."

Anita shook her head and sighed. "Well let's hope you're one of the lucky ones who don't put on any weight when you have kids because it happens to us all you know." Anita patted the lower part of her stomach. She left the bedroom now after she placed the food on the side.

Tracy walked over to the plate and nicked a couple of chips from it. Licking her fingers she lay back on her bed. Checking her phone she scrolled down it and read some of her old messages. Her legs were crossed and as she looked at her phone she rolled on her side. The sound of a message alert could now be heard. Quickly bolting up from the bed her eyes cast over the message. Searching the floor she found her red high heeled shoes. Squeezing her feet inside Tracy stood admiring them in the full-length mirror. She was ready. Her black handbag was slipped over her shoulder and she quickly searched inside it before she left the room. The box she held in her hand said contraceptive pill and some other words were on the side. With a grin on her face she threw them back inside her handbag without taking any of the tablets.

Sticking her face into the front room she quickly said goodbye to her parents. They thought she was off out with her mates and never asked any questions. "See you later love" Her mother shouted and her dad joined in telling her not to be late.

"Have you got your key" he moaned.

"Yeah don't worry, see you later." Tracy struggled to walk in her shoes as she quickened her pace. She wasn't short of male attention and she had a fuck buddy called Mark. They had been on and off for over two years now but neither of them were ready to make any commitment. Mark wasn't short of cash and he made sure he treated Tracy well. In a way she liked him but Kevin was the man she held in her heart and until that was over she couldn't focus on anyone else.

Night was drawing in as she pulled her collar up around her face as the wind picked up. With her head dipped she knocked on the front door. Quickly looking about she could see Kevin's car parked up in the distance. The door opened now but you couldn't see anyone you could just hear a voice.

"Hurry up in then slug."

Tracy smiled and entered the house closing the door behind her. "Fuck me it's warm" she moaned. The heat from all the weed plants was sickening. Kevin headed upstairs and Tracy followed. The smell of the marijuana made her cover her nose. Once at the top of the stairs she was led to the bedroom she had seen so many times before. Kevin was lay on the bed now. His arms were looped underneath his head. Tracy smiled and walked towards him.

"How long have you been here, did you bring any beers or what?"

"Oh yeah they are in the bag downstairs, run down and bring them up." Tracy kicked her shoes off and obeyed his orders. The sound of her running downstairs could be heard. Kevin lay on the bed with one hand down the front of his jeans. He looked sexy as the bottom part of his toned stomach could be seen. Hearing Tracy coming back upstairs he sat up on the bed and stared at the door.

"Fucking hell you took your time. Sandra would have had it here faster than that," he giggled as he took a bottle of Budweiser from her grip. Tracy stood with a cocky look on her face as her hand waved about in front of her.

"Sandra would have been in the fridge for at least five minutes first. You know what she's like for eating. What is it she always says?" her head looked over at the wall as she tried to remember. Within seconds her face changed with excitement. "Oh yeah little pickers wear big knickers. She's so full of shit isn't she? Our Sandra will always be fat. Why she spends all that money on miracle diets is beyond me." Kevin grinned. He didn't like Tracy slagging his wife off but he could feel his cock throbbing and patted the bed for her to join him.

Kevin never really wanted to end up sleeping with Tracy but even from an early age she was flirting with him endlessly. He was a man and he knew she wanted him by the way she acted around him. It all started when

she was fifteen. She had fallen out with her mother and
Sandra had brought her home so they could both cool
down. She was only meant to stay for a few nights but
she ended up staying for months. Kevin noticed the way
she looked at him and she was always eager to be in his
company. She wore short skirts and never had a second
thought about bending down in front of him. She teased
him constantly. One night Sandra had gone to bed early
and Kevin had been sat downstairs watching his usual
porn DVD. He had a large collection of porn and Sandra
had often commented on his late night habits. She had
sworn he had learnt to speak German by the amount of
it he watched. Once the film was over he still felt horny.
Walking up to bed he could see a small gap in the bedroom
door where Tracy was sleeping. The small lamp inside the
bedroom gave off enough light for him to see inside. His
body froze for a second and before he knew it he was bent
over, peeping through the door getting a glimpse of his
sister-in law. That night changed him forever. He planned
his perverted glimpses and even moved the mirror in her
bedroom so he could get a better look at Tracy when
she was getting undressed. Kevin never took it further
than that. He knew it was wrong but just couldn't help
himself.

One night he was sat downstairs on his own when
he could hear footsteps coming down the stairs. Thinking
it was Sandra he switched his DVD off. He knew she
would have gone mad if she had seen him sat watching
porn. As the door opened he was surprised to see Tracy.
She looked ill. Immediately he went to her side and felt
her head. "Are you alright Tracy, you don't look well?"
He always remembered that night and that was the start
of their seedy secret. As he felt her head she pulled his

hand from her forehead and placed in down her vest top. Kevin didn't need to be asked twice and could tell by her face she wanted a good shagging. Not thinking of the consequences he made sure it was safe and took her virginity. Their affair had been on and off since she was fifteen and he had even tried to end it a few times especially when she got pregnant. Luckily he'd talked her round and promised her the world to make sure she got rid of the child. Of course she believed him and since then he couldn't get rid of her. Now she demanded the affair went on otherwise he knew she would tell the world and his wife about his sordid secret. A lot of people knew about their affair and at one point Kevin was on his knees begging one of Sandra's friends not to tell her. Everyone thought that they had stopped seeing each other a long time ago and that's the way Kevin liked it.

Tracy moved her hair from her face and leant in towards Kevin. The smell of the weed all over the house was making her feel stoned.

"Why can't we go to a hotel or something? This place knocks me sick."

Kevin smiled and pulled her towards him. The mattress was stale and even Kevin commented on how rough the place was.

"The grow's nearly ready now, so it will be sorted soon, don't worry. When I get some cash from it I'll book us into The Midland in Manchester. It's one of the best yanno, and I'll treat you like a princess. I promise." That was enough for Tracy and she started to undress. Kevin watched her as she slowly peeled her clothes from her perfect body. She had grown a lot since she was fifteen and now stood before his eyes was the body of a woman. Her underwear made his cock throb and as he rushed to get his jeans off his erect cock was stood to attention and ready for action. Tracy had been shopping and she knew exactly what to buy to turn a man on. Her breasts looked firm and you could just see her pubic hair through her pink lacy knickers. Tracy would have shaved her monkey fluff off years ago but Kevin urged her to keep it saying it turned him on.

They pair lay on the bed completely unaware of the video camera behind the curtain. Their love making began and it wasn't long before their hot sweaty bodies were moving all about the bed. Tracy sucked his cock like it was a lollipop. She sank it deep to the back of her throat and licked his shaft. Kevin could be heard moaning and she knew it was time for them both to explode. Climbing on his erect member she sat down hard and grinded on top of him until she could feel a wave of pleasure riding through her body. Kevin held her waist and you could see his arse moving underneath her. Tracy screamed out with pleasure and lifted her hair up in her hands squeezing it. Now Kevin found orgasm and joined her. His fingers gripped her arse and you could see her skin turning white. It was all over now and two bodies lay exhausted at the side of each other. Kevin was still struggling for his breath as he reached for his cigs.

"That was bang on, that Tracy. I don't know where you keep getting these new moves from but they are the dog's bollocks," Kevin commented as he lit his cig. Tracy smiled and moved herself onto his chest as he smoked with one hand around her body. She knew she shouldn't but she couldn't help it she wanted him and continued with her usual moans.

"Kevin when are we going to be together properly? You said you were going to tell Sandra years ago but I'm still waiting." He sighed and took a deep drag from his cig.

"For fucks sake Tracy why do you always have to spoil it? We've just had top sex and you're going on, ruining it." Kevin knew she would back down now, she always did and he could hear her huffing.

"I'm not moaning Kevin, I just need to know if it will ever happen. I have Mark there if I want and he'll look after me. I mean he's got cash, the car, everything." Her eyes focused on him as she lifted her head. She loved making him jealous and knew the thought of her with someone else made his blood boil.

"Well if you want to be with Mark, off you pop. Don't let me stop you." He was on one now and he reached down to stub his cig out. Tracy pulled his arm towards her.

"Kevin I want a family with you. When I got rid of our baby you told me it was best because the timing wasn't right. When is the time ever going to be right ay?" Kevin felt agitated. She suffocated him and he knew this set up would have to stop before someone got seriously hurt.

"It's hard Tracy. I don't love Sandra but we do have kid's yanno?"

Tracy jumped in. "Kids! They're nearly men Kevin. Fucking hell, maybe a few years ago that would have washed with me, but not anymore." He looked angry.

"Tracy I'm married to your sister. Do you think everyone's going to welcome us with open arms?" She looked sad and she chewed on her finger nails as he continued, "It's just going to take time. If you want to go and find someone new that's a chance I'll have to take, but at the moment I'm not ready to do anything." Secretly he wished she would fuck off with Mark. The first time she'd told him about her new boyfriend he was jealous, yes, but eventually he got used to the idea and it got him off the hook every now and then. Tracy could see he was angry and wanted to make friends so she back-pedalled.

"Kevin you know I love you, and you have said you love me too. I'll wait until you are ready but it better be soon, because I can't stand it any longer." Gripping her back onto his chest he lay staring into space. Silence filled the room.

★

Barry sat with his crew watching the house. He'd watched both Kevin and Tracy go into their love nest. They were all set to make some money once they'd left. Barry had already got somewhere to store the weed and had a buyer waiting to take every last plant off his hands.

Kids like Barry had to wheel and deal to get by in life. To earn this kind of money was a chance in a lifetime for him and he wasn't coming away empty handed no matter what. Slurping on his can of Coke he spoke to his mates. "Right lads we're like fucking ninjas tonight. No fucking about, straight in and out. Maxine has sorted out where we can store it so we're on a winner."

One of the lads piped up in an excited voice. "Defo Baz, I'm gonna get them trainers I've seen in Foot Locker. So we'd better not fuck up." Barry smiled. He's also seen some smart sneaks and knew if this job wasn't pulled off he would have to say goodbye to them too. All dressed in black, they kept their heads dipped and watched the house carefully.

Over an hour passed before they saw Tracy and Kevin leave the house. Barry went mad and told them to get ready. He was rubbing his hands together in excitement. They watched Kevin lock the front door and turn his head scanning the surrounding areas. Tracy had left five minutes earlier. Watching him walk across the small field toward his car they all remained silent. Barry was nervous and it was written all across his face. He fidgeted and rocked about watching his every move. Kevin was gone.

Barry drove the van outside the house and they gathered the tools they needed to get inside the front door. He'd lost the key he'd been given. It was just past midnight and they knew they would have to keep the noise down. They'd seen how to get into houses loads of times on telly and with two great whacks with the iron pipe they'd brought along they were inside. Each lad had a bin liner and they all ran about shoving the plants inside. The lads scattered into each room. Barry made sure the mission ran smoothly and every few minutes the lads were shoving the drugs into the back of the van. It was nearly cleared, even the lights were in the back of the van. Barry stood still and looked like he'd forgotten something. Quickly he ran back up the stairs as the other lads shouted after him.

"Come on Baz we've cleaned it out up there!" Barry didn't answer and ran into the bedroom. He quickly grabbed the video recorder and slung it inside his coat. He ran to join the others. Once in the car they drove from the scene of crime.

"Yo, Maxine. It's Barry. Right it's sorted I'll see you in five." Placing his mobile phone back in his pocket Barry shouted at the others. "Fucking result lads, get in there." The lads were cheering and even the ones in the back of the van could be heard. The roads were quiet and they knew they needed to get off the main road as quickly as possible. Barry took the back streets and kept a low profile.

★

Kevin sneaked into his bed next to his wife. Sandra was fast asleep or so he thought. She could smell her sister's perfume all over him. She knew it well because it was Tracy's favourite fragrance "Britney Spears Fantasy." Her stomach churned as she felt his hand drop onto her waist. Lying still beside him her heart sank. The man she'd loved with all her heart didn't love her anymore. It was official. Yeah he'd given her a beating a few times in the past but didn't that happen in every marriage? What had she done to be treated like this? Anger built up inside her. Her alarm clock ticked loudly at the side of her and she knew in time the bastard would be the one lay wide awake listening to it too. Her list of pay backs were getting bigger each day and she knew if she kept her mouth shut all would go to plan.

Maxine welcomed the youths into her house. She'd been with them to store the plants. Her hands were covered in soil and she chuckled as they all seated. "Come on the lads lets sample this weed." Barry had kept one of the plants and pulled it from the black bin liner. Once he'd sorted it out, he passed the Rizla papers to his wingman to skin up. Maxine now grabbed the video camera from the side and held it with a smile on her face.

"Sandra will be buzzing with this lads, well done. I'm sure she'll have more grafts for you in the future."

Barry sat with his legs apart and nodded. "Any graft she's got, we are the men for it aren't we lads?" The group nodded and loved they were earning some cash. Maxine now spoke to them about getting the money and how they would all split it. With a joint now being passing about they all laughed about the moment Kevin would find out he'd been robbed. They had covered their tracks well and now they were safe in Maxine's house no one would ever know Barry and his mates were the culprits.

Tracy lay in her bed and looked through her window into the night. She wanted Kevin more than ever and planned a way to get him to be with her forever. If the reason he wouldn't leave her sister was that they had children together, surely if she had a child to him he couldn't leave her either. With her palm she stroked her tummy with a cunning look on her face. Reaching in her handbag she squeezed every contraceptive pill from the silver foil. Placing them in a small tissue she planned to flush them all down the toilet the following morning. Placing her earpiece inside her ear she lay listening to her iPod. Her feet could be seen moving underneath the bed covers as her head nodded to the beat of the music. As her eyes closed she planned to take her sister's husband forever.

8

Sandra sat at work behind her nail station. The client was talking to her and she just nodded her head every now and then. She wasn't really listening and apologised a few times to the customer for making her repeat herself. Her mind was all over the place and she constantly stared at her mobile phone at the side of her waiting for the call from Kevin telling her his world had fallen apart.

Maxine had phoned her on the way to work and told her she had the video evidence. They had arranged for Sandra to call after work so she could watch it. The client screamed in pain as Sandra filed her nails roughly. She'd cut her.

"Oh I'm so sorry love" she pleaded. Reaching for a tissue she placed it over the bleeding finger. Her thoughts had been with Kevin at the time and her anger must have seeped through into her work. "I just don't know what's up with these new files they are so coarse. I'm sure they've changed them." The client didn't reply and you could tell by her face she wasn't impressed. With an angry tone she sucked the blood from her finger and sat back in her chair for a minute.

Once the bleeding had stopped she placed her hand back on the table. Sandra now offered her some free designs on her nails to make up for her error. The lady smiled and accepted. She didn't want the cheap design, she wanted something top of the range that would take Sandra a lot more time to complete. Sandra reached over to her mobile phone and plonked it in her bag. It was making her nervous and she had to concentrate.

Once the client was gone there were just another two appointments that day. They were only for waxing so they shouldn't take her long. Sandra popped outside for a cig after she finished with her client. She needed it desperately to calm her nerves. With each drag she felt better. The sound of her phone ringing could be heard. Quickly she ran in the shop and grabbed it, leaving her half smoked cig still alight on ledge outside.

"Hello Yeah I'm alright. Maxine has got that video" she quickly walked back outside the shop and picked her cig up and continued speaking. "I know Tina, I'm shitting myself. Tell you what, meet me at Maxine's after work. Alright speak to you later." Holding the phone in her hand she sighed. This was going to be the moment that changed her life forever. How would she feel seeing her husband for the first time shagging her sister? Flicking her cig onto the pavement she smiled at her next client and led her to the back room where all the waxing was done. The lady was foreign and didn't speak much English.

The beauty room was calming. There was a massage bed in the middle and lots of different coloured pots were scattered on the shelves across the back wall. Sandra now asked the lady which part of her body she wanted waxing – the client wanted her legs, bikini line and tash doing. Sandra heated the pot of wax and told her to lie down. For fucks sake, she moaned as she went inside the small cupboard at the side of the room, why didn't she just want her eyebrows waxing or something simple? She began waxing.

Once the legs were done she asked her what kind of waxing she would like on her bikini line. The woman spoke in broken English and told her she wanted all her pubic hair off. Watching her slide her pink knickers off, Sandra stood looking shocked. "Fucking hell" she whispered under her breath. She had never seen as much monkey fluff in her whole life. The lady's pubic hairs were growing all down her inner thigh and her pubic mound looked massive. Rolling her sleeves up she started to wax the overgrown motty. The woman was screaming in a foreign language and Sandra stopped a few times to ask her if she was okay. Her client was now biting on a towel and nodding her head. Sandra could see her full fanny as her legs hitched up higher. Sandra was disgusted and she couldn't help but stare at what looked like a chicken's napper. The woman's vagina looked like nothing she'd ever seen before. Sandra decided she would check her own lady garden out in the mirror later on that night to see if hers was like that. It was a disgrace.

The screams went on for a while longer and she didn't hear her mobile phone ringing in the other room. Once the client was finished she helped her down from the bed. The woman was walking as if she'd shit her knickers and Sandra turned her head away from her as she chuckled. "What us women go through for beauty ay," she muttered. Her client made no comment and searched her purse for the money to pay for Sandra's services. Once the cash was taken the woman left the shop still walking in a peculiar manner.

Clock watching, Sandra pulled her phone from her bag. She hadn't looked at it in ages and when she saw Kevin's name on the missed calls list she panicked. Sucking on her bottom lip she knew she had to remain calm. Taking deep breaths she went into the toilet and dialled his number. Sitting on the pot she waited for him to answer. His voice was loud and Sandra could be seen holding the phone from her ear.

"Just calm down Kevin. I can't make out a word you're saying." Her head nodded as a smile appeared across her face. She looked mischievous. "Orr no way, Kevin what are you gonna do, I mean Zac and that are gonna want their money from you now aren't they?" She held the phone from her ear again and you could hear someone ranting at the other end of the line. The call ended after a few minutes. Suddenly she punched her clenched fist into the air. "Get in there! You dirty bastard. I'll show you who can take the piss. Let the games begin" She sat for a moment just nodding her head. She could hear someone shouting her from outside. Quickly she opened the door and saw the smiling face of her work mate.

"Are you alright love? I heard shouting"

Sandra smiled. "Oh it was me moaning at Kevin on the phone." She held her phone out in front of her to show her friend his name on the screen. Her friend smiled and left the doorway. Sandra was like a new woman now and she had a spring in her step. She wasn't the underdog anymore and to hear Kevin upset was enough to make her smile from ear to ear.

Sandra lit yet another cig, she had been smoking like a trooper all day long. As she pulled into Maxine's estate she felt her stomach churning like a washing machine. Once the car's engine was turned off she sat with her head resting on the steering wheel. Her head slightly lifted **as** she looked at Maxine's house. Her fingernails tapped on her teeth. Springing from her seat she opened the car door and left. "It's now or never," she whispered. Her face looked worried and you could see her searching her bag. Once she pulled her twenty cigs from it she knocked on the door.

Maxine looked sympathetically at her. She must have watched it already otherwise why was she looking so sheepish. "Come in love. I won't be a minute I'm just sorting this woman out and then we can sort you out." Maxine led her to the front room and as always, all the knocked off stuff was spread across the furniture. Maxine could be seen rolling all the clothes together and shoving them into black bin liners. Once she'd taken the cash from the woman, who looked rough as fuck, she escorted her out. Sandra lit a cig as she phoned Tina to ask her where the hell she was. Tina told her she was on her way and she wouldn't be long. Sandra needed her now, her heart was pounding inside her chest and she thought she was going to pass out. Maxine could see she looked hot and offered her a cold drink. If she would have had some Whisky at hand, she would have poured her a large glass of it, after all she was going to need it.

Sipping at the orange juice Sandra chatted with Maxine. She told her the weed was now sold and they would all get payment later that night. They were now arranging a big celebration for later. After all ten grand was the kind of money Sandra had never seen in her life and she was sure as hell going to enjoy it.

Tina arrived at last. She was wearing a pink vest top and at the side of her foot you could see a large white plaster stuck to her skin. It was obvious she couldn't wait to show the girls what was underneath it. Peeling the plaster away from her skin she looked squeamish. Once the last bit of sticky tape was off it she shoved her foot into Sandra's face. "I've had a tattoo, it didn't even hurt much either. Steven said I was so brave, as he'd seen grown men cry before when they were having tattoos. I'm a warrior aren't I?" The tattoo was in dark blue ink and it read "Carpe Diem."

Maxine was now stroking the design as Sandra chirped in "What does fucking 'Carpe Diem' mean?"

Sandra now stood to look closer and smiled. "Ya fucking mad head."

As Tina slowly replaced the protection her voice was jolly. "It means seize the day." Her face was smiling as she continued. "And that's what I'm going to do from now on ladies, seize the fucking day." They all giggled and Sandra shook her head. Tina was truly a couple butties short of a picnic.

All the doors were locked by Maxine now and she set the video camera up for them to watch the footage. Tina sat by Sandra and held her hand in a tight grip. She looked like death warmed up. Maxine now sat down and they all stared at the TV screen waiting for it to start. The picture was dark to start with and Sandra squeezed her eyes together to try and make out what was happening. She could now hear talking and recognised Kevin's voice. There it was right in front of her eyes, her husband's infidelity for all to see. The sex scene began and Maxine offered to turn it off.

"Don't you fucking dare turn it off!" Sandra screamed. She sat on the edge of her chair now and bit into her knuckles. Maxine took the abuse from Sandra quiet well. If anyone else would have talked to her like that normally she would have twisted them up big time, but this woman was upset and she backed off.

The noises of sex could be heard. Tina could be seen squeezing Sandra's arm and dipping her head away from the TV. They all listened now as they heard Tracy speaking about the baby she aborted. Tears streamed down Sandra's face. There were no sobbing noises, just heartbroken tears gliding down her cheeks.

Once the footage was over they all sat in silence for a moment. Tina passed the cigs around and they waited for some of reaction from Sandra. It took a while but when it did come she was frothing at the mouth.

"Dirty cunt, both of them are. I'm going round to my mam's now to kick her fucking head in. Do they think they can take the piss out of me?" Tina stood up with Sandra and grabbed at her arm.

"Don't you dare give her the satisfaction! Your mam will only protect her, the little slag. And at the end of the day she'll say it was just once that she shagged him. Just take a minute and think about it."

Maxine agreed and joined in the conversation. "You can hurt him in other ways, love. Think about it, you've

just had his grow away and he'll be devastated. Do you
think Zac is just gonna let him get away with it. They
will torture his sorry arse until he pays every single penny
back. Believe me. You just need to chill ya beans for a
while and think about it. It's a lot to take in, I know."
Maxine shot Tina a look as Sandra paced the front room.
She paused at the window and slowly sank to her knees
as if she was melting. Her friends were by her side within
seconds. Sandra was a broken woman.

Like witches sat round a cauldron the three of them
sat planning Kevin's fate. Oh, they were evil bitches. Some
of the things they were saying would have made them
spend a long time in prison if they were ever caught.
Maxine was the brains behind the discussion and she
made them both be quiet as she sat back down with a cig
drooping from the side of her mouth.

"What's our motto now?" she chuckled, "Don't get
angry, get even."

Tina smiled, she loved that saying and it reminded
her of her deceased father. Tina now made the sign of
the cross on her body and looked up towards the ceiling.
"You always said it to me. Didn't you dad?"

Maxine now planned out step by step how Sandra
would deal with her situation. Sandra hung on her every
word and liked her tactics. She was right revenge was
sweet and Sandra was going to make sure her cheating
husband would be sorry about this day for the rest of his
life.

After sitting for a few hours Sandra picked up the
video evidence. She held it in her grip as if her life
depended on it. She'd arranged to meet the girls later
on that night for a good piss-up. Tina was just about to
decline when Sandra grabbed her by the shoulder. "And

don't think you're backing out of it. It's my treat. You can see lover boy later on okay?" Sandra stared at her as Tina sighed. Her friend knew her so well and she agreed to join them later on, under protest.

There was a karaoke night in The Hip pub on Monsall and everyone was saying it was set to be a top night. So that's where they planned on going. Hugs and kisses were exchanged between them all. Sandra was leaving the house when Maxine pulled her back. "Let's sort it girl. Don't worry it will all turn out for the best." She looked cunning as Sandra thanked her. Maxine was one dangerous woman.

Sitting in her car, Sandra watched Tina go in the opposite direction. She'd offered her a lift but Tina had other plans. Turning the engine over Sandra sat for moment in deep thought. The kids playing nearby were waiting for her to move as she was parked in their goal area. One of the kids was now getting impatient and you could see by his face he was getting angry. He waved his arms in the air and urged her to move.

"Little shit" she mumbled as she pulled away. Her mind was working overtime and she didn't want to go home ever again. Her life would never be the same now and her husband had hurt her in the worst way possible. Her phone was ringing and as she glanced at the number she saw Kevin's name flashing in the window. Screwing her face up Sandra spoke to the phone resting on the passenger side. "Oh you want me now don't you? You selfish cunt. Every time you're in trouble it's always the same. Well fuck you arse-hole. I'm going to show you just how much you've hurt me." Heading home she listened to the radio. Why the fuck did they always seem to know when you were upset, because all that they played on the radio was depressing love songs. She switched it off and sat driving in silence.

Sandra's house stared back at her. The front door seemed to be smiling at her and taking the piss out of her situation. Grabbing her belongings she trudged toward it. The curtains could be seen moving and as she looked closer she could see a hand holding the net curtain back slightly. Searching for her keys she entered the house.

There he was, stood right in front of her and he looked a mess. All his hair was stuck up and he looked white in the face. He grabbed at her arm dragging her inside. "Quick, get away from the door. Zac wants to see me and he's not stopped phoning me all day. He knows the drugs have gone missing and I'm sure he thinks I've had them away." She pulled her arm from his. Her face looked angry. "Well you need to sort it out then don't you, instead of hiding away like a coward. Just phone him and arrange to meet up." Sandra held her hands out in front of her. "Fucking hell what's the worst that can happen. Just be honest and tell him the truth."

Kevin grabbed her face in his hands. His knuckles were white as he screwed his face up. "Oh do you think he'll believe me. He's a fucking nutter. He could kill me. Don't you care about me dickhead?" Sandra didn't give a flying fuck and her face told him that. As she jerked her face away from him he lost his temper. Dragging her by the hair he threw her to the floor. Her face was pinned to the ground and held against the carpet. As he stood over her he let rip. "You're never there for me, are you? You've always been the same. All for your fucking self. That's you. The one time I really need you and all you're doing is giving me grief." He launched his fist into her face. Sandra was used to the beatings he gave her and just took it as usual. Once he walked away from her she pulled herself up from the floor and headed to the kitchen. Kevin could be seen walking in and out of each room panicking. He tried to speak to her.

"Do us a drink Sandra." He stood at the kitchen door and looked sorry for his actions. Walking towards her he gripped her waist. She cringed as he kissed her and apologised before heading back into the front room. She was alone. The fridge door was now opened and his precious chocolate milkshake stared at her. Now was the time to start putting into action all the things she had discussed with Maxine.

Checking he was settled in the living room, she crept to the small cupboard where she'd hid the weight gain powder. Pouring it all into a big container she scooped several heaps from it and placed it into his glass. See could still see the powder floating around at the top of it. "Fuck" she whispered. Finding an old bottle she poured all the brown liquid into it and shook it vigorously. Once it was done she poured it back into his glass. "Job done" she chuckled. In the future she would mix it up in one batch. She couldn't take the chance of ever getting caught. He would kill her for sure. Stroking her throbbing face she went to give him his drink. The side of her face was starting to swell, it looked red. She went to leave the room but he shouted her back.

"Sandra get your arse sat down here a minute. I need some help. This shit is doing my head in." He patted the seat next to him on the sofa. Passing him his drink she obeyed his orders. Sandra listened to him and knew she had to pull herself out of the dark hole and speak back to him. She spoke as if she cared. "Just phone him and meet him. There is no point hiding away is there? It just makes thing worst. Zac knows these things happen all the time so he can't blame you, can he?" He sat forward, his head was dipped between his legs as he dragged his fingers through each strand of hair.

"Yeah, yeah you're right, I'll phone him in a minute and arrange to meet up. I need a bath and that first though. I stink like a donkey's arsehole." Sandra watched him gulp at his drink. Her face smirked as she watched him drain the last little drop. "Run the bath for me will you? I'm all over the place and can't think straight." Sandra stood up immediately and headed back into the kitchen to get some toiletries to take upstairs.

Entering the bathroom she locked the door behind her. Tears fell and she threw the toiletries on the bathroom floor. Watching the water fill the bath, the steam filled the bathroom and it made it hard for her to see, her eyes focused on the floor. The hair removal cream she'd just thrown to the floor stared right back at her. The tears stopped as she bent over to grab it. Sandra read the words on the label. Her hands shook as she reached for Kevin's hair conditioner. He always liked expensive stuff for his hair. She carefully unscrewed the lid from his Tony and Guy conditioner. She inhaled its fragrance. It smelt like lavender. Quickly she opened the hair removal cream and squirted the lot inside the red and white container. Her hands now held the hair treatment in her hands and she stood and shook it with all her strength. Pulling the lid back off from it she stuck her nose to the bottle and inhaled deeply. There was no trace of the hair removal fragrance. A smile crept over her face as she placed it back by the bath. Kevin loved his locks more than anything and Sandra knew he would be devastated if he lost one strand of his hair. The bath was now full. Checking there were enough towels in the bathroom, she left to tell him the bath was ready.

Kevin could be heard coming up the stairs and she rushed to the bedroom trying to look busy. The hair loss plan set her thinking and she knew her sister would be getting some of it as well. No one would ever know it was her and that's what she liked about it. She could hide behind her cloak of deceit and never go detected.

Kevin came into the bedroom. Searching his wardrobe he handed her a pair of jeans and a multi coloured top for her to iron. "Run the iron over them babes." Sandra said nothing and took the clothes from him. As she stood to go and get the ironing board out from the cupboard she told him she planned to go out tonight with her friends. His body froze at the bedroom door as he screwed his face up. He looked angry but left the room just huffing. Sandra placed her two fingers into the air and shoved them in his direction. "Wanker" she whispered.

Sandra turned on the CD player and listened to some tunes whilst she was ironing. She ironed her black dress at the same time. Music made her feel giddy and as she listened to The Mavericks track "Dance the night away" she shuffled her body to and fro around the ironing board. Kevin could be heard coming back out of the bathroom, he looked in shock. As she looked at him she could see tears in his eyes. Holding his hand out in front of him, he revealed a mass of hair in his palm.

"Sandra my fucking hair is falling out. Look!" Her eyes stared at the black hair he held in his hands. He kept running his fingers through his hair pulling even more of it out. Sandra looked concerned. She didn't think the hair removal would have been that good but looking at her husband's face her plan had worked even better than she'd expected. She came to his side and comforted him. As she held him she smiled from ear to ear. She was becoming ruthless in her quest to ruin him. She offered some words of comfort.

"It's all the stress Kevin. You just need to stop worrying and it will grow back." As she looked more closely at his scalp, she nearly burst into fits of laughter. The fucker was completely bald in parts. She straightened her face and offered him a solution. "You're better off shaving the lot off. You can't walk about looking like that. You look a right twat." He ran to the mirror for a closer look. His face was showing signs of distress. "Will you get the shavers and do it for me Sandra? I think they're in our John's room. He had them the other day shaving his barnet." Sandra hurried in search of the clippers. Once she'd found them she told him to sit down while she shaved the rest of it off.

Holding the black shavers in her hand she felt like never before. She felt in control for the first time in her life. As the chunks of hair fell to the ground she watched his distressed face in the mirror. His face now looked long and every flaw on his skin seemed to stand out. He looked a right prick. His ears looked massive. Sandra lied when it was finished and told him how much he suited his new hair style as Kevin stood before the mirror turning from side to side. He hated it and she could tell. His mobile phone was now ringing on the bed and he could see the familiar name of Zac spread across the screen. While he answered it Sandra cleaned up the hair from the floor and listened at the doorway as she heard Kevin setting up a meeting with the drug dealer. As he held the phone in his grip he paced around the bedroom with a frightened look on his face. The meeting was now set and Kevin was ready to meet his demons.

Sandra sat in the mirror applying her make-up as Kevin pulled up his jeans. Every time she looked at him she wanted to burst out laughing but she managed to keep a straight face. As he said goodbye he bent down towards her and kissed her cheek.

"Wish me luck Sandra. It might be the last time you see me."

Sandra kept her cool. "Don't be daft. Nothing will happen to you. Just tell him straight."

"Well let's hope you're right ay," Kevin huffed. He left the bedroom. Once she heard the front door slamming, she jumped up from the bed and peered through the top window at him. She could see him getting into his car. He looked a right twat with his new hair style and Sandra pissed herself laughing again. She placed the curtain back and returned to get ready. The smile on her face couldn't be removed and she couldn't wait to tell the girls about her first couple of victories. Quickly reaching for her diary she told it that she was getting stronger and how she'd made her husband lose his precious hair.

9

Kevin drove to his destination with a look of desperation on his face. He knew this man wouldn't take any shit and he prepared himself for the worst. Driving to a deserted car park inside Heaton Park, he turned his engine off and sat trembling inside. Looking into the rear view mirror he checked his face. His hair was a disgrace and he knew it. He looked like he'd escaped from a concentration camp. Gritting on his teeth he blew from his mouth to try and remain calm.

Ten minutes later a silver BMW pulled up at the side of him. Zac was driving. He was a large white man with several tattoos across his upper arm. His white vest-top showed off his bulging biceps. Another two men sat in the back of the car. One of them was black and the other was white. They too looked like they worked out. They looked like warriors. Zac gave the signal for Kevin to come and join them. With hesitation he unlocked his car door and made his way towards the car. The passenger door was now flung open.

The atmosphere was tense. Kevin could feel the guy's breath in the back of the car filtering down his neck as the car pulled out of the car park. Kevin didn't say anything he just sat there fidgeting about with his coat. Zac turned the music up and nodded his head to the beat. He was driving like a mad man and Kevin thought about trying to jump out of the moving vehicle. Zac must have been watching his eyes checking the doors through the rear-view mirror and pressed the central locking at the side of him. Kevin was trapped now and he would have to take anything they had planned for him. He was shitting himself and small droplets of sweat could be seen forming on his forehead. Licking his lips he coughed and began to try and make conversation.

"Where we off to lads?"

Zac turned to him and grabbed his knee as the traffic came to a standstill. Kevin fell back into the chair as he felt his leg being crushed.

"You don't need to know where we're going mate. You just need to know where my fucking bud has gone." Kevin tried to answer but a hand come from behind him and squeezed his shoulder.

"Shut the fuck up" the voice shouted. Kevin felt sick

and knew if he came away from this alive he would be a lucky man.

Zac was a well known drug dealer who ran the drug scene in Harpurhey and Collyhurst. Everyone feared him and knew you didn't fuck with him unless you were willing to take a bullet. Stories of his ruthlessness were always being told in the area. Even though you didn't know Zac personally, you knew he was a man you didn't fuck about with. Kevin had always got on with him and had never had any trouble from him but that was before his weed was stolen. Now was a different story and he was just about to find out exactly what this man was capable of.

The music was turned off now and the two men got out of the back of the car. Fuck me they were massive. Every inch of them was toned; even their fingers looked as if they had been on steroids. Zac led them inside an old scrap yard. A few cars were still lying about but it obvious the place had been closed for a while.

Kevin and Zac walked in front as the two foot soldiers walked behind them. They were watching Kevin's every move. He was walking as if he'd shit himself. He looked weak, as if his legs were about to buckle. A small door was now opened in front of him and Zac led him inside.

The room was quite long and old chairs were scattered about the room. An old desk was situated on the back wall and Zac parked his arse on top of it. A chair was pushed to Kevin and he was made to sit on it in front of him. The two men were now at either side of him. They both stood with their arms folded and awaiting instructions from Zac. The main man now cleared his throat. He could be seen skinning up. Once his spliff was made he lit it and choked as he took a deep drag from it. His face now looked serious and he chewed on his fingernail as he spoke.

"Right Kevin, firstly let me just tell you how much of a twat you look with a bald head." The others chuckled at the side of him and Kevin tried to explain but Zac shut him up straight away. "Shut the fuck up. I'm not here for chit-chat. I want my fucking money back!" Kevin tried to speak again but a fist came from his right side and landed right into his eye. He screamed out in pain. The man now pulled his head up from behind him and made him look at Zac.

Kevin slavered as he spoke. "Mate I don't know what happened. Some fucker must have been onto the grow and had it away." A fist pummelled his face again and this time he fell to the floor like a dead weight. Covering his head with two desperate arms he could feel his body being kicked and punched. Zac's soldiers now dragged him back up and threw him back onto the chair. His eyes were nearly closed and he was struggling to see. Blood trickled from his nose and every bone in his body felt like it was on fire. He struggled to remain on the chair.

Zac now stood up and walked towards him. Gripping his face he screamed. "Nobody has me over you prick. I want what you owe me and I want it now!"

Kevin nodded. You could just about hear Kevin's struggled words. "I'll get it for you. I'll have to sell my car and that." He could feel teeth sinking into his face now and screamed out in pain. Zac pulled a piece of flesh from his face with his teeth and spat it onto the floor.

"Selling your fucking car won't be enough to repay me you wanker."

The drug dealer now walked from him and left him coughing blood from his mouth. Zac stood thinking for a minute he paused.

"Right twat bag. You can start selling brown for me. You'll work for fuck all and do all the running about. That means picking parcels up and bagging it. Do you get me?" Kevin heard his words and doubled over in pain. He would have done anything at that moment to stop the beating and agreed. His head was being knocked about still and as he put his hand up to defend himself he could see blood pouring from his hand. He'd been slashed.

The men stood and watched him suffering. Usually they would have cut his fingers off but they let him off lightly because he'd agreed to deal the hard stuff for them. In the past Zac had showed off people's fingers in the pub that he kept in a steel tin. That was his way of letting everyone know that if they fucked with him that's what would happen to them.

The men left Kevin for a few minutes then dragged him from the chair and carried him back to the car. They handed him an old coat and told him if he got blood on the car seats he would have to pay for that as well. His body was shaking uncontrollably and if you listened carefully you could hear him crying.

The men seemed to have no remorse for the beating they'd just given him and it seemed as if it was all in a day's work for them. Kevin shuffled about placing the coat all around his body. His head rested on the window and his face looked to the floor. He was in a bad way.

Once they were back in Heaton Park, Zac told Kevin he would be in touch. As he started to leave the car Zac stretched over to grab him back inside and looked him straight into his eyes. "Don't forget what I want. If you don't answer your phone when I ring you, I'll be coming through your front door, team handed and you and your family will suffer. Do you hear me?" Kevin nodded and left. He struggled to walk back to his car and when he heard them screeching off, he fell to the ground. He struggled for breath and he tried to find his mobile phone in his pocket. As he located Sandra's number he listened as it went straight to answer phone. Kevin curled up on the floor.

★

Sandra was having the time of her life. She was pissed as a fart and enjoying the company of Tina and Maxine. When she'd told them earlier about how she had put hair removal cream in her husband's conditioner they roared laughing. She was on top form tonight and she mingled with everyone feeling more confident than she ever had in all her life. The night was going well until her sister appeared in the pub. Sandra kicked Tina under the table as they watched her approach. Tracy looked sexy. As always she had everyone's eyes in the pub looking at her, especially Reggae Ronnie the DJ.

Tracy came to their table and leant over to kiss Sandra on the cheek. Sandra accepted and screwed her face up at Tina as Tracy's lips connected on her face. Tracy was dressed in black skinny jeans and a red vest top. Her breasts looked as perky as ever and Sandra could feel herself comparing her own breasts to her sister's. Maxine nodded her head as she gazed at the slut. By the look on her face she wanted to do her in there and then and she whispered to Tina, "Who the fuck does that tart think she is? We should deal with her you know and show her what happens when she fucks around with the big girls." Tina agreed, she'd hated the spoilt brat for years and would have loved to have knocked that cocky smile right from her face. Sandra was her best mate and she needed to step up her game to help her.

Maxine was whispering down her ear. "Let's get the fucker on her own. I've met her sort loads of times and she needs knocking down a peg or too." Tina agreed. She looked about and made sure no one was listening.

"What's that rape drug called where if you take it you can't remember a fucking thing the next day?"

"Rohypnol?"

"Yeah, that's it."

Maxine smiled as a plan hatched in her mind. Tina's phone could be heard ringing and as soon as she saw Steven's name on the screen she hurried to the corner of the pub to answer it. The noise from the music was deafening and she was struggling to hear him.

Sandra was knocking the brandy back, glass after glass. After all she could afford it now. Tina looked down in the dumps and when Sandra asked her what was wrong she sighed. "Oh it's Steven. His dad has just been taken into hospital so he won't be coming home tonight." Sandra grabbed her and held her close.

"Looks like the Anne Summer's rabbit is back in employment then doesn't it."

Tina smiled. She was sad but with help from her best friend she was back on the mend in minutes. Tina looked towards the dance floor and looked shocked to see Tracy and Maxine dancing together. Nudging Sandra in the waist she shouted over the music. "What's Maxine doing dancing with that slag?" Sandra looked over and hunched her shoulders.

"Two faced fucker isn't she?" Tina agreed and pulled her friend from her seat to join her on the dance floor.

The two friends danced away strutting their stuff.

Sandra could feel eyes on her from a man at the side of them both. She asked Tina if she knew him and she told her she'd never seen the guy before. Sandra carried on dancing and kept turning to the man who was more than interested in her. When the song finished they both headed back to their seats. An arm now grabbed Sandra. As she turned it was the man who'd been staring at her. Sandra became defensive at first and asked him to take his hands off her. The man smiled and moved in closer to her.

"Sandra it's me James." She looked at him in more detail. She definitely didn't know him.

"James who?"

The tall man now giggled. "Fucking hell don't say you don't remember me. Did you go out with a lad called James Perkins in St Thomas More School?" Sandra looked at him closely. Then as if someone had pressed a button her eyes became large as she wrapped her arms round him.

"Fucking hell, no way is that you James. You've changed so much."

Her eyes were all over him like a rash now. Fuck me he was sexy. He was tall, dark and handsome and everything a woman could ever wish for. He spoke to her again.

"So you remember now then do ya?" Sandra grabbed him and swung her arms around his shoulders. Back in school they'd had a bit of a fling but they only shared a few kisses, nothing serious.

"Course I do now you've told me who you are, you look so different." She stood back from him now and looked him up and down. He was definitely a fanny magnet. Back in school he was full of spots and had long greasy hair and wasn't really Sandra's type at all. She'd only kissed him as a bit of a laugh anyway.

It was his turn to look her up and down now and she felt uncomfortable as his eyes looked at every inch of her. Sandra glanced at Maxine. She was talking to some well-known drug- dealers.

Sandra invited James to come and sit with them. He carried his drink over and stood at the table. Sandra was now shouting at Tina.

"Guess who this fucking is? You'll never guess in a million years." Tina looked at the man and smiled. Had she fucked him in the past she wondered.

With not a clue in the world she said, "He looks familiar, but I'm fucked if I know who he is." Sandra dragged him to her side now and screamed in a loud voice.

"It's only James fucking Perkins!"

Tina looked amazed. He was just her sort of bloke and if she wasn't in a relationship he would have definitely been in her bed later on that night.

"No fucking way is it. Do you mean James with the spotty face and greasy sweaty hair?" James now stepped in, he felt like a right prick just standing there while they both examined him.

"Ay cheeky, I was never as bad as you're both making me out. Anyway you two were no better than me. Tina you had hair like a poodle if I remember rightly." Sandra screamed laughing as Tina patted at her hair remembering her spiral perm back in the day. He now turned to Sandra. "What are you laughing at? You were just as bad with your big hairdo too."

He was right, Sandra and Tina both had big perms back then and they chuckled as she carried on. "Anyway what are you doing around these parts? I thought you moved abroad?"

James sat down and started to fill them in on the missing years of his life. He spoke about his life and how he married young. His face screwed up as he told them about his ex wife. "It was all great at first, but you know how it gets when you have been married for years. You just become like sister and brother don't you?" Sandra was nodding frantically in agreement. He now asked Sandra if she was married. Before she could reply, Maxine was shouting Tina over. She was holding Tracy in her grip. Tracy looked pissed out of her head. Tina left them and went to see what all the commotion was with Maxine.

Sandra stared into James's eyes. They were so blue. She seemed mesmerized by them and wasn't really listening to him as he spoke. His face just looked so beautiful. Given the chance she would have ripped her knickers off there and then and jumped all over him. So what if she was married? If it was good enough for her husband, then it was good enough for her, she thought. Licking her lips slightly as she spoke, she told him all about the problems in her marriage. He was very sympathetic towards her. Holding her hand he whispered quietly into her ear. "I think you're still fit though."

Sandra felt alive. No one had called her anything remotely sexy for years. She giggled. "Me fit? You must be joking. I've never felt so ugly in all my life." Gripping her fat around her stomach she lifted it up from her dress. "How can you say I'm fit with this blubber?"

James smiled. He looked like he was going to kiss her but stopped. "Why do you put yourself down like that? You look amazing."

She was defensive. "Do I fuck" she ranted. She looked shy now and carried on talking to him. Tina now joined them for a few seconds. She quickly swigged her drink from the table and told Sandra she was taking Tracy outside for a bit of fresh air. Sandra didn't care and carried on gazing into James's eyes.

Tina prompted her again. "If she's no better we'll take her home. Are you gonna be alright here on your own or are you coming with us?"

Sandra stretched her eyes at her. It was obvious she didn't want to go with her and she made excuses. "No I'll stay here. You should just leave her to rot on her own" the little tart. James looked at her and wondered what had happened to the lovely woman he'd just been speaking too. She could see his shocked face and explained. "We've been like that for years James. You don't know the half of it, believe me." That was all he needed to know and he carried on talking to her, making her feel like a woman again. Tonight Sandra had re-discovered the woman she had once been and as she talked to her long lost boyfriend she could feel all her confidence returning.

Maxine struggled until Tina came back outside the pub. No one was about and she was holding Tracy up against a nearby wall. She spat into Tracy's face a few times and spoke to her in an animated voice. "You naughty, naughty little girl" Shagging your sister's husband are you? You're dealing with the big girls now and you'll learn not to take your knickers off as quick next time, you dirty slag."

Tina was now by her side. She grabbed Tracy's other arm and helped Maxine to support the drunken woman. "What the fuck are we doing with her then? Are we taking her home or what?" Maxine smiled.

"Let's take her to your house, it's not far from here is it."

Tina agreed and they set off. Maxine kept bursting into fits of laughter. When Tina asked her what was so funny she cackled. "I've given her something so she won't remember a fucking thing."

Tina stopped walking. "What do you mean something that she won't remember?"

Maxine giggled as they carried on walking. "I got some of that rape drug didn't I? One of the lads brought it in before so I popped it into her drink. We can do whatever we want to the hussy and she won't remember a fucking thing." Tina looked shocked but as she looked at Tracy she knew the home-wrecker deserved everything that was coming to her.

Tina opened her front door. She'd had to get Maxine to hold Tracy up on her own whilst she searched for her keys in her pocket. Once she opened the door she helped bring her inside. Throwing her lifeless body onto the sofa they both sat back looking at her exhausted. Tina and Maxine now burst out laughing.

"Get me a fucking drink I'm knackered," Maxine moaned. Tina entered the kitchen and searched the fridge for a nice cold drink. All she could find was a full bottle of Vodka. Grabbing it from the fridge she swigged at it and went back to the living room. Maxine was now sat admiring Steven's tattoo stuff. Everything was set up and ready to use. Tina joined her.

"Ay if you want a tattoo I can do you one. I've been practicing."

Maxine smiled and spoke in a cocky voice. "Oh have you now. So are you telling me you can use this stuff then?" Maxine was holding the tattoo gun in her hands and twisting it slowly in her fingers.

"Yeah Steven's been showing me for a while now and

I think I'm ready to have a go on a real person." Maxine turned her head slowly towards the sofa. She didn't speak for a few seconds and Tina wanted to know what was wrong with her. "I can do it, don't you believe me?" She was now grabbing at Maxine's arm. "Orr go on let me have a go on you." Maxine slowly grabbed the Vodka from her hand and took a big massive gulp. Once the bottle came from her mouth she spoke.

"Let's tattoo that slag." Tina followed her eyes to Tracy.

"What tattoo Tracy?" she asked with caution in her voice. Maxine was already pulling Tracy towards her.

"Yeah we'll show her not to fuck about with stuff that doesn't belong to her."

Tina paused she looked apprehensive. "Fuck it. Get her over here then." She now helped get Tracy in the position for the tattoo. Once she was lay at the side of them, Tina looked at Maxine.

"What design do you think she should have?" Tina asked as she necked more alcohol.

"Design! Fuck that she's having no design just write 'Slut' on her face."

Tina asked her to repeat what she'd just said. Once she'd heard her right, she dug the tattooing needle deep into Sandra's sister's face. Tracy moved about underneath her but Maxine held her face so she couldn't move anymore.

The girls drank more and more vodka. Before long the words could be seen on Tracy's cheek bone. The both looked at the design and looked proud of their work. Maxine stood quickly and ran to the bathroom. When she came back she was holding a razor in her hands. "Right just let's give her a new design." She quickly scraped the razor into her fringe and took it back to the middle of her head. Tracy looked a mess. As they both giggled Maxine told Tina they would have to get her home now before anyone started missing her. They planned to leave her in the front garden of her parent's house. Tina and Maxine made a pact that this was their secret and no matter what happened they would never tell anyone about how they'd abused Sandra's sister. They smoked a few cigs and finally set off to deliver the faulty goods back to her house. Tina and Maxine now searched for big coats. They needed to make sure no one could ever identify them and dressed for the occasion.

Sandra finished her drink. Checking her watch she knew it was time she was heading home. James was more than willing to walk her but she declined. As he grabbed his coat he walked outside with her. The moonlight now seemed magical and seemed to draw the two of them together. James pulled her out of sight and sunk his sexy lips onto hers. Sandra didn't fight him and enjoyed the moment. She felt like she was back at school and gripped him closer. His lips felt soft and the way he kissed her made her feel like taking him somewhere and shagging his brains out. As she kissed him she could feel his erect trouser missile pressing against her. She wanted him so much and tried her best to fight her feelings. James now held one hand over her head as she stood up against the wall.

"Do you want to come back to my place? We can have a good laugh. Not for sex or out, just a talk."

Sandra smiled and thought she would have a bit of fun with him. "If there's no sex I'm not coming back with you. What do I want to talk for?"

He could see by her face she was having a laugh and raised her up off the ground. He was so strong and she felt protected by him. "Are you coming or what then?" His eyes stared into hers and she was a prisoner of the moment.

"Course I am you dick-head." He kissed her again and this time he used his tongue. Sandra felt on fire inside. They both laughed as he stepped onto the main road and flagged a taxi. Sandra didn't have a care in the world now and she was living for the moment. This was the start of the new her. No more hang ups just fun, fun, fun.

Sandra was still pissed and when they got to James house she still felt on fire. As they entered his house, they both set about each other like there was no tomorrow. He couldn't get her black dress off fast enough and they both laughed when it got stuck going over her head.

The house smelt of flowers and everywhere looked clean and tidy. Leading her into the bedroom she looked around in amazement. "Fuck me it's so clean. Do you live here on your own?" He nodded as she continued. "Are you fucking gay or something? No man can clean like this."

Gripping her by the waist he pulled her onto the bed. "You're so cheeky Sandra. I love the way you just say it how it is." Her laughter could be heard throughout the bedroom. As he stroked her legs she looked horrified. She just remembered she had her period knickers on. She wasn't on her period or anything she just grabbed them because they were the nearest pair at the time. James could see that something was wrong and enquired what was troubling her. She bit onto her tongue and smiled.

"Fuck it" she thought and told him straight. "I've got

the worst knickers on you have ever seen. I didn't think anyone was going to be looking at them. So I just shoved on my Old Faithfuls."

He looked as if he was going to burst with laughter but he kept a straight face. "Oh it doesn't matter. Just as long as your bush is trimmed, we can move on." Her hands now covered her eyes. She remembered that her lady garden hadn't been trimmed for months. Why should she cut it just for Kevin? After all he just fucked her and never took the time to even look at her muffin. She removed her hands from her face.

"James I'm a walking wreck. Can't we do this some other time when I'm more prepared?" His hand stroked her face.

"Sandra do you think I give a flying fuck about what your knickers are like or how big your bush is, because I don't. I like you for being you, nothing else." Sandra listened to his words. She would store them in her mind vault and remember them forever. Kevin had never spoken to her like that. Not even when they first met. They both melted into each other's arms and before long he was caressing her body. Sandra cringed when James ran his fingers across her lower stomach area. Her stretch marks were in full view and he didn't seem to care about them and at one point he kissed them.

Sandra felt loved and special. She responded to his every touch and became the porn star she'd always wanted to be. Sitting on top of him, she grinded down on his erect penis. She watched as his face changed with excitement. Her moves had come from nowhere and she was surprised at herself at how much of a good lover she really was.

Sex was brilliant. As they finished they lay exhausted

in each other's arms. The room was warm and her face was on fire. Throwing his body flat onto the bed he turned her face towards him. "That was amazing Sandra. I'm not being crude or anything but you are one horny fucker." She dug her head inside his waist with embarrassment. James started to joke with her. "My ball- bag must have been massive. I've not had sex for months. Do you need a towel or anything I bet you're covered in bob monk?"

Sandra screamed laughing. "You cheeky fucker. What are you saying!"

James back-pedalled. "No, I'm just saying I don't sleep with anyone. I am quite picky." He was forgiven and James lit two cigarettes. Passing Sandra one he stared up towards the ceiling. "Well I'll tell you more about me and you can get to know me a bit better." She felt cheap. He was right, she'd only known him a short time and there she was bouncing about on his cock. She pulled the blankets over her body feeling ashamed of her actions. What was wrong with her, since when had she been so easy to get into bed. Her thoughts were over the place and James could tell she was regretting her night of passion. "I don't want this to be a one night stand Sandra, I would love to see you again. I know you're married and all that, but if you tell me it's over and you don't love him anymore then that's fine by me."

Sandra rolled his words around in her mind. She didn't love Kevin anymore he'd been shagging her sister so how could she ever love him again? Taking his masculine hand she squeezed it and rested her head onto his chest. She didn't want to look at him when she confessed how much of a mess her life was in. Her words were endearing and she found him so easy to talk to. She told him everything about her life and how her husband had treated her over the years.

James sighed and shook his head and asked the question she'd asked herself a million times in the past. "Why do you put up with him? Why haven't you left him, the prick?"

Her face was regretful and she hunched her shoulders. With a big gasp of her breath she tried to explain her life style. "It's not as easy as all that, James. We have kids together and I just thought… Well I don't know what I thought. I just thought it would get better in time but it never did."

He cradled her and his face looked angry. "Just fucking leave him. I'm not saying come and live with me. I'm just saying if he's not changed over all these years he never will. Leopard and spots and all that."

Sandra looked at the clock at the side of the bed. She bounced up as if she'd had an electric shock. "Fucking hell. Is that the time?" James watched her as she picked her clothes up from the floor. She was mumbling under her breath. Once she was dressed she stood at the side of the bed staring at him. "Listen I'll be in touch. I like you a lot. And as for jumping in bed with you on the first night, that is so not who I am. I just…"

He smiled and interrupted her. "Here is my mobile phone number. Phone me when you can." He passed her a small white business card that he'd got from the drawer at the side of the bed. As her eyes quickly scanned the number she read his job title. "Business Developer."

"Posh fucker you, aren't ya?" she giggled. He tried to grab her back onto the bed but she moved away laughing. "Right James I'll be in touch. Don't miss me too much ay" She quickly bent over towards him and kissed him goodbye. She let herself out.

Walking from his driveway she was in a panic. It was nearly four in the morning. What the fuck would she tell Kevin about her whereabouts? Her heels clicked along the pavement as she made her way down the garden path towards a taxi.

10

Kevin sat watching the clock tick away. He was in severe pain and needed Sandra by his side. His son had tried to come in the bedroom earlier but he'd stood behind the door and told him he was busy. That was all he needed, his son knowing all his business. He was filled with anger, rage was pumping through his veins. Where the fuck was his wife? She'd never been in this late before and if his body wasn't in such a state he would have gone out searching the streets looking for her. He was shaking in pain and a few times he thought his life was going to end. The sound of the front door could be heard. Lifting his aching body from the bed he tried to sit up.

Sandra tiptoed up the stairs. "Please be asleep" she mumbled under her breath. Every stair made a noise and she cursed at them as she made her way to the top. "Fucking noisy bastard stairs." Her breath was struggling now and she inhaled deeply before entering the bedroom. The small bedside light gave off just enough light to see her husband sat up in bed. She didn't give him any eye contact and sighed as she sat on the side of the bed taking her shoes off. "That fucking sister of mine she spoilt our night. Pissed out of her head she was." He wasn't listening and started to cough. Turning her head she looked at him. Her face was in shock. "What the fuck" she said standing up and walking round to his side of the bed. "Kevin, what's happened? Who's done this to you?"

His lips quivered and he sunk his head low as he told her. "It was Zac and his heavy men. Look at the state of me Sandra, they've nearly killed me." Forgetting about her night of passion she ran to the bathroom. She had a medical kit there. She could at least clean the wounds up and assess the damage.

Entering back into the bedroom she dabbed the white fluffy balls of cotton wool onto his face. She'd brought a small bowl of warm water to dip it into as well. As she wiped his face he screamed in pain. "Fucking hell, take it easy will you?" His face screwed up and he looked in pain. Her hands shook as she wiped the dried blood away from his skin. She could see a big chunk missing from his cheek. He definitely needed medical attention.

"Kevin you need to go to hospital you're a mess. I'm going to phone an ambulance." She stood from the bed as his hand gripped her pulling back towards him.

"Don't fucking phone anyone, you silly twat. Do you want the dibble involved, because they will be you know. And then what?" Her face changed. She tutted as she remembered the man sat before her like a wounded animal. He deserved everything that was coming to him, the wanker. She stood from the bed carrying the small bowl of water in her hands. Kevin now shouted after her. "If you phone an ambulance I swear I'll twist you up?" His voice got louder. "Do you hear me?" Sandra nodded as she left the room.

Slowly she tipped the water down the plughole. Running the water to clean the bowl she was faced with her own reflection in the mirror. She'd changed. She no longer looked like the weak, scared, Sandra she'd always seen. She looked different.

Sandra took her clothes off and got into bed. Kevin was still lying on the bed feeling sorry for himself. As she turned away from him he dug his clenched fist into the small of her back. "What the fuck are you doing going asleep, I need some help here, don't you care that I've been beaten half to death you inconsiderate bitch."

Sandra slowly turned round and glared at him. She spoke with a calm voice and meant every word. "You ever touch me like that again nob rash and I'll take you to the fucking cleaners. Do you think you can just punch me like that and I'll just take it?" Her face leant into his. Their noses were nearly touching. "Don't ever raise your hand to me again. Do you understand?" Oh she'd really overstepped the mark now and he wriggled about in the bed gripping her hair.

"Who the fuck are you talking to? Do you think you can chat shit to me?" He screamed as he tried to stand up. He couldn't deal with her at the moment and she knew it. A smile filled her face. Turning her body away from him she spoke in a cocky manner.

"Get in bed you daft cunt. No wonder you got twatted. You probably deserved it." He was fuming and fell back onto the bed. Staring at the back of her head he lifted his hand back and swung at her. She accepted the blow and just pulled the cover over her head. She had other things on her mind at the moment and he certainly wasn't one of them. Snuggling in to her pillow she smiled as her night of passion came to her mind. She was having an affair and she loved every minute of it. Sandra closed her eyes and pretended to be asleep. She could still hear the moaning fucker at the side of her. She felt no remorse for him and prayed that the pain he felt would be enough to wipe the smile from his face for good.

Kevin stared into space as he watched his wife sleep. He needed her but the snoring noise coming from the side of him told him she was fast asleep. As he cried in pain he pulled his mobile phone from his pocket. As he searched the screen he looked for any new text messages. The inbox was empty. His fingers now pressed at the black keyboard on his Blackberry phone. "Where are you, I need you!" he wrote. Pressing the send button he watched the screen button until the sent message symbol appeared. Trying to get comfy he rested his head back onto his pillow. Sleep was a million miles away and he lay staring at the ceiling. He was in deep shit and couldn't see a way out. A tear formed in the corner of his eye as he sighed.

Tracy lay in her parent's front garden as the morning broke. She looked weird. As she lifted her head from the grass, she took in the scenery around her and realised where she was. Struggling to stand she swayed and had to grab a nearby wall to help her balance. Her fingers now felt the front of her head. She felt the prickled hair that was her fringe. As she stroked her hairline her face became white. She knew something was wrong and ran to her parent's front door. Her clenched fist now hammered on the door. She was frantic. "Mam, mam open the fucking door" she screamed at the top of her voice.

Standing back from the front door she looked at the top windows. She could see her mother's face appearing at the window. Tracy shouted for her to hurry. Her mother could see she was in some kind of trouble and she left the window to open the door. Tracy sank to her knees and rested her hands on the front door.

Tracy's mother screamed when she saw her daughter's face. Helping her up from her feet she brought her inside shouting upstairs at the top of her voice. "Graham, get down here quick it's our Tracy." Tracy was screaming when she was gripped in her mother's arms. She knew her hair was missing and pulled from her grip to find the nearest mirror inside the front room. As her eyes focused on her face she noticed the tattoo on her cheek bone. Wetting her finger in her mouth she rubbed at her skin vigorously. Her face was now distraught and her mother was at the side of her trying to rub it off too.

"Will you fuck off!" Tracy snapped. Her face was swollen and within minutes she realised the words were permanent. Anita was still at her side and read the letters on her cheek out slowly. S, L, U, T. You could see at that moment it clicked in her mind exactly what the word meant. Her husband was now at her side and he too was trying to clam Tracy down.

"Who's done this to you cock? Because I'll have them done in. The cheeky cunts thinking they can get away with this!" He paced the floor in the front room as Tracy broke down crying. The front of her hair was missing and she didn't have a clue who'd done it.

"That's it" her mother cried out. "I'm phoning the police." Quickly sitting in the armchair she pressed the buttons on the phone. Tracy was folded in two now on the sofa, crying her eyes out. Her mind was blank and every time her mother asked her a question she screamed that she didn't know. Her father sat at the side of her and stroked the back of her hair.

The phone call to the police was over and she spoke quietly to her husband telling him they were on their way. Anita switched the kettle on. It was the only way she knew to calm the situation down. In a timid voice she spoke to Tracy. "Do you want a brew love? It will help calm your nerves?" There was no reply and she watched as her daughter's shoulders jerked up and down as she sobbed.

The police sat with Tracy and they could tell the attack on her had been planned. She told them all what she could remember and that left them with nothing much to go on. She gave the name of the pub where she had been and told them she was with her sister and her friends most of the night. The officer wrote down everything she'd told him. He'd seen this so many times before and asked Tracy if she'd been spiked. Her face looked vacant. "What do you mean spiked?" The female officer now explained in more detail. "Rohypnol is a drug that will make you forget most of the night. The way you are describing what has happened to you it sounds like it's the effect of the rape drug." Tracy shook her head. She was shivering now and her teeth were chattering together. Her mother grabbed her cardigan from her shoulders and placed it around her child.

Tracy took a moment to speak. She stuttered. "So I've been raped as well"? Her head fell between her legs now and she jerked her knees up and down.

Graham was saying the word out loud. "Rape, you mean my daughter could have been raped?" The officers felt his pain as he sank in his chair. Everyone's eyes were now on Tracy as they told her she would have to go to the hospital to be checked out.

Tracy dragged at her skin and sunk her nails deep into her arms. "I feel dirty. I'm not going anywhere until I've had a wash." The officer explained she couldn't have a full wash as the doctors would have to take specimens from her body.

Tracy ran upstairs. She could hear her mother talking to the people sat in the room. "Surely she would have known if she would have been raped. She can't have been raped surely?"

Locking the bathroom door behind her Tracy held her back against it. Her chest was moving rapidly and she looked as if she was having heart attack. Ripping at her clothes as if they contained some lethal disease she threw them on the floor at the side of her. Standing there in just her knickers she slowly peeled them down her legs. Looking at the knickers in her hands she searched for signs of sex in them. Her eyes scanned the crotch of her underwear. There was no trace of anything. Her knickers were dry. Of course she had a few piss stains in them but that was normal. Bending over slightly she stuck her finger inside her vagina. As she pulled it out she held it to the light. She found no evidence of her having sex. With a flat palm she wiped the mist from the mirror as she stared at her face. She looked like a mental patient. The word across her face made her shake her head. Tears streamed down her face. She was a mess.

With each stoke of the sponge across her face she tried to make herself feel better but nothing worked. A black cloud hung over her and the face she'd always been proud of was damaged. How could she ever rid herself of the name branded across her face for the world to see? Her mother's voice could be heard outside the bathroom.

"Tracy, are you alright? Come on love the police are waiting. The sooner you get to the hospital, the sooner they can catch the bastards who've done this to you." Tracy huffed before she replied. She struggled to stand and her body felt weak.

"I'm coming now. Just leave me alone mam. I'll be ready when I'm ready." Anita shouted to her again.

"I've phoned our Sandra she's on her way love." Tracy didn't reply and dragged the white fluffy towel from the radiator to wrap round her body.

All eyes looked at Tracy when she walked into the living room. Sandra was distraught when she saw her baby sister in such a mess. The headband Tracy placed around the front of her head hid the missing hair, but no amount of make-up could hide the blue tattoo on the side of her face. She looked so different. Sandra came to her side and hugged her but her eyes focused on the word on her face. Who would do such a thing? Sandra looked as if she'd seen a ghost and walked from the front room. Perhaps Zac and the boys knew she was shagging Kevin and messed her up too.

She searched for her mobile and hurried to a quiet place in the garden to inform Kevin what had happened. She knew he wouldn't tell her his thoughts but he would know in his own mind that there could be a chance Zac and his boys were showing him they weren't taking any shit and that they meant business by hurting his bit on the side too.

Tracy sat in the police car. She felt like a grass as the neighbours on the estate were out in full force staring at her. Four women stood at a garden fence sipping their morning cuppas whispering to each other. Sandra now joined her and held her hand in the back of the police vehicle. Her sister looked a mess and she'd never seen her like this before. She looked so defenceless and vulnerable. The officers joined them and the journey began to the hospital. The two police officers spoke briefly to Tracy and told them she would be given an examination when she reached the hospital. They also told her she would be checked for the rape drug to see if it was in her system. Sandra gripped her hand and comforted her shaking sibling.

The hospital was quiet and Tracy was led to a side room. The nurse asked them if they wanted a drink, "Tea with two sugars please" Sandra replied. Two chairs sat in the medical room and the desk in front of them was piled high with paperwork. Sandra could see the police outside talking to the doctor who kept turning to the room and gazing at the victim through the window. Sandra now held her brew in her hands. As she blew it to try and cool it down, she spoke to Tracy. "I wonder who it was. I mean to do something like that to you it must have been some sick bastard." Tracy looked at her blankly. She just sat listening as Sandra continued. "Dad's on the estate as we speak, you know what he's like, he thinks he's fucking Columbo, he said to my mam that he won't rest until he gets the bastards." Tracy raised a smile as Sandra continued. "I can't believe you can't remember a fucking thing though Tracy. Just try and remember something. At least then you've got something to go on."

Tracy broke in. "Sandra will you fuck off doing my head in? I don't remember a fucking thing. Do you think if I knew for one minute who'd done this to me I wouldn't tell anyone? Get a fucking grip will you."

Sandra looked embarrassed, "I was only trying to help." The room was filled with silence and Sandra sat playing with the plastic cup running her finger round the rim of it.

The doctor now appeared. He looked sympathetically at the victim. "Hello I'm Doctor Barnes and I will be dealing with you today." He told Tracy she would be given a full examination and that a sample of her blood would be taken. The women followed him to another room.

Once inside a nurse was also present and she handed Tracy a white gown to put on. Tracy now disappeared into a cubicle. After a few minutes she came back out and looked stressed. She looked so weak and fragile. Sandra was straight at her side giving her support. "Once this is done love, we can go home. Just try and be brave." Tracy climbed onto the bed, tears were forming in her eyes as the doctor took a swab from her vagina. She could be seen gritting her teeth as the examination continued.

Once the tests were over the sisters sat waiting for the news. Tracy was rocking to and fro as Sandra chewed on her fingernails. The word rape sent shivers through Sandra's body and the thought of someone forcing sex onto her baby sister made her stomach churn. All the hate for her had disappeared from her mind. Gazing at her constantly Sandra prayed she hadn't been raped.

The doctors came back into the room after several hours had passed. His face looked serious and he sat down next to the women. As he spoke he kept his eyes firmly fixed onto the sheets of paper in front of him. "Your results are back my dear and there are no signs that you have been raped." He looked up from his paperwork and stared at Tracy. "You do know that you're pregnant, don't you?" Tracy felt her face going red. She sat fidgeting as the doctor waited for an answer. Sandra looked pale. The colour seemed to have drained from her face as she too waited for Tracy to reply.

"Yes I already knew." Sandra stood from her chair. She wobbled as if her feet couldn't carry the torment inside her head. She told them she needed the toilet and staggered to the exit like a wounded soldier.

A few people were already in the toilets as Sandra rushed inside. She found an empty cubicle and quickly went inside locking the door after her. Holding her back against the door she dragged her fingers through her hair. Her breathing was rapid and she was panting like a dog in hot weather as she tried to regain her breath.

"Dirty pair of bastards!" she cried. Covering her mouth with her hands she broke down. She knew the unborn child was her husband's no matter what anyone else would try to tell her. She had to pull herself together and remain calm. Pulling her knickers down she squatted on the toilet. Her head felt heavy as it fell between her legs. Any sympathy she felt for Tracy now left her as she stood up and flushed the toilet. Her hands shook as she unlocked the door. Stepping towards the mirror she looked at herself. Smeared mascara was visible round her eyes and she knew she would have to get rid of it because they would have been able to tell straight away she'd been crying. Grabbing some tissues from a cubicle she wet it and slowly dabbed it near her eyes. Once it was gone she headed back to her sister.

Tracy looked straight at Sandra and she could tell something was wrong with her. "There's a trace of the rape drug in my system." Sandra just nodded. Her fists were tightly clenched at the side of her and you could see she was struggling to keep from pummelling Tracy's face. Tracy looked cocky now. She sat with her palm flat across her stomach. A cunning smile on her face.

The doctor left them both and told them the police would want to see them before they went home. As soon as he left Sandra made no secret that she was upset.

"So who's the dad? You don't even have a boyfriend." Tracy sat swinging her legs and turned to her.

"What do you mean I don't have a fella? Who the fuck is Mark then?" Sandra screwed her face up.

"Mark! You haven't seen him for ages. Since when have you ever called him your boyfriend?" Tracy flicked her hair from her face.

"Listen he's the dad. I know who I've been sleeping with, you daft cow." Sandra could tell she was lying, she hated her with a vengeance. All her hate came to the surface and she wished her sister dead, the lying little slag.

The journey home in the taxi seemed to take forever. Sandra gazed through the window and didn't say a word. She could see Tracy still holding her hand across her stomach and she wanted to beat the baby out of her there and then.

Tracy's parents were sat at the window waiting for them to return. As soon as they stepped from the taxi they were by her side. Her father now held her and she was escorted into the house like a war hero. Tracy now told her parents about the drug being in her system and her dad was fuming pacing the front room. "The dirty no good bastards, who do they think they are putting stuff like that into people's drink. You could have died!" He dragged his fingers through his hair. The love of a father for his daughter now came to the surface. Graham came to her side and cradled her in his grip. "The main thing is that you are alright. You're so lucky you know." Sandra watched the commotion and felt sick inside. Lighting a cigarette she sat with her legs crossed at the dining table, she wanted to wipe the smile of everyone's face. Clearing her throat she casually spoke.

"Oh Tracy tell them your good news."

Anita and Graham both looked at her with vacant

faces. She had their full attention now. A smile formed on Sandra's face as Tracy looked uncomfortable fidgeting about on the sofa. Her parents were waiting anxiously looking at Sandra then back across to Tracy. Sandra couldn't wait any longer. Taking a drag from her cig Sandra broke the silence.

"Our Tracy is pregnant!" Anita and Graham looked shocked.

"What do you mean she's pregnant?" Sandra chuckled.

"Well apparently Mark is the father. He's been her boyfriend for a while hasn't he Tracy?" Tracy was livid and couldn't get her words out quick enough.

"Me and Mark have been together for ages. Just because I don't tell everyone my business, it doesn't mean he's not the father."

Her parents were gobsmacked. Tracy had slept with Mark a few times in the past, everyone knew that, but she was lying through her teeth when she said he was her boyfriend. They were just fuck buddies.

Sandra finished her cig and left her parents still staring at their beloved child. Her father was disgusted and he couldn't hide it. He'd always wanted better things for his youngest child and now he looked at her with disappointment in his eyes shaking his head.

"Right I'm off," Sandra announced. Her mother just nodded. Graham seemed in a world of his own and made no reply. No big hugs goodbye, just a nod of the head.

"Typical!" Sandra mumbled as she left the house.

★

11

Sandra headed home. Her head was in bits now. Her husband had fathered another child. This was the end and there was no way on earth she could ever forgive him. It was the ultimate betrayal. Picking up her mobile phone she got in touch with Tina and told her she was on her way round to her house. After all she couldn't go home yet she was a mess.

By the time she knocked on Tina's door she couldn't even speak. Steven opened the door to her and could tell something had happened. "Come in love, come in. I'll get Tina." Sandra followed him like a lost sheep sobbing. Tina came out of the bathroom with a towel wrapped around her head. As soon as she saw her best friend's tears, she knew she needed her. Tina gave Steven the eyes to disappear and shouted to him as he left the room for him to put the kettle on.

Both girls sat down and Sandra dropped her head onto the table. Her hands guarded her face and Tina had to pull at them to get a glimpse of her face. "Fucking hell Sandra what's wrong. Come on tell me?"

Sandra snivelled. Her eyes looked red raw as she lifted her head up. As she spoke her lips trembled. "He's got her pregnant, Tina. The dirty twat has got my sister pregnant."

Tina looked horrified. "How do you know? I mean what makes you think that?" Sandra started to tell the story of Tracy's attack. Tina went white in the face and she hoped the police wouldn't be knocking on her door any time soon. Tina stopped her and made her go over the details of the attack in more detail. Tina looked like she'd seen a ghost. Her hands were shaking as she reached for her cigs.

Sandra struggled to get her words out. "I know its Kevin's kid even though the tart is saying Mark is the father. Come on, we all know she just uses Mark for money and that don't we?"

Tina nodded, then focussed on the other part of the story. "So let me get this right, someone drugged Tracy and tattooed her face. And now she's found out she's pregnant."

"Yes," Sandra sighed.

Steven returned carrying two brews. He held his hand on Sandra's shoulder and squeezed it. "Are you alright love?" he asked. Sandra sniffed up and smiled at him. He could see she was far from alright and tried to make conversation. "Ay while you're here let me do ya a tattoo." Sandra looked at him. She didn't know if he was joking or being serious. Tina now jumped into the conversation. They were trying to take her mind off the situation.

"Yes Sandra, get the same as me 'Carpe Diem'. Maxine can get one too and we can all say we have survived cheating bastard men." She rubbed at Steven's leg as he stood beside her. Sandra looked as if she was thinking. She knew she had a long way to go before she was a survivor but this was a start surely. She agreed.

Tina rang Maxine and she got there just as Steven began tattooing Sandra's foot. She was screaming out in pain. Her head was turned to the side, and biting into her clenched fist. At one point she screamed out, "For fucks sake this is worst than child birth!" Tina chuckled as Maxine prepared herself for her turn.

Sandra was now finished and the words "Carpe Diem" read across her foot. Looking at it in more detail she looked happy with the design. The art work made her feel strong inside and it just reminded her that one day she would be over all this mess. Steven placed a white bandage over it and taped it down. He was telling her how to look after it as Tina piped up. "Ay Sandra I can tattoo now, can't I love" She looked at Stephen for support. He smiled and nodded as prepared to do Maxine's tattoo. She was sat next to him now with her leg placed on his lap. Stephen continued.

"Yeah she's getting good, Sandra. I'll have to watch her because she'll be nicking all my clients soon if I don't watch out." Sandra praised Tina then a look came across her face that told everyone she was in shock. Tina offered to get her a cold drink of water and thought it was the effect of the tattoo that had made her feel sick. Sandra followed Tina into the kitchen area.

Watching her best friend run the cold tap water she bit down on her bottom lip. Surely she'd got it wrong in her head? She had to get the question from her mouth before she sent herself crazy. Tina passed her the glass of water and told her to take a sip. Once the liquid hit her mouth Sandra told Tina to sit down for a minute. Tina knew by her face it was something important and quickly sat down. Taking a deep breath Sandra began.

"Tina it was you wasn't it?"

Tina looked her straight in the eyes. "What was me? What are you going on about?"

Sandra took hold of her hand and softly shook it. "You did that tattoo on our Tracy's face didn't you?" Tina couldn't keep eye contact with her she was twisting and turning her head in all directions trying to keep the secret she held firmly placed on her tongue. It was no good Tina couldn't hold it any longer. Sandra was her best friend and she needed to know the truth. "Yeah I did. She's a slut and deserved it. How do you think I feel seeing the little tart shagging your husband right in front of everyone's eyes?" You could now hear Maxine screaming in pain from the other room. Sandra looked towards the door. Her eyes cast back over to Tina.

"Was she involved too?" Tina nodded and waited for her reaction. "Fucking hell. So you two have done that to her just for me?" Tina smiled unsure of what her next move was. Sandra now reached over to her and hugged her tightly as she cried. "Thank you so much. Nobody has ever stood up for me before like you two have." Sandra now pulled away from Tina and held her head to the side. "So let me get this right in my head. You two drugged her and tattooed "slut" on her face?"

Tina looked apprehensive at first before she became cocky as she spoke waving her arms about. "Yep that's right. And to tell you the truth I would do it again to anyone who fucks about with another woman's man."

Sandra sighed and twisted her fingers. "You two are fucking ruthless," Sandra smiled.

"Well anyway like you said she deserved it. The police haven't got fuck all to go on so I think there will be no comebacks."

Tina now told her about the whole episode and laughed as she told her about when they shaved her fringe off. Maxine limped into the kitchen balancing on one leg. She held one hand on the door frame

"That killed. It was like a needle being dragged deep into my foot." They examined each other's tattoos now and together they looked invincible. The words on their feet bound them together and from that day on the three of them would deal with anyone who got in their way.

Sandra now told Maxine she knew who the attackers

were who'd dealt with Tracy. Maxine looked at Tina for guidance, but as soon as she saw the look on her face she knew their secret was out. The three of them huddled together in the kitchen and spoke about their next move to finish Kevin off.

★

Kevin sat in his front room bagging the heroin. The scales in front him helped him to weigh out the right amount of smack that would go into each bag. His face still looked swollen and you could see he was still in immense pain. He knew the task of paying the money back to Zac would never end. Kevin needed some help and as he heard his son come in through the front door he shouted him to come and join him.

John walked into the living room and stared at his father's face. "Dad what's wrong? Who's done that to you because I swear I will do em in!" Kevin looked at his son and blew a laboured breath. He felt embarrassed at where his life had taken him. His hand now reached across to John and he gripped his hand.

"Mate I know we haven't seen eye to eye in the past but I'm in deep shit and I need your help," John was now bouncing round the front room. He was fuming.

"Dad just tell me who it was, and I'll get a few lads together and we'll go and sort them out. My mates got a gun so I'll pop a cap in their arses." Kevin raised his voice and told him to sit down.

"Listen you don't fuck about with these kinds of people. They mean business and won't think twice about coming through our front door and dealing with us all. Your mother included," Kevin looked serious. John sat down cracking his knuckles. He looked stoned, his eyes were glazed over. Kevin bit down on his bottom lip as he continued. "They would hurt us son. Without a shadow of doubt, so for now we have to leave it." John shot his eyes at the drugs on the table. He'd dealt in weed before and knew this was some other kind of drug. John's hand reached over and he picked up a small bag of the brown powder. Looking at his dad he asked what it was. Kevin shook his head in disgust. He hated that he was now getting his son involved, but he had no option.

"It's smack, Heroin." John opened the bag and started to smell it. Kevin coughed loudly and told him that he needed to sell it to pay back the money he owed to the dealers. This job sounded right up John's street. He now looked at his father.

"Right I can sort out some runners and that, but we need some phones don't we?" Kevin nodded. They both sat for a minute in silence then Kevin swore him into the secret they now shared.

"Nobody must ever know about this. Not even your mam, or your brother." He stared at his son waiting for a reply. John nodded and agreed. Whilst his father was distracted John pushed a small bag of heroin into his pocket. Once it was secure in his jeans he helped his father bag the rest of the smack up.

By the time Sandra had got home all traces of the drugs had gone. She wanted to dive onto Kevin there and then and plunge a sharp knife deep inside his chest and rip his heart out. Looking at him with hate in her eyes she sat down and started to tell him about her sister's ordeal. As she told him she watched his face drop. He looked white and ready to collapse.

Kevin had introduced Tracy to Zac and his gang in the past and they knew he was shagging her brains out.

Perhaps they'd done this to Tracy just to show him that they meant business?. His words were shaky as he spoke. "So is she alright then or what?" Sandra now sat forward in her chair as she dropped the bomb shell on him.

"Yeah she's fine. She wasn't raped and the tattoo can be removed so she got off lucky didn't she? Mind you her hair looks a mess at the front. But I suppose it will grow back wont it?"

Looking at his wife Kevin agreed. Sandra now turned from his view and spoke. "Well anyway that's the least of her worries. When they examined her the doctor found out she was pregnant. Fancy that ay!" Kevin couldn't speak and nearly choked as he took deep drags from his cig.

Sandra pushed him for a reply. "So what do you think about that then? Apparently its Mark's kid." Kevin stood from his chair. He needed to regain his balance as he stood up. Sandra loved the look on his face and spoke to him in an animated voice.

"Oh how's your leg. You look in pain?" He just mumbled and left the room without replying. She could hear him in the kitchen.

A look of malice was etched on Sandra's face. She stood to her feet and walked to the kitchen. Peeping around the corner she could see him texting rapidly on his phone. The phone was shaking in his hands and she knew he was falling apart. Sandra headed upstairs. She was knackered and needed some sleep. Searching underneath the thick mattress she found her diary. She'd always written one since being a young girl and found it helped her get things off her chest. Reading through the previous months entries she giggled. She was an evil cow she thought as she read what she'd previously done to her husband. Today was a good day for writing and she had so much to tell her diary before she went to sleep. Checking that the bedroom door was firmly closed she started to write up the day's events. Her head was in bits and she secretly planned more payback of her cheating husband.

Later, John looked at the drugs in more detail. He'd been dying to have a go of smack for a long time. He loved a buzz and this stuff looked like it could offer it to him. A few of his mates had tried it in the past. Sitting in his mate's flat he showed them what he had in his hand. At first they looked shocked and wanted nothing to do with it. John's best mate Jason told everyone to get a grip and fuck off out of his flat if they were scared of a little bit of smack.

Jason was twenty-one and loved drugs. He'd had heroin in the past and wasn't afraid to try it again. The others left the flat. John now told Jason the situation his father was in. Jason rubbed his hands together. "Count me in mate. I need to earn some decent cash." John watched as Jason prepared the heroin for them to smoke. John watched with anticipation at his mate tooting from the silver foil. Now it was his turn. John copied everything Jason had done and before he knew it he lay on the floor staring into space just like his friend. His eyes looked vacant and he seemed in a world of his own.

12

Tracy stood in the full length mirror and turned to the side. Her belly looked massive now and she looked disfigured as she stood in her white wedding dress. Tracy and Mark had announced they were getting married a month before. He'd paid for her to have the tattoo removed from her face and was over the moon that he was going to be a father. Tracy had told Kevin about his child but he told her point blank to get rid of it as he wanted nothing to do with her or the baby. She had no option but to marry Mark.

Sandra had been planning this day in her mind for months. This was going to be the day she watched her sister fall to the ground like the little snake she really was. Maxine and Tina had helped set everything up and the plan was ready to wipe the smile from a lot of people's faces.

Sandra stood next to Tracy in the bedroom. My, how things had changed. Sandra was now the thin one and her sister looked like a beached whale. Sandra hadn't really noticed her weight loss until now and as she looked in the mirror, she knew she looked good. The bridesmaid's dresses were a soft lilac colour. Sandra hated her dress and only wore it to keep her mother happy. The two younger bridesmaids were Mark's sisters. They looked so cute, unlike Sandra.

Tracy's mother was like a fly round shit. Every couple of seconds she would come up to Tracy and pull her dress straight. If it wasn't the dress she was touching, it was her daughter's hair. Sandra watched them both with a look of disgust on her face. The sound of a message alert could now be heard. Once Sandra checked her phone she realised that she had a message from James. Heading to the toilet she held her phone tightly in her hands.

James and Sandra had been seeing each other regularly. They'd become quite close and he'd already told her he loved her. Sandra loved him too but knew she couldn't be with him yet until she'd sorted out her own mess. James knew she was up to something but kept his nose out of it knowing Sandra would tell him when she was ready.

Sandra read the message and held the phone to her heart. James was so nice and he'd said in the message that she should have a great day and let her hair down. Her fingers quickly typed a reply back to him telling him she loved him too and she would see him later that night. Her mother was shouting her.

"Sandra, are you in there? Come on, the car's here for us. We don't want to be late do we?" Sandra rammed two fingers into the air behind the door. Anita pissed her off so much and for years she'd just taken it. Today was going to be so different though because by the end of it, everyone would know just how much of a low-life tramp her sister really was, including her mother.

"Right I'm ready," she replied, "don't get your knickers in a twist. I'm coming now!" You could hear footsteps walking away from the bathroom door. Sandra looked at her face in the mirror and gave herself a cheeky wink. "Right girl let's show these fuckers what it's all about."

Sandra quickly ran to see her sister before she left. Tracy was stood looking out of the window and didn't hear her come in. As Sandra placed her hand on her shoulder Tracy jumped. "Fucking hell you shit me up then!"

Sandra giggled. "Right I'm off to the church. I'll see you there." Tracy leant over and kissed her sister's cheek. As she left her she mumbled "Fucking Judas" under her breath.

The car pulled up at the church and Sandra could see her husband smoking at the side of it. She smiled and looked at her mother. "Look at that fat dick-head of mine. Don't you think he's piled some weight on?" Anita looked over to where he stood. She giggled.

"Well, me and your dad thought the same thing but

we didn't want to say anything. You know how touchy Kevin can be. He just seems to have given up on life hasn't he?" Sandra smiled. Her plan was working and her other half was heading for rock bottom at record speed. Just a few more things were left to do and her job would be complete.

Sandra stood behind the two younger bridesmaids as they walked down the aisle at St Edmund's on Monsall. The organ played and all eyes turned to watch the bride make her big entrance. Graham stood at his daughter's side and escorted her to join her new husband. He looked proud to be there.

Maxine and Tina were stood near the front of the church and they could be seen whispering and laughing as Tracy walked towards them. Mark now turned his head as she neared. His eyes looked filled with love as his bride got nearer. The small scar on Tracy's face was still visible. No amount of make-up would ever cover the letters that had previously sat on her cheekbone.

Kevin looked anxious. Tracy noticed him as she walked past him and smiled at him as he dropped his head. Kevin had enjoyed his time with her and in a way he was relieved their affair was now over. He'd told her straight that he would never be a father to the unborn child and as far he was concerned Mark would always be its dad.

The ceremony went on forever. Everyone looked hot as the temperature rose in the church. Little children could be heard crying now and when the couple finally said "I do" it was a relief to everyone present. Tracy kissed her new husband and they left the church arm in arm. The photographer now stood outside organising all the pictures. Sandra grabbed Kevin's arm and told him she needed him to stand with her sister and her new husband for a photograph. He tried to get out of it but Sandra insisted, calling him a miserable fucker. Once the photographs were taken they all headed to the reception at Corpus Christie's. It was a large function room that sat on a road on the outskirts of Miles Platting.

Maxine and Tina were now at Sandra's side and everything was going to plan. Sandra had the video camera and she made sure the reception had everything she needed to uncover her husband's little secret. Tina was nervous. It was her job to load the video when Sandra was doing her speech.

The wedding meal went well and all the speeches had been done except Sandra's. As she stood to say a few words the guest clapped and cheered. A white screen was now placed at the front of them for everyone to see. Tracy was smiling and wondered if her sister was going to play some old footage of them together when they were children. Sandra began. Her voice was shaky and she scanned the room to make sure Kevin could see the screen too.

"Well thanks to everyone who came today. Everyone looks lovely." Her eyes looked over to Maxine who looked anxious. "I'm so happy for my sister Tracy and I know she will love Mark just as much as she has loved my husband." A few giggles now could be heard from nearby tables as she continued. "Tracy has always been jealous of me and even as a kid she always wanted what I had." Anita could now be heard telling Sandra to stop being nasty. Sandra's face looked like it was on fire as she made sure she had everyone's full attention. She'd waited a long time for this moment and she spoke every word carefully. "Well Mark I hope you know what you have taken on with my sister and here are some video clips of what you can expect in the future." Sandra could see Kevin moving closer to the screen. Sandra nodded her head to Tina and she quickly pressed the play button.

The room was filled with silence and you could have heard a pin drop. The images of Kevin and Tracy now came onto the screen. You could hear people sighing in the room. Anita was up at the screen looking at it in more detail. She turned her head to Tracy in disgust. There it was for the world to see. Sandra's husband and her sister at it like two rabbits. You could hear all the conversation between them and everyone hushed as they heard Tracy saying she'd had an abortion to Kevin in the past. Tracy was screaming for it to be turned off. She ran towards the screen and tried to cover her sins. Sandra stood in front of her. Her face was stern and she looked ready for war. Tracy was screaming at the top of her voice but no one was listening, they wanted to watch the rest of the footage. Once it was over Sandra grabbed her sister by the scruff of her neck. She located where Kevin was stood and spoke so everyone could hear her.

"This little slut deserves everything she gets. The baby she is carrying is Kevin's. So don't let her fool you anymore!" Sandra now spoke directly to Mark. "She never loved you and just wanted you for your money. I hope you can see her now for what she really is." Mark was on his feet pulling at his clothes. His best man was at his side and he was trying to calm him down. Sandra threw Tracy to the side of the room and she headed to her husband who was stood not far from her. You could see Kevin was scared and he held his hands up over his face as she launched her fist into his body.

"Sandra please, it's not what it seems," he pleaded, "she was the one who wanted me all the time. I told her

I loved you but she wouldn't leave me alone!" Everyone watched as Sandra spat in his face and made to leave followed by her two sons.

John ran back before he left and punched his father right in his eye. "You dirty pervert" he shouted in his face.

Maxine and Tina held Sandra up. She was shaking from head to toe. Paul, her other son, rested his head on her shoulder. He was devastated and hated what his father had done. Screams from behind them could be heard and as they looked back Tracy was running towards them. Maxine now stood in front of Sandra. She'd been through enough and she couldn't see her go through any more pain. Tracy was at her side now screaming.

"You just couldn't see me being happy could you? Why wait until now. Why didn't you just say you knew?"

Maxine grabbed Tracy's face in her hand. She scowled at her as Sandra took over. "Let the tart go Maxine. I can deal with her." Tracy was livid but the woman she saw in front of her now looked strong and full of strength unlike the sister she'd known in the past.

"You are nothing but a slut. Why should I let you have happiness when you've destroyed everything I had? I hate you and hope you never have any luck. In fact as far as I'm concerned you're dead to me. Do you hear me, dead!"

Tracy fell to the floor as Anita tried to help her up. Her mother now looked at Sandra. "Are you happy now? Look at the state of her."

Sandra looked her mother in the eyes and meant every word she said. "She's a slag mother; do you think it's right that she's been shagging my husband for years?"

Anita shook her head and puffed. "I don't think its

right but to do this on her wedding day. I'll never forgive you."

"Fuck you mother!" Sandra ranted as she left the building. Graham stood watching Anita and shot her a look as he shook his head.

Kevin sneaked away through a side-door. Mark wanted his head on a plate but Kevin was in no condition to fight him. Once he'd got out of the area he fell onto a nearby bench. His world had collapsed around him and he wished he was dead.

Sandra headed home. Months of planning had now got to her. Her son Paul was constantly at her side comforting her. John had fucked off, he couldn't cope with the pressure and left his mother to fend for herself. Sandra's phone was constantly ringing. Kevin's name was flashing on the small screen. "Get to fuck" Sandra ranted at it every time it rang. Maxine and Tina were like her lieutenants. They kept asking if she needed anything and answered the landline constantly.

Everyone was still in shock at the day events and it wasn't long before they were all getting pissed as farts. Tina didn't feel comfortable at Sandra's house and told her that she and Paul should come and stay at hers until things had quietened down. It was settled. They all went to Tina's house and continued to get pissed there.

Kevin watched them all leave his home. He'd wanted to shout Sandra and ask if he could speak to her alone but she looked so angry and he knew he would have to wait a few days before he approached her. Watching them go out of sight he dug his hand into his trouser pockets and searched for his front door key.

Loneliness filled the air. Kevin sat down in the front room as his world fell apart right in front of his eyes. He was a broken man. The ticking clock on the wall seemed to be calling him names and each stroke made him cringe inside. Kevin headed upstairs. His energy was low and he struggled to climb the stairs that faced him. His phone was ringing and Tracy was trying to get through to him. He launched the phone onto the floor.

Lying on the bed he tried to keep sane. How could he ever win his wife back now? Reaching in Sandra's bedside drawer he searched from some writing paper. Perhaps he could write her a letter. He was searching for a few minutes. No luck. All he found was some old make-up and a book his wife had been reading. Holding his hands on the side of the bed he dipped his head under the bed searching for a pen and some paper. His body froze as he saw a small book sticking out from the slats underneath the bed. Throwing his body to the ground he crawled underneath it like a sniper. His hands now pushed the mattress up and he gripped the small pink book. Struggling to get out from under the bed he gripped it tightly in his hands.

Kevin started to read the first page of the diary and flung himself on the bed. These were his wife's thoughts and hopefully he could find something inside it that told him she still loved him. As he turned each page he was gobsmacked. He was now sat up on the bed and couldn't read her thoughts quick enough. "Cheeky bitch!" he screamed as the words jumped out from the page. He was now pacing the bedroom with one hand still holding the book. His fingers kept dragging at his hair and when he read how cunning his wife had really been, he spat at the white pages in front of him. "So it's you, who's been trying to have me over? All this fucking time it's been you. You conniving bitch!."

As he finished the last page he was furious. It was his wife who'd nicked the weed and even his weight gain was the result of his wife's sick mind. "Oh you're so gonna pay Sandra. You just watch you fucking mental case!" Kevin rolled back under the bed and placed the diary back in its normal place. He sat in deep thought as the midnight hour set in. Tomorrow was a new day and his wife would see just what her husband was capable of.

This was war.

13

Sandra hadn't slept a wink all night. Her eyes looked like piss holes in the snow. She'd had so much to deal with today and no matter how long she stayed at Tina's, her problems would still be there when she got home.

Sandra had slept on the sofa and her son Paul had slept on the floor next to her. Checking her phone she could see twenty six calls from her husband. There were also six missed calls from her mother. Sandra felt a bit bad at the way she'd uncovered her sister's secret but she stood by her word and promised herself she would never talk to her again. The phone started to ring. Kevin's name was flashing. Frozen for a second she answered the call.

"What do you want wanker?"

Sandra could be seen listening to him as he spoke. She was screwing her face up and clenching her fist as he tried to get her to meet him. Once he told her he was sat in their family home she was like shit off a shovel and headed home with haste. Before she left she shouted to Tina where she was going. She tried to stop her but Sandra was fuming and wouldn't listen to anyone "That bastard is sat in my house thinking he can just go on as normal. Well I've got news for him he's getting flung out as soon as I get home." Tina told her to be careful and kissed her on the cheek as she left.

As if a hurricane was dragging her along, Sandra reached her front door in record time. As she entered the house she ran into the front room looking for her cheating husband. Her voice was loud as she shouted his name. "Kevin, get the fuck out of this house now. If you don't I'm gonna phone the police." Still there was no reply. Running up the stairs she swung the bedroom door open. She could see him spread out on the bed wearing nothing but his boxer shorts. One hand resting on the doorframe she struggled to regain her breath. "What the fuck are you doing here? I want you out now!" She screamed at him. "Out!"

Kevin looked calm and smiled. "Oh what are you getting all stressed about? Come and talk to me first then I'll go." Was he lying? Sandra thought as she stayed at the door. She approached him with caution. Sitting on the edge of the bed she watched as he patted his large stomach. "Fucking nothing but a fat cunt me, now aren't I?" His hand made a slapping noise against his bare skin. She didn't answer him. As she sat staring at the four walls she could feel his eyes burning into the back of her head. Turning quickly she urged him to leave again. "What are you waiting for? Just go will you?"

"Do you know what," he chuckled, "I didn't think you had it in you girl, but hats off to you, you had me big-time Sandra!" She looked at him with concern on her face. What the fuck was he going on about had he lost the plot or something? Pulling his cock from his boxers he waved it about on the bed. "If you suck me off then I'll leave." Sandra turned and spat into his face. He jerked forward and grabbed at her hair dragging her face down to the bed. "Old Kevin's, back again now love. So don't ever think you can take the piss out of me!" Sandra tried to fight back but he was too strong. He twisted her up on the bed and sat on top of her as she screamed out loud. Kevin pinned her down. "Shut the fuck up and suck my cock." He now held his knob in his hands and tried to push it into her mouth. Knowing she was fighting a losing battle she tried to get him to calm down.

"Right get off me then and I'll suck it."

He looked at her and wondered what she was planning. Speaking in a calm voice she told him she would suck him off as long as he promised to leave straight after it. Kevin agreed and lay back on the bed. Kicking his boxer shorts off his erect penis stood in front of her. The look on Sandra's face was one of disgust. Her eyes now cast over to the bedside cabinet at the side of her. Her nail glue was sat facing her. As she placed his knob in her mouth for the first time she reached over for the small bottle and held it in her grip. She needed it to be out of sight. Telling Kevin she was cold he lifted his arse from the blanket and she slid underneath it. She was now out of sight. Her hands trembled as she carefully unscrewed the lid from the resin glue. All the time she was stroking and caressing his body. Sticking her tongue down his jap's eye she saw her chance. Slowly she sneaked the tip of the glue to the opening of his penis. Kevin was moaning with pleasure. The moment was right and she squeezed the glue all over his cock. She held her fingers tightly across the slit in his nob until she heard him scream in pain. Throwing the blankets from her body she stood watching him trying to unfold his penis. He was screaming at the top of his voice.

"You mental cunt! Are you right in the head woman?" Reaching for the phone he dialled the emergency services. When the voice at the end of the phone asked him which service he required he told them ambulance and police. Throwing the phone to the ground he lay on the bed in pain. Sandra knew she would be in trouble but she didn't give a fuck as this moment it was more than worth it. Kevin was screaming out in pain.

The police let themselves into the house as the front door wasn't locked. As Kevin heard them he shouted in a distressed voice that he was upstairs. Sandra sat looking out of the window and didn't seem to care that she was in deep trouble. As soon as Kevin saw the police at the bedroom door he pulled his boxers down and showed them his throbbing cock. Sandra was sure she saw the officer smiling as he glimpsed Kevin's red raw throbbing penis for the first time. Kevin now reached frantically under his pillow. He passed the officers the diary belonging to Sandra. He'd previously pulled the pages out about the grow and what she'd done. He wasn't that daft and didn't want to end up getting in trouble himself.

"She's a fucking crank officer. She needs locking up and her daft mates as well. Just read that diary and you'll see she's a fucking lunatic." Sandra saw the evidence in the police woman's hand and knew she was in deep shit. She didn't deny pouring the glue down her husband's japseye and was read her rights before they took her away in the police van. As they led her off, Kevin was shouting at full pelt. "You should be sectioned you crank, you're not right in the fucking head woman." The policewoman told him to keep his voice down as she could see the woman was upset. She presumed he deserved everything he got because his attitude towards women was atrocious.

Kevin was now led to the ambulance in severe pain. He struggled to walk and looked like he'd shit himself.

Sandra had a smirk across her face as she watched her husband being led to the ambulance. "Tosser" she whispered. All the neighbours were out in full force and when they spotted Sandra in the back of the police car they were banging on the window to her asking if she was alright. Sandra didn't answer them she just smiled and turned away from their view. They were nothing but nosey fuckers anyway and she didn't want to fill their mouths with more gossip. They would find out soon enough anyway. Sandra was just glad her own two sons weren't there because John would have caused World War Three with the police who'd attended.

The sound of the ambulance leaving the street could be heard. Sandra turned her head towards it and listened as sirens screamed out. Quickly sneaking her mobile phone from her pocket she texted Tina.

Police know it's you and Maxine who attacked our Tracy. Sort ya shit out quick.

As soon as the message was sent she deleted it and shoved the phone back in her pocket. As she looked into the front seats she could see the female officer reading her diary. She could see her grinning and spoke to her with a cocky tone. "It's everything he deserved the wanker. I'm not sorry one little bit, he's treated me like a sack of shit for years so what does he expect?" The officer calmed her down and told her she should wait until her interview before she started speaking. Sandra sat back in her seat. She was frustrated. Head resting on the window she looked at all the other cars in the traffic. She felt like a goldfish in a bowl. Everyone was looking at her and at one point she stuck her middle finger up at a woman who was looking at her longer than she needed to.

Tina read the text message and immediately phoned Maxine. She was a wreck and was shaking from head to toe. Maxine had told her to come round to her house and as soon as she ended the phone call with her she ran all the way there. Maxine was stood at her front door with a can of Stella in her hand. This was the norm for her and she didn't hide the can from anyone. Maxine was still dressed in her pyjamas. Her black Ugg boots covered her feet as she stood waiting for Tina with a serious look across her face.

"Fucking hell Maxine, the shit's hit the fan. What the fuck are we gonna do?"

Maxine grabbed her by the arm and pulled her inside the house. "Keep ya mouth shut eh, telling the world and his wife our fucking business. You know what these nosey twats are like round here." Tina was pulling at her hair and pacing the front room, she looked flustered.

"Oh Maxine what the fuck are we gonna do. I can't do jail. Sandra said the police had fuck all on us. What's changed?" Maxine was now smiling and looked at her with a smirk across her face.

"A bit of lettuce licking never did anyone any harm love. The women will love you in jail."

Tina scowled. "Will you fuck off. I'm being serious. I'm not a lesbian and even if I went to jail I wouldn't munch no woman's rug."

Maxine opened another can after she'd swilled the remains of the first one. "Right we don't even know what the script is yet do we? Show me the message she sent you." Tina's hand could be seen shaking as she searched for the message. Once she'd found it she passed it to Maxine. "She might be fucking about with us. You know what Sandra's like."

Tina shook her head. "No she wouldn't do that. She's not the kind to have us on about something like this." She grabbed her phone back from Maxine. "I tried phoning her straight back but the phone went to voice mail." Maxine parked her arse on the sofa. Sucking on her lip she looked in deep thought. Tina was up at the window peeping through the net curtains for any sign of the police.

Sandra sat in the cold cell at Grey Mare Lane police station. She'd been there on a few occasions to bail John out in the past but never as an inmate. As the door closed behind her she made her way to the small wooden platform at the back of the room. A small window gave off very little light and she could see the steel bars behind it. Sitting on the thin mattress her eyes started to read the bits of graffiti that previous occupants had written. One read "I'm fucking innocent." Sandra moved nearer to read the next one. As her eyes cast upon it she could just about make out the words. "I love you always Mandy loves Peter." Blowing her breath through her lips she sat with her back against the cold wall. The noise from outside kept her amused. You could hear people who were also locked up shouting their heads off.

One man must have been next door to her because she could hear him coughing and farting singing an old Collyhurst song. She remembered the song and smiled as she recalled her dad singing it years before when he was drunk.

When I was young and lazy, as lazy as can be.
I said fuck off to the mother-in-law and off I went to sea.

Sandra drew her legs up to her chest and waited for the singer to belt out the chorus. She joined in as he sang louder.

Collyhurst Road, I am forsaken,
and it's not that my poor heart is aching,
it's the whisky and the rum that I've been takin.
For that charming little girl down Collyhurst Road.

The sound of the police officer banging on his door could be heard. The man next door was shouting abuse at whoever was at his door and it didn't deter him from finishing the song. Hours passed and Sandra was bored. She picked at her nails. Pulled a string of cotton from her sleeve and was ready to start banging on her own door too. Suddenly the door opened and a female officer told her to follow her whilst she took her finger prints and photograph.

"Are you having a laugh." Sandra joked. "I've put super glue on my fella's nob not robbed the Bank of England"

The woman turned and smiled. "It's procedure. Everyone who gets arrested has to go through this."

Sandra huffed. "Well if you ask me it's a waste of fucking time. Come on," she said sarcastically dragging at her clothing, "do I look like an arm robber or summat?" The woman led her into a small room and started to fill out some paperwork. Sandra scanned the area and felt a bit scared. The officer now placed a white piece of paper under her fingers and started to roll the end of her fingers into an ink pad. Once this was completed she rolled each finger onto the piece of paper. All that was left now was to have her picture taken. Sandra started to straighten her hair as she stood in front of the white background. The photo was taken.

Sandra was led back to her cell. When she asked the

officer what was happening next, they told her they were waiting for the duty solicitor to attend so they could go through the interview. "Interview?" Sandra repeated, "Interview for what? I've said I've done it so what else do you need me to do? Give me the charge sheet and I'll attend court."

The police woman looked at her in disbelief. She felt sorry for her. "It's not as easy as all that love, you can't just go without us interviewing you. Your husband is in a bad way. You could have killed him."

Sandra raised her eyes to the ceiling. "Could have? What! Don't tell me he's not fucking dead?" The door locked behind her and she was sat back in the small room. Her eyes felt tired as she lay flat on the stinking foam mattress.

Maxine and Tina were both arrested later that day for everything they'd done to Tracy. They denied any knowledge of the attack and both protested their innocence. The police had taken all the tattoo equipment from Tina's house and her case wasn't looking good. They were also taken to Grey Mare Lane police station. As Maxine was led to her cell she was shouting at the top of her voice as they pushed her inside. "Sandra if you can hear me, we're innocent. Tell them fuck all. Don't say a word until your brief gets here!" Sandra sat in her cell and she could hear her friend's voice.

"Maxine, is Tina with you?" she shouted. Her ear was placed against the thick steel door now and she couldn't hear any reply. Darkness soon fell and Sandra pulled the crusty thin blanket over her body. It stank of cheesy feet.

Just as Sandra had nodded off a hand was shaking her body. As her eyes struggled to open she remembered where she was. She could now see a man stood in front of her. As she scraped at her eyes she saw it was a police officer. "Come on Sandra your solicitor is here. We can start the interview now." Sandra silently rose and followed him.

As she walked into the room she could see a small fat man wearing glasses at a table with two chairs on either side of it. Placed on the dark wooden table was a tape recorder. All the walls had black panels on them and as Sandra felt one, the solicitor told her it was to help keep any noise out. The man now introduced himself as Daniel.

Daniel looked about forty-five, his receding hairline made his face look round and fat. The white shirt he wore looked too small for him and the buttons dragging across at each side of it, told you it didn't fit well. Clearing his throat he pulled a writing pad from his briefcase. As the two of them sat at the table Sandra started to tell him what had happened. His face looked horrified. Grabbing a drink of water from his paper cup you could see he was disturbed by it all. As he touched his own manhood she told him about shoving Super-glue down her husband's penis. Sandra didn't care anymore and she told him everything about him shagging her sister and getting her pregnant. Her eyes looked menacing as she cracked her knuckles as she spoke.

"At the end of the day," she said scratching her head, "sorry what's your name again?"

"Daniel" he replied as he rolled his silver Parker pen around in his fingers.

"Yeah Daniel. At the end of the day he's treated me like shit for years physically and mentally." She now rolled her sleeves up and started to point bruises out on her arms. "Look I'm covered in signs of abuse but does anyone give a fuck about me? No. I have to just put a smile on my face and pretend everything is fine. Well I can tell you it's not. Why do you think I have done that to him?" Daniel kept his eyes on the paper as he carried on writing. This woman made him feel uneasy and he kept looking at the door checking he could get out if she attacked him. Sandra was livid.

Daniel read the evidence from the police. Looking up at her he spoke. "The diary they have found suggests that you have been doing lots of other things to him too." His eyes were burning into her as he waited for a reply.

"For fucks sake Daniel," Sandra chuckled. Her hands were waving about in front of her. "Don't you think they are taking this too far?" Daniel looked shocked as she continued. "I mean I've pissed in his mouthwash a few times and made him put a bit of weight on. Come on that's not a hanging offence is it? And he's not dead."

Daniel stared at her. He tapped his thumbnail on his front teeth. He didn't know if she was serious. Surely she must have understood why she was under arrest. He sighed and placed his paperwork down on the table. His face was serious. "Sandra you need to listen carefully. There are some serious allegations against you and if they are proved you will be looking at a lot of time in jail." Her eyes scanned his face. Swinging back on her chair she looked at the door to make sure no one was listening. She'd watched lots of crime programmes on TV in the past and knew they would have to prove beyond reasonable doubt she was guilty. Daniel continued. "You have written in your diary that your two friends attacked your sister. They also drugged her, tattooed her face and dumped her at your parent's house. If you don't understand how serious this is you're in for a big shock." Sandra wiggled about in her seat. She really didn't understand that she could go to jail for a long time. There was complete silence in the room as she pondered her thoughts.

★

Kevin lay in the hospital bed as he held his penis in his hands. It looked sore and the medical team were doing their best to take away his pain. Lots of doctors and nurses kept coming in to look at him and you could see the disbelief in their faces as they saw the damage his wife had caused.

Two nurses were stood outside the door of Kevin's room and you could hear them whispering as they giggled outside. "Fucking hell he must have deserved it" said one.

"I know, what a great idea, if my fella is unfaithful to me he's getting the same treatment. I'm gonna stock up on super-glue," replied her friend. The laughter from outside the room could be heard now and you could see an older middle aged nurse holding her belly as she exploded with laughter.

The press had got wind of the story and lots of journalists were eager to see the man who'd been attacked. The police were guarding Kevin and making sure the media didn't get to him whilst he was still getting treatment. The doctor injected his penis with some pain relief. As the needle pierced his skin he howled like a wounded animal. Everybody in the room cringed and the men in the room sympathised with his pain. Kevin was ranting at the top of his voice. "Doctor, am I going to be okay? You're not going to cut my nob off are you?" The medical staff explained to him that the glue had burnt the inside of his manhood and hopefully with some extensive treatment he should make a full recovery.

Kevin started to relax as the pain relief kicked in. He now spoke to the nurse at the side of him. "She's a fucking crank you know, I mean who would do something like this, sick she is. Fucking sick in the bastard head. I hope she rots in jail. The fucking slag." The nurse tried to make him relax as the police officer now came into the room. Kevin sat himself up from the bed and sat with a cocky face as he opened his legs. "I hope she's not getting bail?"

The policeman now sat down at the side of him as the medical team left the room. Once he knew they were alone he told Kevin about the press outside waiting to talk to him. Kevin's eyes lit up and his face had a cunning smile. "Yep let em in. I'll tell the world what Sandra has done. Ay I might make a few quid as well might I?" The male officer kept his eyes in the note paper in front of him. You could tell he wasn't a fan of Kevin's and just got the information from him that he required. Once he'd finished he didn't hang around to chat. The man was acting like a complete arsehole and he couldn't wait to get out of his company.

"Right Kevin, I've got all I need for now. If I need anything else I will be in touch." The officer now left as Kevin sat up on the bed. Pulling the cotton sheet from his parted legs he glanced at his throbbing member. His face screwed up and he yelled as his hand stroked the shaft of it. Mumbling under his breath he cursed Sandra.

14

Maxine and Tina were interviewed. The case was not looking good against Tina. The police had been to her house and retrieved all the tattooing equipment. She was fucked. Tina sat in the interview room and sobbed. She didn't admit anything and was advised by her solicitor to go "no comment" all the way through her interview.

Maxine sat in another interview room just down the corridor and she seemed much calmer. She'd been through this process so many times in the past and it was like water off a duck's back to be sat in some police station. They had fuck all on Maxine. She had an alibi and was confident she'd get bail. She knew the entry in the diary was the only evidence they had. Her face looked weather-beaten as she sat in the room waiting for her interview to begin. Maxine still had her pyjamas on and she'd tucked the bottoms into her Uug boots so they wouldn't trail on the floor. The female solicitor smiled at Maxine. She'd met her lots of times in the past and defended at her at court a few times.

Tina was questioned by two male officers. Chewing on her fingernails she struggled to talk. Even telling the police her name made her throat close up. She looked as if she was suffocating and her red face suggested she wasn't feeling too well. Questions were being fired at her like bullets from a gun. Grabbing and pulling at her hair she looked distressed. The police officer told her they had evidence that she was the one who'd tattooed Tracy. Her fingerprints were all over it. They'd even traced the ink back from the tattoo gun to Tina's house. Fidgeting she looked at her solicitor. He nodded to remind her of her answer.

"No comment" she replied.

The interview went on for over an hour. Each question they fired at her resulted in a "No comment." The interview ended. Once the police left, Tina and her solicitor were alone she pulled at his arm. "Am I going home or what?"

He sighed and shook his head slightly. Pulling at his grey suit he removed her hand from his. "Tina I don't think you'll get bail. The evidence against you at the moment doesn't look good."

"What do you fucking mean?" she screamed "That I'm staying here?"

He nodded slowly as he watched her fall to her knees. Her head was touching the grey cord carpet and her hands squeezed at her hair. Reaching down to console her he patted her back. "Just try and be calm. We'll know what the bigger picture is when everyone has been interviewed. You're co-accused might say something that helps us." Dragging her body up from the floor she collapsed onto her chair.

"I can't be locked up. I'll go crazy. You need to get your arse out there and tell them I'm innocent." Her solicitor now gathered all his belongings together. As he slid the paperwork inside the black briefcase he shook his head at her because he knew there wasn't a cat in hell's chance she would be getting bail.

Maxine stood at the charge desk in front of the custody officer. His eyes cast over her as he read out the allegations. Smirking she waited anxiously to see if she was getting bail. As he read the allegations out aloud she could tell by his tone of voice that she was going home. Kicking at the floor she was starting to get bored. Passing her a pink bail sheet she folded it quickly and shoved it in her pocket. She had to attend the police station in a few weeks to see if they were charging her with any offences. As she gathered her belongings she could see Tina walking down the corridor with a police woman at the side of her. She didn't look good. Maxine was quickly hurried out of the station to her freedom and before she went she shouted to Tina. "Keep your chin up love. You'll be home soon." The officer now urged her to leave, pulling at her arm.

Both Sandra and Tina were charged. There was to be no bail for either of them. Once Tina learnt she was being held in custody she broke down and sobbed out loud. "I'm fucking innocent. Get my solicitor back here!" Her screams could be heard throughout the police station and she wasn't taking the news well at all.

Sandra sat in her cell. Blowing hard she shook her head. She'd tried consoling Tina through the cell walls but her sobbing could still be heard. They were going to court the following morning and they were told it was more than likely they would be moved to a prison after that. Sandra had heard about prison life in the past. A few of the girls from the estate had spent many a month in there for different charges. She looked frightened.

Kevin sat with the press. He played the victim well and kept showing signs of pain in his face as the questions were asked. The flashing of cameras in his face made him squint. His story was going to be big and he'd already signed an exclusive deal with a big name paper. A few of the female reporters were sat with him in the room. You could tell by their faces they wanted him to open up more as they didn't believe for one minute a woman would do something like this without being provoked.

A blonde journalist now stood up and got his attention. "Kevin, have you ever hit your wife in the past?"

He looked embarrassed. He knew what he'd done in the past but lied. "I have never raised a hand to Sandra. I've treated her like a princess since we've been together. She has mental health problems. I've tried to help her all I can, but this is how she repays me." His face now showed pain and he soothed his crotch again as he continued. "Sandra has always been jealous of me. She hates it if I even talk to a woman. I've threatened to leave her loads of times because of it but she always said she would get help and change." The reporter looked at him with disbelief. She knew there wasn't any smoke without fire and left the room in search of the truth. Kevin was going to be on the news and feature in most newspapers. The story was massive and he was set to earn a right few bob.

Darkness fell in the police cells. Sandra dragged the small blanket over her body. She looked like it was all hitting her now and she started to regret her actions. The following morning she would go to Manchester Magistrates and every one would know what she'd done to her husband. Looking at the tattoo on her foot she smiled. As she mumbled under her breath you could see a single tear falling onto her pillow. "Bastard, you won't get the better of me. I promise you." Her eyes closed.

Morning came and shouting could be heard outside Sandra's door. As the door opened a female officer stood looking at her. Sandra and Tina were the talk of Grey Mare Lane police station and everyone wanted to see the woman who'd shoved super glue down her husband's penis. The officer placed her hand on the cell door frame and smiled at Sandra.

"Come on love we need to get you to court. I have to tell you there is a lot of press attention and the reporters are outside in full force."

Sandra looked confused, "Fucking hell why are they interested in me?"

The woman smiled. She checked no one was listening and stood inside the doorway. "They are interested in you because you gave your cheating husband exactly what he deserved, the scum bag."

Sandra smiled before replying, "he deserved a lot more, the wanker. And I've not finished with him yet. We'll see whose laughing at the end of this. What's that saying now…" she looked to the ceiling as she remembered, "Those who laugh last, laugh longest. I'll show that shit-stain don't you worry."

The officer led her to the car park and protected her as the press tried to get a photo of her face. Sitting in the white sweat box, she smiled. Her mind was working overtime now and she shouted to see if Tina was inside the van too.

"Tina are you in here love?" She placed her ear to the door. There was no reply. She shouted again and this time she could just about hear her friend's voice.

"Sandra I'm here love. I'm shitting myself." Sandra sat in the small space and gazed out of the window. Her eyes were struggling to see anything outside. She replied as she blew her warm breath onto the window.

"Tina we'll be fine. Don't worry love, just keep calm." She could now hear the broken words of her friend. She couldn't make out what she was saying as the traffic from outside was too loud. Her fingers now wrote her name in the mist she'd created on the window.

The two women were soon sat inside the courtroom. They were secured in the dock by a thick piece of glass. Two Group 4 guards sat at either side of them. Reporters were present in the courtroom and they were watching their every move. They hid their identity well from the usher because if he knew for one minute they were reporters they would have been carted from the courtroom without a doubt.

Tina's hands were shaking and Sandra gripped them tightly as they watched Steven and James enter the court room. Tina tried to stand up to go to the glass but the security quickly told her she had to remain seated. Sandra smiled at James. His face looked endearing. He was dressed in jeans and a grey t-shirt. He looked sexy with the stubble that was present on his face. Sandra now spotted Maxine. She was waving her hands above her head to get their attention. Sandra smiled at her and waved back slowly so no one could see. Maxine now stood up from her chair and told them she was on it and would help get them out as soon as possible. She gave them a quick wink as the female usher told her to sit down.

Judge Maloney now came into the courtroom as everyone stood up. Everyone kept their heads low as he sat. They treated him like royalty. Sandra and Tina's solicitors were both rearranging pieces of paper and preparing to speak on behalf of their clients. They were both applying for bail. The solicitors knew they were fighting a losing battle but promised to give it their best shot.

The prosecution was the first to speak. He was dressed in a long black gown and a grey wig. The man spoke in a posh voice. As he read from the white pieces of paper in front of him his voice was distressed. He was speaking about Tina and Sandra as if they were murderers and a danger to the public. Sandra whispered to Tina. "Fucking hell what's he going on about? Why is he making us out like we're fucking nutters?" Her face looked angry as she sat forward listening to all the evidence against them. The judge kept lifting his head and staring at the two women sitting in the dock. As the prosecution told him that the women both had the same tattoos on their feet he tried to make out they were involved in some kind of cult that were against cheating men.

"For fuck's sake," Tina whispered, "it's a tattoo that's all. They need to get a grip." Sandra locked her fingers together now. She wanted to stand up and shout out that her husband was an out and out twat but it looked like she was struggling to speak.

The prosecution carried on reading extracts from Sandra's diary. The hair loss, weight gain, and spitting in his food were all mentioned along with lots of other things that made the courtroom giggle. The solicitor applied for bail.

The judge told the woman that their case would now be adjourned and they would both remain in custody until the date he'd set. Tina shook her head. She was fuming and couldn't hold her tongue any longer. Her flat palms now fixed themselves against the glass as she ranted at the judge. "Remanded, are you having a laugh you old cunt. You need to see this for what it really is. Kevin is a lying bastard. He's made her life a misery for years" she pointed her finger at Sandra so everyone knew she was the one who'd been abused. "You need to get your facts right before you start judging us. Kevin is the one who needs locking up, not us!" Tina was being pulled from the courtroom.

Sandra stood up and smiled at James. "I'll write to you" she mouthed. James nodded as he blew a kiss to her.

Maxine looked angry and pushed the usher out of the way as she left court. The reporters were having a field day. The pens in their hands were writing ten to the dozen and one of them followed Maxine outside.

Jenny had worked for The Sun newspaper for years. Following Maxine down the stairs she hurried to catch up with her. "Excuse me love" she shouted after her. Maxine halted. As she faced Jenny for the first time she scowled. Jenny could see she was in no mood for anything and approached her with caution. "Hi love. I'm a reporter and would love to help your friends. I'm interested in the truth and I could help getting your names cleared." Maxine carried on walking and once they were outside the courts she searched her pocket for her cigs. Lighting one she looked at the woman in front of her.

"Right what are you going on about?"

Jenny smiled. Maxine was rough as fuck but she there was something likeable about her. The reporter stood against the wall and spoke casually. "I know there is more to this story than meets the eye and I would love to help Sandra and Tina."

Maxine held her head to the side. "How the fuck can you help them? You're a reporter" she moaned taking a deep drag from her cig. Jenny asked if she would come and have a cup of coffee with her to discuss it further.

Maxine told her straight as she took the final drag from her cig. "Listen I'm not a grass or owt. I've not got a pot to piss in at the moment so I can't be buying any coffees."

Jenny knew she was dealing with a strong woman and told her straight. "Oh don't worry I'll get the drinks. I don't want you to grass. I just want you to clear your friend's names." Maxine stood in thought for a minute. Checking her watch she agreed to have a quick brew with her.

"Right you can have five minutes, but if you're chatting shit I'm getting off, alright?" Jenny smiled and walked with her to the nearby Costa coffee.

Sandra and Tina were getting shipped out to Styal

prison. They both sat together before they were parted and cried in each other's arms. Sandra was the brave one and comforted Tina. "We'll be fine love. Trust me. We'll sort something out I promise you. Plus Maxine is helping us. You know what she's like. She won't let us rot in here trust me." They both entered the sweat box that was taking them to prison. Reporters took photos and Sandra couldn't help but smile at them and yank her two fingers into the air. Their faces would be all over the tabloids the next day and she prayed someone out there would help them to get free.

Jenny took shorthand notes as Maxine spoke. Some of the things Maxine told her made her piss laughing. Jenny warmed to her. She was a diamond in the rough without a doubt. The conversation was coming to an end and Jenny came to the conclusion that Sandra was the victim and not Kevin. After all, he'd shagged her sister for years and there were rumours that she was pregnant. Surely that alone would be enough to push any woman over the edge? Maxine told Jenny that the tattoos were just something that stated that they wouldn't take shit anymore. She told her of all her own personal turmoil she'd dealt with in her life and that "Carpe Diem" meant that from that day onward all the three of them would become stronger in relationships. Jenny nodded. She had been hurt in the past and could identify with the women. Jenny held her foot out to the side. "I might get that tattooed on the side of my foot too."

Maxine giggled as she slurped her coffee. "Go for it chick."

Jenny was looking anxious. She told Maxine that she had a plan to get every woman all over the world behind the pair of them. She rubbed her hands together as a story unfolded. "The way I see it – Sandra and Tina are icons for women worldwide. I mean, come on; it's about time that men see that we won't take any shit from them anymore. Kevin abused her for years, where is his punishment? I'm going to do a big story and get the right people behind us."

Maxine thanked her from the bottom of her heart. She was on bail for the charge and she had to go back to the police station in a few weeks to see if she was to be charged as well, so any help at the moment would be more than appreciated. "Thanks Jenny. When I first met you I thought you were up ya own arse and all that, but ya sorted you are. Thanks love."

Jenny hugged her as they made to leave. Maxine looked at her with cunning eyes. She didn't trust anyone and she let her know that if she was having her over, she would find her and make sure she dealt with her. Jenny looked scared and she could tell by Maxine's face she meant every word. They exchanged phone numbers and Jenny told her she would be in touch in the near future. They both left. Maxine had bigger fish to fry now and she set off with speed to try and get her friends out of prison.

★

Kevin sat in his front room. The house had an eerie silence to it. His two sons sat looking at him. He could see Paul had hate written all across his face. He'd always been a mummy's boy in the past and he clenched his fist as he looked at him.

John seemed in a world of his own. His eyes looked dark underneath and he looked like he'd lost a lot of weight. Kevin spoke to him. "What's up with your eyes?

You look fucked."

John stretched his eyes open and struggled to speak. "Nar. I'm alright. I'm just tired and that. It's all this with my mam and you. It's fucked my head right up. You should drop the charges and get her out."

Kevin stood from his chair. Holding his crotch he screamed. "Get her out! Are you having a fucking laugh or what? She tried to kill me ya muppet. Look at my nob! Look at what the barmy bitch has done." Pulling his cock out he walked to John. Paul had a look of disgust on his face and left the room. John cringed as he saw the shrivelled penis.

"I know what she'd done dad, but she's your wife. You can't leave her in there can you, I mean what did you expect? You shagged her sister." Kevin wobbled back to his chair. As he sat down he yelled out in pain.

"She can rot in there for all I care. Anyway you need to deliver this." Kevin held a bag of smack out in front of him and watched as John took it from his grip with eager hands.

Kevin started to tell John about Zac and how the money from the paper stories would at least pay some of his debts off. "John stood at the door as Kevin answered a phone call. You could see small droplets of sweat forming on his forehead and he looked anxious. Kevin held his hand out to him and told him to wait as he spoke on the phone. It was just another drugs order and John listened as Kevin shouted out the address.

John took the other parcel from his dad's hideout and helped himself to another two bags for himself. He'd been tanning the gear left, right and centre these last couple of months and he was now an addict. Going back into the front room he told his dad he was going to drop the drugs off. Kevin didn't answer him and he could be seen examining his nob in more detail. John left without saying goodbye.

★

Sandra and Tina began their prison life. The jail was horrific to look at. As they went through the motions they could see prisoners nearby looking at them like vultures waiting to pounce. Tina stood by Sandra and the tears left her eyes. She knew this was a dog eat dog environment and she wasn't going to let anyone take the piss out of her or her friend. Sandra's face looked hard and she now had a menacing look in her eyes. If this was the place she was going to be for the next few months she was sure as hell going to make the most of it.

The two of them were escorted to their cells. As they walked along the long landing the inmates stood at their doors clocking them. Sandra gazed over at them and could see most of them had that hard look in their eyes. There were around fifteen rooms on each landing. As they passed an inmate, she patted Sandra on the shoulder and shouted out at full pelt. "Good on ya girl. You should have cut his cock off not just glued it." Sandra smiled as other inmates joined in.

"We're proud of you girls. It lets these men know that we won't be taking any shit in the future!" The woman patted Tina's shoulder as they made their way inside their new cell. They were like returning war heroes. Once they were inside the cell Tina smiled.

"Fucking hell Sandra, how the fuck do they know what we have done?"

Sandra shrugged her shoulders. "It's probably been on the news. There must have been reporters inside the court room?"

Tina walked to the small window in the middle of the cell. She started talking. "Yeah but fucking hell Sandra, I didn't think people would recognise us. I bet our photo is all over the fucking TV."

Sandra threw herself onto the bed as she patted her hair down. "I hope I looked okay" she giggled. "I bet that bastard Kevin has given them a photograph of me when I was about twenty stone. The sad cunt."

Tina now lay on the bed opposite her. Looping her hands behind her head she sighed. "I'm sorry Sandra. It's my fault you're in here. I never meant for it to go this far. Maxine just got some stuff from some guy and the rest just followed. I suppose we just got caught up in the moment."

Sandra was now sat up on her bed. She looked upset. "Listen here you daft cow. I was the one who wrote it all down in that stupid fucking diary. Without that none of us would be here. So it should be me apologising to you." Tina joined her on her bed and they hugged. Sandra now banged her fist on the side of the bed. You could see her knuckles changing colour as she gritted her teeth.

"He thinks he's a smart arse. But I swear Tina, he'll get what's coming to him. I won't rest until I know he's been paid back. Who does he think he is having us locked up in here?"

Tina agreed. "I know, love. For the first time in my life I've been really happy and have a fella and that crank of a husband goes and fucks it all up, I swear if you don't do him in, I will." Tina now wrapped her arms around herself. "Orr I'm going to miss Steven you know. Did you see him in court? He looked fit as fuck."

Sandra giggled. "I know he did but what about James.

No way did I think he would come to court. I hope he comes to visit me in here."

Night was drawing in and the cell was going dark. Tina flicked the light on and stared at the walls around her. It was social time soon and they would be able to mix with the other inmates. Sandra looked tired. She hadn't slept a wink in days and her lack of sleep was catching up with her. Stretching her arms above her head Sandra farted. Tina chuckled and held her belly. "You dirty bastard. Oh no, it smells like the sewers!"

Tina covered her nose with her hands as Sandra laughed rolling about on the bed. "It's my nerves love. And if we're pad mates we'll have to get used to each other's habits and all that."

Tina giggled and fell back on her bed. "You're a skunk Sandra."

The cell door opened and three women were outside. Tina stepped out first and thought they were waiting to do them in. She walked outside with caution. As soon as her feet touched the landing, arms were flung around her neck. Tina felt uncomfortable. Sandra could now been seen getting the same treatment. The women were being treated like action heroes. As they walked down the stairs in the middle of the landing the rest of the convicts started chanting and whistling. Sandra stared at Tina with disbelief as she lifted her hands up at the side of her mouthing, "What the fuck?"

They were welcomed into Styal prison with open arms. Prisoners gathered round them as they told their story. One woman even said she would pay big money for her husband to experience the same kind of treatment. Lots of the women told stories about their own partners cheating on them and how they felt. For the first time in her life Sandra didn't feel alone.

One convict told her own story and dipped her head as she told them of the abuse she'd suffered for years from her partner. "My old man was a mental cunt. He used to stub cigs out on me when he was pissed. One night I woke up and the bastard had soaked me in lighter fuel. I thought I'd pissed myself at first when I started to wake up." Everyone laughed but as she continued the smile left their faces. "He shaved my hair too. I stayed in for fucking months. Nobody knew anything about it, I just kept it to myself. I suppose that's why I'm in here now. He fucked with my head that much, drugs were all I had left." Arms from different directions now cradled the woman. Tears formed in Sandra's eyes and you could see all the women in her presence feeling her pain.

Tina now had the women laughing their heads off as she told them the time Sandra shook her husband's can of coke beyond belief and when he opened it he was covered in it from head to toe. Sandra smiled. "I've done some great things to pay him back, ladies. If I would have just kept my mouth shut and never written it in my fucking diary I could have finished him off." The women hung on her every word and discussed the charges she faced.

The hour of association was soon up and the women headed back to their cells. Sandra lay on her bed and looked at the prison issue letter and wondered who she should send it too. Her parents had disowned her so there was no point in writing to them. She knew her dad hadn't fallen out with her but he was ruled by her mother and wouldn't dare cross her. Should she write to her kids or should she pour out her feelings out to James. Finger shoved inside her mouth she asked Tina her thoughts on it.

"Write to James love. I'm not being funny or owt but your John or Paul won't be arsed writing back to you. At least James will."

Sandra paused for a minute. "Yeah you're right. The lads will come up on a visit, they won't be arsed with any writing. I'll write to James then." Stroking the lined white paper in front of her she lay on her bed, she was struggling to find the words at first. The words she wanted to say were stuck inside her heart and she couldn't bring them up to the surface.

The letter was tossed aside for now. Sleep was more important and Sandra snuggled into her bed pulling her white quilt over her body. Tina was drifting off to sleep too. Darkness fell and the women were sound asleep.

15

The weeks passed and Kevin was making a full recovery. The media attention had died down now and all he had left was a few hundred quid from selling his story. The house felt lonely as he sat watching a film. His kids barely spoke to him anymore and he knew they hated him, especially Paul. His debt was still being paid off and his own flesh and blood was running here, there and everywhere trying to end his debt to the dealers.

Zac had been in touch when he'd heard of Kevin making a few extra quid from the media stories but Kevin hid away from him like a scared animal. Zac wasn't happy with Kevin and he'd arranged to meet him later that day to discuss how he was going to pay the debt off more rapidly. His arse was flapping at the thought of another beating from the heavy mob.

John sat in his room injecting heroin. Nobody but

a few friends knew he was now a baghead. His youth seemed to be disappearing right in front of his eyes and there wasn't a thing he could do about it anymore. He was a junkie. John sat in his room listening to NDUBZ. The drugs had just hit his veins and he'd fallen back onto his bed. The posters on the wall of David Beckham stared back at him and he remembered when all he wanted in life was to become a professional footballer. His dream had been to play for Manchester United... His eyes seemed to sink to the back of his head. John's clothes hung from his body. As he wriggled about his t-shirt rolled up over his stomach. You could see his ribcage. There was more fat on a chip. If he'd turned sideways you would have reported him missing he was that thin. All the signs of drug use was scattered about his bedroom. Nobody ever came into his room these days and he felt safe that no one would ever know his seedy secret. The sound of footsteps coming up the stairs didn't cause him to stir. He was oblivious to anything around him.

Kevin waddled up the stairs. His penis was still sore and he still felt like he had a hot poker between his legs. Hearing music from his son's room made him halt. His head looked towards John's room. Grabbing the handle on the door he paused. His face looked as if he was debating his next move. His fingers gripped the handle on the door and slowly he twisted it until the door opened slightly. He was half expecting his son to shout for him to get out of his room. That's what he'd done in the past but today he heard no noise.

The carpet stopped the door opening any further. It was a job he should have fixed months before but couldn't be arsed doing it. The door needed planing down after the new carpets were fitted but he never seemed to find the time. With one hard push he opened the door fully. His eyes stared about the room. "Scruffy twat" he mumbled. Sandra was always telling him in the past that the lads needed to clean their rooms more often but he always thought she was overreacting. Looking around the bedroom he shook his head as he walked further inside. "Ay John you scruffy cunt. Get this room sorted out. It's a shit tip in here." There was no reply. Walking to his son's bedside he kicked at the base of the bed. "Do you hear me or what?" John now turned round and struggled to see who was talking. Kevin looked at him closer. He looked like death warmed up. He sat down next to him on the bed and dragged him up by his clothes towards his face. "Are you fucking stoned again? You need to get a grip and curb smoking that shit all day long." John jerked his body away from him. Kevin now turned to leave but his eyes focused on the hypodermic needle at the side of the bed. There was brown liquid left in it at the bottom. Gripping the needle he looked anxious. His eyes now scanned the floor area and there it was before his own eyes. His son was using heroin.

"John!" he screamed at the top of his voice. "John you prick. You better wake up now or I'll fucking waste you." John turned his body slowly. Spit hung in the corner of his mouth and he slowly tried to wipe it with his scrawny hands. "What the fuck is this?" Kevin picked up a needle as John tried to focus. Thrusting the pin towards John's face, Kevin started shouting. "Please tell me you're not injecting heroin!" His hands pulled at his hair as he paced the floor in the bedroom. John just lay lifeless still trying to focus.

Kevin lifted the net curtain and stared through the bedroom window. He could be heard huffing. Suddenly

he ran back at John and dragged him up from the bed.
"You fucking prick. You know what heroin does to people
and you're fucking injecting it. You're a daft twat! How
long have you been on it?" John sucked on his lips and he
looked like he was in slow motion. He struggled to speak.
Kevin launched his fist into his face causing him to fall
back on the bed. His voice was hysterical as he screamed
at him again. "How long have you been taking this shit?"
John shrugged his shoulders. His dad now grabbed his
face, squeezing his cheeks together in his hands. "You
must fucking know how long you've been on it. Don't
take the piss out of me. I said how fucking long?" John
crumbled. "Since you've have been selling it." His voice
was shaky and he looked scared. He'd seen his father's
temper in the past and knew he wouldn't think twice
about smashing his head in.

Kevin dragged him up and shoved him towards the
bathroom. He dragged him to the mirror and held it there
as he ranted. "Look at the fucking state of you. You silly
bastard. Did you think I wouldn't find out? Look John,
look at the state of you!" John tried to focus in the mirror
but Kevin knew he was fighting a losing battle. His son
was off his head and he didn't give a fuck about anything.
Kevin looked at the water left in the bath from earlier. He
dragged him to it and shoved his head beneath the water.
John struggled but his dad held his head firmly under the
water. He lifted him up for a few seconds before shoving
him back down again. John was struggling for breath and
his body was jerking about trying to break free. Kevin's
hands were shaking and he knew he had to stop before
he killed him. John was soaking wet as he dragged him
back to his bedroom. Throwing him back inside Kevin
ran downstairs.

John tried to regain his breath. He was a mess. He could hear the downstairs door banging. He needed to get out of the house as soon as possible. Dragging his wet clothes from his body he searched for some clean ones to put on. His head was inside the wardrobe but he froze as he heard someone at the bedroom door. Kevin was now stood with a hammer in one hand and some long nails in the other. John tried to grab some clothes but his dad kicked him to the floor. Rolling about in just his boxer shorts Kevin dragged the set of pine drawers behind the door. Pushing it securely behind it he gave John another kick on the way as he passed. Kevin lifted the net curtain right up and grabbed several large nails from the side. His face looked mad as he hammered each nail deep inside the window frame.

"You won't be going anywhere now will you sonny boy?" John sat shivering from head to toe. His body was covered in goose pimples and his teeth were chattering together. "You fucking dirty smack head. Haven't I brought you up better than this?" His movement stopped as he carried on speaking to his son. "My own son a heroin addict!" he gasped.

John didn't reply and grabbed his quilt cover from his bed. Wrapping it around his shoulders he drew his knees up to his chest. Tears filled his eyes and his bottom lip shook as he let rip at his father. "You brought me up to hit women dad. What father gives their son drugs to sell? You don't give a fuck about no one but yourself. Look what you have done to my mam."

Kevin jumped from the window ledge. He was frothing from the mouth. "You cheeky cunt. What do you mean by that?"

John swayed as he pulled himself from his bed.

With the quilt fixed firmly round his neck he answered. "Exactly what I said. You've treated my mam like shit for years and you deserve everything she's done to you. I mean you shagged her own sister. You skank!" Kevin wrestled him to the bed. His hands lunged into his son's face. Blood was splurging all over the walls and as Kevin moved away from the bed you could see John was the one who was injured. Screams filled the room. Kevin slammed the bedroom door behind him and left his son struggling for breath.

Within seconds you could hear banging on the bedroom door. John kept his head under the covers. As the hammering noise continued he peeped from his bed. He could now see the end of silver nails coming through the side of the door. As he ran to the door he tried to open it with frantic hands. He realised that he was now a prisoner in his own room. He screamed like a wounded animal. "Dad, dad, please." The hammering continued but no one answered him. His body keeled over behind the door and he raised his knees up to his chest as he wrapped them in his arms. "Please dad. I'll sort it out, let me out please." John sobbed rocking to and fro banging the back of his head on the door.

Kevin marched down the stairs like a mad man. The hammer was still held tightly in his grip as he pummelled it against the walls in temper. "Bastard, bastard, bastard" he ranted. Entering the front room he fell to his knees. The pain in his loins seemed to disappear and the pain he felt in his heart seemed a lot worse. Banging from upstairs could be heard and he could hear the voice of his son pleading with him to set him free. Covering his ears with both hands, he tried to drown out John's call for freedom.

Kevin cried like a baby. "Why, why,"? he sobbed. The front door could now be heard opening. Jumping up from the floor he dried his eyes trying to hide his pain.

Paul stood at the doorway looking shocked. Looking at his father he could instantly tell something was wrong. "What's going on dad? What's up?"

Kevin fell into his chair and held his head in his trembling hands. A loud banging noise filled the room and Paul looked at his dad as he heard the noise from upstairs. "Will you tell me what's going on or what?" Paul started to walk out of the room as the voice of his brother calling him made him look distressed.

Kevin jumped up from the chair and grabbed Paul by his shoulder. "Leave him where he is."

Paul scowled. He'd witnessed fights between his father and brother in the past but nothing as bad as this. "What's he done now?"

Kevin chewed on his bottom lip and Paul slowly came back into the front room to listen. Paul urged him to speak. He was shouting now in desperation. "Dad fucking tell me. What's wrong?" Kevin's eyes looked dead inside. Holding his stomach area he looked like he was going to spew his ring up.

"He's on gear" he mumbled. You could tell by Paul's face that he didn't understand.

"What do you mean he's on gear?"

Kevin snapped. "Fucking smack, brown, heroin, you dickhead. Your brother is a junkie."

Paul's eyes opened wide as he covered his mouth in disbelief. "No way dad, stop lying, tell me the truth."

Another squealing voice came from upstairs. Paul looked at his dad and made his way up the stairs with Kevin running behind him.

"He's a smackhead Paul. He's going nowhere until he is clean."

Paul stood at the bedroom door shouting. "Our kid, are you okay?" John could now be heard.

"No Paul I'm not, the fucking nutter has locked me in here; he's nailed the windows down as well. Please get me out of here." Paul looked at his father. You could tell he didn't know who was telling the truth. He blew a hard breath and walked about the landing thinking. Kevin sat on the top stair as Paul spoke with his brother again.

"Are you on gear John? Dad's saying you are. Just tell me the truth and I'll help you." The silence seemed to last forever before John sobbed.

"I've only had it a few times Paul. That prick thinks I'm an addict or summit." Paul felt sick as his face fell. The thought of his brother being a junkie made his skin crawl. He rubbed at his arms as if he felt dirty. He struggled to speak. Looking at the sadness in his father's eyes he knew it was true. Paul now ran to the bathroom. You could hear him retching into the toilet bowl. When he came out he was wiping his mouth. Tears filled his eyes as he barged past his father. Kevin followed him downstairs.

Paul reached for the TV remote. As he flicked through the channels he looked at his dad who was now sat facing him. "It's all your fucking fault, yanno. You better get my mam out of nick. We need her here to sort this mess out." Kevin knew he was right but it had all gone too far now. He'd sold his story and imprisoned his wife and never thought for one minute that it would affect his family this much. His mobile phone now started ringing. As he looked at the screen, Tracy's name flashed. She'd been phoning him endlessly for weeks. He knew sooner or later he would have to speak to her. She was carrying his child after all and there was no getting away from the fact. He would have to speak to her, but not now. Kevin left the phone ringing and placed the pillow over it to silence the repeating ring tone.

"Dad do you hear me? We need my mam here. You need to sort it!" Paul stood up and walked up to his father. You could see his temper boiling and by the look on his face he was thinking of revenge on his father. Kevin just sat shaking his head. The media stuff all seemed right at the time and now it had hit home he started to regret phoning the police on his wife. Huffing he grabbed his coat from the side.

"I'm doing fuck all. Your mother is a crank and she deserves jail!" Paul didn't have a chance to argue back with him, he was gone and the sound of the front door slamming could be heard.

Kevin walked to the car. Grabbing his phone from his pocket he dialled Tracy's number. As he spoke to her you could tell by his voice he was upset. "Yeah it's me. Meet me at The Hip pub in about five minutes. Right okay, see you there." Throwing his phone on the passenger seat he set off. Nothing seemed to make sense anymore. His life was a sham. Looking at his eyes in the rear view mirror he didn't recognise himself anymore.

Pulling into the pub car park he could see Tracy waiting anxiously. "Fucking tart" he whispered under her breath. Once the engine stopped, she walked quickly to the car and sat inside. "Fucking hell, face of thunder. What's up with you?"

"Nowt why?" Kevin snarled.

Tracy pulled the mirror down and started checking her make-up. "I'm just saying you look angry or summat." He wanted to throw her out of the car there and then but he desperately needed some loving. He grabbed her and kissed her. As he kissed her there was no passion involved just a hunger for some affection. He was just another rampant male searching for some quick fanny. Tracy welcomed him and gave him the attention he required. He wanted some sex and told her straight he wanted to shag her brains out. Tracy smiled. Her hand stroked his cock as he tried to fight off the pain he felt inside. His cock was nowhere near ready to be used and he felt frustrated. Tracy looked at him with an endearing look she knew he was in pain.

"Is the beast ready for action yet?"

He wanted to say yes but he was in pain and he knew sex was a million miles away. Tracy hugged him. "We can just spend time together. We don't have to have sex. I mean it has to heal dunnit?" He looked angry as he yelled back at her.

"I know it has to heal, you daft twat, but when? It's been months now?"

She felt rejected and moved back over to her seat. "It's not my fucking fault you know? Look what the barm pot done to me. You can't see me moaning can you?"

She looked hurt. Kevin turned the key in the ignition. "Where do you wanna go then? Don't think I'm walking around some park with you being all lovey dovey. It's not my game."

Tracy looked out of the car window. She fidgeted around and swept her hair back from her face. "I'm not arsed." Kevin drove out of the car park with a cob on. He could see her hand stroking her stomach. He looked disappointed.

★

Maxine was like a blue-arsed fly. She couldn't rest knowing her friends were locked up. She'd booked a visit for later on that day and she hoped she would have some news to tell the girls if everything went to plan.

Stood waiting outside The Broadway pub in New Moston her eyes focused on every car that went passed. She'd arranged to meet Zac here. Maxine had been friends with him for a long time. She's put him onto some good jobs in the past and he always treated her with cash from successful grafts. She never let on that she was the one who sold his last grow from Kevin because, after all, he was loaded and would never miss the money. She was a snidey cow.

A silver X5 BMW pulled up at the side of her. The tunes were pumping inside and Zac sat smiling at her. He'd shagged her in the past but they were just fuck buddies. It was a drunken mistake on both parts, even though they got on like a house on fire. They were still good mates and she scratched his back and he scratched hers. That's just the way it was.

Maxine jumped into the passenger seat and slammed the door. He smiled as he watched her get comfy. "Where do you wanna go?"

She thought for a minute and replied. "We can go in the pub if ya want?"

He shook his head. "Nar lets fuck off from round here. I don't want people seeing us together you know what they are like, the nosey fuckers."

Zac kept looking at her as he drove. He could tell by her body language that something was on her mind. The music played and he drove them to a nearby park. Pulling up he turned the engine off and slid his seat back so he could stretch his legs.

"Right what's up with you? I can tell you're upset." Maxine positioned herself to face him. Taking a few seconds to get her words right she began.

"I need a favour love, a big fucking favour. It's Sandra's husband Kevin."

He knew exactly who she meant and looked angry. "Why what's up?" Zac had seen the news and read the papers and knew Sandra and Tina were in nick. It was the talk of the town and everyone was gossiping about it.

Maxine held her head to the side and looked sad. "I need you to get Kevin to drop the charges?"

Zac rested his head on the steering wheel. Lifting it up after a few seconds he looked confused. "How can I do that? He's a full-time prick. He's been all over the news. He's not gonna say he was lying is he?"

Maxine grabbed his hand. "Right this is what I was thinking. I know where there is a big grow of weed and if I put you on to it then you can say to Kevin, that if he drops the charges, he won't have to pay you the money back what he owes you. Do you understand?"

Zac snapped. "How the fuck, do you know he owes me money?" his teeth were gritted together.

"Tell you what, he's gonna get a dig now for talking about my business to people. The big mouth cunt."

"No, No, Zac, Sandra told me that's how I know." Zac's nostrils were flaring and his muscles on his arm seemed to be growing. Looking out of the window he lit a cig. He seemed in deep thought as Maxine watched him in anticipation.

"Right tell me more about this graft? It better be big!"

Maxine filled him in and told him he would get more then what Kevin owed him. He smiled at her. "You're a devious bitch you are Maxine, remind me never to get on the wrong side of you."

She playfully punched him in the arm. "I want to be there when you get Kevin though. I still want him to get a few digs and feel the pain that his wife is going through."

Zac rubbed his hands together. "Right I'll see what I can do. It shouldn't be a problem. He's just a little nob head and I bet he jumps at the chance of wiping his debt clean. The skank."

Maxine agreed. Zac now told her that he would ring her later on to let her know the script. He told her he would get hold of Kevin and set a place and time for a meeting and let her know when it was taking place. Maxine sighed with relief.

"Orr thanks Zac I owe you big time. If I can pay the favour back anytime. I will ya know." He smiled and looked at her with a cocky face.

"What about sucking me off then?"

She loved the way he joked with her and answered him back. "Ay you had your chance, remember our one night of glory?" she was giggling now, "that should be enough to last you a life time."

He chuckled and held his head back in his seat. "Yeah you were an alright ride Maxine." His body folded up as Maxine's hand, karate chopped him. They both sat pissing themselves. Maxine was serious now. "Nah, I'll get you some smart clothes. I'm in town later so I'll sort you out. I'll do you a good price."

Zac coughed as he choked. "Fucking hell I thought you were giving them me for nowt. You tight cow!"

"Fuck off" she chuckled. "We all have a living to make yanno." Zac turned the ignition and drove Maxine home.

She kept her head dipped as she neared familiar ground. She didn't want anyone putting two and two together.

★

Kevin was back in his house. Tracy was all over him like a rash. Baby this, baby that was all she talked about. He'd made a rod for his back without any doubt. Tracy was making plans for their future and she wanted them to be a couple. A proper couple she said. Making himself a drink he remembered John, locked upstairs in his bedroom. There were no moans coming from upstairs, it was silent. Slowly he poured his milkshake into the glass. Sipping at it he walked to the bottom of the stairs. He looked worried and went to investigate

Once at the top stair he held his ear to the door. No music played, no nothing. "John" he shouted. Still no reply. "John answer me now otherwise I'll come in there and give you another beating." His chest could be seen moving rapidly. Quickly running down the stairs he located the hammer. Jumping two stairs at a time he started yanking the nails from the wooden door. Once he'd pulled enough out to gain entry he barged the door open with his shoulder. His eyes frantically moved about the bedroom. "Where is the little bastard?" he mumbled. The white net curtain was flying around the window. Running over to it he screamed. "Little prick." John had smashed the window right out and escaped.

Glass was all over the bedroom floor and a few jagged pieces were still in the frame. His head peeped through the broken window with caution. He couldn't see him anywhere. "For fucks sake!" he screamed. Bending to the floor he started to pick the broken glass up from the beige carpet. He now found a football trophy wrapped in a jumper nearby. John must have used it to break the window. Slowly peeling the jumper from the trophy his eyes focused on the engraved message. The award had been given to his son for football when he was twelve years old at St Patrick's junior school for man of the match. His fingers touched the name of his son. He'd had so much hope for his lads when they were kids but now they were older he knew they wouldn't amount to much. Paul was just happy getting along on his job seekers allowance and didn't care that he was always penniless. Even from an early age he knew John was nothing but trouble. Tears ran down his cheeks as he cleared the mess. His body was weak and he felt as if he was at breaking point. He'd failed as a father.

The mobile phone in his pocket started to ring. As he dug his hands deeper into his jeans the ring tone stopped. Looking at the screen he saw the missed call from Zac.

"Fucking hell, can this day get any worse!"

16

Sandra and Tina were on bang up. They were locked up for most of the day. Prison life was hard and you could see the signs on both their faces that it was hitting home where they were. Steven had been to see Tina weeks before and told her he'd moved out of her home. As you can imagine she was devastated. Every night for weeks she'd cried herself to sleep and promised herself she would never fall in love again. He'd told her it was all too much to take in. He just wanted to live a normal life. Tina told him she wouldn't be in prison forever but he told her point blank that he was a man and he had needs. He wasn't willing to wait for her.

Sandra sat on her bed she looked in a world of her own. The prison mail was due soon and she prayed she would have a letter from James. He'd been to see her a few times over the last few weeks but she wasn't sure he was going to stand by her although he'd told her a hundred and one times that he would. Tina had now declared she would never fall in love again. She'd told Sandra in more ways than one that she was thinking of becoming a lesbian. She said it would be a lot easier and wouldn't end in heartbreak all the time. Sandra just listened to her waffling on and knew she loved men too much to become a lesbian.

The screw stood at the cell door with a load of letters in her hand. Passing them to the girls she smiled. "Looks like you two have a big fan club outside these four walls doesn't it?" Sandra stood from her bed and took the pile of letters from her hands. They were addressed to the both of them.

Tina looked up from her bed. "Are they all for us?"

Sandra nodded. Tina now sat up and looked like she had a burst of energy. "Pass me some then." Sandra split the pile of around twenty-six letters and sat on her bed. The first envelope she opened was pink and looked pretty.

Tina ripped her first letter and started to read the words inside. After a few minutes she screamed out, "We're fucking famous love! This lady has told me her life story and says good on us for not taking any shit from men." She now waved her hands in front of her face. Her eyes were welling up as she continued. "This woman has just been out and had a tattoo done the same as ours on her foot saying 'Carpe Diem'. Fucking hell Sandra we have a following."

Sandra's eyes were still reading her letter. As she

finished it she held the letter to her heart and spoke. "It's so sad Tina. All these women have been hurt and betrayed by the men they've loved. This woman says..." she sat back on the bed and placed a pillow behind her head, "where was I? Oh yeah, she says her husband beat her for years and slept with her best mate. She thinks we've made a stand against men and wishes she had paid her husband back for the way he treated her in the past." Tina was ripping another letter open. "Sandra I think we've got lots of support from women out there. I mean why on earth would they write to us otherwise?" The room was silent. You could have heard a pin drop as they read the letters. They both read their own piles and swapped letters.

Tina now lay on her stomach and kicked her legs up behind her as she held the letter in front of her. The cell door was now opened and a few inmates stood at the door. "Fuck me where's all the letters from?" The butch prisoner snarled.

Tina turned over and looked at her as she smiled from cheek to cheek. "They're from our fans. Apparently me and Sandra are icons for a lot of women. Here have a read of this." She held the letter out to the convict and watched as she trudged towards her. Her face was green with envy. The woman was now holding the letter in her hand and it was quite obvious that she couldn't read very well.

Another inmate joined her, "give it here you thick cunt. We'll be waiting all day for you to read that, I'll read it for you." The jailbird started to read the letter out aloud as Tina and Sandra looked at her. The other woman gritted her teeth and you could tell she was upset at her friend's comment.

Once she'd finished the letter she cheered at the

top of her voice. "Get in there girls, it's about time these men learnt, that we're not no fucking doormats." Sandra smiled, she was still holding a letter in her hand that she'd kept back from Tina. The letter was from someone called Jenny from "The Sun" newspaper. Once the other inmates had left the room Sandra pulled herself up from the bed and closed the door. Tina was still reading the letters and wasn't interested in what Sandra was doing. Walking to the window Sandra sighed. "Fucking hell Tina, I've got a letter from a journalist from a national newspaper."

Tina stopped what she was doing and looked at her. "Which one? I haven't read it."

Sandra looked at her as if she was daft. "I know you haven't read it you fucking idiot, because I didn't pass it to you," she giggled.

Tina stood up and tried getting the letter from her grip. "What does it say? Come on you know I don't like secrets?"

Sandra sat back on her bed. Jenny wanted to help the two of them and was investigating their story. She told them that she would help them all she could and try and get them some support from "Women's Aid" and other groups against Domestic violence. Her letter was three pages long. Jenny had said she wanted to see if she could arrange a visit to come and see them both before their trial. Tina was jumping up and down on her bed now. She sprung from it jumping right onto Sandra's body. "We might get out of here after all. Orr fingers crossed she's not a bullshitter and she really means what she says. Fucking result." Sandra agreed. They both danced about the cell in excitement.

Sandra dragged some writing paper from the wooden drawer. Searching for a pen she looked frantic. Once she'd found one she sat on her bed chewing the lid from it in her teeth. "What the fuck do I write back?"

Tina joined her as they both stared at the blank piece of paper. "Erm, just say thanks for her letter and we would love any help she could give us. Don't lick arse in it though. Just tell her about how Kevin has treated you over the years."

Sandra sat thinking for a moment. "Do you think I should tell her about when he put the hot iron on my leg and when he raped me?"

Tina rubbed her arms. You could see small goose bumps appearing on them. Slowly she rubbed her best friend's shoulder. "Sandra, tell her everything. That bastard deserves everything that's coming to him. Why should people think he's the victim? You're the fucking victim not him!"

Sandra smiled. You could see she was remembering her past and placed the paper on the bed. "Do you know what Tina? When I look back at all the shit that worthless dickhead has put me through I feel sick inside. Was I that much of a knob-head that I let him treat me like that?"

Tina held her head back against the wall. Her face looked serious as she rolled them both a cig. "Sandra, I did tell you but you were in love and didn't see it. I mean he was always a womaniser wasn't he? Everyone knew it except you. I mean…" she took a long drag from her cig, "he's been shagging your sister for years and you must have known it because everyone else did."

Sandra threw her legs off the bed and turned her body to face her. "No I fucking didn't. Did you know?"

Tina looked edgy, she sighed, the secret she'd hid had been held on her lips for years but now her friend was in her face, asking her the truth, she couldn't lie to her. "I'd heard he was shagging her, yes, but I didn't know for sure. It was just rumours on the estate. You know what it's like on Monsall for gossip?"

"No I fucking don't know what it's like, tell me Tina."

Sandra was angry and her face was going red. Tina blew a laboured breath and shook her head. Sandra now stood up from the bed and bent her face down towards Tina's screaming. "You're my fucking mate, even if it was only people chatting shit, you still should have told me." She turned and walked to the window gasping for breath. "What else do you fucking know about? You snidey bitch?" Sandra shook her head from side to side. "Fucking best mate my arse, best friends don't keep secrets." Tina held her head down low, Sandra was right she should have told her.

Sandra stayed at the cell window until she'd finished her cig. Flicking the butt through the bars, she turned back round.

"Come on Sandra don't be like this," Tina pleaded "I kept it from you for the right reasons. You wouldn't have believed me anyway. Kevin's word was gospel and you would have just brushed it off as per usual."

Sandra snapped. "What are you saying that he's cheated on me lots of times?"

Tina stood up and they both faced each other. "Yeah, if you want to know the truth I'll give you the fucking truth. He's shagged fucking loads of women. Remember Lilo Lil? Lesley fucking Ward? Well he was shagging her for ages. I saw him loads of times coming out of her house in the early hours." Tina was on a roll now and didn't stop for breath. "Gemma Cocks, Lindsay Fulham, the list is endless. There, are you happy now?" Tina flung herself on the bed.

A screw walked into the cell after hearing the commotion from outside. "Is everything alright in here ladies?" Sandra collapsed onto the bed as Tina spoke and she got up to leave the cell. "Yeah Miss. Just a bit of misunderstanding that's all." Tina pushed past the warden. When Tina had left she asked Sandra again. "Are you okay?" Sandra was ready for bursting. She quickly nodded to the officer and watched her leave.

Heartbroken, Sandra jumped up from her bed and slammed the door behind her. "Dirty cheating bastard Kevin. I'll show you now you low life fucker." Her face looked white. She was grabbing at her neck as her temperature rose. Finding the pen on the bed she gripped it tightly. Her hand was still shaking as she began to write the reply to Jenny.

Tina sat down at the bottom of the landing. She looked distressed as she held her head in her hands. One of the inmates was now at her side. "What's up love? Are you okay?" Tina lifted her head up and saw a smiling face. The woman was around forty-five and had long dark hair tied back in a ponytail.

"Yeah women troubles that's all," Tina huffed. The woman introduced herself as Penny and sat next to Tina nudging her in the waist. "Come on cheer up, things can only get better." Tina smiled and replied. "I've just had a raging argument with my best mate. I've never fallen out with her before; I mean we've known each other since being kids." Penny just listened as Tina told her all about her problems. Once she'd finished Penny asked her for a game of pool. Tina joked. "Fucking pool? I've never played it before. I'll be shit."

Penny grabbed her hand and pulled her up from the

staircase. "I'll learn you, how long you in for anyway?" Tina now explained that she was on remand and told her a bit about her case. Penny laughed out loud. "Oh right, so you're one of the women that everyone's talking about. Your mate stuck glue down her other half's willy didn't she?"

Tina giggled, "She sure did and lots of other stuff." Walking to the games room they both giggled at the things Sandra had done to her husband.

Penny now froze and looked at Tina. "So you got a man on the out or what?"

Tina shrugged her shoulders. "Nope. I did have but he binned me when I got put in here the tosser, I'm fucking sick to the high teeth of men. I never have any luck with them. I'm just gonna turn lesbian and have done with men forever." Penny smiled. She looked at Tina with endearing eyes and you could tell she had the hots for her. The two of them played pool and Penny was all over Tina. She was teaching her the game of pool and every time she took a shot she was behind her holding her body in the correct position.

Sandra licked the envelope and sat looking at it lying on the bed. She's told Jenny everything and hoped she could help. She looked lonely as she sat twisting her hair on the bed. Wiping the tears from her eyes she went to make friends with Tina. After all it wasn't her fault that she'd married a complete arse was it? Straightening her hair she went to make peace with her best friend.

The prison looked quiet. Only a few women walked across the landing. A few stood talking to each other and as she passed them the butch prisoner from earlier could be heard talking. "Fucking thinks she's a hero now that one, bit of glue down her bloke's cock doesn't make her

216

a criminal."

Sandra heard her and stopped dead in her tracks. Her anger returned and she walked back to the two prisoners. She was fuming. "Listen, gobshite. Keep your snidey remarks to yourself. I don't claim to be any fucking hero, so keep your beak out of my life alright?"

The convict stood tall and grabbed Sandra by her clothes. "Who the fuck do you think you are? Talking to me like that, I'm not your husband. I'll twist you up you daft slag." Sandra could feel her grip tightening around her neck and her face looked scared as she stood on her tiptoes in her grip.

Shouting could be heard coming from the stairway and Tina could be seen running towards them with a face of thunder. Tina was screaming. "Take your fucking hands off her. You big rug munching twat!"

The prisoner screwed her face up and threw Sandra to the side of her as Tina was now at her side. She was shouting in Tina's face. "Do you want a bit then?" Tina held her hands out in front of her now and waved them in the inmate's face. "Yeah bring it on ya lettuce licker. Let's have it. Come on then." The two of them pounced on each other and they were going for it, punching and kicking, Tina was holding her own. Sandra now stepped in as did the other inmate's friend. Once they'd split them up they were both shouting insults back at each other. Sandra dragged Tina away from the landing. She was trying to break free to try and get back to the fight.

"Sandra let me fucking go. I'll waste the big fucking trollop." Sandra was struggling to control her. The other woman was still shouting at the other end of the landing and it was obvious that Tina had now made an enemy.

★

Maxine sat waiting with Zac as they shared a spliff. Kevin was due any minute now and she wanted to make sure that they got him to drop the charges against Sandra. Zac sat on the chair dressed in a black vest top and a long pair of canvas shorts. His trainers looked brand new and he kept removing specks of dirt from them with his index finger.

Maxine passed him the spliff. "Zac, I need you to proper shit this fucker up. He needs to know that if he doesn't drop the charges he's gonna get wasted."

Zac choked as he inhaled the weed. "Since when do you need to tell me my job? I'm not no prick yanno, he'll shit bricks when he sees me he always does. I can give him a few digs tonight if you want?"

Maxine chuckled. "Just do what you have to do to get the daft twat to drop the charges. I'm gonna go out of the way while you speak to him though. I don't want him knowing I'm owt to do with it. He's a grassing cunt and I can't take the chance. Do you know what I mean?" Zac nodded.

Kevin walked into the old shop. It had been a meeting place for a lot of gangsters in the past and it was a safe place to sort out any deals. Kevin looked old. His once shining skin now looked dry and cracked. He'd not been on the sunbed for months and his tan had disappeared completely. His hand shook as he tapped on the back door of the shop. He could hear footsteps nearing and he struggled for his next breath. Zac stood at the door, looking like a man who could have killed him with a single blow.

He coaxed Kevin inside. "Come on slug. Get ya arse inside before anyone sees you." Kevin hurried in but was still walking with a struggle. His penis was still sore and the doctors said it could take years before it felt normal again. Closing the door behind him he followed the drug dealer inside. Maxine hid in another room and watched Kevin enter.

"Fucking rat" she whispered.

Kevin sat down on the chair at the side of him as Zac jumped up onto the old counter. As he swung his legs out in front of him he joked with Kevin. "How's the old cock then? Is it still fucked up?"

Kevin raised a smile but hesitated to answer. He looked terrified. "Yeah it's getting there mate. Fucking loony women for ya innit?"

Zac watched Kevin's face as he held his crotch. He could feel his pain as he watched him try to get comfy. Zac coughed loudly before he began. "Right I've got a business deal for you." Kevin looked shocked, his face was blank. Kevin sat forward and hung his hands between his legs. "What kind of deal?" he asked in a quiet voice.

Zac sucked on his bottom lip. "I see it like this mate. You still owe me a lot of cash don't you?" Kevin nodded slowly and waited eagerly for him to get to the point. He couldn't rush him. He hung on his every word. "Well I want you to drop the charges on Sandra and Tina and your debt will be cleared."

"Are you having a laugh or what? Are you serious?" Kevin chuckled.

Zac jumped down from the counter, he looked intimidating. "Fucking dead right I'm serious. I want you to go to the dibble and drop all the charges against them. So get into Tracy's head too because she needs to drop all her charges as well. Once you've done that, you won't owe me fuck all. You'll be debt free." Kevin stood up, he looked uneasy; scratching his head he paced the floor.

Zac was watching him like a hawk. Laughter could be heard and Kevin walked back to Zac with a cocky face. "Alright yeah I can do that. But I hope this is not bullshit and you're not joking."

Zac swung his fist right into Kevin's face. "Do I look like I'm a fucking bullshitter?" he ranted.

Kevin covered his face and fell to his knees. "I know mate. I'm just saying it's hard to believe that you're gonna let me off with the money if I sort Sandra out."

Zac pulled him up from the floor as Kevin wiped the blood from his mouth. He guided him back to his chair. "Right I want you to do it tonight. Don't fuck me about though because if you don't I'll find you and make sure it's more than ya cock that gets injured this time. I'll cut the fucker off. Do you hear me?"

Kevin jerked his head up and down rapidly. You could tell by his face that he knew Zac meant every word he said. He was a bad arse and wouldn't think twice about cutting his dick off. He'd heard of some ruthless things he'd done in the past. Kevin agreed to do it.

They sat there for a moment and Kevin was itching to speak. He didn't want to wind him up anymore so he approached him with caution. Clearing his throat he coughed slightly. "Zac can I just ask you one question."

Zac screwed his face. He squeezed his fist tightly and was getting ready to tune the cheeky fucker right in. "What now, what do you want to know?" he replied.

Kevin spoke quietly. "Why are you interested in helping Sandra?"

Zac yawned. He wasn't ready for the question. Stretching his arms above his head he answered him. "Just let's say that I don't like seeing women who I've known for years being slammed in jail. Fuck me man, she's your wife. Haven't you got no morals?"

Kevin gulped; his mouth looked dry as his tongue slid across his bottom lip. "Yeah I know mate. I feel bad about it all you know; it's just that the daft cunt tried to ruin my manhood."

Zac giggled. "Women are mad fuckers mate, and word on the street is that you were shagging her sister. What do you expect?" Kevin knew it was the truth. He walked over to him and held his hand out for Kevin to shake it. Kevin was wary but shook it anyway. He told him to make sure he went to the police station tonight and Kevin agreed before he left.

The shop door closed and Maxine came out of hiding. She waited for Zac to return and hugged him as he entered. "Thank you so much love, did you see the cocky fucker? I'm so glad you punched the lowlife skank."

Zac checked his knuckles and rubbed at them with a smile on his face. "Yeah well he was getting fucking cheeky wasn't he? He knows not to fuck with me."

Maxine stroked his muscles on his arm as he chuckled. "He better get his sorry arse to the police station tonight, because if he doesn't, I'll chop his one eyed worm weasel right off and send it up in the sky tied to a helium balloon." Maxine roared laughing, "Yeah imagine that, that would be the dog's bollocks that. I might have a go of that myself if my fella ever cheats on me."

Zac looked blank and hunched his shoulders. "Since when did you have a man in your life?"

Maxine hesitated. "I mean if I ever get one. I'm having a drought at the moment but men are like buses aren't they, none for ages then they all come along at once."

Zac dragged her by the arm towards him. "Right let's get down to business. Where's this weed stash?"

Maxine kept to her side of the bargain and filled him in on the whereabouts of the grow. Twisting his fingers together he joked with her. "If we get a good earner on this I might take you out for a night on the town." She looked embarrassed as he continued. "That's if you have a wash and that you scruffy cunt." Maxine patted her hair down and giggled. "Ay fuck off will you, I've not had time to get ready this morning. My mates are more important at the moment than looking good." He walked towards the exit with Maxine following closely behind him. She liked him and it was so obvious, this was her chance to get into him. "Don't worry, when you take me out, you won't recognise me. I'm quite a stunner when I've got my slap on."

He turned back to her as his fingers turned the key in the door. "I'm sure you do love, just make sure you wash your motty though. It was a bit whiffy last time." Maxine playfully pushed him out of the door. They loved the banter between them. The desire for each other's bodies was written all across their faces. Zac kissed her on the cheek and they went their separate ways.

17

John sat in his mate's flat. His body was weak. The cut on his hand still looked sore. He'd wrapped an old sock round it to stop it bleeding. All that was on his mind was drugs. He knew his mother was locked up but he didn't have the courage to go and see her. Sandra could spot a drug addict from a mile off, she'd done it in the past so many times. They would be sat in the car and all of a sudden she would get his attention "Look at that baghead. You can just tell they're on drugs cant you." He remembered her conversation and knew she could never see him like this. Drugs were hard to get hold of now. And since he was no longer delivering them for his father he had to turn to crime to pay for his habit.

Kevin had been to the flat where he was staying over the last few days looking for his son but John always hid away and got his friends to lie for him. His life was in a state and every day he was falling deeper into a hole of desperation.

Kevin sat in the reception of Grey Mare police station. Dropping the charges on Sandra would be a small price to pay to clear off his debts. He'd told the policewoman behind the reception counter why he was there and he was now sat waiting to see someone about it. Chewing rapidly on his gum he read the notice boards all over the walls. The drugs notice seemed to grip him and he stood up to read it properly. Shaking his head he typed the phone number of the helpline in his mobile phone. Sitting back down the Domestic Violence data stared right at him. The picture showed a woman sunk in a corner with a man stood over her shouting at her. His face changed. He'd led Sandra a miserable life and he knew it. She just wound him up so much with her gob. A voice could now be heard and Kevin answered to his name being called.

Kevin walked into a small side office. He was told to sit down while the policewoman got all the paper work she required. Once she joined him again he couldn't wait to get the words from his mouth. "I want to retract the statement I made against my wife and drop all the charges."

The policewoman read through the file in front of her and shook her head. She was aware of the case. After all it had been all over the news. The officer now spoke

"I think it might be a bit late for that." Her eyes carried on reading the notes in front of her as Kevin watched in disbelief.

"Listen," he said in a stroppy tone, "I don't want to press charges. I want to drop all of them. I mean how hard is that? Just give me the form and I'll sign it to that effect."

The policewoman sat back in her chair. "You may want to drop the charges but the prosecution might still want to carry on with the case without your evidence. It's not as easy as you think. Your wife committed a crime and she won't just walk away from it just because you have changed your mind."

Kevin was up in arms. "If I tell you I deserved it and I pushed her to it, then surely that must count for something. I know Tracy will also drop the charges on Tina as well, so there won't be a case." The policewoman took his statement and told him that in her experience the police would still carry on without him. He looked demented. Giving a big sigh he left the police station.

Walking from Grey Mare police station he phoned Zac to tell him the job was done. He didn't tell him what they said about it not being over for Sandra. He just told him he'd retracted his statement. A smile filled his face and he felt himself again. He was debt free and his struggle to survive was nearly over. He had the spring back in his step.

Kevin's son lay heavily on his mind now and he decided he would go looking for him. Kevin knew who was selling heroin on Monsall and felt certain John would sooner or later make contact with them for a fix. Making his way to Big John's he set out to capture his son.

Big John was a middle aged man who lived in the

block of flats on Monsall in Manchester. Kevin had known him for years and had often had a pint with him in the local pub. Pressing the button outside the flats he waited eagerly for John to answer. Kevin now spoke into the intercom. "Hiya mate its Kevin. Let us in." The door made a buzzing noise and within minutes he was inside the flats. Walking to the right of him he located the lifts. John lived on the fifth floor. Kevin stepped inside the lift and pressed the floor number he required. The lift stank of piss. As he looked down on the floor he could see the wet liquid rolling about near his feet. "Scruffy cunts," he mumbled.

John was stood at his front door waiting for him. They shook hands and John invited him inside. The flat was nothing like Kevin expected. He thought John was a scruffy twat but as he looked around the front room he realised how wrong he was. John had the latest TV and the smell from his brown leather sofa told him he hadn't had it long. Everywhere looked spick and span.

John brought two cans of lager from the kitchen and passed one to Kevin. "Get that down your neck lad. From what I've heard you've earned it!" Kevin opened his Stella and slurped from the top of it. John held nothing back and came straight out with it. "How's your love sword lad. Bet you want to do the tart in don't you?"

Kevin raised a smile. "It's getting there mate. Still a bit sore but the old fellow will be back in action soon don't worry." They both chuckled.

John made himself comfy in his large armchair. "So to what do I owe the honour then? It's not often I get a visit from you what's up?"

Kevin sighed. He looked deflated; you could tell he was trying to find the right words. After a few moments he spoke. "It's our John. He's on gear."

Big John sat forward in his chair, his face looked traumatised. "Fuck off, are you joking or what?"

Kevin shook his head. "Nar mate. I found him injecting in his bedroom a while back. I locked him in there but the fucker smashed the window and done one."

Big John took a big gulp from his drink. You could hear him swallowing the lager. After a big burp he placed his hand down his grey tracksuit bottoms and scratched at his ball bag. "Bad news that mate. I mean once they start on that shit it's very rare they come back." Kevin agreed. The mobile phone at Big John's was ringing constantly and you could hear him speaking in drugs terms and organising drop offs.

Kevin knew he didn't have long as he needed to go out now and asked the question that was lying heavily on his lips. "I need you to tell me when John or his mates phone you to score. I've looked everywhere for the little prick but can I find him? Can I fuck! Just ring me when you're doing a drop and I'll do the rest."

Big John agreed. He knew Kevin's son and wanted to help him as much as possible. "Yeah as soon as he rings I'll phone you don't worry, I want you to sort him out, it's no life being a smack head." Kevin thanked him and they left the flat together. John told him he would be in touch. He checked he had the right phone number for him and once he knew he had, he left him to go and drop the drugs off.

Kevin felt better. He would catch the fucker, he knew it. Now Big John was on side it was just a matter of time before he got his hands on the little bastard. His phone started to ring. Tracy's name flashed.

"Hello sexy" he joked. His mood had lifted and as he

touched his crotch he knew it was ready for action. He arranged to meet Tracy and a night of sex was all he had on his mind. Kevin had to get Tracy to drop the charges now against Tina. Once that was done he could sit back and enjoy his new life with her. Tracy's parents seemed to have disowned Sandra and accepted that he was now with Tracy. Well Anita did, Graham always looked at him as if he wanted to plunge his fist deep into his face every time he saw him. Kevin thought it was wrong how Anita had sold out her eldest daughter but ay, if it made his life easier he didn't give a flying fuck. He headed to meet Tracy at her parent's house.

Tracy was lying on the sofa when he got to her house. Her mother was running round after her as per usual. Ever since she'd told her she was pregnant she'd been at her side for her every need. Walking into the front room Kevin was greeted by Anita.

Tracy was wearing a small pair of shorts that obviously didn't fit her anymore. Her stomach hung over the shorts and she looked huge. Her breasts were two large mounds that stood on her chest like a small mountain range. Pulling her face she moved her legs for Kevin to sit down. Tracy could see there was something on his mind because he sat quietly and that wasn't like him.

"What's up?" she moaned.

He turned to her and placed his hand on her bare leg. "Erm," he said struggling to find the words. Tracy's parents were waiting on his next words and he could feel their eyes burning into his head. "I've just been to drop the charges on Sandra. And I think you should do the same for Tina."

Tracy bolted up from the sofa. "Are you having a fucking laugh or what?"

Kevin expected this reaction and tried to calm her down. "She's my wife and I feel bad, the kids need her." He sunk his head down knowing she would feel sorry for him. Forcing tears into his eyes he snivelled. "Tracy, Sandra's been through a lot, we're together now no matter what. Don't you think that's enough punishment for her?"

Tracy sat back down. Her mother was now at the side of her stroking her hair. "He's right love. We all know she's been a silly cow but she's your sister and you've hurt her too."

Tracy blew through her mouth. Chewing her fingernails she turned to Kevin. "Fair enough but Tina and Maxine shouldn't have got involved in it. They drugged me and tattooed my face are you forgetting what them mental cunts did to me?"

Kevin held her hand and looked deep into her eyes. He could always win her over and once he showed her a bit of affection he knew she would be butter in his hands. "I just want it to be over. How can we move on with our lives with this hanging over our heads? Let's make a break for it. Drop the charges and move away. We're having a baby now and this is our time not theirs."

A smile appeared on her face and she held her head high. He was telling her they would move away together and be a family. That was all she ever wanted. So what, she'd stolen her sister's husband. As long as she was happy that was all that mattered? "Okay I'll do it," Tracy said at last, "I better not get into any trouble." Kevin smiled, he was a devious bastard. Tracy's dad sat watching him eagerly. He'd always known what kind of man he was, but just sat back and went with the flow. Kevin had already hurt one of his daughters and now he'd moved onto the next. He was chomping at the bit to twat him, he reminded him so much of someone from his own past.

Tracy looked happy. She kept placing Kevin's hand across her stomach. "Orrr Kevin it's kicking! Feel it here." Kevin couldn't feel a thing, his eyes raised to the ceiling as she kept his hand there for ages. His mobile phone started to ring and he removed his hand from her stomach quickly. Walking out of the front room they all listened to his conversation especially Graham. He was watching the sly fucker like a hawk. When he came back into the room he told Tracy he had to go out and that he had business to sort out. Her face sank, but once he told her he would be straight back she seemed okay. She was an irritating bitch. Standing up to kiss him, her parents watched. Her father pulled a face and his wife nudged him knowing exactly what he was thinking.

Once he'd gone, he whispered to his wife so Tracy couldn't hear. "Business my arse . He's probably got another woman on the go. Once a womaniser, always a womaniser. I'm onto him don't you worry and when I catch him I'll do more than Super glue his fucking dick." Tracy turned to hear the conversation but her mother changed it straight away. She didn't want her darling daughter getting upset for anything. She'd been through enough already.

Kevin was running through the estate. His breathing was frantic. He'd not been to the gym for ages and his fitness level had dropped. Getting to the meeting place he could see Big John in the distance. Standing still he checked the area, heading to a nearby bush he hid behind it. "Come on you little fucker" he mumbled. His breathing was calming down now and his eyes were peeping from the bush like a sniper waiting for the enemy. Big John could be seen stood near a wall. He looked dodgy as fuck; if the police would have driven by he would have been nicked without a shadow of doubt, because it was obvious what he was up to.

Kevin heard footsteps at the other side of the bush. As he dipped his body completely out of sight he saw his son walking past. John was acting as if he'd shit his pants. Leaping from his hideout Kevin pounced on him and dragged him to the floor. John was screaming and didn't realise it was his dad who was attacking him. Big John now ran over and helped Kevin pull his son out of view. That's all they needed a fucking scene. He was screaming like a girl so Big John covered his mouth with his big fat fingers. "Shut the fuck up ya crying fucker" he yelled. Kevin's teeth were showing now and you could see the rage all across his face. He looked like the incredible hulk.

Dragging his son to an entry at the side of them he pinned him up against the wall and yelled into his face. "Don't ever think you can take the piss out of me. I told you I would find you didn't I? Now I'll show you what the big men are all about." Scanning the area his eyes focused on a large piece of wood. It looked like it used to belong to someone's fence. He told Big John to hold him while he went to get it. John was still wriggling about trying to break free. Kevin returned. His eyes looked menacing. Pausing for a minute he told Big John to move his body out of the way. Swinging the piece of wood he attacked his son's legs. You could hear every whack he gave him and John fell to the floor in severe pain. "You won't run away now will you? You bell-end!" Big John helped carry him to his car. He told Kevin he'd drop him off at home with his son. John was screaming in pain as they tossed his bony body into the back of the car. Kevin sat next to him and kept his son's head firmly pushed onto the seat.

The screams from his son could be heard and it was heartbreaking to watch. Kevin knew this was his mess and he'd planned to right his wrong. If he hadn't have been selling heroin this would never have happened. His face was white with anger. He decided he would sit with his son round the clock until he was clean. He told Big John this too and you could tell by his face he meant every word.

★

Sandra sat at the table in the visitor's room wearing a red bib. Lots of other inmates were on the visit and she was watching all the goings on around her. The inmates looked so happy to see their loved ones and you could see the pain of being locked up away from their family inside in their eyes. The woman at the side of her was sat nurturing her child. You could hear the little girl saying "Mummy when are you coming home?" Sandra felt emotional and missed her own boys, not once had they written or been to see her, her heart was broken in two.

Visits were the highlight of any convict's day. She knew a lot of women would be getting things into the prison today because she'd heard one inmate explaining to another just how she planned to conceal it. Drugs were still getting into the prisons every day and some of the stories she'd heard would send shivers down your spine. One woman told her she would swallow the drugs once her boyfriend had passed them to her during a kiss and then she'd just wait until she had a shit later on to get them out. Sandra had looked shocked and the woman had to explain the whole process of searching your shit to get the drugs you required. Prison life was hard and Sandra hated every minute of it. A woman now sat down at her table and Sandra smiled as Jenny introduced herself. Jenny recognised her straight away from her picture in the newspaper.

"Thanks so much for seeing me Sandra. I didn't think you would."

Sandra shook her hand and smiled. The journalist now asked her if she wanted something to eat from the canteen. Looking at her she smiled and just asked for a coffee. Jenny walked away and Sandra sat alone tapping her fingers on the table. This woman was her last hope of telling the truth and when she came back to the table she planned to pour her heart out to her.

"Oh it's hot. Watch your hands," Jenny giggled, as she passed her the drink. With the journalist seated, it was like they had known each other for years and the conversation never stopped. "I know bits of the things your husband has done to you, but it would be better if you told me your side of things and then we can take it from there."

Sandra took a slow sip from her drink. Her face looked serious. "I don't know where to start Jenny, do you want to know how he was as a husband?"

"Yeah let's start there if you don't mind?" Jenny nodded.

Sandra gripped her arms and rubbed at them. "He was always a wanker. I just didn't see it at the time; I was the fat girl that no one ever took much notice of."

Jenny reached over and stroked her arm. "Orr don't say that sweetheart you're lovely."

"I suppose when Kevin took an interest in me I was over the moon," Sandra continued, "everyone fancied him and he was hot I can tell you!" Sandra chuckled. "I got myself pregnant on purpose you know?" Jenny sat back in her chair she was intrigued by her honesty. "When I got pregnant I knew he would have to marry me. He's like that, he likes to do the right thing plus my dad was threatening to do him in if he didn't do right by me." Jenny smiled and started to eat her bar of chocolate. She hung on Sandra's every word "Things were great at first but slowly day by day he was destroying me. He called me fat. He called our sex life, everything in fact. And it wasn't long before I felt worthless. I put loads of weight on you know?"

Jenny jumped in she knew exactly what she meant. "We all put weight on after child birth. I was like a fucking sumo wrestler after having my two." She giggled.

Sandra was so funny and she made Jenny smile with her bluntness. "I think I knew he was cheating on me but I could never admit it to myself, he was all I had. Even sex with him was crap. He just used to roll on top of me and empty his load. The cheeky fucker told me I was a fat cunt and said I was lucky to get sex because I didn't turn him on anymore."

Jenny looked shocked. "Why did you let him speak to you like that?"

Sandra didn't hesitate with her answer. "Because I needed him Jenny, he was the best thing I had in my life. I mean other than the kids, he was my prize and even though I didn't win him fairly he was still, all I had." Sandra filled up and a single tear rolled onto her cheek. As she wiped it away she took a deep breath and continued. "He treated me like a slave. Even removing his plate from the table was my job. He didn't lift a fucking finger. I did tell him I was sick of it and that's when the bastard started hurting me. I thought it was just a one off but how wrong was I? It became a regular occurrence. I became his punchbag. He beat me black and blue many a night." Jenny suggested they had a break as she looked upset but Sandra declined and continued. "I hid it well and no one ever knew the truth. No one knows what goes on behind closed doors do they?"

Jenny was hanging on her every word. She encouraged her to continue. "So tell me about the affair with your sister, how did that happen?"

Sandra gritted her teeth and flexed her fingers in front of her. She was fuming and her payback to her slag of a sister was far from over. As she spoke Jenny could see the anger in her face. "She's a dirty little tart. And she'll get what's coming to her trust me. She's always been the same since being a kid. It's my mother's fault, she treated her like a princess. I was always the fat kid at the back that no one noticed." Jenny shook her head from side to side. She could tell this woman had endured so much pain in the past and she promised herself she would do all she could to help her. Sandra continued in a cocky tone. "After years of abuse I just couldn't take it anymore. Kevin shagging my sister was the last straw so to speak. That's when I started to do things to pay him back." Jenny was on the edge of her seat. It was like watching a film and if she would have had any popcorn she would have sat munching it as the story unfolded.

This was what Jenny was waiting for; Sandra smiled cunningly and giggled, "I've always done little things to him like spitting on his food and shrinking his clothes on purpose. But when I found out he was a lying cheating bastard I suppose I just went wild. I hated him with a passion you know?" Jenny loved her outlook on life and told her she would get her story all over the media. She urged her to continue as the visit was nearly over and she wanted all the dirt on her cheating husband. "I used to shake his canned drinks before I gave them to him. Once he opened it, I would watch as it went all over his expensive clothes. I pissed laughing every time you know" Her face looked sad as she told her the consequences she had to pay for her actions. "Yeah he would kick my fucking head in after it, but I didn't give a shit. I became immune to any pain he gave me and to see him upset was worth any beatings he gave me. I put hair remover in his shampoo but he deserved it. He loved his fucking hair so that was the only way I could hurt him. He was a proper vain cunt and to take that away from him put a smile all over my face every day."

Jenny listened for the last twenty minutes of the visit and before it was over she had enough evidence on Kevin to ruin him. The screw now came over to the table and told them to finish the visit. Jenny stood up and looked at the inmate. "Sandra you are a very strong woman and I know I can help you. Too many women out there are living with domestic violence and they too think they are alone. I'm going to do a big campaign to bring awareness and hopefully your case will show just how bad things are for some women."

She quickly rolled her jeans up over her ankle. At the side of her foot she showed Sandra her new tattoo. "It says 'Carpe Diem'. I've been a victim of abuse myself you know and these words on my foot mean so much to me. Just as they do to you. Every time I look at them I know I'm not alone in what I've been through, and I'll never ever put myself in that position again." Jenny hugged Sandra, she told her to watch out in the national newspapers for stories about domestic violence. Jenny told Sandra she would be working with her solicitor to get her out of prison as soon as possible. Sandra reminded her about her co-accused Tina. Jenny told her she was working for the pair of them and not to worry. As she left she raised her arm in the air and shouted "Carpe Diem." Sandra smiled and sat back at her table waiting to go back to her cell.

Watching all the visitors go home made her feel sad. There was an ache deep inside her chest and she could feel her eyes filling up. Her life was in such a mess and it felt like just at that moment, everything had come to head. Sobbing, she dug her head into her folded arms on the table. Her tears were like a river of sadness. The woman from the next table stood up and rubbed her head softly. "Come on love. It gets better with time you know and before long you will be home."

Sandra lifted her head and looked at the inmate. "I know love, I know, it's just that today it all seems to have hit home where I am. I'm such a fool aren't I?" The lady went back to her table and listened as the screw told them all to make their way back to be searched.

As they entered the small room they could hear a commotion. A woman could now be seen being dragged out of it by two guards. She was angry as she told them to "take their fucking dirty hands" off her. Sandra looked behind her at the other inmates. They seemed oblivious to it and it didn't bother them.

"What's going on?" Sandra asked a woman in front of her.

The convict covered her mouth as she spoke. "She's been caught with a parcel or summat. They are taking her down the block."

Sandra shook her head. "Fucking get me out of here" she mumbled under her breath.

Returning back to her cell Tina was waiting for her. As soon as she sat down she was on her. "Come on what did she say, is it good news?" Sandra wasn't in the mood for talking and lay onto her bed grabbing the bedding over her body. Her eyes looked swollen and Tina thought Jenny was full of bullshit.

"I knew she was chatting shit. Why did I even think Jenny could help us? She's just like everyone else. Full of fucking shit."

Sandra stopped her dead in her tracks. "No love, she's gonna help us both. She is trying to get our story all over the media using domestic violence stories. She said she's going to work with the solicitor on our case. So it's not all doom and gloom is it?"

Tina looked confused and placed her hands on her hips. "Well if she said she's going to help us, why is your face like fucking Chief Black cloud?" Sandra rolled over to face the wall. Tina could see her shoulders shaking; she sat on the edge of her bed and placed her hand onto Sandra's waist. "Orr come on chick. What's to do with you? Talk to me will you?" There was no reply. Tina lay next to her now and held her, as the tears continued. "We're gonna be alright yanno. You're just having a bad day that's all."

"A fucking bad day," Sandra screamed "it's the worst time in my life, I've lost my kids, my husband, I can't see them queuing up to come and visit me can you? My mother's disowned me. So don't tell me everything is gonna be alright. We're fucked Tina and the sooner we get used to that the better!"

Tina held her and spoke into her face as her hands

trembled. "Just calm down will ya. I know you're upset but we can get through this together. Trust me love, everything gonna be sweet." Sandra didn't reply. The night hour set in and they both lay in each other's arms terrified of the days that lay ahead.

Every day that passed in prison was more or less the same. Tina had a new friend Penny and everyone knew Penny wanted Tina as her girlfriend, Sandra was always joking with her and telling her she was Penny's bitch, but she just took it on the chin and laughed it off. "I'm fucking fed up not hard up" was her reply to all the jokes Sandra threw at her.

Jenny had been in touch constantly over the last few months and today was the day the domestic violence story was set to be in the paper. Jenny had changed Sandra's name to avoid any mither from the police. If they found out Jenny had been to see Sandra in jail she would have been in deep shit. Walking out of her cell Sandra made her way to collect a newspaper. As she walked up she could see the women looking at her. As she neared, they all started clapping and cheering. "Fuck me Sandra, you're all over the news papers." Sandra cast her eyes over the paper the inmate was holding up. Once she saw the story she giggled. Sandra sat down and she read every word that Jenny wrote. The girl had done well; she'd done exactly what she said she would. Sandra was a victim of domestic violence and now everyone knew what women put up with when they had abusive partners.

Tina came running down the landing. "Is the story in or what" she screamed.

Sandra waved the newspaper in the air. "Yeah it's in. Come and get ya arse here and have a read." Tina squeezed her arse cheeks next to Sandra as they both sat down to read it together. The other women were all behind them and hugged them as they were passing. They all knew the story was about Sandra's life even though the names had been changed. Tina made sure everyone knew.

"Good luck you two. I hope you get off with it, from what I've read that husband of yours deserved everything you did to him" an inmate shouted.

Sandra smiled. She felt strong again. Tina now looked concerned and shook her head. "Sandra all this news is about you," she knew she was right and tried to comfort her.

"You were helping me love, I'm your best friend surely that counts for something. You did what you did to help me. Don't worry." Tina knew what she was saying was true. Sandra's solicitor had told her the same thing though. Tina was in deep shit and she could be looking at a long time inside. The court case was two weeks away and both of them were preparing themselves for the worst.

★

John had been off drugs for months now. Kevin had nursed him back to health. Locking him inside his room for over a week was the worst time ever for John. He had to go cold turkey and he'd shit himself on more than one occasions. His brother Paul helped him a lot and he'd often gone to sit with him when he was going through it. Their family had been torn apart and in Paul's eyes his father was the one to blame.

Kevin spent a lot of time at Tracy's now. He'd brought his tart to the family home a few times but he knew she wasn't welcomed by his boys. Paul was the one to watch these days. He seemed to be the one in charge and even John his brother listened to him. Paul had been to visit

Sandra now and he hated that she was locked up. Kevin had a lot to answer for and in his son's mind he knew he'd be answering to him one day soon. He hated him with a passion and he promised once his mother was cleared of her crime he would deal with him properly. John had confided in his younger brother that it was his dad's fault that he'd ended up on gear. He told him he had him selling heroin. Paul's blood boiled at the thought of his father telling his son to sell drugs. He'd always thought he was a prick but this information confirmed it. Both Sandra's sons were backing her now and they were both going to court to give evidence that they'd witnessed the violence between their mother and father in the past.

Maxine had done all she could to help her two friends. She'd been back to the police station months before and they told her she was in the clear. They didn't have fuck all on her and from day one she knew they could never make an arrest.

Zac and Maxine had been out on a few dates now and she really liked him. He liked her too. He was always ringing her now and they were more or less an item. Maxine dressed differently now and any shoplifting she'd done in the past had stopped. Zac gave her everything her heart desired and she wanted for nothing. They were so like chalk and cheese but somehow it worked. Maxine was the happiest she'd been in a long time and the grey cast of sadness over her face had completely disappeared. All she wanted now was her friends to be released. The trial was due to start the following day and she prepared herself for the next three days being sat in court.

18

The steps of Manchester Crown Courts were packed with people carrying banners. "Carpe Diem Girls" was written over a large white poster that two women were carrying. Over five hundred others were scattered about the entrance of the courts and Jenny was among them showing her support.

A TV crew was interviewing a few of the women and when they told them why they were there, they knew Sandra and Tina had a fan club. Lots of banners were held up as the TV crew walked between the women. A few of the protesters even showed new tattoos they'd had done in support of the two prisoners. They sang at the top of their voices as people walked into court and it was clear they wanted justice for Sandra and Tina.

"Women's Aid" a domestic violence group was also present in the crowd of supporters and Kerry, their spokesperson, told the news crew all the statistics about domestic violence. Her words were strong and everyone was quiet as she raised her voice. "We want respect from men, we're not slaves, they don't own us. Sandra has suffered enough. We want it recognised that she was the victim not her husband." The women cheered as she finished. One of the banners stood out from the others and a few people smiled as they read it. "Off with their nobs" it read. It was painted in thick black paint on a white sheet. Jenny was mingling with these women and she wanted them to make as much noise as possible.

The sweat box pulled up outside Manchester Crown Court. The reporters were holding the cameras into the small dark windows at the side of the van, hoping to get a photo of the woman everyone was talking about. The story was massive and everyone in the nation was aware of the trial. Sandra sat in the sweat box and could hear the cheers and rants from the people outside. Tina was banging on her wall next to her. "Can you hear them Sandra. Fuck me it's mad innit!" Sandra giggled; she was shitting herself and this was what she needed to pick her mood up.

Once they were inside they were escorted to the holding cells. The solicitor was on his way down to see Sandra. He told her he wanted to speak to her one last time before she went inside the courtroom. Tina was quiet now. There were no more rants coming from her cell. She too knew that in the next few days she would face her punishment. Her barrister had told her to expect up to four years. Her arse was twitching and her face betrayed her nerves.

Sandra's solicitor came to see her after about half an hour of waiting. Once they went into the small interview room he smiled at her sympathetically. "Sandra this is it! When you take the stand you have to do your best to let the people know exactly what you've suffered. As I've told you in the past, if this goes the other way you could be doing three to six years in prison." His words sent shivers down her spine and she had to hold her hands together to stop them shaking. Her mouth felt dry and she asked him for a drink of water.

Once she quenched her thirst she held her arms tightly around her body. They looked like they were holding her together. Her words were shaky as she spoke. "I can only do my best that's all. What will be, will be won't it?"

Her solicitor smiled. He loved her outlook on life and knew if he'd been the one sitting in her position he would have been crying his eyes out. He left the room once he's hugged her. "Good luck Sandra. I hope this all goes your way." She smiled and watched him leave.

The girls were escorted to the dock. Lots of people could be seen in the public gallery and they were waving and blowing kisses at them both. Tina looked serious. "I'm shitting my knickers Sandra. I just need this to be over now!" Sandra nodded. The room looked busy and lots of people were coming in and out of the courtroom.

Four people sat at the first table in front of the judge and two other people were at either side of them. One of them looked like they were taping the court case.

The prosecution was a man. He looked stern. His grey wig didn't fit his head properly and you could see his raven black hair sticking out from underneath it. The black gown he wore covered his navy suit. All you could see was his highly polished black shoes sticking out from underneath his gown. He looked a posh fucker and Tina nudged Sandra as they sat waiting for the judge to come into the court room.

"Fuck me he looks a right twat, doesn't he?"

"I was just thinking the same" Sandra whispered. The courtroom door opened and Sandra froze as she saw Kevin for the first time in months. Their eyes locked and they stared at each other. She could feel Tina holding her hand now as she carried on her look of disgust at him. Tracy now entered with her parents. This was the first time she'd seen them too. Her mother had written a few letters in the past, but that was only to tell her how ashamed she was of her.

Sandra's mother Anita was now seated with Tracy at the side of her, Tracy looked huge. Tina was giggling at the side of her. "Fuck me, who's ate all the pies or what? She looks like she's not stopped eating for nine months."

Sandra didn't reply and cast her look over to Tracy. Her sister looked edgy, she knew it was far from over with Sandra and she looked scared as she dipped her head to the floor. Tina was still going on, at the side of her. "Ay she won't be wearing them skimpy fucking knickers anymore will she? She'll need a fucking hammock to cover that fat arse now. Won't she?"

Sandra chuckled. "I know Tina, she doesn't look like herself does she?"

"Welcome to the real world Tracy," Sandra snarled as she shot a look over to her sister. Tina now started waving as Maxine entered the courtroom. The security guard at the side of her had to pull her back to her seat. She shrugged him off but obeyed his command.

"Maxine looks mint. She's really changed since she got with Zac. Orr I hope things work out for her" Tina whispered.

"Yeah me too" agreed Sandra. As the time passed James and her two sons came into the courtroom. Sandra broke down in tears when she saw them for the first time. They looked like grown men now. John looked ill and she wondered if that was the reason he'd not been to see her. She nodded her head to them both and the love of a mother for her sons could now be seen.

They were all told to stand now as the honourable Judge Cassidy came into the courtroom. Everyone kept their heads low until he was seated. His robes were quite colourful and the purple gown looked crisp and clean. The judge looked old. He was a fossil. He must have been at least in his seventies. Once he was seated he cast his eyes over to the dock to the two prisoners. Kevin was coughing loudly now and Sandra mumbled under her breath. "Choke you bastard." Once he'd controlled his coughing there was silence in the courtroom. Sandra kept looking at Kevin. Was this the man who'd she once loved? Because now all she felt in her heart was hate. She looked at him as if he was a piece of shit. He must have sensed her look because every now and then he was twisting his head to look at her. Each time he did turn his head she growled at him and he soon turned back around. He knew it was far from over with her.

Sandra knew he'd dropped the charges but she still hated him with a passion, she hated the fact that he must have been thinking she owed him a favour. He could rot in hell for all she cared. He would never get a drop of thanks from her, never in a million years.

Sandra's dad smiled at his daughter sitting in the dock. She knew he was ruled by her mother and his life wouldn't have been worth living if he'd gone against his wife. Sandra loved her dad. He was dressed in a white shirt and a black pair of pants. You could tell he didn't feel comfortable dressed the way he was and she knew her mother was behind his outfit. The usher now sat down and gave a look to the public gallery. She placed a finger up towards her mouth and urged them to be quiet.

Judge Cassidy now told the usher to bring the jury in. As they walked into the courtroom they gazed at the two women. There was a mixture of ages in the jury between eighteen and fifty years old. There were seven men and five women. They all just looked like normal everyday people. One of the jury members was holding a notebook and pen and she could be seen writing something as soon as she sat down. The judge now asked if they were all sworn in and did they know any of the women stood in the dock. Once they'd all told him "No" the judge asked Sandra and Tina to confirm their names and addresses.

Sandra was shaking from head to toe and the judge asked her to speak up as he was struggling to hear her. Sandra cleared her throat and spoke louder. Tina now confirmed who she was. Sandra's mother was now covering her mouth and whispering to her husband. "She looks ill doesn't she? She lost way to much weight don't you think?" Graham agreed and told her to be quiet. He was in no mood for her bitching today and told her point blank that it was a court case not a fucking fashion show.

The defendants were now told to be seated. Tina felt faint and at one point she lost her balance and nearly keeled over. This was it, their fate was here and by looking at the two women's faces they were scared to death of the outcome.

The prosecution began. As he started to speak he looked over at Kevin and told the judge that the victim had now dropped the charges but the police were still carrying them on. Kevin smiled over at Sandra looking for praise. She gritted her teeth and gave him a look that would have killed. The prosecution now read out the first statement that Kevin had given to the police. His voice was loud as he spoke and his gaze kept flickering from the judge to the jury constantly. After the statement was read out he now turned to the jury and held one hand on his hip as he paced the courtroom floor.

"Sandra Partington is a danger to any man who crosses her. She planned what she was doing and with the help of her friend Tina Dixon they both nearly killed her husband." Gasping and sighing could be heard in the courtroom. The usher looked at the spectators and gave them the look that meant be quiet. As he read the list of things that Sandra had done to her husband he paused between each sentence. "Mrs Partington placed

Immac hair removal cream into her husband's shampoo and caused him to lose a large amount of his hair." One women in the jury looked like she was struggling to stop laughing, as was the woman and man sat next to her. He continued. "Mr Partington was oblivious to his wife's acts and just thought he was losing hair because of the stress he was under. He even thought about seeking medical help about this ailment." The judge looked at Sandra and Tina and was seen writing. The prosecution continued. "Sandra wasn't happy with her husband losing his hair, oh no." His voice was now even louder than before and somewhat aggressive. "She wanted to hurt him badly and continued to put weight gain powder into his milkshakes." Now there was giggling from the public gallery and the judge looked over to them and warned them that if there was any more noise he would have them removed from the courtroom.

The prosecution continued. "Mr Partington gained a severe amount of weight over the months that passed. Before this he was a regular member at the gym and took pride in the way he looked." Sandra whispered to Tina. "Yeah we all know why, don't we. The fucking cheating bastard had to look good for his dirty slags." Sandra sat forward in her chair and you could tell she was struggling to keep her mouth shut. The prosecution now held Sandra's diary up to the jury.

"Sandra Partington logged everything she did to her husband inside this journal she kept. The acts she carried out on her husband are endless." The judge asked if the jury all had copies of the entries in the diary. The usher now confirmed they did. As the prosecution wound up his evidence on Sandra he now started to speak about Tina's part in Kevin's downfall. As he told the courtroom about the charges Tina faced there was silence and you could have heard a pin drop.

Tina's chest could be seen expanding in and out at a rapid pace. She breathed heavily to calm herself down. "I'm fucked aren't I?" she whispered to Sandra.

Sandra gripped her hand and squeezed it. "Just think positive love. We haven't spoken yet. This is just all their evidence. It always seems bad at first." They both sat looking like they were waiting for the death sentence. Sandra couldn't keep still and she was fidgeting all the time.

Sandra's barrister now took control. He read out all about Sandra and the life she'd led in the past. He made her sound weak and a pill away from a breakdown. The first witness was called.

Maxine was now sworn in. She repeated the words the court member told her to say and looked directly at the judge as she repeated them. Maxine was dressed to impress. She wore a black pants suit with a light pink shirt underneath. Her hair was tied back in a neat plait. The barrister now asked her some questions.

"Can you tell me how long you have known Sandra Partington?"

Maxine sounded confident and you could tell she was talking in her best voice. "I've known Sandra for many years. She is a good friend and a lovely woman."

The barrister continued. "Can you tell me what you know about her relationship with her husband Kevin?"

Maxine looked directly over at Kevin who was now sat slumped into his chair. He looked embarrassed and hated that his life was being discussed. "Where do I start?" Maxine said in a sarcastic manner. "He's always been a womaniser. He treated his wife like a piece of dirt and it's common knowledge that he beat her up regularly. I mean, I've seen her with more than one black eye in the past." Kevin stood up and walked from the courtroom. He could feel everyone's eyes on him. He felt like a coward. Tracy was trying to pull him back down by his coat but he let her know there was no way he was staying inside the courtroom. Maxine continued. She knew she was doing well and seeing Kevin leaving the courtroom was just what she wanted. Now she could go to town on his name.

"Sandra was always a confident person. As soon as she met Kevin he seemed to suck all the life out of her. She lost all confidence, and wasn't the same person I knew before. Many a time I've seen bruises on her body" she rubbed her arms as she continued. "And she has even told me that he was the one responsible for the marks. He's led her a dog's life. He treats her like she's his own personal slave. He's possessive and a control freak."

The barrister seemed pleased at her evidence. He read from his notes and kept her standing for a moment longer. Walking round towards her he tilted his glasses onto the end of his nose. "Is Sandra a violent person?"

"Definitely not. She's the most laid back person I know" Maxine ranted.

The barrister continued. "Does Kevin have other women in his life?"

Maxine went for gold now holding nothing back. She mentioned a few names and looked over to Tracy. "Kevin even slept with his own sister in law. The cheap whore she is." The barrister apologised to the court for Maxine's foul mouth and finished his interrogation. Now it was the prosecution's turn to cross- examine her.

"Maxine would you say, you are a trustworthy

person."

She swayed about in the dock and hesitated. "Yeah I would." He continued.

"So is shoplifting something an honest person would do and supplying drugs." Her head was all over the place. The barrister had told her to expect this from the prosecution and she now stood her ground.

"Listen I'm not the one on trial here. I'm here because my friend has been shit on all of her life and suffered more than anyone will ever know. So deal with that issue and not my past." She was crumbling. The barrister knew he had to get her out from the witness box as quick as possible. He could see her dragging at her clothes and looking like she was about to give him a piece of her mind. He objected to the courtroom. The prosecution stopped just in time and Maxine was told to leave the stand. As she left she looked over to Sandra and Tina and raised her eyes to the roof. Tina nodded back at her. As she sat back in her place you could see her red faced talking to Zac.

Jenny was now called to give her evidence. She'd interviewed lots of people from the Monsall estate where Sandra lived. She had passed all the signed statements to the barrister. Now he was asking her questions. Jenny told him about the life Sandra had led. She told the courtroom about the screams from her house that had been reported in the late hours and how one neighbour had seen her estranged husband Kevin dragging Sandra up the path by her hair one late night. Jenny had done well in giving her evidence. Sandra could see the jury members shaking their heads as they looked at her. She felt like she had them onside. The barrister now read out the statements from her two sons. As he started reading Kevin re-entered the courtroom. He kept his eyes to the floor as he made his way to his seat.

The barrister held his hand towards his heart as he read the statements from Paul and John. You could see he was deeply touched by what they had said. His voice was low and the emotion from the letter was held in his voice. It was Paul's letter who caused a few people in the courtroom to cry. He'd told them that his mother was his world and his rock. She was also a devoted mother and a caring kind loving parent. Paul had told the barrister that he'd heard the violence between his parents on many a night and struggled to sleep because of it. All he wanted was his mother to be home where she belonged. One woman was now sobbing her heart out and the usher passed her a box of tissues. The courtroom was touched by both her sons' testimonies. Now it was Sandra's turn to take the stand. The Group Four guards now led her to the dock. He knew she wasn't likely to escape and stood at her side with ease.

Sandra looked like a nervous wreck. Her lips were trembling and they looked a dark blue colour. She could feel the eyes of the courtroom on her. She turned her head to her parents and gave a half-hearted smile. Her father smiled back at her but her mother sat stone-faced looking straight through her.

"Old hag" she muttered under her breath. Sandra's clothes hung from her frail body frame. She was easily a size twelve now. Her face looked drawn and her cheekbones stood from her face like a supermodels.

Everyone's eyes in the courtroom were now fixed on Sandra. Kevin had settled back in to his seat and stared at his wife. He could be seen sighing as she told the courtroom her full name. "Sandra Jane Marie Partington" she told them in a distressed voice. She looked cold as she folded her grey cardigan around her body.

Her barrister now began. "Sandra can you tell me more about your marriage to Kevin?" Everyone was hanging on her every word. People hung over from the public gallery to get a better look at her. She paused and looked over at Kevin. You could see the hate in her eyes as she began.

"My marriage has been a sham from day one. He never really loved me if the truth was known. He just married me because I was pregnant; I suppose I have always known that from the start."

The barrister stepped in with another question. "If you knew he didn't love you, why did you stay?"

Sandra huffed and her lips quivered as her warm breath passed through them. "I just always thought he would change. I had two children with him and I wanted to be a family." Sandra's mother was shaking her head as she looked over to her. Sandra could see the look of disgust written all over her face.

"Was he violent towards you or your children?" he asked her with a firm voice.

Kevin's eyes glared at her now and that was the sign for her to turn the tears on. "Yeah from day one he treated me like a skivvy. I was more his slave than a wife." She looked at Kevin directly and started to cry. "He's used me as a punch-bag for years. If anything in his life went wrong, I would always cop for it." Tissues were passed to Sandra and she got the message over to the court members that Kevin was an out and out bastard. When she'd finished giving her evidence the prosecution were next to try and rip her apart. Sandra held her own with the barrister but several times through her interrogation she lost it and started shouting. This was a woman suffering from domestic violence and everyone knew in the courtroom her emotions were no act.

Tracy screwed her face up at Sandra. She whispered to her mother at the side of her. "Fuck off she's lying mam. I mean, you know Kevin isn't like that. He's so laid back, it's fucking her, the stress head. I hope she get what she deserves the lying cunt."

Anita looked at her daughter. She'd never heard all the allegations before. She looked at her husband. "Do you think all that's true what she's saying or what?"

Her husband looked at her with a sarcastic face. "Well our Sandra's no liar, what does she have to tell lies for? He's hit her alright. Just look at the coward sat there fronting it all, as if he's the victim. I'll tell you what Anita, if our Sandra gets sent down today he's getting a piece of my mind." Anita calmed him down and told him to be quiet. They all watched Sandra leave the dock. Her head was held low and as she passed James she gave a half-hearted smile.

The court adjourned for dinner and everyone was told to come back before two o'clock. They all stood as the judge left. Noise filled the courtroom now and Sandra and Tina were taken back to the holding cells. Kevin stood up and waited for James to walk at the side of him. He'd read all about him in his wife's diary. "Fucking lover boy" he muttered as James was now at his side. Kevin made sure Sandra's family was out of the way. Tracy was moaning at her mother and you could see she wasn't happy with everything that was going on inside the courtroom. He saw his chance and grabbed James's arm pulling him to the side of the stairs. "Oi, can I have a word?" James looked at him.

James knew who he was and made no secret that he wasn't afraid of him. "Yeah, what do you want?"

Kevin now waited for a few people to clear from the area. Once they were gone he stood in front of James and placed his hand in front of him on the wall. James felt intimidated and quickly pushed his hands out of the way. "Shift your hands away from me alright."

Kevin looked shocked. He must have thought James was an easy target, he back-pedalled.

"No worries, I just want a word that's all." James's nostrils flared. His chest looked firm and you could see his fist clenching at the side of him. He was ready for whatever this prick had to throw at him. "So you're Sandra's new fella?"

James nodded his head. "And?"

Kevin kicked his foot at the ground. "Well I'm Kevin her husband. Surely she must have mentioned me?"

James dipped his head to Kevin's face, he spoke directly to him. "No she hasn't spoken about you, you're her past mate. Why would she want to waste time chatting shit about you?" Kevin hated that he wasn't in control. He thought he was going to bully James but by the looks of it all, he was the one who looked more afraid. James now started to walk away from him. As he passed him he spoke in a cocky tone. "Sandra's with me now, I can look after her and treat her how she should have been treated. Abuse it and lose it remember." With that James was gone.

Kevin stood looking lost. It was real, Sandra was gone out of his life and he looked sad. Shaking his head he walked to meet the others. As he walked up to Tracy he sighed. He knew he'd made a big mistake by losing Sandra and he wanted her back in his life. Was it too late and was she gone forever with her new lover boy James? He stood with Tracy. Anita and Graham were stood looking at him. He could see the evil look his ex father in law was giving him.

At last Tracy piped up. "Where the fuck have you been?"

Kevin struggled to answer. "I just went for a piss. Why what's the problem?" she huffed and linked his arm.

"I don't want to stay here all day; I've listened to enough bullshit, we don't have to stay do we? Let's fuck off and go and get something to eat at Nando's, I'm starving." He couldn't tell her he wanted to stay throughout the trial and the look on his face told everyone he was struggling to give into her. Graham could read him like a book and stepped in.

"Yeah she's right. No need for you to stay son. You can go home." Kevin sucked his bottom lips. His eyes met Graham's. He wanted to tell him to fuck off but he could see he was in a no win situation and agreed with a low tone.

"Yeah all right, let's do one Tracy." Anita and Graham watched them leave arm in arm. She looked at her husband and suggested they went for a coffee.

Maxine and Zac sat in a nearby Cafe. As Sandra's parents walked in Maxine mumbled under her breath as she clocked them both. "Fucking hell here she is the old battle axe." Zac turned his head and smiled. Maxine lost the plot straight away and stood up to go and speak to Anita. She hadn't spoken to her for months and wanted to set the record straight. Graham was ordering their drinks and Anita was seated at the other side of the room. Maxine slumped down beside her in the leather armchair. Anita's face was on fire and her temper was about to explode. Maxine stopped her dead in her tracks and spoke first.

"Anita I know I haven't been to see you about all this mess, but come on, you're not the easiest of people to speak to are you?" Anita's eyes searched for Graham, she needed his back-up. Maxine continued. "Listen all I want to say is that Sandra has put up with a lot, you don't know the half of it, Tracy is a little tart and I don't know how you can just accept, that Kevin has moved from one daughter to another."

Anita held her hand up in front of Maxine's face with a flat palm. "You cheeky cow. I don't just accept it at all; I can't help it if Kevin loves Tracy."

Maxine moved her arse on the chair and looked like she was getting up to leave. "She's your daughter too you know, perhaps if you could see the wood through the trees you would see who the wrong one is. Sandra needs you, all her life it's been Tracy this and Tracy that, it's time to see her for what she really is."

Anita wasn't listening and shook her head; she was now speaking over Maxine. "Piss off back over there. You don't know what you are talking about woman." Maxine stood and hovered for a minute. Seeing Graham coming towards her with two drinks she turned to leave. She paused.

"Like I said, Tracy is the wrong one. Be a mother and step up to the mark." Anita didn't reply. Maxine left and smiled at Graham as she passed him to go back to her seat. Anita looked deflated and she was pulling at her jumper round her neck. Graham asked her what Maxine wanted, but she just changed the conversation and spoke about Tracy and the baby.

Sandra sat in the cells. She could hear crying in the next pad. Apparently the woman had just been sentenced to seven years. Sandra stared at the floor. Holding her head in her hands she felt weak. Tina was the next to hit the stand and her heart told her it wasn't looking good for her best friend. The trial was set for three days and Sandra didn't know if her heart would stand all the stress. Her fate sat with the jury members. She just hoped she'd done enough to become a free woman again.

19

Today was the day when Sandra and Tina would learn their fate. The last few days had been hard on them both and it showed across their faces. Sleep had been a million miles away for them both and they looked tired. Dark circles were present under their eyes and they seemed to have aged in the last few days. Tina knew her case wasn't looking good. After all, she'd drugged and kidnapped somebody, so she had to expect some kind of custodial sentence.

The Group Four guards led them both up to the courtroom for sentencing. Some other prisoners were wishing them well as they passed; Tina couldn't raise a smile and ignored them completely. The door opened to the dock and both women were led inside. Tina looked edgy. She couldn't keep still and she was constantly chewing her nails.

The spectators eyes were all glued to the women. They watched their every movement. One woman shouted to them both. "Good luck girls. We're all here behind you." The Usher seated the spectator straight away and warned her to be quiet.

The press gallery was packed. Notepads at the ready, they were waiting on an exclusive story for the papers. This trial was something the entire nation was talking about. Jenny was sat up straight and she could be seen crossing her fingers together and holding them up to the girls.

"Could the courtroom please rise", the usher spoke in a stern voice. Judge Cassidy now entered the courtroom. Once he was seated everybody else did as well.

Tina was whispering to Sandra. "Orr I hope his wife sucked him off last night or something, perhaps then he might be more lenient with us, if he's in a good mood."

Sandra giggled. "Will you fuck off making me laugh? My arse is twitching, I think I'm gonna shit my knickers."

Tina held her hand and spoke with a low tone. "No matter what happens" she held her tears back as she looked at her. "You're my best friend and I know you won't sell me out."

Sandra choked. "That goes without saying love. If I get out of here I'll make sure I look after you, I promise." The judge lifted his head up from his notes and asked for Tina to be removed from the courtroom.

Tina turned her head from side to side. "What the fucks up?" she asked the security guard. He told her that she would be sentenced on her own. Her face dropped. This wasn't good. She quickly kissed Sandra on the cheek and wished her luck. She now left the dock. Whispering could be heard throughout the courtroom. The jury members were all sat inside the courtroom now. They'd taken all afternoon to come to a decision. This was a nail biting moment for everyone.

The judge now asked the spokesman for the jury if they had come to a decision about Sandra. A middle-aged man now stood up. He was dressed in a grey suit and looked very smart. Sandra was clenching her fists. She looked white as a ghost. The member of the jury now spoke. "Yes we have your honour." The courtroom was on edge. A pin could have been heard dropping. Women huddled together and one woman hid her face in her friend's shoulder. The suspense was too much to cope with.

The judge read out the charges and asked what the verdict was. The man looked at his paper in front of him and cleared his throat before he replied.

"Not guilty"

Sandra looked about the courtroom. Did she hear him right? Her head was turning rapidly. Jenny shook her hands above her head. That was one of the charges out of the way. Now the charge of her injuring her husband's manhood was read out. The judge asked if they had come to a verdict. The spokesman looked nervous. The paper was shaking slightly in his grip.

"Guilty" he answered.

The noise in the courtroom was out of control and one woman was told to leave the public gallery. Her anger was there for everyone to see. She was removed from the courtroom still shouting. The usher spoke to the spectators and told them that quiet must be maintained, otherwise they would all have to leave. Sandra fell back onto her chair. She looked as if she was going to faint and the guard used his radio for help to get her a drink of water. The judge adjourned for half an hour and told Sandra he would sentence her when they came back after the break. She was led from the dock back to the holding cell.

Once the judge had left, Maxine was bouncing about the courtroom. "It's a fucking liberty. The man beats the living shit out of her every other night and she's suppose to do nothing. The law in the country is shite."

Zac calmed her down. "Come on Maxine she might not get slammed yet, there are other options you know." She wasn't listening and continued ranting.

"Who the fuck do they think they are playing around with people's life's. They know fuck all about the real world these fuckers."

Anita sat sneering at her, Maxine could feel her eyes burning into her and looked directly at her. Their eyes clashed and at one point it looked like Sandra's mother was going to launch at her. Graham smiled gently at Maxine. He knew she was talking sense, but to side with her was more than his life was worth. Anita was a stubborn bitch and for years he knew it was her way or the highway.

Jenny was now talking to the supporters. After all, she was a journalist and needed a big story for the national newspaper. Her hand was moving quickly as she wrote everything down that was going on. Kerry from Women's Aid, was right in her face now. "See what I mean, Domestic violence means nothing to anyone. When is someone going to start listening and start helping these women?"

Jenny looked up from her notebook. "I know Kerry; I don't think people really understand what goes on behind closed doors. Anyway, that's why I'm here to help get the message out." Kerry stomped off and started talking to the other women who were stood nearby. As she watched Kerry talking, she could see a scar across the side of one woman's face. Being nosey she closed her writing pad and joined them. Jenny stood listening. The woman with the scar on her face was quiet. Jenny just knew she had a story to tell and made her way to the side of her.

Kerry was still furious telling everybody they must do more to end this reign of terror on women. Jenny smiled at the woman; she was about fifty and looked like she'd been through the mill. Her eyes looked sad and the lines across her face told Jenny this woman had seen some hard times.

"Hello love," Jenny said with a smile on her face. The woman smiled softly and said hello back to her. "Are you a friend of Sandra's honey? I've been covering her case and trying my best to help her."

The woman shook her head slowly. Her words were low and full of sorrow. "I hope someone does help her, I wouldn't look like this if someone would have helped me."

Jenny was like a dog with a bone now. "Why, what's up with the way you look?" Jenny looked at her up and down and knew the woman was right. Her clothes hung from her scrawny body and she looked like every drop of life had been sucked out of her. "You look great," Jenny lied.

"Are you having a laugh love? I have eyes you know. She giggled. "When I look in the mirror each day I see what that husband of mine did to me and I hate myself for letting it happen."

Jenny placed her arm on the woman's shoulder. Her voice was sympathetic towards her. "Why what happened to you?"

The woman was a bit cagey at first and pulled her arm to bring her closer. "My husband did this to my face; don't tell me you can't see the scar." Jenny cast her eyes to her right cheek. There it was in full view.

She looked closer, "Bloody hell sweetheart, why did he do that?"

The woman shook her head and held it back as she sighed. "Phew I wish I knew, he was pissed as usual and just sliced my face with a Stanley knife. He said I deserved it for making his life a misery." The woman softly touched her cheek; her fingers seem to be soothing her scar. Her face now turned to Jenny. "That's life isn't it love, I should be glad to still be alive shouldn't I?"

Jenny looked startled. The lives of all these women she'd met lately were really making her feel sick. Each of them had a story to tell and each incident was as bad as the next. Jenny whispered to the woman. She was lost for words at her ordeal and struggled to speak. "Carpe Diem sweetheart. You're a survivor. Don't ever forget that."

The woman quickly slid her black scruffy shoe from her foot. "Look I spent my job-seekers allowance on it. I've not got a pot to piss in but I wanted to be part of something."

Jenny gazed at her the foot. She chuckled. There it was in small writing on the side of her foot. 'Carpe Diem' it read. The woman now said goodbye and joined Kerry who was still putting the world to rights. Jenny left the courtroom, she needed a cig. This was all getting too much for her. Whatever happened to her normal life, she mumbled as she left the woman's side?

Sandra sat inside her cell yet again. She could hear Tina shouting. "What's going on Sandra? Did you get slammed or what?"

Cupping her two hands up to her mouth she shouted back, "I've got to back in a bit for sentencing. I got a guilty verdict." Sandra listened for her to reply but it never came. Tapping her fingers on her knees she rested her head on the cold wall. Gliding her fingers over the painted grey brickwork she looked as if she was trying to contact the dead, as her eyes were firmly closed, concentrating.

Prison life had taken its toll on her and she dreaded

returning back to serve her sentence. Sandra was questioning her own strength. She looked like she was having a panic attack. She paced the floor and dragged at her hair. Dropping to the ground she started blowing her breath rapidly from her mouth. Small droplets of sweat were visible on her forehead. "Please God; please don't let me go back to prison, I'm not strong enough, Please help me." Sandra was a Catholic girl and had gone to church regularly as a child. Since being an adult she'd lost all her faith and stopped going to church. Her words to her mother in the past were "God has given up on me so what's the point." She needed help now and the only person who could help her was the big man in the sky. She crossed herself, she was shaking. Wrapping her arms closely around her she squeezed herself tightly. Her fate was minutes away.

The judge re-entered the courtroom. The usher had already warned the people in the public gallery that if there was one squeak out of them they would be out of the courtroom in an instant. Judge Cassidy sat. Sandra was a mess. Her father looked over at her and mouthed "I love you, you'll be fine." Anita didn't see him and he looked like he was going to cry. The members of the court now prepared themselves for sentencing. You could hear the prosecution taking bets on how long she would get. They didn't care about her one little bit. It was someone's life they were talking about not a horse race and if anyone would have heard them they would have been in big trouble. The judge twisted his pen in his fingers. No one could see his movements as his hands were out of sight. He was nervous. He was aware of how much publicity this case had had and he didn't want to let anyone down. Judge Cassidy had taken a long time to find the right sentence for Sandra and her crimes. The defendant was now asked to stand before the court.

"Sandra Partington," he began, "taking into account that your husband has withdrawn his statement…" Everyone was on the edge of their seats and Maxine was chewing her fingernails as if her life depended on it. The judge continued. His voice was firm. "…I have decided to sentence you two year's suspended sentence, forty hours community service and an anger management placement order." Sandra heard the two years but didn't understand what it meant. Maxine was smiling over at her. Sandra looked confused as she held her hands up at the side of her face. The judge now explained his sentence so she fully understood. "This means if you break the law at any time during the next two years you will be recalled to serve two years in prison plus whatever you get sentenced for the crime you have committed." Sandra looked relieved as he continued. "The anger management course will help you control the temper you have developed and make you think of the consequences you will face, if you carry out any more of these ridiculous acts." Sandra stood, taking in all the information she been was given. She was a free woman. The Group Four guards escorted her from the dock back to the holding cells. As she left the courtroom she punched her tightly squeezed fist in the air. "Get in there" she mumbled.

The atmosphere in the courtroom was electric. The onlookers were all smiling and loved that Sandra was now a free woman.

A short time later Tina entered the dock and the room fell silent again. Tina wafted her hand in front of her face. Her cheeks looked on fire. She'd pleaded guilty to her role in the kidnap and the drugging of Tracy. They had too much evidence on her and her solicitor had told her point blank that if she pleaded guilty she would get a third knocked off her sentence. Tracy sat down and waited for the judge to return. Twisting her hair about in her fingers she looked as if she was going to break.

The judge now returned. The look on his face gave her little hope. He looked pissed off and in a bad mood. Reading from his notes he reviewed the case history and reminded Tina what she was being sentenced for. As he told her to stand up her legs buckled and she had to use the chair at the side of her to help her to her feet. Everything just went so quickly and when he told her she was being sentenced to three years and eight months in prison she collapsed. The guard looked flustered as he tried to revive her.

The women in the courtroom were gasping for air. Once they'd brought Tina back around she sat sipping a cold drink of water as the judge continued speaking to her. Her face now boiled with temper. After all she had nothing to lose now because the grumpy bastard had already sentenced her. She threw her plastic cup to the floor and stood up with her face squashed up against the glass. Everyone watched as she opened fire. "You miserable twat, what's up, didn't you get a leg over last night you grumpy wrinkled fucker!" Giggles could be heard from the spectators in the public gallery. Maxine knew her friend had a temper and cringed as she listened to her continue as they dragged her out of the courtroom. "You know fuck all about the laws of life; you're up your own arse, never wanted for owt in your life I bet, well fuck you and fuck your sentence I'll do it on my head." The dock was now empty. All the members of the public started to leave. They were all talking amongst themselves.

James thanked Jenny and hugged her, she told him where to go to meet Sandra. With a spring in his step he ran all the way to meet her.

Anita left the courtroom with an angry face with Graham following closely behind her. He was over the moon his daughter was free and knew Anita was upset that she didn't get a custodial sentence. She was a bitch and he hated the woman she'd become. For years she'd abused his love and always spoke to him as if he wasn't good enough for her. They'd had their problems in the past but for some reason he always stood by her no matter how much shit she gave him.

Tina was kicking and screaming as they launched her into the cell. "Take your fucking hands off me. You fucking dirty pervert, what is it ay? Do you want a quick feel of a real woman?" The door was slammed behind her. Banging her clenched fist on the steel door she shouted abuse at the male guard. "Bet your wife is at home taking it up the arse from your neighbour. I don't blame her seeking a real man because all you lot are fucking dinner mashers, you gay fuckers!" She screamed. With one last hard kick on the door she walked to the back wall. She sank to the floor like butter melting onto toast. Her body was rocking and she gripped her arms tightly around her arms. She was devastated. Tears now rolled down her face. "Mam help me please. I can't do this "she sobbed.

The cell smelt of misery. It smelt like a room where a dead person lay. Tina had died inside and the look of distress was written all over her face. Looking about the room she hoped to find something that would help her kill herself. She couldn't go back to prison, she just couldn't take it anymore. Tina bit hard onto her skin and drew blood. Wiping the blood all over her face she hoped she would convince the guards she wasn't of sound mind. Within minutes she'd bitten all over her body and smeared the bright red blood all over her skin. Tina now lay sprawled across the floor. She stared at the ceiling and wished she was dead.

★

James kicked his foot at the floor as he waited at the exit where Sandra would come from. He was now joined by all the women who were supporting Sandra and Tina. The press were there too and he could see them taking photographs of him. The flash from the camera was hurting his eyes and his hand was now up to his face guarding his eyes from the flashing lights.

The door opened and the cheers from the crowd could be heard. Everyone was pushing past James to get next to Sandra. The TV crews now shoved microphones in her face. They seemed to come from nowhere and before long five or six microphones were sticking near her mouth.

"How does it feel to be a free woman Sandra?" The questions were like bullets being fired at her. Her mouth felt dry and she was pushing the TV presenters out of the way. They weren't giving up for love nor money.

Finally she snapped, "Right, right calm down will you, what do you want to know?"

A voice was heard from a reporter at the side of her and a woman spoke. "Sandra, do you now feel like you represent all these women who've suffered violence from abusive partners?"

Sandra grinned. She gave a gasping breath and continued. "I don't think I represent them I think I've helped them to recognise that they don't have to take crap from men anymore."

The reporter continued. "What about all these women who have had 'Carpe Diem' tattooed on their feet. Surely they are all part of your group now?"

Jenny was at Sandra's side now. She dealt with the reporters and spoke on her behalf. "This lady has just been released from prison. Please give her some space." She now held Sandra's arm and led her to her car.

The reporters were taking loads of photos and Sandra chuckled, "They're all fucking up it."

James sat in the back of the car with Sandra. He smiled at her and held her hand in his tight grip. She felt safe. Her head was spinning and she looked confused. Jenny pulled off at speed and left the reporters still stood at the roadside. "We'll have to wait for Tina" Sandra shouted with a frantic voice. She placed her hands on the back of Jenny's seat.

Jenny stared at her through the rear view mirror as James took over. He gripped her waist and sat her back in her seat. "She got time love, she's not coming home."

Sandra screamed out like a wounded animal. "What do you mean? How long did she get?"

"Three and a half years love." James said as he tried to calm her.

Sandra shook her head. Her tears were genuine and you could see the news had devastated her. "She won't be able to do it on her own, she needs me. I can't just leave her, she's my best friend." Her shoulders were shaking now. Her head banged against the car window as James tried to console her. Jenny now asked where they were heading to.

Sandra spoke with a low voice. "Kevin's letting me stay at the house. Apparently he's moved into a new place with Tracy." Quietness filled the car; Jenny continued driving and knew the days ahead were going to be hard for Sandra.

Pulling up at her home Jenny could see more reporters. She sighed. "For crying out loud why don't they just back off?"

Jenny now smiled at James, "I can see now how I treat people when I'm on a story, you just don't think they need a bit of time alone do you?" James agreed. They all got out of the car. Jenny threw her jacket over Sandra's head. She led her by the arm to the front of the house. Sandra's neighbours were out in full force and some of them were shouting at Sandra.

"Get in there love. You showed them that we won't take any shit anymore!" Sandra tried to smile underneath the jacket but her heart was broken. They made their way inside the house.

Sandra looked strange. She looked lost. She froze for a minute before she went any further into the house. James was by her side and offered to make a drink of tea. Sandra just nodded. Walking slowly to the front room she could see her two sons sat there waiting for her. They both stood up and ran at her throwing their arms tightly around her body. Paul was crying as he squeezed his mother. "Mam I'm so glad you're home. Things have been shit without you."

John looked upset. His hands were shaking. His lips trembled as he spoke. "I love you mam. Please just let's get back to normal. I can't take anymore of this shit." Sandra dug her head between her two sons. They all shared a special moment and Jenny stood crying at the doorway watching the emotions between them all. James now came to join them and asked everyone what drink they wanted. John looked at him and scowled. He'd heard from his dad that his mother had a new boyfriend but he still looked at him with hate in his eyes. Sandra could see her boys looking at James and knew it was time to introduce him.

"Lads, this is James. He's helped me all the way through this nightmare and I would be glad if you would show him the respect that he deserves." Paul backed down and hugged him and thanked him for his help. John was more laidback and just nodded at him. He didn't trust anyone anymore and he whispered to his brother that they would have to watch him in the future.

They all sat chatting and Jenny got her exclusive interview with Sandra and her family. Jenny now stood to her feet and hugged Sandra. "You're an inspiration, you are Sandra and I wish you all the luck in the world, I'll keep in touch with you don't worry but I'm going to leave you for a few weeks to find your feet."

Sandra squeezed her. "You don't have to wait love, you come here whenever you want, I owe you a lot and without you, I would have rotted in jail for years." Jenny smiled and said goodbye to everyone. The sound of the front door could be heard closing.

Four people now sat in the front room. James looked uncomfortable. He fidgeted inside his pocket. "Sandra I'm going to get off now. You have so much to come to terms with and I know you want to spend some time with your lads." Sandra nodded he was right. Walking him to the door they shared a long passionate kiss, James told her he would be back in touch and he left.

John was now pacing the front room. Sandra dropped to the chair she just couldn't believe she was free. Her home looked so different to her and she kept letting out gasping breaths. The time that had passed was now discussed. Paul told his mother about John's addiction. John sat staring at the floor and felt ashamed. Sandra couldn't believe she was never told of any of this and jumped to John's side. "Oh son. Why would you go and do that?"

He snivelled and months of emotion broke free. "Mam I just got mixed up in it all. My dad asked me to sell it and I just thought I would see what it was like. I hate myself for doing it, I'm clean now though mam, honest." John sat with his hands crossing his heart. "I swear to God mam, I'll never touch it again." Tears fell from his eyes and he sobbed. Paul joined them and they all shared a special moment. Their mother was home now and that was all that mattered.

Sandra trudged up the stairs to her bedroom. Throwing herself on the bed she sobbed her heart out. Tina was on her mind and she couldn't believe she wasn't by her side. Smelling the duvet cover she cringed. She could smell her husband's aftershave on it and jumped from the bed as if someone had poured boiling water on her. She dragged the cover from the bed and looked angry. She was now on a mission and opened the wardrobes in the bedroom. The cheeky bastard had left some of his clothes inside. She dragged them out from the wardrobe as if they were on fire. Within ten minutes she'd cleared the bedroom of any possessions Kevin owned.

Stood looking at the pile of clothes, a cunning smile filled Sandra's face. She gripped a large pile and ran downstairs towards the back garden. Throwing them onto the grass at the end of the garden she ran back upstairs to get the rest of them. Sandra sprayed hairspray all over the clothing. A neighbour popped her head over the fence and asked if she was okay. Sandra giggled to her and told her she was just getting rid of a few things she didn't need any more. The neighbour could see she was upset and told her she was coming over.

Anne had been her neighbour for years and knew the torment Sandra had suffered. When she came into the gate she was dressed in her pyjamas. In her hand she was carrying a half bottle of Vodka. Sandra smiled at her as she spoke. "Here get two glasses love. We'll have a drink, and then we can get rid of that shit." Her finger pointed to the clothes on the patch of grass nearby. Sandra left Anne alone for a minute and returned with two glasses. Pouring two large shots of Vodka they celebrated her freedom. The glasses clinked together and they both necked their drinks.

"Right let's get this job done," Sandra huffed. Anne watched as Sandra sprayed more hair spray on the clothing. She now stood with her body held back as she flicked her yellow lighter at the pile of clothes. They were on fire. They burnt quickly and shrivelled up within seconds. Sandra stared at the yellow flames and turned to Anne. "I feel better now. I want every trace of that cunt gone from my life." Anne was by her side and offered her a cig. She dragged two garden chairs from the side of the house and both of them sat watching the flames eat at her husband's clothes. The Vodka kept coming and both of them were pissed as farts as the night went on.

Anne smiled as she gripped her hand. "You're gonna get through this you know. You're strong and you're a survivor."

Sandra nodded as she watched the dying flames. "I know love, I know," she mumbled.

★

20

Sandra was a true friend to Tina. Maxine also made sure she played her part too and sent a postal order to her friend as often as she could. Sandra wrote her endless letters and told her that she would be free soon and to think positive. Tina had had a few bad months in Styal prison to start with but as time was going by she seemed to be coping.

Sandra had heard about Tina self harming and told her straight that she needed to stop. Penny, another inmate, was now mentioned in all Tina's letters and Sandra had a feeling they were now lovers. She knew Penny from when she was in there before and it was quite obvious she fancied the pants off Tina.

Sandra was now back at work, her job as a nail technician was doing well. Lots of women wanted appointments with her and in a way she became an agony aunt for a lot of her customers. Kevin had not been near her and the last she'd heard from him was that him and Tracy were living together in New Moston somewhere.

Anita sat in her front room, she was such a moaning fucker and it was a wonder Graham hadn't strangled her over the years. As they sat watching a film, Graham seemed to drinking his cans of lager at speed. He looked pissed, Anita sat moaning about the film again when Graham snapped, he stood from his chair and screamed out. He'd had enough, "Will you shut up fucking moaning woman? I'm sick to death of you, everyday it's the same, you're never happy."

Anita screwed her face up. This was so out of character for Graham and she fought back. "What the fuck is up with you. Who's rattled your cage?"

Graham walked to her chair where she sat. Anita looked scared. Bending his head down to hers he spoke into her face. "It's like history repeating itself isn't it?" she looked at him as if he's lost the plot.

"What the fuck are you going on about Graham?" He growled at her now, years of stored emotion now came to the surface.

"Tracy is just like her fucking mother. She nicked her sister's husband and got pregnant, just like you did with my brother."

Anita went white in the face; she fidgeted and tried to get up from her chair. Graham pushed her back down. "You stay right fucking there, you need to hear what I'm saying. For years I've held it in, but no fucking more." Anita held her hand up to her face, she didn't trust Graham. He was acting so strangely and he was frightening her. He carried on and his voice sounded menacing. "Tracy is my brother's child; you treat my child like she's shit. What is it? Do you see yourself in Tracy?"

Anita looked gobsmacked. "Graham you're pissed just go to bed will you?" He made his way back to his chair and sank back into it.

Reaching for his can of lager he slurped a large gulp. "Secrets ay. Don't you think it's time to tell Tracy that I'm not her real father? We can tell them both the real story about their mother's sordid past can't we?"

Anita went to stand up but he threw his empty can at her. "Sit fucking back down." Anita slowly sank back into her chair. She was white with fear. She watched him light a cig and he just sat looking at her with disgust in his eyes.

"Why are you bringing this up now?" Anita piped up, "It's years ago and you forgave me didn't you?"

His eyes danced with madness. "I forgave you yes, but I've never forgot. You treat Sandra like she's not good enough. Just like the way you've treated me over the years." Anita tried to answer back but he stopped her dead in her track. "You had an affair with my brother, and then came back to me when the shit hit the fan. I should have kicked your sorry arse to the kerb there and then shouldn't I?" Anita looked devastated. She'd always been in control of their relationship and she knew she'd pushed Graham too far this time.

"Sandra is my child too. I don't treat her differently at all," she protested unconvincingly.

Graham laughed aloud. "Are you having a fucking laugh or what woman? It's Tracy this, Tracy that, she's a dirty little slag but you treat her like a princess. What is it? Do you see our John in her or what?"

She snivelled. "No do I fuck, you daft bastard. Why are you saying that? You're pissed, I'm going to bed, I'm not listening to your shit anymore." Anita moved her hair from her eyes as she stood up to leave. Graham stood too.

"You don't have to listen to my shit love. You go to bed and hide away from the truth. Things are going to change in this house and from now on if you don't sort your attitude out I'm fucking off and leaving your sorry arse to fend for itself. I should have done it years ago." Anita huffed and walked from the living room. As he heard her going up the stairs he shouted. "It's about time people knew the truth about you anyway. Tomorrow I'm going to let your precious daughters know just what kind of a mother they really have."

Anita ran back down the stairs, she was in his face now. "Why are you doing this Graham? Please think about this, I'm sorry for the way I've treated you. I'll change, I promise." She fell to her knees now and touched his legs. "Please Graham. I'll change. I'll go and see our Sandra tomorrow and put the record straight." Her tears fell now and Graham just carried on drinking his drink as he left her sobbing between his legs.

His face held a smirk across it. "No more the fool Anita," he muttered, "I'm me not my fucking brother. So from now on treat me with respect, otherwise I'm gone. Do you hear me?" Anita nodded her head as she looked into his eyes. Her reign of terror was now over.

★

Tracy lay in bed next to Kevin. She could hear his snoring and felt restless. The baby was kicking and keeping her awake. Grabbing her housecoat from the side she headed down stairs. As she stepped from the bed she held her lower stomach. She froze for a minute and blew from her mouth until the pain had passed. Regaining her balance she went to the toilet. They'd had a curry earlier that night and she thought that was the reason her guts were hurting. Stepping into the toilet the pain came again. This time it was a lot stronger and she held the wall as the pain surged through her body. Yanking her knickers down Tracy sat on the toilet. Her eyes focused on her knickers and she could see something that looked like jelly inside them. Scratching her head she smiled, "Fucking idiot" she mumbled under her breath. She'd had sex with Kevin earlier and she thought it was just his man muck in her underwear. Sticking her fingers into it she brought it up to her nose and smelt it. "Yeah it's definitely sperm." Her arse now exploded and she shit like a newborn baby. Her face looked hot and she had a red glow all over her face.

After about twenty minutes she wiped herself and headed downstairs. Sleep was a million miles away and she went into the kitchen to make herself a drink. Her finger pressed the switch for the kettle. As she stood preparing her brew the pain returned. Her body keeled over the kitchen side and this time she screamed with pain. "Kevin help!" she shouted. Her voice was low and she looked terrified. As the pain passed she walked back up the stairs slowly. Sitting on the side of the bed she shook Kevin's shoulders. "Kevin wake up. I think I'm in labour."

You could hear moaning from the body in the bed but he snuggled back into the covers and dragged them over his head. Tracy dragged the sheets from him. He was livid, "What the fuck are you doing you nobhead?"

Tracy's face told him something was wrong as she fell on the bed at the side of him. Another pain strangled her body and she rolled about onto the bed. "Kevin help me please." Rubbing at his eyes he looked at her in more detail. He'd seen this look before in his wife and knew she was in labour. Jumping up from the bed he switched his side lamp on. Tracy was still dealing with the pain and he sat on the side of the bed stroking her head. "You're fucking boiling" he whispered as he felt her forehead.

"Get me to hospital" she screamed into his face. Kevin searched for his phone. He couldn't drive her to the hospital, he was still pissed. He'd had at least eight cans of Stella earlier on. "Hello can I have an ambulance please. My girlfriend is having a baby." Throwing his phone onto the bed he helped Tracy to her feet. "Here, stand up and walk about for a bit. That's what Sandra used to do." She screamed into his face. "I don't give a flying fuck what Sandra did, I'm Tracy not fucking Sandra."

He snapped at her. She'd been a right moaning

fucker lately and he was finding it hard to still be in a relationship with her. He tried to calm her down. "I'm just saying, that's all you moody bitch. Carry on like this and you can go to the hospital on your fucking own." She didn't reply and doubled over as another labour pain took over her body. Tracy was screaming at full pelt and Kevin knew she was going to be a drama queen throughout her labour. "Phone my mam," she shrieked. Kevin sat on the bed. Checking his watch he knew Anita would be sleeping. Tracy screamed at him again, "What the fuck are you waiting for? Just fucking phone her." His face looked angry as he gritted his teeth. Pressing the buttons he dialled Anita's number, Kevin listened to the ringing tone, "There's no answer" he told her.

"Keep trying please, keep trying" she pleaded.

Anita lay in her bed as the phone rang at the side of her. Her eyes were swollen. The sidelight was still on at the side of her. Graham was fast asleep. Glancing at the small alarm clock at the side of her she could see it was nearly four o'clock in the morning. Lifting the receiver she spoke in a low voice she didn't want to wake her husband. He'd only just gone asleep. "Hello" she whispered. "It's Kevin, can you come round, Tracy is in labour" he didn't let Anita get a word in. "And to tell you the truth she's doing my fucking head in. She's crying out for you all the time. Can you come now? I've phoned an ambulance already so it might be best to meet us at the hospital"

Anita replied "Okay" and the phone line went dead. Usually she would have demanded that Graham should wake up and take her, but now things were different and she decided to go alone. Creeping out from the bedroom she collected her clothes from the small chair at the side of her bed. Anita finally saw her reflection in the bathroom mirror. She looked a mess. Swilling cold water over it she hoped the swelling under her eyes would go down. Grabbing a small white towel at the side of her she patted it on her face. Her tears were hard to fight away and she sat on the toilet for a while crying. Graham had told her straight and she knew he was right – her past was catching up with her.

At the hospital Tracy lay in the bed wriggling and screaming. The midwife had given her pain relief but she was still demanding more. Kevin covered his face as she screamed at the midwife. "Get me something to take away the pain you silly bitch, I need more pain relief you daft black twat."

The African nurse looked at her and let her have it back. "Don't you ever speak to me like that? You need to learn some respect lady." Kevin stared at the floor looking embarrassed, Tracy was still screaming. The nurse could now be seen filling a syringe with some clear liquid. She now told Tracy to roll on her side whilst she injected Pethadine into her body. As she rolled her long t-shirt up the nurse had a smug smile fixed onto her face. She dug the needle deep into Tracy's arse cheeks. Tracy was howling as the needle pierced her skin.

"How long does it take to work, because I can't take much more of this fucking pain?" The mid wife didn't reply, Tracy had pissed her right off and you could tell by her face that she was struggling to attend to her needs.

Anita now entered the medical room. Kevin looked at her with relief. "Fucking hell she's only having a baby there's no need for all them tears," he moaned.

Anita tried to crack a smile. She had to cover up her own torment. "She's still my baby and I feel her pain," Anita replied as she comforted her. He knew Tracy was

Anita's life and in her eyes Tracy could do no wrong. The midwife was now joined by another nurse. They both examined Tracy. The African nurse now spoke. "Right miss your cervix is open and you're ready to give birth. You're going to have to be brave." Tracy looked like a woman possessed; her eyes were rolling all over the show as she sucked on the thin white tube of gas and air. "Get this baby out of me you black cunt!"

The other nurse now stepped in. "If you continue this racial abuse you can give birth to this baby on your own. We don't have to take this kind of talk from you. Do you hear me?"

Tracy continued to scream with her legs wide apart on the bed. The midwives both stood at the bottom of the bed and encouraged her to push. "Right you need to listen to us. When we say push, you need to push with all your might." Anita was now relaying the message to her daughter as she sat by her side squeezing her hand. You could see where Tracy had already dug her nails into her mother's hand. There were red patches all over them. Kevin sat at the other side of Tracy, he looked bored. He'd seen all this before when his own son's were born and he couldn't stand the noises Tracy was making. She was like an actress; surely she couldn't be in that much pain.

Tracy yelled at him as she finished another big push. "I'd like to see you squeeze an eight pound turd from your arse-hole because that what it feels like you daft bastard" Kevin grinned and shook his head, her mouth was foul and she didn't care who heard what she had to say.

"I can see the head" the midwife shouted. She asked Kevin if he wanted to come and see it but he declined telling her he would much rather sit at the top end of the bed. Anita wanted to look; she made her way to the bottom of the bed. "Oh Tracy I can see loads of dark hair. A couple more good pushes and it will be all over love." Tracy prepared herself for the next push. She sucked on the gas and air.

Her feet started to curl up now and you could see the pain returning in her face. "Fucking bastard" she yelled at the top of her voice. Anita was spraying cold water onto her face. Kevin had squirted it into her eyes on purpose so she demanded that Anita had to take over. "Push" the midwife yelled. The African nurse now joined her; she'd been at the side of the room preparing everything for the baby when it was born. Everyone now screamed at Tracy. "Puuuuuuuush."

The pain on Tracy's face was now gone. The baby was out and the nurse was clearing its airwaves before she passed it back to Tracy. The sound of a baby crying now filled the room. Everyone's face looked relieved. Tracy was anxious to see her child. She sat up on the bed and held her hands out to the midwife.

A baby was now passed to her in a green cotton blanket. Tracy's face dropped as she looked at the baby for the first time. She checked the sex of the baby and announced it was a little girl. Anita was now at her side and her face looked shocked as she shot a look at her daughter. She looked at the baby closer and knew what she seen was right, the baby was black.

Kevin now held his hands out to Tracy. He was sat in the chair next to the bed. Tracy passed him the baby with caution, his eyes now looked at the baby in more detail.

Opening the blanket he looked shocked. "It's fucking black," he screamed.

Tracy started to cry. "No she's not, she's just a bit

tanned."

Kevin handed her the baby back. "You dirty slut, that baby is black. I'm not fucking daft." His hands were dragging at his hair now as he paced the floor.

Anita took the baby from Tracy to look at her in more detail. Kevin was shouting at the top of his voice. "I've lost everything for nothing, everyone told me you were a trollop but I didn't listen. I'm gonna be the talk of the fucking town now. What a daft prick I've been, I can just hear them now, all laughing behind my fucking back." He walked to the bed and spat right into her face. The African nurse was smirking at the side of the room and didn't know where to put herself.

Tracy wiped her face and tried to get up from the bed but her body was weak. "Kevin, don't go, we can sort this out." He turned his head as he left and growled at her. She knew by his face he would never come back to her now.

Anita looked at the baby then looked at Tracy. "Well who's the father, because this baby is definitely mixed race?"

Tracy struggled to think, and then it came to her like a bolt of lightning. She'd had a knee trembler with the black DJ Reggae Ronnie one night when she was feeling lonely. She'd had sex with him on more than one occasion and she'd often drop her knickers in the pub toilets for a bit of affection. "It's Reggae Ronnie's the DJ from the pub."

Anita knew who he was straight away without asking anymore questions. "Have you never heard of condoms?" She now touched the baby's skin. "Well what's done is done; you can't turn back time now can you?" Tracy sobbed, she'd lost the man of her dreams and she knew he'd never come back to her again. Anita comforted her daughter, Tracy had definitely dropped a bollock and before long everyone would know about it.

Kevin ran through the early morning streets at speed, he looked like he was suffocating. His breath could be heard as he stopped for rest at a bus shelter. Sitting on the small plastic bench inside it, Kevin held his head in his hands. "I'm such a fucking idiot, I've lost it all for nothing." He cried like a baby. Snot now hung from his nose and he wiped it on his sleeve. The traffic was starting to pick up now and he knew before long the public would be out on the street. He trudged from the bus shelter and made his way back to his home.

Anita kissed Tracy on the cheek; she had her own demons to face and couldn't stand Tracy's moaning any longer. When she told her she was leaving, Tracy grabbed her hand and begged her to stay with her a little longer. Her mother broke down and told her she had to go home. She didn't tell her she had her own problems to deal with.

Everything was a big mess and Anita told her time would heal everything. Anita left her granddaughter in the small cot next to the bed. Tracy hadn't even named her yet and it was obvious they weren't bonding. Tracy's mother left, leaving her alone with the baby for the first time. The baby started crying. Tracy pulled the covers over her head and hid away under the blankets. She was ashamed of her sins.

The nurse returned to the room. She'd been outside telling all the others about Tracy's mis- fortune. Anita had heard them gossiping earlier and went outside to tell them that they could hear every word they were saying. They didn't seem bothered that anyone could hear them.

The nurse started to clean everything up. Hearing

the small infant crying she went over to the body that lay under the sheets. Lifting the cover up she saw Tracy crying. "Come on love. Your baby needs feeding. Everything will turn out right trust me." Tracy yanked the blankets from her body.

"I don't want that baby anywhere near me. Take her away, she's the reason Kevin's not here with me. Get rid of her, put her up for adoption, I don't fucking want her."

The nurse looked concerned. "You can't say that, this is your daughter."

Tracy screwed her face up and looked into the cot at her child. "I feel nothing for her; I'm not going to feed her she can starve for all I care. When can I go home?" The nurse now left the room holding the baby. The way Tracy had looked at her made her think that the baby wasn't safe left alone with her, so she took her outside to feed her away from any danger.

Tracy saw the nurse leave with the baby. Looking at the open ground floor window nearby she knew she had to get away. Searching the small black sports bag at the side of the bed, she grabbed a pair of knickers and a pair of jogging bottoms. She'd had four stitches in her vagina where the baby had ripped her and she was struggling to bend down.

Tracy stood for a minute with one hand held to her head she felt dizzy. Making her way to the window she dragged a nearby chair and climbed on top of it to make her escape. Tracy could be seen dangling out of the window. There was a small drop outside and it wasn't dangerous. Her strength was weak and she looked like she was struggling, Tracy was gone.

Anita opened her front door. She could smell the cigarette smoke that meant her husband was up. With caution she made her way into the kitchen. Graham was sat there reading the newspaper. She tiptoed past him. Graham dropped his paper down from his face and turned his head to her. He looked sorry for the way he'd acted the night before. He spoke in a soft voice, "Switch the kettle on love, I'll make us a brew."

She looked relieved; she now walked to the table and broke down crying. "Graham I'm so sorry for everything. You're so right I don't deserve you. I promise you I'll change."

His heart melted, after all he still loved her. "I'm sorry love" he whispered. "It's just that I can't take it anymore."

She gripped his face in her hands, "No don't you be sorry, I deserve everything you said. Even everything you said about our Sandra. You're right I haven't had the time for her." She kissed his face softly and placed her arms round his neck. "From now on Graham you'll see just how much I love you and the girls. I've just been so wrapped up in our Tracy that I didn't see what was going on right in front of my face. I love you with all my heart and from this day on, I'll never treat you bad again."

Graham sighed and wiped a tear from his eyes. He now stood up and forced Anita to sit down. "Let's have a nice cuppa, it always sorts out our tears doesn't it?" Anita was still sobbing but nodded her head as she tried to smile. Graham got two cups from the cupboard. "Where have you been anyway?"

Anita blew hard from her mouth. "Make them drinks and sit down; I think you should put a drop of brandy in them because when I tell you what's happened, you won't believe it."

Graham placed the drinks on the table. Anita looked at the ceiling and raised her eyes. "Our Tracy went into labour last night. Kevin phoned me about four o'clock in the morning to go to the hospital." Graham now looked upset that he hadn't been there with his wife. He tried to apologise but she stopped him dead in his tracks. "The baby's black, it's not Kevin's." Looking bewildered he asked her what she meant. Anita now told him about the whole experience.

Graham held a smirk for a while and Anita had to remind him that he was smiling. "No love, I'm not smiling, but it's nice to know that fucker has got his comeuppance."

"Yeah, but what about our Tracy? She's heartbroken!" Anita protested.

He tried to see things from Tracy's point of view but couldn't help feeling that she'd got her payback too. He jumped up from his chair and told Anita he was going round to see Sandra. After all she had a right to know what had happened and he didn't want anyone else telling her. Anita told him to finish his brew and said she would come with him to tell their daughter the news.

Tracy was banging on the front door of their house. "Kevin I know you're in there please just let me talk to you." Her body was knelt at the letterbox and she had her mouth pushed inside it shouting inside. Tracy could hear the window above her being opened. She dragged her body from the floor and stepped back hoping to see Kevin. Clothes were now landing all over her body. She lifted her hands above her head to try and protect herself. Kevin could be seen at the window with a frantic look on his face.

"Here you go shag-bag, get all your stuff out of my

life." Shoes were now being hurled at her from the window. The heel of one hit her on the mouth, her bottom lip was now pouring in blood.

"Orr Kevin my lips cut, let me in, please I need to sort it out."

"Fuck off you black man's blanket. You can bleed to death for all I care. Sandra is the one I love not you, so fuck off out of my life, you life wrecking slut!" The window closed. Tracy looked at all her clothing scattered in the garden. She made an attempt to try and gather it together but her body was shaking. Sliding against the front door she tried to get Kevin to speak to her. Over an hour had passed and there was still no reply from him.

Anita and Graham drove to Sandra's house. Anita hadn't been there in a long time and guilt was written all across her face. Graham was now singing along to the radio and seemed on top of the world unlike Anita. As they pulled up they could see John walking up the garden path. He turned and smiled at them both. He now waited for them to lock the car up.

"Hiya Nana, what are you doing here?" She hugged him and tried to make light of the matter.

"I've come to see my gorgeous grandsons. Why is that a crime?" He chuckled and opened the front door.

"Mam! Nana and granddad are here." Sandra was upstairs and didn't know if she'd heard him right. Surely her mother wasn't here, he must have been joking. She bobbed her head over the landing and looked down. She could just about see a woman's legs. She jerked her body back out of view.

"Fucking hell, what does she want?" she whispered.

Running to the bathroom she straightened her hair. She looked a nervous wreck. John shouted her from downstairs. "Mam are you coming down? Nana is here and my granddad."

"Yeah I won't be a minute I'm just getting ready," she replied. Sandra looked flustered as she ran about the bedroom trying to find a clean top. "Fucking hell, the house is a shit tip and she decides to visit me. Just my fucking luck!" she moaned.

Her legs looked shaky as she held the banister heading down the stairs. She wiped the fluff from her black pants as she got to the bottom of the stairs. Her father was waiting for her and hugged her. "You're mother's in the front room. I'll pop the kettle on." Sandra looked anxious. Had someone died and they were coming to tell her? I mean why else would Stoneheart be here she thought. Stepping into the front room Anita smiled at her. Sandra tried to raise a smile back but it was hard for her. After all her mother had never given a shit about her all the time she was locked up in prison. Sandra spoke in a cocky manner. Her mother didn't scare her one little bit anymore and she was ready for anything she had to throw at her. Sandra sat down. John could see them both looking nervous and knew it was time to leave. They had so much to sort out and he felt in the way, he went to join his granddad in the kitchen.

"So to what do I owe the honour?" Sandra laughed nervously. Anita cleared her throat, how had she let things get so bad between them? She moved over next to Sandra and hugged her. You could see Sandra felt uncomfortable and pulled away from her. Anita felt embarrassed but what did she expect.

"I'm sorry love," Anita spoke in a low tone. Sandra didn't trust her and treated her like the enemy.

"Sorry for what? Not being a mother?"

Anita dropped her head down, she felt ashamed. "Yes love and I'm sorry for not sticking by you when you needed me most."

Sandra looked around the room. Was someone playing a prank on her? She searched the room for the TV crew? "Mam stop fucking about. Am I on TV or something? This isn't like you. You're scaring me."

Her mother stood up and paced the front room floor. "I want us to be friends, I know I have always favoured Tracy and I'm sorry for that." Sandra started to listen. Grabbing her cigs from the table she inhaled deeply as her mother continued. "Tracy has wronged you and I should have sorted it out there and then." Sandra nodded in disbelief as Anita continued. "Well our Tracy has got her payback now and I'm sure she won't be anywhere near Kevin again."

Sandra sat forward in her chair as she stubbed her cig out. "Why have the lovers had a tiff or something?" Sandra asked in a sarcastic tone. She now watched Anita sit back down.

"The baby's not Kevin's… she's black." Sandra took a minute to take it all in. Had she heard her right? She asked her to repeat herself.

"I said the baby is Reggae Ronnie's from down the pub. You know the one who does the music for all the disco?" Sandra hesitated, she looked in deep thought. She knew who she meant straight away. Bursting out laughing she rolled about on the sofa.

"So you're telling me Tracy has got a black baby and it's not Kevin's kid?" Anita nodded. "Fucking hell there is a God." Anita knew she wouldn't get any sympathy out of Sandra for Tracy and let her have her moment. Sandra was dancing about the living room and she ran into the kitchen to tell her son.

She bounded off to tell John but he looked at her as if she'd lost the plot. Explaining it to him again, he too laughed out loud. "Fucking hell, get her on that Jeremy Kyle show with that story, it's mint!" Graham gave a snide smile to his daughter. She knew without him saying that he felt the same way. Anita now joined them and she too couldn't help but laugh at the whole episode. She now sat at the table and laughed as she told them all about Kevin's face when he'd seen the baby for the first time. Sandra was smiling from head to toe. She ran to the phone and relayed the news to Maxine. Everyone could hear her laughing her head off at the other end of the phone. Sandra knew that within the hour everyone would know Tracy's story. Maxine had told her straight that she couldn't wait to spread the news.

Sandra returned to the table and sipped her coffee. The table had heard so many secrets in the past and as her hand stroked over it she knew it would have been laughing its head off at the latest news.

Paul now entered the house. Seeing his grandparents there he looked shocked. He was ready for trouble and if his Nana said one word against his mother he was throwing her out of the house. He called John into the hallway.

"What's going on?" John filled him in and Paul told him what he'd planned for his Nana if she was starting any trouble.

"Nar she's being alright, honest her and my mam are getting on great." Paul walked in to meet them with caution on his face. Anita smiled at him. Sandra stood up and ran at Paul.

"Tracy's had a black baby. It's not even your dad's

kid."

Paul fell about laughing. He forgot that his grandparents were there and screamed out. "Serves her right, the slapper" Anita didn't stick up for Tracy and Sandra wondered what was responsible for the big change in her. She's also noticed that she was treating her father differently as well. Had she had a breakdown or something because this definitely wasn't the mother she knew.

★

Tracy made her way back to the hospital. She couldn't leave her child there. She'd tried to but her heart was calling her back to see her baby daughter. Blood was trickling down her legs and she knew if she didn't get back to the hospital soon, she would surely collapse. Her head was all over the place and her world had fallen apart right in front of her very eyes.

Walking back into the labour ward her body fell onto the floor. The midwife pressed the emergency buzzer as soon as she saw her. Within seconds the medical team were around her. They took Tracy's lifeless body into a nearby medical room. The doctor examined her and told everyone she was haemorrhaging. They quickly put her on a bed and within seconds they were pumping blood into her. Her face was grey and her eyes looked vacant as she stared into space. The doctor spent at least twenty minutes attending to her. Once he'd finished he sighed with relief. This woman was lucky to be alive.

★

Kevin sat in his bedroom. He played his "Take That" CD at full pelt. "Back for Good" played out loud as he cried his eyes out. Lay on the bed he held his stomach. He couldn't think straight and his face looked white. Standing from the bed he looked from the bedroom window. His eyes cast over Tracy's clothing in the garden. He could see a few neighbours looking at them and gossiping. As they looked up towards the window he jerked his body back and hid behind the cream blinds. "Nosey twats!"

Returning back to the bed he searched for his shoes. He couldn't stay in the house a moment longer. He felt as if he was going mental. Grabbing his keys from the side he headed down the stairs. Walking out from the house he could feel the glare from two women who were stood at their fences. Lifting his head up to face them he shoved his two fingers in the air. "Get a life you nosey cunts" he shouted. The two women huddled together, one of them returned the fingers back at him as he set off at speed down the road.

"Give me a double brandy," Kevin moaned at the barman. The man was in his forties. He turned to the bar to get his order. He'd seen heartache lots of times in the past and this man was definitely a candidate for it. Placing his drink onto the wooden bar Kevin handed him a ten pound note. The man watched as he necked it back and slammed the glass back onto the bar. "Same again mate." The barman shook his head he knew it was going to be a long night and sighed.

Kevin continued drinking until he was smashed out of his face. He was sat in the corner of the pub drowning in self pity. He heard laughter and noticed Maxine and Zac coming into the pub. Maxine noticed him straight away and he could see her nudging Zac in the waist.

Zac ordered drinks for them both and Maxine couldn't help but rub salt in his wounds. Walking towards Kevin she was grinning from ear to ear. Seeing her feet on the floor near him he struggled to raise his head. "Hello Kevin, are you celebrating the birth of your baby?" she now giggled and held her head back. "Are you fuck celebrating, I mean how could you celebrate the birth of another man's child that you thought was yours."

Kevin darted his eyes at her, "Fuck off will you. I just want to be left alone"

"Oh I'll leave you alone Kevin, but I'll leave you with this. You'll end up a lonely old man. You've lost the best thing you had in your life, I hope you rot in hell you tosser." Kevin's fist could be seen clenching on the table but Zac came to her side just in time. Kevin let his grip go because he knew he'd be fighting a losing battle.

Zac smiled at him with a cocky grin. He could see his pain and didn't want to stick the boot in. "You live and learn don't you mate." Kevin didn't reply and his head crashed to the table. Maxine and Zac went to sit on the other side of the pub but Kevin could still hear Maxine's loud laughter. He knew he was the centre of all her jokes. He drained his glass and staggered out of the pub.

Kevin started walking home. The rain was now hitting his face hard and it felt like he was being slapped on the side of his face with each droplet. His legs were struggling to carry him and a few times he fell to the floor. No one came to help him and he remained there for over five minutes. Lifting his face up from the mud he used a nearby tree to help him up onto his feet. He fell back down a few more times but eventually he managed to stand up. Kevin now walked along Fernclough Road with thick mud smeared all over his face and his clothing. He looked like he'd been fighting. He just wanted to go home and go to bed. He dragged his legs as if they were lumps of lead. Once Kevin found his key he fell into the house. He kicked the door shut behind him and lay where he fell for the rest of the night.

★

Tracy woke up in the hospital the following morning and thanked the doctors for saving her life. She was now brought her daughter, as she held her in her arms she cried. The little girl was beautiful and looked defenceless. Tracy waited until the doctors had left her bedside and whispered to her infant. "It's just me and you now, I hope me and Kevin can work this out but I doubt it." Smelling her baby's skin she cried.

Her tears were now visible on the baby's face. The days ahead were going to be hard for her but Tracy knew somehow, someway she'd get through it. She looked at the clock on the wall and knew anytime now her parents would be there to see her. Cuddling her baby she watched the minutes pass as she waited for them.

21

Sandra handed the visiting order to the woman behind the reception desk. She glanced over the yellow piece of paper and asked if there were two people going in to see Tina. Sandra confirmed both hers and James addresses and then sat down.

Months had passed now and Sandra looked well. She'd struggled to cope for many weeks when she first got out of prison but every day that passed, she seemed to be getting back on her feet. James was her rock and understood when she needed to be alone.

Sandra looked around the room and gazed at all the visitors. The women were dressed to the nines and some of them wore skirts that didn't leave much to the imagination. The men in the room looked like they were at their wit's end. They shouted at the children with them constantly and one man could be seen smacking his child's arse for not listening.

The few toys in the centre looked like they'd been there for years. They were battered and bruised. A man sat near them looked like he was going to sleep. He stank of stale beer and cigarettes. The lady now started shouting names out and Tina's name was called.

The visitors now went into another room that wasn't far from where they sat. Each of them was asked to show their ID. Once they had confirmed who they were they were asked to take their shoes off. James thought they were having a laugh and looked at Sandra. "Are they being serious or what?" Sandra confirmed he had to take his shoes off. He now told her that when he'd come to visit her in the past, things weren't as strict as they were now. He was now led to a box where he had to stand while he was searched. The prison officer told him to hold his hands out to the side of him as he got frisked.

James was now stood with his mouth open as the guard looked inside it. Sandra followed the same procedure. They were both asked to stand on a yellow line now that was painted across the floor on a long corridor. Altogether, five visitors stood on a single line. The guard now told them that they were to look in front of them and not to touch the dog, James looked mortified. The Springer spaniel, who the officer called Jay-Jay, now sniffed each visitor in turn, once he'd finished they were told they could go upstairs to the landing where the visits would be held.

About twenty people were sat in the room and all

the chairs were taken. You could see people handing in personal property like knickers and socks. James couldn't take it all in and kept firing questions at Sandra. "It wasn't like this when I was coming to see you, yeah, I got searched but not like that." Sandra told him that when he was visiting her she was on remand and now Tina had been sentenced everything was a lot stricter. He gasped "Fucking joke it is. They treat us like convicts too."

Sandra told him to stop moaning and hugged his arm. "I've missed her so much you know, I can't wait to see Tina." James smiled and kissed the top of her head. Tina's name was now called.

Walking into the visitor's room sent shivers down Sandra's spine. It was all coming back to her and she felt sick inside. She could now see an arm waving in the air at the bottom of the room. Her pace quickened, grabbing Tina, she squeezed the living daylights out of her. Sandra wiped the tears from her eyes before she sat down. James now asked what Tina wanted to eat and drink as he could see the queue getting bigger and didn't want to spend all his time stood in it waiting for food. Tina looked at him and smiled. "I'm fucking starving today; just get me a butty a drink and some chocolate. I need chocolate, I'm hormonal."

"Too much information Tina," James laughed "Did I really need to know that?"

She giggled and grabbed Sandra's hands from over the table. "Orr love I've missed you so, so much"

"Me too Tina," Sandra replied, "I've been having it hard you know, at one point I thought I was fucking losing it"

Sandra stroked Tina's hair, she giggled and hid her face for a minute, "Let me tell you something that will make you piss laughing."

"Come on then, I could do with a laugh." Sandra now told her about Tracy having a baby to Reggae Ronnie, Tina was holding her stomach as she exploded with laughter. "It's made my fucking day that. I can't believe it!" Sandra told her all the rest of the gossip and told her there were talk of Maxine and Zac getting married. Tina looked amazed. "Fucking hell, it's all happening isn't it?" Sandra agreed.

Tina now looked for James in the queue and knew it was time for her to tell her best friend her bit of news before he returned. "I've been doing a bit of rug munching Sandra." Tina sat back now and covered her face with embarrassment.

"What! You've become a lesbian?" Sandra gasped.

"No" she screamed. "Well maybe a part-time one while I'm in here."

Sandra dragged her hands away from her face and chuckled. "You're so funny, what are you like? I mean how can you be a part-time lesbian?" Tina told her to lower her voice as people nearby were looking over at them both.

"I mean when I get out, I'm back to cock," Tina sniggered, "it's like they say, when in Rome…"

Sandra sat back in disbelief. "Tina you make me laugh so much, I say whatever makes you happy, go for it."

Tina started to blush. "Don't be telling Maxine, you know what she's like she'll tell everyone." Sandra assured her that her secret was safe.

James now returned, as he placed the drinks on the table he looked at them both and could see them giggling. "What so funny?" he now started checking his clothes, he thought they were laughing at him.

"Nothing love, it's just Tina telling me some of the stories from in here. She's off her fucking head you know."

James sat down and stuck his cheek over to Tina for a kiss. She gripped his face and pressed hard with her lips. "Oh you smell so fucking hot, my fanny's twitching."

Sandra slapped her arm. "Ay you horny bitch, hands off he's mine."

"I'm joking you lunatic, my names not Tracy." They all giggled and spoke about all the goings on, in life behind the walls of the prison.

The two hours passed quickly and before they knew it their time with Tina was over. Sandra kept kissing her and touching her face. She felt guilty that she wasn't in there with her. Tina now looked at James with a serious face. "You look after my friend you, she's special you know."

James agreed. "You don't have to worry about me Tina, I would never hurt her, she means too much to me."

"That's good then" Tina said with a chuckle in her voice. Tina felt sadness as she watched her visitors leave. Before Sandra left she turned back and blew Tina a kiss. Tina pretended to catch it and put it in her pocket. The visit was over; the prisoners were all took back to their cells now. Time was flying for her in the prison and Tina knew it wouldn't be long before she too would be a free woman.

As James pulled away from the prison car park, Sandra looked deflated and he could tell she needed cheering up. Stroking her neck with one hand he spoke, "Do you fancy a night of porn tonight? We can get some food and just lock ourselves in the bedroom." Sandra stared at him; she found him sexy and wanted to sit on his face there and then. Pulling herself up from her depression she reached over to stroke his manhood. He looked happy as he tried to concentrate on his driving.

Sandra now unzipped his jeans as he held his belly in so she could get to his trouser snake. He now lifted his arse up from his seat as she helped him pull his jeans down slightly. Sandra now leant over and rested her head on his lap. Sticking her tongue out she teased the end of his penis with her tongue. Sandra could feel his excitement and started swallowing his member like a hungry animal. James was struggling to keep his eyes open as her mouth slid up and down his shaft. Resting one hand on her head he tried to drive with the other. The car kept going faster and then slowing down and she could feel her head being jerked about. James was now ready to come. She placed her hands round his throbbing penis and sucked on the tip of it. His moans could now be heard and you could hear a car honking its horn from behind them. James nearly lost control as he was shooting his load. He just managed to gain the control back before he crashed.

Sandra still stroked his love shaft and lifted her head up from his lap. "You filthy animal" he laughed.

Sandra wiped her mouth and felt naughty, "Ay it's my turn when we get home, it's a boomerang wank, I want one back." The two of them now laughed their heads off. They got on so well and each of them bounced off each other. Sandra now knew she held deep feelings for James. She didn't tell him though, she was scared of getting hurt. She could tell he felt the same and he told her all the time that she was a drug and he was addicted to her.

Kevin had rung Sandra's phone a few times over the last couple of months. He never spoke but she knew it was him, she had a gut feeling. Her hate for him was still there and if she never set eyes on him again, it wouldn't have mattered. She was well and truly over him. She'd also been to her mother's house and seen Tracy and the baby. She couldn't help but feel sorry for her sister and she sometimes let her guard down and forgot what she'd done in the past.

Tracy was like a new woman and she looked after Mia the best she could. Anita had taken a step back and made her realise how much hard work children really were. Anita and Graham looked like a new couple. Graham was a happy man now and didn't sit in the shadow of his wife anymore. They were both equal in their relationship.

Anita had arranged a family meal for the family one Sunday afternoon. All her grand children were there too. Sandra's mobile phone kept ringing all the time and you could see it was doing her head in. Her dad was onto it and asked who was calling her. With distress in her voice she told him, "I think it's that nobhead Kevin. He's been at it for months. He just rings and never speaks the fucking weirdo."

Graham pulled his face. He grabbed her phone and examined it. "Why is he still mithering you? He had his chance and fucked it up; he should just get on with it."

Sandra agreed. "I know dad. If he would speak I would tell him straight, but he never does the wanker."

Tracy carried on talking to the baby. Just the mention of Kevin's name brought back all the lies and betrayal she'd given to her sister in the past. Sandra gazed over at her and it was obvious she knew Tracy was listening to her conversation. Anita now shouted her family to the dining table. She'd done them proud and everything looked perfect.

Throughout the dinner Sandra's phone kept ringing.

Her sons looked at each other as did Anita and Graham; this was going beyond a joke. Anita now piped up.

"Why don't you go to the police and get him done for harassment?" Sandra carried on eating her dinner and spoke with a mouthful of food. "I just want him to stop, it's over, I want to get on with my life. Is that too much to ask?" Tracy now left the table as her baby could be heard crying in the other room. She told them she was going to take her out for a walk as she'd been cranky all afternoon. Anita didn't seem to mind and she left the dining table.

Anita served ice-cream for dessert and watched as her family devoured it. The sound of Sandra's ring tone started again. "For fucks sake" she moaned. Grabbing the phone she went into the back garden she could now be heard shouting "Hello" down the phone. The phone call was different this time and Sandra could now be heard talking to someone. Tracy was at the side of her putting the baby in the pram. "Right where?" she moaned. Sandra stood for a few seconds and said "Okay" to the caller before she pressed the button to end the call. Smiling at Tracy she went back inside the house.

"Told you it was him didn't I? He wants to talk to me and promises that once he has had his say then he won't bother me anymore."

Anita looked mortified. "I hope you told him where to go, you owe him fuck all." Sandra glanced at the pine kitchen clock on the wall and sat back down at the table. She pushed her ice-cream away, she'd lost her appetite.

John looked flustered, "Well it's up to you mam, innit. Just go and speak to him and see what he wants."

Paul looked enraged. "Nah. Like my nana said. It's over. He just has to deal with it." The sound of Tracy opening the back gate could be heard. You could see her pushing the pram out of the garden.

Sandra sat smoking like a chimney, her eyes focused on the clock as she stood up. "Right here goes, I need to get this over with don't I?" Grabbing her black leather bag from the side of the chair she kissed her parents goodbye. John now stood with her and told her he was going now anyway and he would walk with her. Paul just nodded his head at his granddad as he finished his second bowl of ice- cream.

Sandra kissed her parents goodbye. Her dad looked at her with a serious face. "Be careful with him love, you know what he's like." She nodded. "Don't worry dad, I'll be okay."

John and Sandra left the house at the same time. John was extremely quiet as they walked along Rochdale road. As he got to where the estate was he kissed his mother on the cheek and said goodbye. "Mam ring me if you need me." She nodded. He could now be seen jogging off in a different direction. Kevin had asked to meet Sandra at a place they used to meet when they were younger. They'd shared many an hour sat on the top of the flats in Kingsbridge Court in Harpurhey. She smiled as she remembered the first time they'd had sex there. Kevin was probably trying to rekindle the love they once shared and by setting the scene at the top of the flats he must have thought that Sandra would have been an easy target.

The rain started and she fastened her coat up. The traffic was busy as she crossed Rochdale Road. Everybody just seemed in a rush. Her eyes now focused on the block of flats. She looked closer to see if she could see Kevin at the top of it. There was no sign of him, pushing the door open to the flats entrance, she remembered when she was a young girl and she couldn't wait to get to the top to meet Kevin. Her legs felt weak as she pushed the button for the lift. Once the lift had come she pressed the button to the top floor. Turning to the mirror inside the lift she straightened her hair, and used her finger to wipe the mascara that had smudged under her eyelids. The doors opened and she looked scared as she made her way to the roof top. It felt eerie.

Looking about she couldn't see him anywhere. She walked slowly around the rooftop. You could hear her heels clicking. Glancing over the edge she felt sick and quickly moved her body back to safety. A loud coughing noise could now be heard behind her. As her body shook with fear she turned around slowly. There he was stood right in front of her. She quickly weighed him up and down it was obvious he was drunk. She waved her hand in front of her face and spoke to him. "Are you pissed?" She waited for a reply but he remained silent. "You are aren't you? Because I can smell it from over here." He gave her a smile. Sandra sighed, he looked rough. His face was covered in stubble from a week of not shaving. His hair was stuck up all over the place and his clothes looked dirty. My, how things had changed.

Kevin now came to the side of her. She was cautious, as he approached and spoke frantically. "Right I haven't got long, what do you want?" Kevin now led her to their old hideout. As she looked down on the floor she could see he'd placed a blanket across the concrete floor. "What's the blanket for? She asked in agitated voice"

He smiled. "I just thought it would be more comfortable for us to sit on it while we chatted, God shoot me for caring" he moaned as he sulked.

Kevin sat down first and patted the spot next to him. "Come on Sandra, park your arse then."

"I'm not staying long so say what you have to and get it over with," she sighed. Kevin tried to grab her hand but she pulled away from him.

"No, don't even think you can touch me." His head dropped, he looked sad. Sandra's phone started ringing and she could see her dad's name flashing in the screen. She ignored it and placed it back inside her pocket.

"Who's that? Is it lover boy?"

Sandra gritted her teeth, "It's got fuck all to do with you anymore; you lost that right to ask me questions when you fucked my sister, alright knob-head." Her head was bobbing about now and he knew she was right. Her anger was making her fidget and he placed his arm on her shoulder telling her to relax. She shouted at him again and this time she looked furious.

"Don't fucking touch me, you make my skin crawl you pathetic bastard. Hurry up and say what you have to say then I'm off."

Kevin looked angry, "Fucking hell chill ya beans will you? Since when did you become so aggressive?"

"Since you had me put in prison and slept with my sister. That's what it does to you, you know?" He licked his bottom lip and looked up at the sky. The rain had stopped now and some bright clouds were trying to break through.

"It's always been you Sandra. I made the biggest mistake of my life sleeping with your slag of a sister. If I could turn back time, I would. You're everything I want. I can't live without you."

Sandra chuckled and chewed on her thumbnail. "You should have thought about that before you slept with her shouldn't you? What is it? Is it because you didn't father her child? It serves you right for all you've done to me."

Kevin wrapped his arms around her waist and cried. "Please Sandra, I'm nothing without you. I'll change, I'll never raise a hand to you again. I swear on my kid's lives," Sandra looked sad. The man she saw before her eyes was just a shell of his former self. He now tried to make a joke as he lifted his head up from her waist. "You glued my cock Sandra. Fucking hell you nearly killed me, we've both done bad things but I'm willing to forgive you and start again." A loud noise now made them look over to the exit. They couldn't see properly and it sounded like a door opening. Kevin jumped up to investigate. Running over to the exit she watched him go out of her sight. He was only gone a few seconds then returned. "It must have been the wind banging it." He made his way back and sat by her side. "Can you give me one last chance babes? Things will be so different, I swear to you."

Sandra had heard enough. She pulled herself up from the floor and stood over him. He now reached to a blue plastic bag at the side of him. Pulling out an unopened bottle of Brandy he held it up to her. "Don't go, we can drink this together. Remember how we use to get pissed and shag like rabbits up here?"

She looked white in the face. "I'm going now Kevin. It's over" He panicked now and he stood in front of her trying to stop her leaving. The look on her face told him he was fighting a losing battle. As she started to walk off he screamed. "I'll kill myself. I swear Sandra, if you don't come back here. I'll neck this brandy and jump off." She halted. Turning her face back to him she looked fierce. The wind gripped her hair and she had to move it from her mouth. Standing looking at him she held one hand out in front of her.

"Do it Kevin. It would save us all the misery that you

bring. I'm off, you sad cunt." He was screaming behind her but she just kept walking and never turned back.

Kevin sat on the rooftop. The brandy never left his mouth, he was as pissed as a fart. His eyes looked like they'd cried a thousand tears. Every now and then he thought he'd heard her returning and kept looking behind him. His legs now hung over the edge of the roof. His brandy was at the side of him. He could be heard singing "Endless Love" by Lionel Ritchie and Diana Ross. He was tone death and sounded like a cat crying out in pain. The brandy was nearly empty. His eyes looked as if he couldn't focus properly. He heard something behind him. His head slowly turned and he could see a blurred vision of someone behind him. Kevin was now rubbing at his eyes.

The figure was now at the back of him. He was losing his balance as he tried to turn around. A hand now moved in and gently pushed at his body. Kevin lost his balance and fell from the rooftop. You could see the figure watching him fall from the top of the roof. The sound of running footsteps could now be heard as the murderer headed for the exit. Kevin lay at the bottom of the flats and he wasn't moving. A foot gently kicked his body then walked off at speed.

Kevin was dead.

22

Kevin's death hit his family hard. Sandra felt guilty and regretted ever leaving Kevin in the state he was in. The police had interviewed her about his death but after endless investigation they came to the conclusion that Kevin had taken his own life.

Sandra's sons were devastated and couldn't stop crying. Sandra had done her best to console them but the tears still fell. Everyone knew how depressed Kevin had been over the last few months and reports from the community had told them that he'd been pissed out of his head for days on end. It was a sad time for the family.

The morning of Kevin's funeral came. Quite a lot of his old friends had turned up to say their last goodbyes and Sandra thanked them from the bottom of her heart for attending. The black hearse pulled up at the front of her house. James was by her side as she led her family outside.

The neighbours had gathered and they crossed themselves as the flowers were put at the side of Kevin's coffin. Maxine stood waiting for Sandra and as soon as she walked down the garden path she hugged her tightly. "It's going to be fine love, just get today out of the way and you can move on." Sandra never replied and used the white handkerchief she pulled from her pocket to wipe her tears. Kevin's family all looked at her before she stepped into the car. She could tell by their faces that they all thought it was her fault and she couldn't wait to get out of their view.

Kevin's body was taken to Blackley Crematorium. The funeral car drove up Rochdale Road and the public stood on the roadside paying their last respects. Sandra watched her sons and wished she could take away their pain. John had taken it the worst and Paul was at his side every time he broke down.

At eleven o'clock on the seventh of September Kevin Partington's body was brought into the chapel of rest. His older brother and five of his old friends carried his body inside the church. Once they had placed him at the altar the priest placed Kevin's photograph on top of his coffin. Sandra smiled when she saw it. There was no getting away from it, Kevin had been a good looking fucker in his day. Her eyes looked at the photograph in more detail. She remembered him having it taken. He was dressed in a white t-shirt and faded jeans. His face looked suntanned on the photo and his bright blue eyes stood from the picture.

The song her sons had chosen for their dad now finished playing. It was one by Usher. Kevin had loved the singer's voice and often joked saying he could dance like him. The priest now stood in the pulpit. He welcomed Kevin's family to the crematorium. The man of the cloth was dressed in a long black robe with a purple scarf hanging round his neck. He looked about fifty. His voice was daunting and every word he spoke sent shivers down Sandra's spine.

The priest now spoke about Kevin's life. Sandra felt angry and shook her head. Why was none of the bad stuff read out? As she looked over at his family she wanted to shout out that he was a wife beater and a bully but she held her tongue for her son's sake. Maxine sat close to her and you could see her legs shaking. Her face was white and Kevin's death had hit her hard. She was usually a tough cookie but today she let her emotions take over.

Anita and Graham sat two rows behind Sandra and her sons. Anita was crying and every now and then she blew her nose on her handkerchief. Graham looked strong. His head was held high and no emotions were visible on his face. He looked smart in his black suit and could be seen wiping bits from his pants throughout the service. As the priest was praising Kevin, Graham kept whispering insults to his wife. "He was a no good bastard, death was the best thing for him, he can't hurt anyone anymore." Anita urged him to be quiet, she was scared of anyone hearing him.

Tracy cried as she sat at the back of the church. Everybody knew what she'd done to Kevin and they partly blamed her for Kevin's downfall. Motherhood had taken its toll on her and she was just the same as most women these days. No more designer clothes or fancy hair do's. The label sticking out from the back of her pants told you that Primark was her budget store now and that her daughter's clothes came first. Her once flowing locks now looked greasy and were held at the back of head in a short pony-tail. She'd decided months before that long hair was too hard to manage now she was a mother. She went to the hairdressers and had the lot cut off into a short bob.

Sandra stared at the design of the church. It was only small but well decorated. Pictures hung from the walls and each of them had a religious image printed on them. James could be seen squeezing her hand throughout the service. She never looked directly at him but you could tell she was glad of his support.

After the service Kevin's coffin was carried to his resting place. Women cried as they all walked the muddy paths to his plot. As his body was placed down the deep dark hole, John broke down and Paul had to hold him back because it looked like he was going to jump in it with his father.

Sandra stared at the gold plaque on top of the coffin with her deceased husband's name and the date he died. It all seemed like a dream and she couldn't believe he was gone forever. She'd hated him from the pit of her stomach but she never wished him dead. The priest said a few more words and people started throwing handful of dirt onto his coffin. Kevin's sons had brought red roses and each of them in turn dropped one onto the coffin.

People started to walk from the graveside now. They all looked so sad. Sandra and James started to follow them but she realised John was still there. She broke free from James's arms and started to run back. Her dad saw her and told he would deal with him. Sandra agreed and went back to James.

As Graham approached John he could hear him talking to his dead father. His heart melted as he stood behind him. John didn't know he was there. "Dad I'm weak, I can't do this without you. Our Paul's the strong one not me. Why did you do it? Didn't you think about us? We loved you and needed you."

Graham choked back his tears and came to his grandson's side. "Come on lad, it's time to go. You will be fine son, I'm here for you always." John crumbled to the floor. Graham bent his knees to pick him up. As he lifted his head up he could see Paul running up towards them. Once he was there with them both, he looked at his granddad for help. Graham just shook his head and his emotions took over. Paul sobbed. "Come on our kid, we can get through this together trust me." He pulled John from the ground and started to walk off with his brother tightly in his arms. Graham nodded at him and told him he would follow them on. Tears fell from his eyes; he hated seeing his grandchildren upset.

Graham looked down the deep hole towards the coffin, he checked he was alone. Bending to his knees he whispered. "You have caused so much heartache in your life time Kevin. You treated my daughter like a slave and beat her to within an inch of her life. Did you think

I would just sit back and take it? You remind me of my own brother." His face looked angry and you could see him squeezing his fist as they rested on his knees. "He did exactly the same as you and slept with my wife. The only difference is that Tracy is his child. Do you know how much that hurts? People like you deserve to die and that's why I pushed you. I hope you rot in hell, you bastard!" Anita was now shouting his name. He raised his head and stood upright. Kicking some dirt onto the coffin he spoke his final words to the dead body below him. "Carpe Diem mate. Nobody take's the piss out of my family and gets away with it." Graham held a smile on his face as the wind picked up.

As he started walking, Anita ran to his side. She gripped him and sunk her head into the small of his chest. "It's all so sad isn't it love?" He stroked her hair but never replied. They both went to join the others.

Everyone sat in Sandra's house. Some of Kevin's relatives came back but most of them went to a nearby pub to drown their sorrows. Sandra had made a buffet and everyone seemed to be making the most of the situation. Maxine was on top form and was making everyone laugh. She now whispered into Sandra's ear. "Remember when I farted on Kevin's steak before you cooked it?"

Sandra pushed her hands into her side and tried not to laugh. Her voice was low as she replied. "Orr I know we were bad weren't we? The poor bastard drank more balls of snot than anyone I know. No wonder the fucker was always on the shitter all the time."

"That wasn't the snot that made him shit," Maxine giggled, "that was the batch of laxatives you bunged in his brews." They both burst out laughing and Sandra held a hand between her legs as she propped herself up against the wall.

"I'm gonna piss my knickers. Stop it please." They both laughed out loud and people were starting to look at them both. Maxine had to pretend Sandra was crying and wrapped her hands around her doing a distressed face to the other people sat in the room.

The wake went on until late. Music was played and considering it was supposed to be a sad time the party was swinging. Tracy was sat near her parents and didn't mingle much. At one time she would have been the life and soul of the party but these days she'd calmed down a lot. Seeing Sandra passing her, she pulled her to where she sat. Sandra smiled at her. "What's up love?"

Tracy had been drinking and she looked pissed. Her words were slurred. "I'm sorry Sandra. Kevin always loved you, I was a fool to ever think he could love me, I know I was just a bit of a shag." Sandra looked shocked. Never once had her sister apologised for her affair with her husband. Sandra turned her head to the side. Her sister looked so miserable and she knew it was time to build the bridges between them.

"It's gone now love, past is past, don't get me wrong I'll never trust you again with my fella but as far as I'm concerned we can start again."

Tracy snivelled, she grabbed her. "I'm so glad Sandra, I've been so depressed, I've felt like no one likes me anymore because of it all."

Sandra shrugged her shoulders. "Well what did you expect love, what you did was wrong. We have a rule in our circle of friends that you don't touch your family or friend's men, I suggest you abide by that rule in the future." Tracy nodded. She was like a small child who'd just been told off. Sandra stood up and made her way back to James. Tracy looked happy.

John was pissed out of his head and starting to become a nuisance. His voice was getting louder and louder and Paul was trying to calm him down. He so was much like his father and Sandra knew as she gazed over at him that she would have her work cut out with him in the future.

The guests started to leave. Her parents had left about an hour earlier. Graham was pissed as a fart and Anita was holding him up as she escorted him to the taxi. The house was now empty and all that was left was Sandra's children, James, and Maxine and Zac.

Zac was all over Maxine like a rash. They were so in love and he'd asked her to marry him earlier in the night. Maxine had told him straight, that until her friend Tina was out of nick there was no way she would get married. Zac called the girls the Three Amigos. Their friendship was close and he knew no man would ever come between them. He agreed to wait until Tina was free and Maxine was over the moon.

★

Anita had gone to bed and Graham sat downstairs on his own. The small lamp in the corner of the room gave off very little light. Graham was looking at some old pictures in the photo album. His eyes were struggling to see as he reached for his black spectacles at the side of him. As he turned the pages he smiled at the photographs in front of him. Suddenly his face changed. His teeth clenched together. Pulling the old snap from the album he stared at the man in it.

"You're another one who thought I was a useless piece of shit aren't you John?" he laughed menacingly at the photograph. "You were my brother and I trusted you.

That's why you had to go just like that bastard our Sandra married." He reached for his can of beer and gulped a large mouthful. "They all thought you fell to your death too didn't they?" His hands stroked over the face of his brother. A tear fell from his eyes and he wiped it slowly away from his mouth. "That's two men I've killed now. This is your fault, I'll never forgive you and I hope you never rest in peace you cunt." Graham spit at the photograph and ripped it into small pieces. As he stood up he made sure he held all the pieces in his hands.

Walking into the kitchen he flipped the bin's lid and shoved the photo inside it. "In with the shite brother, exactly where you belong." His feet now turned and he made his way to bed. Once he dragged his clothes from his body he snuggled next to his wife. She was fast asleep and never budged. He kissed the small of her back and drifted off to sleep.

23

The months passed and life was hard for Sandra. I would love to say they all lived happily ever after but come on, this is a Manchester council estate story and we all know nothing is plain sailing in the real world. John was going downhill every day that passed and the dark circles around his eyes told you he was using heroin again. Paul had tried to save him from the life set out in front of him but it was too much, John was stubborn and led his own life, his way.

Maxine and Sandra were still close friends and they kept their promise to Tina by visiting her every week. Tina was still having a lesbian love affair with Penny and laughed as she told them both it was just a pit stop while she was in nick. Sandra was still madly in love with James and there were talk of him moving in with her in the near future.

Sandra still worked as a nail technician and was doing really well. Women were coming to see her from all over the place. She was a lot more than a nail technician. She was known as the Godmother of Payback to cheating and abusive partners.

Lots of men would pay the price for their sins in the future and Sandra loved to hear their success stories. Lots of women were now in the news with attacks on their violent husbands. Women were making a stand all over the world. Domestic violence in the area had dropped and some say that Sandra's story scared a lot of men into getting their acts together. Men feared her and knew she could break a man at the drop of a hat.

On the night of Sandra's next birthday, all the girls had organised a night out on the tiles. Sandra looked amazing. Her figure was curved and she no longer felt fat. Looking in the hallway mirror she looked at her reflection. For the first time in her life she felt happy. She no longer hated the woman who stared back at her. Flicking her hair from her face she smiled into the mirror. "Carpe Diem baby," she chuckled to herself as she heard Maxine shouting her name at the front door. "I'm ready now you moaning cow, stop fucking shouting." Sandra opened the door and about twenty of her friends and family stood there cheering.

She locked the door and turned to face them. Sandra shook her head and ran into them with her hands held out. "I love you girls. Come on let's go and have some fun." The women could all be seen walking out of the garden. They were all singing "Girls Just Wanna Have

Fun" by Cindy Lauper. Life was never the same for the women on the council estate. They were a new generation of women who took no shit from men.

So if you ever look down at a woman's foot and see the words 'Carpe Diem' tattooed there beware, because this woman has been hurt before and she will take you to the cleaners, if you ever try to hurt her. She belongs to a big pack of women that all work together, from all around the world – if you fight one you fight them all.

Other books by this author

BROKEN YOUTH

A novel by Karen Woods

"Sex , violence and fractured relationships, a kitchen sink drama that needs to be told and a fresh voice to tell it."

TERRY CHRISTIAN

When rebellious teenager Misty Sullivan falls pregnant to a local wannabe gangster, she soon becomes a prisoner in her own home. Despite the betrayal of her best friend, she eventually recovers her self-belief and plots revenge on her abusive boyfriend with spectacular consequences.

This gripping tale sees the impressive debut of Karen Woods in the first of a series of novels based on characters living on a Manchester council estate. Themes of social deprivation, self-empowerment, lust, greed and envy come to the fore in this authentic tale of modern life.

ORDER THIS BOOK NOW FOR JUST £6
WWW.EMPIRE-UK.COM

Other books by this author

BLACK TEARS

A NOVEL BY KAREN WOODS

"MANCHESTER'S ANSWER TO MARTINA COLE"

WITH EVIL GORDON locked up in Strangeways for 5 years, the characters from Karen Woods' debut novel 'Broken Youth' come to terms with life without him.

Misty, now married to Dominic, gives birth to Gordon's child, Charlotte. Her former best friend Francesca also gives birth to one of Gordon's children, Rico, while staying with Gordon's heroin addicted brother Tom.

Meanwhile, as the clock ticks down on his sentence, Gordon broods on the injustice of his situation and plots sweet revenge on those on the outside.

ORDER THIS BOOK NOW FOR JUST £6
WWW.EMPIRE-UK.COM

Other books by this author

BagHEAds

"An author Manchester should be proud of"

CRISSY ROCK

Shaun was always a child who demanded more than life could give. His mother's stuggle began when she became a single parent, leaving her abusive husband behind. Unable to cope without the family unit, Shaun turns to a life of crime and drugs and eventually ends up in the care system.

ORDER THIS BOOK NOW FOR JUST £6
WWW.EMPIRE-UK.COM